Surviving the Evacuation

No More News

Life Goes On Book 2
Frank Tayell

Surviving the Evacuation: No More News
Life Goes On, Book 2

Published by Frank Tayell Copyright 2020
All rights reserved
All people, places, and (most) events are fictional.

ISBN: 9798642865781

Other titles:
Post-Apocalyptic Detective Novels
Strike a Match 1. Serious Crimes, 2. Counterfeit Conspiracy
3: Endangered Nation & Work. Rest. Repeat.

Surviving The Evacuation/Here We Stand/ Life Goes On
Book 1: London
Book 2: Wasteland
Zombies vs The Living Dead
Book 3: Family
Book 4: Unsafe Haven
Book 5: Reunion
Book 6: Harvest
Book 7: Home
Here We Stand 1: Infected & 2: Divided
Book 8: Anglesey
Book 9: Ireland
Book 10: The Last Candidate
Book 11: Search and Rescue
Book 12: Britain's End
Book 13: Future's Beginning
Book 14: Mort Vivant
Book 15: Where There's Hope
Life Goes On 1: Outback Outbreak
Book 16: Unwanted Visitors, Unwelcome Guests
Book 17: There We Stood
Life Goes On 2: No More News

For more information, visit: www.FrankTayell.com &
www.facebook.com/TheEvacuation

27th February

The Apocalypse So Far
Nanaimo Airport, British Columbia

For the second time that morning, the hangar's small office filled with the buzz of departing helicopters. Pete Guinn abandoned sleep and dragged himself out of the military-grade sleeping bag issued to him by the Canadian police officer.

"Are they leaving?" Pete asked, crossing to the window where RCMP Constable Jerome MacDonald watched the choppers depart.

"Heading to Vancouver," Jerome said. "As we promised. How much do you know about the missing woman?"

"Clemmie Higson? Not very much at all," Pete said, watching the trio of helicopters dart upwards, then buzz towards the chaos that was Vancouver City. "Her mom's the pilot who flew us here. We stayed in their house down in Australia, but I never met Clemmie. She's been studying, here in Vancouver. Do you think they'll find her?"

"We'll do everything we can," Constable MacDonald said in a well-practiced, professional manner that was neither confirmation nor denial.

Pete grabbed his coat, the only item of clothing he'd taken off, tied his boots, and refilled the pockets he'd emptied during the night. It was nine days since he'd left South Bend. Nine days, give or take a hemispheric time zone, since he'd bidden farewell to Olivia Preston in the parking lot of Wall-to-Wall Carpets where they'd both worked. He'd almost… not asked Olivia out on a date, but almost gone for a non-work drink, which, maybe, might have led to something. They'd hung out before, sure, in and out of work. They'd helped each other at the weekend with moving and other multi-person chores, but those were always shrouded in a veil of co-workerly neighbourliness. That last time had been different. Not just the moment out in the snow, but during the few days before when they'd been closing down and locking up the store. Except their stolen moment had been disturbed by a limo, waiting outside to take Pete to the airport.

He couldn't really remember anything about the limo because he'd been transfixed by the passenger, the billionaire Lisa Kempton.

Technically she was his new employer. Or, since the apocalypse had changed everything, his *last* employer. Except he wasn't sure she'd even been that. Kempton had bought the carpet store simply so she could promote him from a shop-floor gopher up to regional management where no one would think it suspicious for him to be sent to a training course in Hawaii. There had been no training course. Yes, they'd gone to Hawaii, but only to refuel, after which they'd continued soaring southward over the Pacific, to Australia.

Nine days. Only nine days, and the world had changed completely.

Beyond the window, snow lay in drifts along Nanaimo's runway, pushed aside by the growing number of conscript-labourers bringing the Canadian airfield back to life. The workers had all come from the nearby town on the eastern edge of Vancouver Island, where some had lived and worked for years. Others were refugees from remote hamlets, while some were escapees from Vancouver City who'd fled across the tumultuous Strait of Georgia by ferry, freighter, yacht, and even dinghy. Now they hastily cleared the snow, preparing for the arrival of more flights, while others strengthened the fence, readying for the arrival of more zombies. Pete wondered which would arrive first.

While the helicopters had gone to Vancouver City in search of Liu Higson's daughter, Liu herself had flown the jet back to Australia, the cabin full of bed-bound children in desperate need of a working hospital. It was the same plane which had taken him to Australia nine days and a lifetime ago.

He shivered with misremembered fondness at the shock of the heat as he'd stepped out of the jet plane onto Broken Hill's baking runway.

Lisa Kempton had sent him to Australia to make contact with his long-missing sister, Corrie. For years, Kempton had known about a group of corrupt politicians and aspirant gangsters plotting to destroy the world and rule over its ruins. She had, apparently, been working to stop them. To assist in that effort, she'd recruited Corrie Guinn, Pete's sister. But Corrie, when she'd learned what Kempton was really doing, had fled. She'd gone off the grid, under the radar, and out of his life for a decade. But

Kempton had finally found her, and she'd sent Pete to play messenger, to hand his sister a sat-phone and a number to call.

Pete was still hazy on the nature of that call, or the code his sister had long ago written and then activated, except that it had something to do with satellites, nuclear weapons, and missile guidance systems. Ultimately it didn't matter, because Kempton's real purpose was sending away two of her once-trusted pilots, Rampton and Jackson, one of whom Kempton suspected of being an agent of the cartel. And that didn't matter either, not really. Not after the outbreak. And certainly not after an airliner had crashed in the outback, outside Corrie's remote cabin, with zombies aboard. He and his sister had fought the undead, and fought their way back to the cabin. They'd nearly died, but had been rescued by an airborne RSAS unit and been helicoptered back to Broken Hill where they'd been billeted with Liu Higson.

Her husband, also a pilot, was missing somewhere in Europe. Her daughter, Clemmie, was studying in Vancouver, leaving Liu at home with her son, Bobby. Pete and Corrie had been given the small one-room annex to sleep in, Clemmie's vacation-time home. For the briefest few hours, things had appeared nearly normal before the nightmare twisted its blade, becoming infinitely worse.

It *always* got worse, he thought. Billionaires, then zombies, then gangsters, then gangsters armed with assault rifles and mortars. It always got worse. Baking heat then freezing snow. He should be optimistic. Olivia was always saying that you should be optimistic because despair solves nothing. It was a saying Olivia had copied from their old boss, Nora Mathers.

Pete's hand strayed to the holster at his belt, and the distinctly non-military gun held there. But things *had* gotten worse in Broken Hill. The cartel had come after them. In a diner, he and Liu had killed a gangster armed with the silenced pistol he now carried at his belt. Pete had found himself helping the police inspector, Tess Qwong, and so became witness to the infected undead arriving at Broken Hill's outer limits. He and Corrie had helped where they could, in the town, at the airport, as refugees arrived, as zombies followed, as the world beyond collapsed. During the

3

search for left-behind survivors, they'd stumbled across the cartel thugs' hideout, and the tortured remains of the pilots, Rampton and Jackson. And then, barely, they had finally escaped Broken Hill by plane as mortar shells rained down on the runway.

The plane had been supposed to fly to Canada, or at least to North America. Liu Higson had received approval of the plan from Canberra, and a promise that Australian SAS soldiers would be sent to travel with them. While Liu wanted to find her daughter, the real purpose of the flight was to learn what was happening in North America. Pete and Corrie were to be the guides, taking the Australian Special Forces east. But while they were waiting for the soldiers, shells had begun exploding around the plane. To save the aircraft, and to leave before the runway was ruined, Liu had decided to take off, with only Pete, Corrie, and Liu's son, Bobby, as passengers. Flying on fumes, they'd landed at Nanaimo.

At least they'd found people here. Survivors. Police officers. Refugees from the chaos consuming Vancouver. A deal had been struck. Liu would ferry sick children down to Australia where there were still hospitals. In return, the helicopters had gone to the city to find Liu's daughter, while Pete and Corrie were being given a flight of their own, inland, to complete the mission with which the missing Australian Special Forces had been tasked: to learn what was happening in the United States. From what Pete had seen of Vancouver Island, it was bad. Worse than Australia.

But he *was* returning to Indiana. He'd return to South Bend. He could look for Olivia. Which was… it was crazy. Beyond dumb-stupid. Sure, down in Australia, he'd dreamed of seeing her again, but he'd not really thought he'd be allowed on the flight north with the soldiers. Not really. In the air, he'd simply hoped they'd find somewhere to land. But the Canadians had asked where they were trying to reach, and now they would help them get to Indiana. It was… it was hard to put into words. Sure, there was one word that explained it all, a word used in songs and poems by Shakespeare and Frost, and every other poet whose name he didn't know. It was a word he didn't feel comfortable using. Not here. Not now. Not until he found her. But he knew he wouldn't find Olivia. There was no chance he'd see her again.

A grumbling rasp behind him punctuated his sister extracting herself from the sleeping bag she'd been cocooned inside.

But he *had* found his sister. Impossibly. Improbably. The sister he'd not seen in years, who'd gone on the run to keep him out of the nightmare Kempton had dragged her into. Corrie might have failed in that, and Kempton had certainly failed to stop the apocalypse, but he and his sister were now, impossibly, together. So maybe there *was* a chance, no matter how slim, he'd find Olivia. Somehow. Somewhere. Out in the frozen wasteland of post-outbreak North America.

Part 1
Hell Comes to South Bend

Indiana and Michigan

Chapter 1 - The End of Dreams
South Bend, Indiana

For Olivia Preston, the whoosh of water whirling through pipes an inch of plasterboard away from her ears was better than an alarm clock.

"I'm up, I'm up," she lied, automatically reaching for her phone, but it wasn't there. Sleep faded, wakefulness returned, and with it came memory. Specifically the memory of her roommate, Nicole, confiscating her phone and quarantining it in the kitchen drawer last night. Not that Olivia needed to check the time. If Nicole was in the shower, she was getting ready for work, so it was on the tomorrow side of four a.m.

Olivia, by contrast, had no job to get up for, but was enjoying the glorious unicorn of a paid vacation while the carpet store was being refurbished. With nowhere to be, and nothing that had to be done, she could go back to sleep, but a routine is a hard habit to kick. She dragged herself out of bed, padded into the kitchen, and flicked on the coffee machine, waiting for Nicole to finish her shower.

Theirs was a small apartment on the western bank of the St Joseph River. A two-bed, one-bath, with an open-plan living-room-kitchen on the fourth floor of a recent renovation on Waterside Drive. The apartments on the east-facing side of the block had river views. She and Nicole did not. By way of compensation, in the summer, with the windows open, they did have a river smell. But they didn't pay rent. The building's owner had wanted new carpet, and quickly, after a tenant had done a midnight flit taking the flooring from their unit. Olivia had laid it herself, for a discount, after hours, and with Mrs Nora Mathers's help. Impressed, the landlord had asked whether they could re-floor some of the other units, which turned into a one-month day-and-night slog through the entire building, its neighbour, a set of suites near the university, and a block of offices near the airport. In return, Olivia had been given a small two-bedroom apartment, rent-free for a year. At the time, Nicole had been sleeping on her couch in a two-sofa walk-up little bigger than a lock-up, so it was the perfect deal at the perfect moment. But that year was nearly up.

The bathroom door opened and Nicole came out, dressed for her daily grind at the grocery store. The two women shared a similar temperament, similar hobbies, and similar foibles, but they were utterly dissimilar in appearance. Where Nicole was a beanpole six-foot-three, Olivia had to stretch to reach five-four. Where Olivia was dark-haired, Nicole was a bottle-blonde. Where Nicole could eat all the junk food she could steal from work without adding an ounce, Olivia gained a pound every time she walked past a bakery, which was why she'd taken up running this year. After two months, her slow jog along Riverside Drive had turned into a quick jaunt the mile and a half to Keller Park, on the return leg of which she often *didn't* stop at the bakery.

"Oh, hey," Nicole said. "Tell me you got some sleep?"

"More than I need," Olivia said, pouring coffee from the battered pot into mugs which bore the legend of her one-time employer, *Wall-to-Wall Carpets*.

"Thank you, Lisa Kempton," Nicole said, taking the mug.

"Thank Mrs Mathers," Olivia said. "She paid for this coffee."

"As long as it's free, I'll say thank you to the world," Nicole said.

The mugs, coffee, and the coffee machine had been liberated from the break-room at the carpet store where Olivia had worked, which Lisa Kempton had purchased, and which was currently being torn apart and rebuilt. The banner Olivia and Pete had hung across the parking lot outside hadn't been lying; *everything must go*, including everything in the staff break-room. They'd had a raffle of sorts, with everyone getting something. Everyone except Pete, of course.

"So, spill," Nicole said. "How many times have you checked your phone this morning?"

"Not once," Olivia said.

"No. Seriously?"

"Seriously," Olivia said. Out of reflex, her hand strayed towards the kitchen drawer, but she raised it instead. "And I'm not going to check it now. Was there anything in the news?"

"One thing, actually," Nicole said. "A state senator got a DUI. On a beach. In a hearse. Which was occupied. With a coffin."

"Wow. One of *our* state senators?" Olivia asked.

"Kansas."

"What beach?"

"In Florida."

"Ah."

"Which means there's a job vacancy," Nicole said. "Or there soon will be."

"I don't think I'm qualified," Olivia said.

"Have you ever taken a hearse on a joy-ride?" Nicole asked.

"Maybe not, but I don't live in Kansas," Olivia said.

"But if you're going to move anyway," Nicole said, and left the thought dangling. She decanted the rest of her coffee into an insulated mug. "My shift finishes around twelve. We'll go out this afternoon, take a drive, and say goodbye to Indiana. So make a decision before then." She tapped the notepad Olivia had left on the counter the night before. "Remember, if *you're* leaving, *I'm* leaving. Kansas could be nice, but moving to Chicago could be fun."

"If it *is* Chicago. Don't quit yet," she said.

Nicole grinned. "Not until I've finished shopping. I'll see you later."

Alone, Olivia took the notepad and her coffee over to the couch. The TV went on, but after a minute listening to the anchors mull over aerial footage of a hearse bogged down on a sandy beach, she muted the sound.

Her dilemma, her two-decades-too-early mid-life crisis, had a name: Pete Guinn. She liked him. She *did*. He was the right mix of funny and serious. Not too stubborn or opinionated. If he had one fault it was that he was a little slow on the uptake, but she'd known him for two years and couldn't find anything worse to say about him. No, if she were looking for one word to describe him, it would be *decent*, and she'd been on enough bad dates to know that wasn't as common as paperbacks made out. She'd probably have asked him out a year ago, except she'd planned to leave South Bend until she got the year's free rent. And over this last year, they'd grown simpatico. She'd spent a week searching for an aptly descriptive word. And during that week's exploration of the dictionary, and her own feelings, she'd realised that maybe there could be something deeper between her and Pete.

She'd been about to ask him out when Mrs Mathers had announced she was selling the store. The shrapnel from that bombshell was still pattering down when Pete had received his out-of-the-blue promotion to regional manager in Lisa Kempton's organisation.

It changed everything. Pete was now her boss. Since opportunities like the six-figure promotion rarely fell into anyone's lap, if they dated and it didn't work out, she'd have to quit. If they never dated, she'd have to quit anyway because seeing Pete drive up to the carpet store in his fancy car, wearing his increasingly fancy suits, would just be too much of a reminder of the life she didn't have. Either way, she couldn't stay working for Lisa Kempton. It was a shame since the pay was good, and the benefits far better than anything Mrs Mathers had been able to afford. But her mind was made up.

That left the dilemma of dating. It almost certainly wasn't going to work. Not now. Not with Pete starting a new job with a ton of training and even more responsibilities. Right now he was training in Hawaii, for heaven's sake. His circles were already infinitely wider than those she travelled in. But she'd give it a go. More than that, she'd make a real effort. Pete, stunned by the sheer number of zeroes in his paycheck, hadn't realised he wouldn't be based in South Bend. Ms Kempton didn't have a corporate office here. Quite why she wanted the carpet store in the first place was still a mystery, but Pete would be working out of Chicago, Detroit, or Cleveland. But not South Bend.

Wherever it was, Olivia would go. She wasn't following Pete, not exactly, but she was willing to put everything she had into this. Give it one huge try. And when it didn't work out? She looked at the notepad. Without a degree, her options weren't great. What made it deeply frustrating was that Ms Kempton would pay the part-time college tuition for any employee without a bachelor's, but only after two years' employment.

She hated retail. Her reaction to hospitality was hostility. Warehousing was a killer, and after she'd seen a fifty-year-old co-worker die on the stockroom floor, she'd promised herself never to do that again. Policing? In Chicago, she might be safer joining the army, but she'd rather not do either. Nor nursing. Funeral home was on the list, a late-night addition while they were browsing horror movies, but, again, she'd be starting at the bottom. No one within a hundred miles wanted a manager for a carpet store. Which left the first thing she'd written on the pad, the very first full-time job she'd had at nearly eighteen, ten years before: working in a care home. Hopefully as a manager this time, thanks to her experience and a reference from Mrs Mathers. But there was a reason she'd opted for a carpet store in South Bend.

She dropped the notepad. Until Pete returned from Hawaii, it was impossible to plan too far ahead.

Finally cracking, she got up, walked to the kitchen, opened the drawer, and checked her phone. He still hadn't called. Of course he hadn't. No matter how gruelling the training course was, he was on an all-expenses-paid-by-a-billionaire trip of a lifetime to Hawaii. She put the phone back in the drawer and returned to the TV, switching to the show she'd been streaming the night before, trying to lose herself in the mystery of vampire murders.

Nicole had decided she was coming with her. Which was… probably a good thing. Probably.

Olivia had moved to South Bend three years ago, picking the city because she knew nothing about it, and no one who lived there. After a few months packing boxes, a few more waiting tables, and a few less stocking shelves, she'd met Nicole and landed the job at Mrs Mathers's carpet store, all in the same week. Olivia had been planning on leaving the city anyway, getting restless the closer she got to thirty. She was loath to admit it, but half the reason she'd stayed was Pete. The other half was the free rent, but that stopped in another six weeks.

What if Pete didn't want to date? Or what if the first one was an utter disaster? What if she didn't have to go to Chicago or wherever? What then? Where then? Like Nicole said, there were plenty of care homes in Florida. And in Florida, they had someone with whom they could stay.

The show she was watching made no sense. The premise was intriguing, sure, but the principal character, the vampire cop, couldn't go out in daylight. The interviews and investigation had to take place at night, so the crime scenes had to be somewhere open after dark, and which jewellery store did that? But the sunrise-scenery was spectacular, and she liked the small-town vibe. Maybe that was the answer, to stop worrying about the job, and think more about quality of life.

She watched to the end of the episode, and the beginning of another, but when the show began buffering, she paused it, and headed for the shower. She was overdue for her morning run, but she deserved a day off.

Studiously ignoring her phone, she made more coffee and returned to the couch. The show was still buffering. Frustrated, she stood, and went to the kitchen drawer, and found her phone had gone crazy with insanely impossible notifications.

Outbreak in Manhattan was replaced by *Viral Outbreak*, and then by *Chaos in New York*.

Assuming the worst, and that her phone had been hacked, she tapped the news app. Half the photos refused to load, and nor would the first story she clicked on. Nor the second. After the third failed attempt, she scanned the headlines, scrolling down until she reached a page of familiarly benign entertainment news. Those stories wouldn't load either.

Phone in hand, she returned to the couch and switched to network TV. The screen filled with a sweating anchor who failed to remain calm as he stuttered through a handwritten note. What he was saying wasn't much more than she'd read on the phone. There'd been an outbreak in Manhattan. Something viral. Something that was spreading quickly. People had died. But how many? How likely was it to spread to South Bend?

Getting frustrated with his slow and stumbling delivery, she switched channels and found herself watching a horror film. A blood-soaked woman in a business suit tore at the flesh of a runner. Except then it cut back to a news studio.

The anchor's words washed over her as another clip began. She picked up her phone, and finally the story loaded. It had little to add to what the anchor was saying, and included an embedded clip that appeared to be a lower-res version of the same footage the TV was broadcasting. A woman in a business suit staggered out of a café, covered in blood. She collapsed to the sidewalk. A runner stopped to help her, but then she attacked. Biting. Clawing. Tearing at his flesh. Almost as if she was eating— No.

Olivia dropped the phone, returning to the semi-sanitised coverage on the TV. One clip replaced another. One anchor replaced another. Slowly, order was restored. The broadcasters were calmer, the clips more professionally edited. The tone was more reassuring; oddly so for the usually strident news channels. But there was no comfort in the message. People in New York were attacking one another. Killing one another. And no one knew why.

One hand on the remote flipped through the channels. The other scrolled up on her phone, then down through the cascade of new news, searching for confirmation that the outbreak was confined to the East Coast. She didn't find it. There was very little real information at all. The networks had the same selection of clips, uploaded by citizen journalists, culled from blogs and social media.

It was like a horror film, but far worse. She skipped from a train station to a busy road intersection to a shopping mall somewhere upstate; it was always the same nightmare repeated against a different background. Someone covered in blood fell out of a doorway or reared up from a car, tearing and ripping at a passing civilian.

But finally, on her phone, she found a clip of police setting up a hasty barricade. Her shoulders dropped, releasing a surge of pent-up tension as the clip played, showing the cops corralling civilians into pushing stalled cars into a line across the road. A police officer suddenly fell, dropping her sidearm as she was tugged under a car. The civilians near her stepped back as the fallen officer's mouth opened in a silent scream. Grateful there was no sound to the clip, Olivia still couldn't tear her eyes away. But whoever was operating the camera felt differently. The image shook and blurred as they ran back a few yards before, again, it focused on the car and the now unmoving cop. Another officer, gun raised, ran forward, grabbed her collar, and dragged her clear. Her foot was missing. Her leg now ended in a bloody stump. Except she wasn't dead. Only a few feet clear of the car, having left a bloody smear behind her, she rolled onto her side. The rescuing officer dropped to his knees, bending over her to apply a tourniquet. She reached up, gripping his shoulders. Not to speak. Not to plead. Not to beg for help, or cry out in pain, but to rip and bite at his neck. The clip stopped.

Olivia stared at her phone, then the TV, her eyes slow to focus on the footage of a shopping mall, but she'd seen that clip before. She changed the channel, and found an image of the train station. She leaned forward, watching a few seconds, then skipped to the next channel, the next, skipping more quickly when she found a shopping channel still hawking paste-jewellery. But as far as she could tell, despite the many different angles and varying quality, there were only five, perhaps six, different incidents.

She picked up her phone, reopening the news app, seeing if anything would load. Perhaps it wasn't as bad as the news anchors were making out. They were so used to portraying every minor crisis as the end of the world, that now, when it might actually be really happening, they'd gone into meltdown. An outbreak? Yes. A terrible one? Yes. But surely it could be contained. Right?

She pressed the remote, flicking to the next channel, and saw the cop die again. Yes, maybe it wasn't so bad. Or, a voice in her head said, maybe only six people were stupid enough to record video rather than run. Either way, there was no getting around what to call it. The news feed already was. The headline on the lead article read *Zombies in New York*.

Morning came and midday went, but it was nearly two when Olivia realised Nicole hadn't returned. She wrote a text and went back to the news app, but it was the same footage as before, so she returned to the text-app to see why Nicole hadn't replied. Nicole *always* replied. Despite company policy, she always kept her phone on her, even when she was working the register, which was why she'd been relegated to morning-openings and stockroom duty. The message hadn't sent. Olivia tried messaging through all the social media apps that Nicole used, but still nothing. In desperation, she tried the rarely used green phone icon. The call didn't connect. Frustrated, she slumped back against the couch, her eyes on the TV where the footage had, finally, changed.

Shaky phone footage had been replaced with aerial shots filmed from news choppers. She left the volume on mute. What the reporters had to say didn't matter. Nor did the slowly repeating words at the bottom of the screen. The stock market had closed, as had airports and bridges, but it didn't tell her *which* airports and bridges. What she wanted to see on the screen was the National Guard being deployed to New York. But so far, in all the pictures, there were police and an occasional civilian or fire-crew roadblock, but nothing else.

A quick and late lunch later, nothing had changed. She still couldn't get through to Nicole. The military were still absent from the footage on TV. Her phone's connection was still erratic. She went to the window to watch the street. It was oddly empty. Eerily so. No delivery trucks rushed by, no soccer-mom SUVs battled school buses heading in the opposite direction. It was too early for commuters, but not too late for shoppers, except there was no one. No, there, a pedestrian hurried along the sidewalk, hand buried deep inside his coat, eyes darting left and right. He turned a corner and was lost from view. A moment later a gunshot rang out, muffled by the window's insulation, but still distinct.

Olivia moved away from the window, retreating behind the kitchen island. The best thing to do was to stay put. Stay inside. And wait for normality to return.

Chapter 2 - Old Dates and Dead Friends
Waterside Drive, South Bend

Olivia jumped awake and to her feet, momentarily uncertain what had been a nightmare and what was reality. That was forgotten as she looked beyond the patched couch to the opening apartment door. For a second, it swung inwards on its own, then two men came in, one carrying the other.

"Who the hell are—" she began, before Nicole entered behind them.

"Help me, Livy," Nicole said.

"What's going on?" Olivia asked. "Is that..." But not only did she recognise the tall man being half-carried, she'd been on a date with him. "Dante Regan? Is that you?"

"Help him," the other man said, while Dante barely groaned.

"Dante was shot," Nicole said.

"Over here, get him onto the couch," Olivia said, switching to automatic, and slipping to the injured man's other side, helping him lower Dante to the couch. "Dante?" she said. "It's going to be okay. What happened? Why didn't you take him to the emergency room?"

"It's a nightmare out there, Livy," Nicole said. "Didn't you see the news?"

"Manhattan, you mean?" Olivia asked. "The virus?"

"Zombies," Nicole said. "It's zombies."

"That's what happened to Dante?" Olivia asked, taking a step back.

"No. Some people tried robbing the grocery store," Nicole said.

Olivia unbuttoned Dante's sodden shirt. "Get the first-aid kit from under the sink. And get some towels and some linen."

She found the wound easily enough, beneath a drenched bandage. Lodged dangerously in Dante's waistband was a Smith and Wesson 9mm. She withdrew it, carefully, with two fingers. "Why does he have a gun?" she asked, holding it up.

"Why does anyone?" Nicole said, taking the gun and handing her the first-aid kit.

It didn't take long for Olivia to do all she could, which wasn't much. "I'm not a doctor," she said, standing.

"She said you worked in a hospital," the as-yet-unidentified man said.

"Who are you? Who is this, Nicky?"

"Morgan Mack," Nicole said.

"*This* is Morgan Mack?" Olivia asked. "Oh."

"What's that mean?" Mack asked.

"Nothing," Olivia said. Now certainly wasn't the time for her to share the horror stories Nicole had told her about the stockroom supervisor. "I worked in a care home. It was years ago, and I just handed out Jell-O and changed bedpans. That's not the same as nursing, let alone surgery, and that's what Dante needs. Try 911."

"There's no point," Mack said.

Olivia picked up her phone and tried anyway. Frustratingly, Mack was right. The call didn't connect. Noting the bloody fingerprint she'd left on the phone, she put the device down, and went to the kitchen sink to scrub her hands. "We have to take him to the hospital."

"We can't," Mack said. "It's chaos out there. The world's ending. It's the apocalypse. The end of days. Judgement. I knew it was coming." He walked into the kitchen nook, and sat down at the small table on which Nicole had placed Dante's gun. He pulled up his grey and now blood-stained hoodie and extracted an identical handgun of his own, placing it on the table next to Dante's. "I knew something like this would happen. I said. For years, I said."

"You saw the news, Livy?" Nicole asked.

"There was an outbreak in Manhattan," Olivia said. "I've been watching it on TV all day." The cat-and-mouse wall clock showed nine-thirty. "Why didn't you come home earlier?"

"After the news broke, we closed up the store," Nicole said. "You know what'll happen. There'll be looting and chaos. It's not like any more deliveries will come in."

"You closed the store so you could keep the food for yourself?" Olivia asked.

"Not really," Nicole said. "Just to stop people stealing. But they came anyway. They broke in. Not at first. Not until a few hours ago. That's when Dante got shot."

"Why didn't you go to the hospital?" Olivia asked.

"Because there are no hospitals anymore," Mack said with furious exasperation. "No cops. No law. No order. No help. It was a cop leading the mob."

Olivia walked back over to the couch. Dante's face was increasingly pale. Eighteen months ago, she and Dante had been on a date. One date. Only one. It had taken twenty minutes for her to realise the man wasn't just pining for his ex, but dreaming of an entire forest. "There's no exit wound," she said. "I think he's bleeding internally. There's nothing I can do. In an hour or two, he'll be dead. But a doctor could save him. How many zombies did you see out there?"

"What?" Nicole asked.

"Zombies. How many are out there?"

"I dunno."

"Well, how many did you see?" Olivia asked. "How many were there at the grocery store?"

"It wasn't zombies. It was people," Mack said.

Olivia nodded. "You didn't see any at all?"

"It's people who did this," Nicole said. "They came to take the food."

"Manhattan is seven hundred miles away," Olivia said. "I seriously doubt, from what I saw, that zombies can drive."

"So?" Mack said.

"So they aren't in South Bend," Olivia said with a firm conviction she didn't entirely feel. "Looters came to your store. Dante got shot. That's all. There's no reason not to take him to the hospital."

"What is it with you girls?" Mack growled. He picked up one of the handguns. "Look at this! It's the end of the world. Survival of the fittest. People are killing each other for food." The gun waved wildly as he spoke.

"Put the gun down," Olivia said calmly. "We can take him to the hospital. Or we can try. He might die in the car, but he'll die on the couch if we don't."

"And we don't really need a hospital, right?" Nicole said. "An ambulance would do. You could save him if we had an ambulance?"

"Me? No. But I guess a paramedic could," Olivia said.

"Why don't you listen?" Mack said, now waving the gun like he was conducting an orchestra. "Why do girls *never* listen? It's help yourselves out there because no one will help each other. You saw it, Nicole. You saw what they did. No one will help."

"Put the gun down," Olivia said, hands raised in front of her. "Just put it down. I can't help Dante. *You* can't. If he stays here, he'll die. And none of us want that."

"Always talking, never listening," Mack fumed. "Never listening!" He turned around and paced the two steps back to the table, slamming the gun down. And, as he did, it went off. The bullet went wide of Olivia by six feet and forty degrees, straight into Nicole's chest. She blinked.

"Nicole!" Olivia said, rushing to her friend's side, catching her just as her legs gave. "Nicole!" All she could do was lower her friend to the floor, cradling her in her arms as Nicole met her gaze, wide-eyed and confused.

"Livy?" Nicole whispered. The last syllable ended in a splutter of blood. A coughing gasp. She went limp.

"Nicole?"

Her friend didn't reply. But there was a desperate cough from Dante, on the sofa.

"I... didn't mean to," Mack said. "I... do something."

Mack had, at last, put the weapon on the table, but he was on a tighter trigger than the handgun. Nicole was dead, and a growing weight in her arms. Carefully, gently, Olivia laid her friend down. Dante gasped again, clearly struggling to breathe. He was still alive, and he might still live, but only if he received proper treatment immediately. Nicole was dead, but Dante might live. Decisively, Olivia stood.

"There's only one thing we can do now," she said firmly. "I'll be back in a minute. Open the door on three knocks."

She crossed quickly to the door, opened it and stepped outside even as Mack asked, "Wait, where are you going?"

Not bothering to reply, Olivia jogged along the corridor, wondering if any of the other apartment doors would open. They didn't. Nor from behind any did she hear a sound. Her neighbours must have heard the gunshot. Maybe they were all calling 911. Maybe. Hopefully. But hope alone saves no one.

She sprinted down the stairs, and only as she opened the lobby door, and a blast of frigid air slammed into her face, did she remember she'd left her jacket upstairs. And her keys. And her phone, her pocketbook, and everything between. She was wearing sneakers and sweats, now drenched in blood. No matter. She knew the way and it wasn't far.

She jogged along the sidewalk, focusing on putting one foot in front of the next, barely registering how deserted the roads were. Distant sirens blared. Nearby, a whiff of acrid smoke tickled her nostrils. There, then gone, and back again as she ran across an empty intersection. Above, light streamed from windows, but just as many were dark. The city wasn't asleep; it was hiding.

After a leg-burning run through the ominously empty streets, the hospital rose like a bright beacon ahead of her. The parking lot came into view, and with it, more lights. Flashing lights. But not from ambulances. A pair of police cars had been zagged across the road, on either side of an ambulance, collectively blocking the entrance. A portable spotlight on each of the police cars' roofs shone on the road, until one swivelled to focus on her.

"Stop!" a male voice called. "Stop there! Don't take another step!"

She raised her hands, and slowed her run to a walk, but she didn't stop. "My friend was shot. Please. I just want to get help for my friend. I need a doctor. An ambulance. No one was answering 911."

"Shot?" the voice asked. Two figures stepped forward. Both men. Both in police uniform. One far younger than her, the other far older.

"What do you mean, shot?" the older man said, and Olivia realised it was him who'd spoken earlier.

"My roommate came home from work less than an hour ago. She came with two men, two of her co-workers. One had been shot in the stomach. I wanted to bring him to the hospital. The other man, he wouldn't let me. He… his gun discharged. He shot my roommate. It was an accident, but she's dead. The other man, Dante, he's still alive, but he won't be for long. He's bleeding out."

"Whose blood is that?" the young officer asked.

"Not mine," Olivia said.

"Are you bitten?" the young officer asked.

"Stow it, Officer Herrera," the older man said. "Two men and a woman? The man who was gut-shot was about six-feet-two?"

"That's right."

"And the other man, can you describe him?"

"Mack? Um…. five-eight, I guess. Wearing a grey hoodie over his work clothes. Long-ish greasy black hair. Not quite shoulder length. Small, sort of wild eyes. I… I never met him before today."

"Where does your roommate work?" the officer asked.

"The grocery store on Western Avenue."

"It's them," the younger officer said. "You're under arrest."

"No she's not," the older man said. "But you will have to come with me. Officer, you stay on watch, but you keep your weapon holstered. We're keeping the peace, not starting a war. Ma'am, if you'll come with me."

It wasn't a request, but she didn't mind. With someone else taking charge, she finally felt able to release a little of the tension that had been keeping her going, and keeping her upright, since the nightmare began.

"I'm Sergeant Tom Wilgus," the cop said, leading her through a parking lot full of quiet ambulances. "What's your name?"

"Olivia," she said. "Olivia Preston. What happened at the grocery store? I mean, something did. Something bad, right?"

"Your friend and her co-workers barricaded themselves inside. When customers came to stock up, they were refused entry. A standoff became a riot. Two of our officers died."

"I'm so sorry," she said. "Did Mack and Dante shoot them?"

"No," Wilgus said. "We got the shooters, but those two stole our officers' sidearms and ran. I'll need your address. I'll send a tactical team, and a medical unit. Until the situation is resolved, you won't be able to go home. In here, please."

Chapter 3 - Impatient Inpatients
St Patrick's Memorial Hospital, South Bend

The police sergeant didn't take her to the emergency room's main entrance, but to a side door guarded by an elderly security guard wearing a holstered sidearm, stab-vest, and a lifetime's worth of worry on his aged face. Though he was armed, both his liver-spotted hands tightly clutched a flashlight as a preventative against shooting at shadows.

The sergeant gave the elderly man a brief nod, and led Olivia inside, into a waiting room, though not one for the obviously sick. Four rows of joined-together chairs were a quarter occupied by individuals on their own, most of whom had their heads buried in their phones. Following the sergeant's direction, she sat while he went to the unoccupied desk at the hall's end. Next to the desk, a pair of swing doors led into the hospital proper. Behind the desk was a small door belonging to a glass-windowed office crammed with ancient filing cabinets. The sergeant went through the small door and into the office, disappearing behind the wall.

Feeling eyes watching her, she looked up and around. Those of the waiting area's occupants who weren't watching their phones were now watching her. She looked down, staring at the floor, trying to make herself invisible.

An achingly long few minutes later, the sergeant returned.

"I'll be back in a few hours to take your statement," Sergeant Wilgus said.

"You've sent an ambulance to my apartment?" she asked.

"I called it in, yes," he said. "So wait here. When the shift changes, I'll be back, okay?"

"Sure. I'll wait here," she said. Even if she wanted to leave, she had nowhere else to go. The growing sense of lonely isolation grew as the sergeant returned outside, leaving her alone with the other... patients? Who were these people? Were they all witnesses to similar crimes? The man on the chair closest to her didn't look injured. Not unless his wound was hidden beneath his thick coat. She realised she was staring at the same time she realised *he* was staring at her.

"Sorry," she said.

He didn't reply, but stood and walked over to a seat on the far side of the clinic.

As her eyes followed him, she realised that nearly everyone was looking at her now, so she looked down, staring at her blood-drenched shoes.

The hospital was clearly working as normal, the police checkpoint notwithstanding. If Nicole had brought Dante here, he would have been treated. She would still be alive.

Nicole.

Nicole was dead.

This morning, they'd had plans. Crazy plans. Driving off into the unknown together. Starting over with all the possibilities of a blank slate. Now they had nothing. One minute Nicole had been alive. Now she was dead. The first real friend she'd made since school, since her parents' divorce, since she'd cut out on her own. Since—

"Excuse me," a woman said. "You're Sergeant Wilgus's witness? Olivia, yes?"

She looked up, and saw a stern-faced nurse towering over her. "Yes. Olivia. Hi," she said.

"Olivia, I'd like you to come with me, please."

Olivia stood and found her feet unsteady.

"Were you hurt?" the nurse asked.

"No, just tired. It's been a long day."

"Hasn't it?" the nurse said, leading Olivia to the desk, then into the office, and to a door nearly hidden behind the gun-metal-grey filing cabinets. A swipe of her keycard got them access to a staff break-room, where tables and lockers battled with burst-seamed armchairs, and where a snoring doctor lay sprawled across a sofa. The nurse led Olivia on, and into a corridor with curtained exam rooms, where sobbing emanated from behind at least three.

"In here, please," the nurse said, pointing to the first set of open curtains.

Olivia stepped inside. The nurse pulled the curtain closed.

"I found you some scrubs to wear," the nurse said, pointing at the neat set, folded on the bed.

"I'm sorry?" Olivia asked.

"Your clothes. The blood. It's scaring the other visitors."

Olivia looked down at the matted brown blood coating the once-blue and white sweats that had been worn and washed to a comfortable grey. "Scaring? I thought, in a hospital, you'd expect to find blood."

"It's the news," the nurse said. "Everyone thinks there are zombies everywhere. Zombies? Nonsense."

"You don't believe it?" Olivia asked.

"It's nothing more than an exotic virus that an air-passenger brought into New York. I'm not saying it isn't serious, but it won't affect us out here." She pointed to the scrubs. "Change into those, and I'll find you some shoes."

The shoes fit almost perfectly, a well-worn pair of sneakers borrowed from the locker of someone not on duty. The scrubs didn't fit her, but they'd been designed not to fit anyone. They were clean, which was one up on her own clothes. With the shoes, the nurse brought two transparent plastic bags. While she didn't describe them as evidence bags, it was clear that was what they were for. A loud scream somewhere further down the corridor had the nurse hurrying away. Feeling increasingly like a criminal, and uncertain why, Olivia placed her old clothes in the transparent bags, sat on the bed, and waited for the nurse to return.

Thinking about what the nurse had said kept her mind off the nightmare of the last few hours. She'd described the people in the room the sergeant had taken her to as visitors. Whom were they visiting? When? And the nurse had been dismissive of the idea of zombies. But there was little reassurance in that. Not when Olivia had spent the day watching the footage on TV. Which brought her back to the apartment, and to Nicole.

Seeking a different distraction, she focused on the sounds outside. Crying. Moaning. Sobbing. Far quieter were the sounds of doctors and nurses practicing their craft. Far, far quieter. The hospital must be understaffed. And why were so many ambulances parked out by the entrance? Or was that because, with 911 down, there was no one to run dispatch? And again, her mind returned to Nicole. Her shoulders slumped as grief again returned, but before exhaustion could give misery a helping hand, her body reminded her of a more urgent demand.

In the corridor beyond the curtained exam room, the bathrooms were well signposted, and a warm-water wash left her feeling alert if not refreshed. But while finding the bathroom had been easy, finding her way back was not.

The further she slowly ventured, the busier the corridors became. The curtained rooms were more densely occupied, with voices running through a procedural list with a practiced resignation that spoke of only one end for the patient on the other side of the curtain.

At the intersection of two corridors, she nearly ran into a young doctor wrestling with a gurney on which lay a gowned and unconscious patient.

"You! Nurse," he called. "Don't just stand there, help me."

"I'm just supposed to be waiting," Olivia said.

"You have arms, legs? Then push this gurney," he said, bending over the patient. "We're taking him to surgery."

"Where's that?"

"Left. Right. Left again. Go," he said with a volume that suggested he'd not stopped in hours. As he headed off in the opposite direction, she heaved the patient left then right, through the still busy corridors. Another left, and she nearly bumped into a nurse.

"This is the pneumothorax?" the nurse asked.

"Um… I don't know," Olivia said.

The nurse looked at the chart. "It is. I've got him."

The nurse pushed the patient on, through a set of double doors that clicked closed behind her. Olivia, again alone, again wondering what to do, began retracing her steps. From the signs, she was miles from the emergency room. From the patients bumping knees in the corridors, emergency cases had spilled into the outpatient facilities.

"Nurse?" a voice called from a partially open door. A bathroom, judging by the sign.

"Um… yes?" Olivia said.

"Please, can you give me a hand?" It was a woman in a wheelchair, with a bandage on her leg, another on her arm. "I managed to get here okay," she said, "but getting back on my own will take hours. I don't want to miss my cab."

"Sure. Of course," Olivia said, relieved. "I can help with that. If you know the way."

"You're new?"

"Pretty much," Olivia said. It was simpler than the truth.

"What a day to start your new job," the patient said. "Down here, then left."

"You're waiting on a cab?" Olivia asked.

"Everyone is," the patient said. "No one can get through on a phone. Can't call Dwight to come get me. They got through to a taxi firm who're sending cars. Or they were supposed to, hours ago. The police won't let us leave on foot. Not an option for me, anyway."

A little more of the picture swam into focus. With no cell service, no one could call a loved one to come get them. With no dispatch, the ambulances couldn't respond to calls. With no pedestrians allowed to roam the streets, the hospital was filling with the almost-walking wounded.

Olivia left the patient in a wide corridor filled with scores of other bandaged injured, and resumed her hunt for signs back to the emergency room. Instead, she saw the nurse who'd given her the scrubs.

"What are you doing here?" the nurse asked.

"Helping," Olivia said. "As much as I can."

"You're a nurse?"

"I worked in a care home for a few years," Olivia said. "I know how to push and carry."

"Good. There was a pile-up at the university an hour ago, and we only just found out. We're going to need all the help we can get."

21ˢᵗ February

Chapter 4 - A New Dawn, an Old Problem
St Patrick's Memorial Hospital, South Bend

A hand on her shoulder brought Olivia violently awake.

"Jamilla D'Souza," the nurse said, taking a step back. "Hi, we were never introduced earlier. I brought you some lunch." D'Souza handed Olivia a steaming mug of instant noodles.

"It's lunchtime?" Olivia asked.

"It's not even breakfast," D'Souza said. "It's three-twenty in the morning, but I think the worst of it is over."

"How bad did it get? I mean, compared to an ordinary night?" Olivia asked.

"I've been through worse," D'Souza said. "But not since I was working for the Red Cross. We're short-staffed, which doesn't help. Most people who were on duty when the news broke stayed, but most of the night shift stayed home. Things will improve when the morning news bulletins report the crisis in New York has been contained. It will be. Trust me. And things will get easier now."

Olivia nodded, sipping at the mug. She'd escaped the chaos for a few minutes' calm inside the nurses' break-room, and must have fallen asleep, though she wasn't sure for how long. Before then, her night had been a hectic jumble of one patient then the next, pushing, holding, helping as best she could.

"How long can you stay?" the nurse asked. "Do you think until mid-morning?"

"I guess," Olivia said. "I suppose I should stay until the sergeant tells me I can go. I… I can't go home." The memories of how she'd come to be at the hospital returned in a flood. She pushed them down. "I can stay."

"Good. How are you with a mop?"

"I almost went pro," Olivia said.

"Great. There's a lot of cleaning up. I'll show you where the supply closet is."

She led Olivia back to the waiting room she'd first entered. It was fuller than before, with people asleep in chairs, and in the aisle between them.

D'Souza opened a large closet filled with cleaning equipment. "One each then, we'll make a race of this."

"Where are we cleaning?" Olivia asked.

Before D'Souza could answer, the doors opened and Sergeant Wilgus staggered in, barely holding up a bloody firefighter.

"Little help!" Wilgus called.

"Get that chair," D'Souza said. "What happened?"

Olivia grabbed the solitary wheelchair, currently unoccupied and sitting in a gap between two seats, and wheeled it over, missing Wilgus's explanation of what had happened. The moment the barely conscious firefighter was in the chair, Wilgus ran back outside.

"Follow me," D'Souza said.

"What happened?" Olivia asked, pushing the chair after the nurse, through the doors, and into the hospital proper.

"Some fools decided the best place to survive the chaos was inside a well-stocked bar," the nurse said. "Then they built a barricade on the street. There was a fight, then a fire. Hundreds are on their way here. Ah. Perfect." She stopped by an empty gurney. "Help me get him up here. On three." They heaved the firefighter onto the gurney. "Go help the sergeant with the others," the nurse said. "Wait, you'll need this for the doors." She pulled an I.D. card from her belt, handed it over, and hurried off without another word.

Olivia took a deep breath, and returned to the blood-and-soot-stained fray.

The curtained corridor became an improvised triage centre. With the barely injured kept in the waiting room, the more serious were moved into the hospital proper. By the third patient she brought in, the corridors were filling with nurses, doctors, and paramedics, as well as with the walking and recumbent wounded. Order was dragged from confusion as the living were dragged back from the gates of death.

Her tenth patient refused the help of the wheelchair, so Olivia helped her walk on unsteady feet through the doors, where she almost collapsed before she could be placed on a gurney. Back in the waiting area, a man with a blood-soaked arm had claimed the vacant wheelchair. Since three of her previous patients had been gunshot victims, she assumed the same was the case with this man.

"This way, then," she said, wheeling him towards the doors.

"Thanks," he said.

"What happened to you?" she asked as she pushed him through the doors and into the crowded corridor beyond.

"I was shot," he said. "Just winged."

"That's a lot of blood for a graze," she said.

"Ah, yeah, I got bit first. Damn dog was going crazy."

"You were bitten?" a passing woman asked. She wasn't a nurse. She wasn't a doctor. She was a wild-eyed woman with singed hair and a smoke-streaked face. "You're infected?"

"Do you see any foam? I ain't got rabies," the man said.

"I don't mean that," the woman said, taking a step towards them so she was five feet in front of both wheelchair and the man. "I mean the zombies."

"It weren't no zombie that bit me," the man said. "It was my dog. Damn thing went crazy with all that smoke, all that shooting."

"A dog, yeah, right," the woman said. "Let me see."

"What?" the man asked.

"Show me your arm!" the woman said.

"Just get out of the way," Olivia said. "There's a doctor waiting down —" She froze. For the second time in twenty-four hours, she found herself staring at a gun. This one, a snub-nosed compact, was aimed mostly at the man in the chair, but the woman's arm waved wildly left and right.

"Please don't," Olivia said, already a vision of the bloody, violent, inevitable future flashing in front of her eyes seconds before it happened.

30

But her premonition was wrong. Before the woman could fire, an arm appeared from behind, grabbing the gun, twisting and turning the woman, pushing her down until she was lying on her front, her hands pinned by Sergeant Wilgus. The woman yelled more in anger than pain as the sergeant quickly cuffed her, then hauled her upright, planting her in a chair.

"He's been bitten," she said. "He's infected! He's going to kill us all."

"Sir, you were bitten?" Sergeant Wilgus asked, as he ejected the round from the chamber of the woman's small gun.

"By my dog!" he said. "Betsy bit me. My dog bit me, not a person!"

"He's lying," the woman said.

"Easily proven," Wilgus said, ejecting the small mag. Like the round, neither the magazine nor pistol went into an evidence bag, but into his pockets. "Sir, can you show us your arm?"

Olivia had to help him with the crude bandage. Underneath, encrusted with oozing blood, was an unmistakable bite wound far too small for any human to have made.

"Told you," the man said.

"Nurse, can you take him for treatment? As for you, ma'am…"

As Wilgus dealt with the nearly murderous woman, Olivia pushed the man on until she found a doctor in whose care she could leave him.

When she returned to the waiting room, she found no more patients, but she did find the sergeant, alone.

"I suppose you'll want a statement?" she said.

"No," Wilgus said. "I sent her home."

"You didn't arrest her?"

"The cells are full," Wilgus said. "The hospital is almost full. The morgue will be soon. We had twelve dead at that bar. Looks like at least another twelve died in the fire. Twenty at the university. Then there was the pile-up, the river, the airport. The list goes on."

"How… how many?"

"At least a hundred dead," Wilgus said. "It's the fires. The flames spread too fast. The fire crews can't be alerted in time." He shook his head. "No, there's no time for paperwork tonight."

"Oh. What about the other statement? I mean, my apartment."

"Ah, that. Sorry, I don't know if Tactical have been yet. Everyone's deployed to the streets. We're a visible presence, responding to what we can see. I'd advise you stay away from your apartment for now. I spoke to D'Souza. She says you've been helping out."

"Just pushing and carrying," Olivia said.

"It's more than most. Is there someone you can stay with? A friend? Family?"

"I suppose. I really can't go home?"

"If Tactical haven't been, they'll go sometime after dawn. If they have, it's a crime scene. Either way, you can't go there unaccompanied. Although…" He trailed off. "Look, honestly, it's going to take weeks to clear up the chaos of the last few hours. If you know somewhere you can sleep, eat, go there, do that. And then come back. I'll be here. I'll take you to your apartment so you can get your things. But one way or another, you can't stay there. You understand?"

"I guess so. I hadn't really thought about it."

"Where do you work?" he asked.

"A carpet store, but it's being refurbished. I'm on vacation."

"Then you can help out here."

While she was still processing what he'd said, a shout had him hurrying outside. She took a step after him, but decided no. He was right; she needed some sleep. Afterward, she could come back and help.

The doors swung open and a paramedic entered, alone except for the chill wind that slipped in behind him. On a chair lay a brown overcoat seemingly belonging to no one. She picked it up and checked the pockets, but they were empty. Pulling it on, she stepped outside.

Chapter 5 - Old Boss, No Boss
Lilac Road, South Bend

Since she'd begun her early morning runs, she'd become used to the quiet frenzy of pre-dawn South Bend. Today, the city sounded different. It looked different. It *smelled* different. Despite the streets being utterly deserted, she could sense the eyes behind every curtain, every door's peephole, watching her traipse across the icy sidewalk. She pulled the coat tight around her shoulders. The chill was worse this morning, beyond a frost and turning to a freeze. There'd been snow the night Pete had left. Most had melted, but a dusting remained, and the air held the promise of more. She thrust her hands deep in the coat's pockets, and wished she was wearing something warmer. That brought up memories of how, for her, yesterday's nightmare had truly begun. Memories she had to avoid at least until she was somewhere inside. She couldn't go home, but she had to go somewhere.

Her phone was in the apartment, and on it was her address book. It didn't have many entries, but since she didn't have the phone, it was academic. What addresses did she know? There was Kelsey Wannamaker, who worked installations in the afternoons, and the projector at the movie theatre in the evenings. But Kelsey had taken advantage of the two weeks paid leave to attend a steampunk convention in California. There were plenty of other co-workers who'd open their doors to her, but she had no idea where to find them. In the safe in her office, Mrs Mathers had kept a giant binder with the addresses of all her employees. But the safe, and the office, had been torn out during the retrofit.

Mrs Mathers! Of course.

Olivia mentally kicked herself for not thinking of her sooner. Mrs Mathers was still in town, but only just. There were a few bits of paperwork to tidy up before her former boss went down to Florida to begin her retirement. Olivia knew where she lived, and so that was where she would go. On foot, in scrubs and borrowed nurse's shoes that were pinching after a night on her feet. In the cold, against which the borrowed coat offered little protection. Through a city that had slept as little as she had.

It was nearly five miles from the hospital up to Mrs Mathers's home on the other side of I-90, just off Lilac Road, near the very northern limits of the city. She'd walked the route before, twice. Though, on both occasions, in the other direction, walking from Mrs Mathers's place to her own apartment. The first time, Mrs Mathers had been unable to drive herself home from work, and so Olivia had driven her, leaving her own car at work. The second time was after she'd loaned her boss her own car after Nora's ancient Studebaker had lost its exhaust on a pothole near the airport. Both times had been in the fall, when the weather was still warm, and in the middle of a day when she'd had no reason to be anywhere else. She'd taken the sometimes-scenic route, mostly following the river. Today, that wasn't an option since it would bring her far too close to her old apartment. Instead, she kept to Portage Avenue, following it north to I-90.

At first she was utterly alone. There were no sirens, no pedestrians, no cars, just an occasional distant shot that made her hurry even faster. There were lights, though. An indication that the city wasn't as empty as it first appeared. At first they were only behind windows, but the further she walked, and as the sun crawled above the horizon, people came out onto the streets. Their bags were already packed and went straight into the backs of their cars before they, just as quickly, threw themselves in and drove away. At one house after another, from one below-ground parking garage and then the next, cars flew by, heading in both directions. When she finally reached the interstate, again she saw cars, and again heading in both directions, though there were more heading west than east.

Where were they going? Why? Where were the police? Where was the National Guard? The questions danced across her mind, her only companion as she hurried north.

Mrs Mathers's house was one of six built in a cul-de-sac off Lilac Road. The dinosaur of a station wagon was missing from the un-swept drive. Now she was looking for it, she realised that none of the neighbouring properties had a car outside either. Ice, and a little lingering snow, crunched underfoot as she walked up the S-shaped path to the un-lit door. She shivered, only partly because of the cold. She rang the bell. There was no answer. There hadn't even been a buzz. She pressed it again, but heard nothing inside. The curtains were drawn in the den's bay window, but it was obvious no one was home.

Not wanting to think the worst, she made her way to the wooden gate that never properly locked. When she pushed upward on the frame, the lock disconnected, and the gate squeaked ajar. Never had she heard anything so loud in all her life. Auditory memories of gunshots and screams flashed across her brain. Fear, exhaustion, cold; it was all beginning to wash over her. In the four-tiered, white limestone rockery, she counted four rocks to the left, and found the fake rock with the hider-key inside. She went to the back door and opened it.

"Hello?" she called. "Mrs Mathers? Nora? It's Olivia. Are you home?"

No reply came. She pushed the door closed, and brushed a foot against the floor. The doormat was gone. As was the dryer in the small utility room. She stepped into the kitchen and found it empty. No stove, no refrigerator, no table, no chairs. No framed cross-stitch on the wall. No photos on the shelf. No alphabetically arranged jars of herbs grown and dried by Mrs Mathers herself. It was all gone. She tried the lights. They didn't come on.

The hallway was just as empty. The den wasn't. She stumbled into the boxes, but with the curtains drawn, there wasn't enough light to count how many. She returned to the hall and checked the other rooms, then upstairs. The house was empty. Mrs Mathers had already left.

She sat on the top stair, head in hands, letting herself wallow in misery for half a beat. First Pete, then Nicole, now Nora Mathers. Gone. All gone. And she was alone.

No.

Despair Solves Nothing: that was the embroidered missive Nora had stitched and hung in her kitchen. After Mr Mathers had died, a misguided well-wisher had given her a 'Bless-This-House' kit with which the grieving widow was supposed to occupy herself. Mrs Mathers had taken out her anger in an utterly Nora way, stitching her own message instead.

Mrs Mathers had told her she was heading down to Florida in a couple of weeks. She'd said she wanted to see what a billionaire would do with her store before she went south. She and Olivia were supposed to be having lunch later in the week, just the two of them. But she must have left early. Left and slipped away, without saying.

As frustrating as that was, Olivia had a house to sleep in for the night. Or, considering the hour, for some of the day. There was no bed. No lights. No heat. No food. Nothing but some old boxes in the den. She went back downstairs. Water still ran from the faucet. The toilet still flushed, and there was a half roll of paper.

"Well, who packs toilet paper when moving across country?" she said aloud. Speaking helped. Hearing words banished the creaking, hissing, auditory hallucinations haunting the dark and empty house. Dark, empty, and cold. Very cold. Increasingly so, now she'd stopped moving about. The house was well carpeted, but insulation wasn't the same as heat.

In the den, she slowly felt her away around the boxes neatly stacked in the centre of the otherwise empty room. She opened the curtains an inch, letting in just enough light to see the pair of folded lawn-chairs. She recognised them instantly, and didn't need to read it to know that *Generation Twelve* would be etched on the frame.

Generation One had been the chairs at the tailgate party some fifty years before when Mr and Mrs Mathers had first met; he drinking with his college teammates, she protesting the university's lack of funding for women's sports. They'd gone through a lot of chairs over the years. Treating them unkindly, roughly, knowing the sentiment was stored in the idea, not the metal and canvas. These were the last pair, bought but never used. Mrs Mathers had left them behind, taking the memories with her instead.

Olivia pulled one out from between the boxes, unfolded it, and sat down, wrapping the borrowed coat around her as she tried to stay warm, finally allowing herself to remember all that had happened over a long and horrific day.

Nicole was dead.

Quietly, Olivia cried.

Chapter 6 - By Dawn's Glaring Light
Lilac Road, South Bend

She didn't sleep. Slowly the sky brightened, then darkened again as clouds swept in from the north.

"Thirsty, stiff, cold," she whispered. "But one of those can be fixed."

Sufficient light crept through the broad kitchen window to see she'd been wrong: the kitchen wasn't *entirely* empty. There was a letter on the counter addressed to Jenny, a nearly-next-door-neighbour who owned the corner house with the blue picket fence. A little younger than Mrs Mathers, Jenny had a sprawling tribe of children and grandchildren for whom working the carpet store stockroom during high-school vacations was as long-running a family tradition as the New Year's Day movie.

Olivia had met Jenny a few times, and been to the New Year's movie day once. An entire screen at the theatre had been booked, the cinema filled with the extended family, eating smuggled-in hot dogs, drinking home-brew cider. She smiled at the happy memory.

The envelope wasn't sealed, so Olivia didn't feel too guilty about opening it. Inside, she found a letter, and a second envelope. The second envelope was affixed with a stamp and inscribed with a very familiar address: her own. She read the letter addressed to Jenny first.

Dear Jenny,

As promised, the boxes in the den are for Malcolm. The contents belonged to Charlie, but they're still in good condition. It would be a sin to bin them, but I don't want to bring those particular memories with me to Florida.

Please could you mail the enclosed letter for me?

I look forward to seeing you in March, in the sunshine, and will speak to you before then.

Yours, as always,
Nora.

Hands trembling, she opened the letter addressed to her.

My dearest Olivia,

You know how much I hate breaking my word, but packing has brought up too many memories. Life has finally caught up with me, and I'm feeling my age. I've left early, and I am deeply sorry I didn't tell you, but once I'd sold the house, I felt as if I was a stranger here with only Charlie's ghost for company. I have to begin my new life, and let him enjoy his eternal rest.

When I sold the store, I told Ms Kempton you should manage it. I'm sorry that she didn't give you the promotion. And I'm sorry that the sale makes your position somewhat precarious. No one knows what the future will bring, but everyone needs a place of their own, so I'm giving you the cabin. It's not much, but like Mark Twain said, no one's building land anymore. Go up there, take a look for yourself. If you think it'll be too much to manage, too far from the city, the realtor who handled the sale of my home thinks she has a buyer. It won't bring in much, but it should be enough to set you up in a new life in a new place, all of your own.

And if you do decide to leave, consider Florida. You'll always be a welcome guest of mine, and a welcome neighbour.

With all my love,
Nora.

Olivia leaned heavily against the counter. She was a homeowner. Owner of a cabin and a few acres of woodland. Or, really, owner of a few thousand dollars with which she could start over. Mrs Mathers had read between the lines, filled in the gaps, and come up with a solution. A cabin, an asset, she could keep or sell, and an invitation down to Florida where there were plenty of care homes looking for an assistant manager. There it was, the invitation that Olivia had been too proud to ask for. A lifeline. A future. It wasn't an answer to all her problems, since it didn't resolve the issue of Pete, but it reframed the question. For the first time, she had a safety net. A secure fallback if her romantic, made-for-TV fantasy failed.

But the world had changed. Pete was in Hawaii, Nora was in Florida, and Nicole was dead.

"Despair solves nothing," she said loudly, as she stared at the dark square on the wall where the cross-stitched motto had hung. "No, despair only distracts, though not from hunger."

Water helped a little, as she drank one cupped handful after another. A cold-water wash with the dish-soap left beneath the sink helped a little more. She didn't feel clean, but she felt awake. And hungry.

It took less than half an hour to confirm that the house truly was empty except for the boxes in the den. Among the jars of screws and bolts, the patched dungarees, and commemorative plates, she'd found an electric lantern, and the batteries to power it, but the glow it gave was softer than that of morning's first light. A complete set of never-used *Fighting Irish* mugs gave her something to drink water from, but the only real find was the four boxes in the middle and bottom of the pile. Left behind by accident, they contained some of Mrs Mathers's old clothes. The volcanic-orange calf-length skirt fit, though only after she'd used a screwdriver to punch a new hole in one of Mr Mathers's heavy-duty belts. A ruffled blouse that had gone out of fashion before she was born, and probably before Mrs Mathers was married, was far warmer than the stained scrubs she'd worn from the hospital.

She sat on the chair, surveying the boxes.

"It's not much, is it?" she said to herself. "But better than nothing."

A comment which only reminded her of how little she'd eaten in the last day. She crossed to the window. She could see Jenny's house, ringed by the blue picket fence. But there were no more signs of life now than there had been by dawn's first light. Like with the other driveways in view, the cars were gone. Everyone was gone.

Her stomach growled, and she sighed. There was no option left but to return to the hospital. Memories of the previous night came back to her, accompanied by a pre-emptive wave of exhaustion at the coming day's arduous labours. She'd return to the hospital soon. But there was no hurry. No reason to rush. She made a nest on the floor out of the unused clothes, curled up, and slept.

A few hours later, she woke, stiff and starving. She wasn't sure of the time since she had no phone or watch, and the only clock among Mr Mathers's hand-me-downs had no batteries. Water filled her stomach, but it didn't trick her mind. There was no food in the house. No money, either. Nor a car. She had no phone. No way of knowing what was happening in the wider world. She had the cabin, sure, but there was no way of reaching it without driving.

It was a nice idea, escaping to the cabin. She and Pete had spent many happy afternoons thrashing out their post-apocalyptic plans, but not with any seriousness. Reality was different. If the police sergeant took her back to her apartment, and she got her keys, she could drive to the cabin. But then what? No. It was far more sensible to return to the hospital, where she'd be assured of something to eat, and probably somewhere more comfortable to sleep than the floor of this unheated room. Before she could change her mind, she left.

Keeping away from the kerb, she kept her head down, but her eyes up as vehicle after vehicle sped by. The sidewalk was as empty as first thing that morning, but the roads were busier as people drove north and south, east and west. The houses, however, were darker, emptier. Outside some properties, the half-full bags abandoned on the driveways were an obvious clue that the owners had spent the night packing, and left with dawn's first light, but had overestimated how much their car could hold.

As she crossed the interstate, she toyed with the idea of breaking in. If the owners had gone, they'd have left some food behind. But when she came to a house where a pair of young men stood in the doorway, crowbars in hand, she changed her mind. Though she was hungry, it wasn't just a single meal she sought. She kept her head down, and hurried on.

But with her head down, she didn't see the car until it was almost too late. As she jumped sideways, the vehicle swerved across the road, narrowly missing her before clipping a streetlight, spinning ninety degrees, and coming to a ragged halt. She picked herself up, and took an uncertain step towards the car, but stopped as the passenger door opened and a blood-soaked man stepped out. It wasn't the blood which made her pause, but the gun in his hand.

She backed up as he staggered on a few paces, turning to face her, raising the gun until a dog bounded over a fence, yapping and barking.

With the gunman distracted, she turned and ran, diving down a narrow alley. Another alley and two roads later, and she was heading south again, determined that the hospital was the right destination. Hearing a sound behind, she turned, expecting to see a person, but it was only a dog, a fawn-coloured Great Dane with a wet-looking coat and a tired look in his eyes.

"You're the dog that just saved me," she said. "Thanks."

The dog gave a tilt of his head that almost seemed like a nod.

"You're not called Betsy, are you?" she asked, remembering the man at the hospital who'd been bitten. The dog wagged his tail.

"No. Probably not. You should go home," she said.

Dogs were like wolves, weren't they? Descended from wolves, anyway. Had this one's owners fled, leaving him behind? He didn't seem dangerous, but nor did he seem to want to leave. Instead, he followed her south, falling into step at her side.

After a block, the dog finally stopped, sitting on the kerb. When she looked back, he was still there. When she looked ahead, she saw the smoke. She could smell it, too. Taste it. An acrid tang that had been growing in intensity. She'd been so focused on the dog, on the passing traffic, she'd not looked up. Ahead, a towering grey pillar tumbled skywards. With a sinking sense of inevitable dread, she kept going until she reached an intersection where a police car was skewed across the road, the engine partially buried beneath a four-ton truck. But she gave the vehicles barely a glance as she looked upward at the growing cloud of smoke. The hospital was on fire.

While she was still debating whether there was any sense in continuing, gunshots sounded from beyond the smoke-filled haze. As the rat-a-tat of automatic fire filled the silent streets, she ducked down, taking shelter behind the police car. A burst came again, longer, then silence. Another burst. This time shorter. Was it a gun battle, or just ammunition cooking in the blaze? Either way, it was an indication she should leave. She turned, about to run when she caught sight of the coat on the police car's front passenger seat. The name read *Wilgus*. It belonged to the sergeant from the previous night. Cautiously, she tried the door handle. It was unlocked. There was no blood on the steering wheel, nor on the seat, suggesting no one had been inside the car when the truck had driven into it. She picked up the coat, checking the pocket, but the gun the sergeant had placed there was gone.

Another burst of unseen automatic rifle fire decide it. In a crouch, she ran, back the way she'd come, only slowing when she reached the kerb where the dog still sat. He tilted his head to one side as if in exasperation at the human who'd not taken his advice, then fell into step with her as she continued walking.

Where could she go? Hunger was an increasingly pressing problem. With no money, she couldn't buy any food. Not that she'd seen any open stores. Her feet were taking her north, but there was no food at Nora's, and there was none on the building site that used to be her place of work. She had no friends to visit. Leaving… where? Her apartment? Except that she didn't know if the tactical unit would have been. If they hadn't, Mack might still be inside. One of the properties with the possessions discarded on the drive? Maybe. She'd find food, but obviously no car. There was Pete's place, of course. She had a key for his apartment on the same key ring as his truck's key, which was in a drawer in her apartment. But his truck was in the garage beneath his building. She'd driven it there herself after he'd been suddenly whisked away to Hawaii. He had a spare set of keys in his apartment, inside a plastic Statue of Liberty. If she could get in, she could get the keys, and take his truck. His apartment door would be locked, of course, but it felt less like a crime than robbing some random stranger.

"Yes," she said aloud. "Pete's."

The dog gave a soft yip.

"I don't have any food," she said. "And if you're thinking of eating me, I'm going to put up a fight. Okay." She stopped. "Seriously, are you called

Betsy?" She bent and checked his collar. The name tag read *Rufus*, beneath was a phone number.

"Sorry, I can't call your owner. No phone," she said. "And I don't think they work anymore. Did you get left behind?"

She found talking to the dog helped. If nothing else, it helped her feel less alone as, on the road, one overloaded vehicle after another barrelled by. Trucks, cars, even an ice-cream van, loaded down with possessions. Those she could see suggested the occupants prized what had been valuable last week over those more everyday items invaluable for survival. But where were they going? No one stopped, and she didn't feel comfortable asking any of the people boarding up their shops and homes.

When she reached Mrs Mathers's house, Olivia went inside, holding the door open, but Rufus sat on the porch.

"You're an outdoors dog? Fair enough. I won't be long."

And she wasn't. She knew what she was after. Among Mr Mathers's boxes was a wide selection of tools. Some were nearly as old as the couple's marriage, but they were meticulously clean. She took the hammer, screwdriver, and a small pry-bar. They went into a tasselled knit shoulder bag that must have belonged to Mrs Mathers. Before leaving, she filled one of the plastic bowls with water and took it outside with her, placing it in front of the dog.

Rufus yipped his thanks, and then began guzzling. She kept going, walking away from the house, briefly glancing back to see the dog happily lapping at the bowl.

"So you were only after a free drink?" she said. "I suppose I should be glad."

But she felt a pang of regret that, once more, she walked the city alone.

Chapter 7 - Breaking the Law
South Bend

Breaking the law, and breaking into Pete's apartment, was far easier than she'd expected. She slotted the pry-bar into the gap between door and lock. One tap with the hammer, one dull crack from the lock plate, and the door swung ajar.

She quickly stepped inside, glancing back along the dark, quiet corridor with its six other doors leading off it. But quiet wasn't silence. Behind at least one of those doors, someone listened, watched, shuffling their feet, breathing softly. She pushed the door closed, and used the pry-bar to wedge it shut.

So far, so good.

Her first stop were the curtains, drawing them to let in a little light.

"Wow, Pete. You're not the tidiest, are you?"

The efficiency apartment wasn't dirty, but it was simply too small for Pete's acquired junk. Barely giving the jungle of cables, forest of bank envelopes, and clutter of collectibles more than the briefest of curious glances, she entered the small galley-kitchen, revising it downwards into a kayak's kitchenette. As she'd expected and hoped, the minuscule pantry was crammed with sugar-laden, unnaturally coloured, gloriously edible cereal. Twelve boxes in total, seven of which were unopened. In the still-humming fridge, she found two sealed gallon jugs of milk. Though Pete hadn't expected to leave town the night he'd disappeared in the limo, it was typical he'd not considered scaling back his purchase of perishables before going away. The milk wasn't sour. The cereal in the open packet was close to stale, but she didn't notice until her third bowl.

Over her more thoughtful fourth bowl, she reassessed her actions, decisions, and options. The hospital had burned down. An emergency clinic would have opened somewhere, but was there any point in looking for it? What did she want? If she could find him, Sergeant Wilgus might escort her back to her apartment, but she couldn't think of anything there she needed. Her car, her clothes, her food, weren't needed while she was working at the hospital. Which, of course, she couldn't now it had burned down. She wanted somewhere safe to sleep and a few square meals. The hospital had ticked those boxes, particularly safety. Or so she'd thought.

Finishing her bowl, she looked about the small living and sleeping room. Pete still had the flea-market chair. The small table was covered in some books, a few dollar store DVDs, and a dusty Statue of Liberty. Inside were the spare car keys and two hundred dollars. She smiled, impressed he'd been able to sequester so much, but unsurprised he kept it as cash rather than in a bank. Even if there was a typhoon on Hawaii, his rainy-day fund was of no use to him now. Pocketing the keys and cash, she turned her attention to what else she could use.

The miniature closet contained more shoes than clothes, and half of those were his old work uniform. The bathroom contained a one-gallon jug of shower gel, one toothbrush, a mammoth tube of toothpaste, a comb, a half-empty crate of deodorant, and a quarter empty pallet of toilet paper stuffed into the narrow cupboard beneath the small sink.

"You like shopping in bulk, don't you?" she said. "Or you hate shopping. Which is it, Pete? I should know, shouldn't I?" A wave of regret washed over her, followed by one of tiredness. She rested her hands on the cold ceramic sink and peered at the gaunt stranger in the mirror. She tried the faucet, intending to splash some on the back of her neck. A wondrously soothing cloud of steam rose as hot water gurgled down the plughole.

She could have a hot shower. She could sleep in a real bed. She tried the light switch and found there was, of course, power. Behind the cereal had been a few cans which she could heat up.

From outside, she heard a faint, sharp bang. Was that a gunshot? Maybe not, but she wasn't safe here with only a pry-bar holding the door closed.

It took longer to find the bags than to fill them. Four near-identical hold-alls that nearly held everything she needed. Food, blankets, pillows, toilet paper, toothpaste, and Pete's toothbrush: once boiled, it would be better than nothing. How she'd boil it was a problem to solve later, but from everything she'd seen that morning, it was going to be weeks before any shops reopened. Some cutlery, some crockery, some clothes, and the bags were nearly full.

What was missing was a spare phone, radio, or even a working TV. His screen was plugged into his laptop through which he got every television channel in a way that he'd insisted wasn't *technically* illegal. The laptop required a password, and she didn't want to waste time trying to guess it. Nothing the news had to say would change her circumstances. Not now. Not yet.

She looked again at the bags, then at the room, and knew why she was reluctant to leave.

"Goodbye, Pete," she said aloud. "Thank you."

She pulled the pry-bar from the bottom of the door, picked up two of the bags, and made her way outside.

Along the hall, the door to number 314 opened. A man stepped forward, though not quite outside, lingering in the doorway with his right hand hidden behind the frame.

Head and shoulders taller than Olivia, the man wasn't athletic, though his clothing was. His face was a riot of battling emotions. Nervous. Anxious. Angry. But not alone. There was at least one person standing behind him.

Before either could speak, Olivia went first. "Oh, it's so good to see people again," she said. "I thought everyone had already left."

"What are you doing?" the man asked.

"Getting my boyfriend's things," Olivia said decisively. "We're leaving town, I think everyone else has already gone. You don't want to be the last here. Did you see what happened to the hospital? I was working there yesterday. But it burned down. No one came to put the fire out."

"The hospital burned down?" the man asked, sounding genuinely curious.

"You didn't know?" Olivia said. "It was a nightmare there last night. Gunshots, car-wrecks, fights, fires."

"Zombies?" another man asked, the other person in the apartment, opening the door a little further so he could see out.

"No," Olivia said. "There were no zombies. Just people acting crazy. I went back to work another shift. The whole building was on fire. Now I'm — *We're* leaving. Everyone out there is. You should do the same. Get out while you can."

As she spoke, she'd taken half steps along the corridor. Now she took full ones, striding along the hallway. Not wanting to wait for the elevator, she took the stairs, walking not running, listening but not looking back. She wasn't followed down to the garage, but it was half empty and nearly pitch dark. Pete's truck was where she'd parked it when she'd brought it back for him, close to the entrance through which bitterly cold light streamed. The two bags went on to the passenger seat. That left two up in the apartment. She took a step away from the car, then changed her mind. She'd brought the food. The clothes and other things could be found elsewhere or she would do without. She put the key in the ignition and drove.

Driving summoned a comfortable memory of familiarity, an illusion of safety that was shattered when a red and silver eighteen-wheeler ambled across the intersection ahead of her. She had plenty of time to brake; the juggernaut barely managed ten miles an hour, but it was travelling southwest along an east-west street, heading from Woodlawn Boulevard but completely missing the diagonal turn onto Wilbur. Instead it rumbled on, mounting the kerb, churning the civic apron of grass to mud before doing the same to the corner plot's front lawn. The truck swerved slightly to the right before it slammed into the brown-brick single storey house. Glass shattered as windows smashed, but the slow-moving juggernaut finally stopped.

Olivia slowly released her grip on the wheel as, outside, the clatter of falling masonry subsided. Slowly, she got out. No one else did. The doors of the truck remained closed. With the house's front door partially buried beneath its massive wheels, she didn't expect the homeowner to come out that way, but no one made their way around from the back of the house. Nor did anyone appear from any of the neighbouring homes. Surely not everyone could have fled the city, not from all of the windows she could see. Not yet. Could they?

A pattering of bricks from within the partially demolished building was followed by an echoing grind. The driver still hadn't opened the door, and there were two possible reasons for that. She suspected the worse, but on the slim chance they were merely trapped rather than dead, she grabbed the pry-bar before hurrying over to the juggernaut.

It had New Jersey plates. She could fill in the rest of the blanks. The driver had taken a few pills to stay awake on the long escape-drive west, but had a heart attack behind the wheel. Except...

When she'd got into Pete's truck, driving from his apartment, she'd slipped into automatic, and had headed back to familiar roads close to her own apartment. The river wasn't far to the east, while the interstate was still a couple of blocks further north. The trucker couldn't have been fleeing, but heading to somewhere specific. This house? Wherever it was, they weren't going any further.

She pulled herself up the steps to the driver-side door. The windows were coated with dust, mud, and spider-web cracks from the collision. But from inside, she heard movement.

"Hello? Are you okay? Can you hear me?" she called.

The handle was jammed. She slid the pry-bar in, and slammed her entire body against it, levering the stuck door open with a grinding crunch. The door swung outward, forcing her to jump down. She landed unsteadily on the rubble-strewn mess beneath the person-sized wheels. Looking down to find her footing, it was a second more before she looked back up and saw she'd been wrong. The driver was dead. The woman, wearing blue dungarees, a plaid shirt, and a green cap, was covered in blood and slumped forward over the steering wheel.

Was there someone else in the cab? Olivia quickly pulled herself back up. There was a man in the passenger seat, and he was certainly dead. He'd been shot, from close range. Twice, by the look of it. Once in the chest, once in the head.

The driver gasped, and Olivia lost her footing, falling once more outside the cab, but landing on her feet among the debris.

"It's okay," she said. "I'm here to help."

Bone grated as the driver twisted her broken neck, flexed her fractured body, tugging against the seatbelt holding her in place. Her arm reached towards Olivia. The forearm was broken in at least two places, giving an unnatural curve to the limb.

"Don't move!" Olivia said. "Don't..." The words trailed into silence as she finally understood what she was seeing. "You're infected. You're... you're..." She couldn't bring herself to say the word aloud, but that didn't stop it being true. The driver was undead. No longer human. A zombie.

Olivia backed off and ran back to Pete's truck, got behind the wheel, and tried the ignition. The engine wouldn't start.

She didn't hear the seatbelt snap, but she heard the crunch as the zombie fell out of the cab. The undead driver landed on broken arms, and crawled more than walked, lurching forward on its four broken limbs before slipping and rolling to its side. In the process, somehow, it managed to get a knee beneath its body. Slowly it unfolded upright. Standing, it staggered on.

Olivia turned the key again. Still nothing. Again. Nothing.

The zombie lurched nearer.

From nowhere, a ball of fawn-coloured fury ran at the zombie. The dog sprang sideways at the last second, circling behind, barking and snarling at the zombie who snarled back in turn. The zombie spun, swiping its broken arm at Rufus who kept circling. Kept barking. Kept snapping. He was trying to scare, to subdue, a task for which he must have been trained, but the zombie wasn't going to be intimidated. On the video footage she'd seen on TV, and on her phone, the undead had advanced into a hail of gunfire, and then kept walking. A dog would be no more trouble than a person. She tried the engine one last time. Still it wouldn't start.

Olivia grabbed the pry-bar and got out, but she couldn't run.

Rufus walked backwards as the zombie swiped its arms towards it. How did he find her? How did he know not to bite? Could dogs get infected? She bundled the questions around her doubts and pushed them aside, to be dealt with later.

"Rufus! Heel!" she called, hoping that was the right command. The dog understood his name, at least, and backed off a step, then darted left, sprinting in a curving half circle until he'd come to stand a little in front of Olivia.

"Now what?" she asked.

Rufus yipped.

"That's not very helpful."

The food was in the truck. And it was the only vehicle for which she had a set of keys. She could run, but carrying the bags, could she outrun a zombie? No.

The broken-armed monster limped closer, dragging its left leg behind it.

"Rufus, get in the truck!" Olivia said.

The dog rose to a half crouch, eyes now on the zombie, clearly ready to charge.

"Stay!" Olivia said.

She looked in the dead trucker's eyes, and wished she hadn't. There wasn't even a spark of recognition in those lifeless depths. She raised the pry-bar and swung it like a bat, straight into the zombie's outstretched arm. Bone snapped, but the zombie staggered on. Olivia backed off. Rufus charged, accelerating from zero to a surging ball of defensive anger, slamming into the zombie's legs. The undead driver flew up before falling down, hard, while Rufus tumbled sideways, across the road.

"Rufus?" Olivia called. The dog whined.

Anger rose, quickly turning to fury, then a blinding rage as memories of the dead and dying at the hospital came back to her, settling on a memory of Nicole. Of Dante. Of Mack. Screaming now, a feral bellow of justified rage, she swung the pry-bar up, and slammed it down on the zombie's skull. But as the bone cracked, reason returned, and she backed off, until her legs hit something hard. Spinning around, she saw she was back at Pete's truck. She spun around again, but the zombie hadn't moved. This time, it was well and truly dead.

She breathed out slowly, and realised Rufus had gone.

She looked up and down the empty street. No one had come to a window. No one had come to a door. No one had come to help her, except Rufus. And now the dog had vanished as mysteriously as he'd arrived.

She got back into the truck. This time, the contrary engine started the first time. She was about to drive off, when she paused. Leaving the engine running, giving the corpse a wide berth, she went to the truck's cab. There was a gun on the floor, beneath the steering wheel: a cheap nine-millimetre, which explained how the passenger had died. She grabbed it. Near the stick was a small wash bag. She grabbed that, too. Neither was what she was after.

She wanted answers. An explanation. She'd settle for a map, but couldn't see one. Her eyes settled on the radio on the dash, covered in gore from the shot-dead passenger. But Pete had a radio in his truck.

Taking gun and wash bag with her, she returned to Pete's truck and turned on the radio, flipping through stations as she drove back to Mrs Mathers's house.

Chapter 8 - Trooper State
Indiana & Michigan

With cold water and bleach, she cleaned the pry-bar, then her hands, then the skirt, all the while wishing she'd gone back for clothes from Pete's. Too big would have been better than damp and smelling of chlorine. After, she sat in the lawn chair in the kitchen, sipping from the gallon jug of milk, considering her options. They weren't great.

On the positive side of the ledger, she had a truck with nearly half a tank of gas, enough cereal to last her a month, a roof over her head, and water coming out of the faucet. She had a firearm. In the truck driver's wash bag, she'd found a spare magazine, a thousand dollars in twenties, neatly tied together, and twelve plastic pill jars that were labelled Vitamin-D, but almost certainly weren't. The pills had gone into the trash. The bills and the gun, now unloaded, were on the kitchen counter.

She ran through the mental list again, but couldn't come up with any other positives. The negatives were far more numerous.

She had no electricity and little clue what was happening in the world. The radio stations she'd skipped through on her drive back hadn't helped. Each frequency still broadcasting had yelled, mumbled, or preached a variation on it being the end of days, the end of the world, and nowhere was safe. What had been lacking was some kind of official government statement about where to go, where to avoid, where to leave, or where to stay. Perhaps that would come in time. Until then, she was on her own, which brought her back to her mental list.

The infected had reached South Bend. One truck driver from New Jersey might be the first, but she wouldn't be the last. There'd be other cases between here and New York, and more every hour. There was no sign of the National Guard. No sign of the police this morning. No fire service either. From the acrid tang settling over the city, the hospital wasn't the only conflagration. She had no phone. No address book, either. Pete was in Hawaii, which might as well be the moon. Nicole was dead.

Mrs Mathers was in Florida. A half tank of gas in an unreliable truck wasn't going to get her far. There was no sign of life at Jenny's house at the end of the street, and in the entire city, she couldn't think of anyone who'd give her a better welcome than a stranger.

Sensing that her list was drifting into a litany of self-pity, she turned to her choices. Essentially, there were two. Her eyes fell on the letter, still on the counter. Either she stayed in the house or she went to the cabin.

Those quiet afternoon fantasy conversations with Pete, usually the morning after the alien invasion series had aired on TV, came back to her. Most of those time-wasting dialogues had been spent discussing what they'd haul up there in the back of one of the store's delivery vans. Sometimes it was two vans. Sometimes it was one of the grocery store's delivery trucks, already conveniently full, collecting Nicole along the way. What they'd not really considered was, in a real apocalypse, they wouldn't be the only people wanting to escape.

No, reality was different from fantasy. The cabin's power came from a generator which was always drained at the end of a stay, and no one had stayed there in months. Not since she'd gone up there with Mrs Mathers to help pack up her husband's old things. A lot of which were now in boxes in the den. There might be a few sticks of furniture left behind, but nothing else. There was an open fire, and the woods were full of trees, but she didn't have an axe, let alone a chainsaw. There was an old well, but she wasn't sure the water was potable because, when she'd gone up there with Mrs Mathers, Nora had insisted they bring water with them. The cabin was four walls and a roof in the middle of the woods. Remote, yes, but that came with dangers as well as benefits. There had to be another choice.

Her eyes fell on the gun. An hour ago, she'd killed someone. That there'd never be any repercussions was more terrifying than the act itself. That she felt no regret was worse still. But she'd been in shock since she'd turned on the TV yesterday. Since then, so much had happened that she was thoroughly numb.

A long time ago, about the time she'd cut ties with her mother, she'd realised that there was a time for emotion, and a time for it to be boxed up, put away. This last year, in the company of Pete, Nora, and Nicole, she'd let her emotions come out. Let herself feel safe. Feel normal. As if life could be lived in colour, rather than in shades of grey. Today, they'd been permanently tinged blood red.

In high school, a counsellor had told her that life could always be split into binary choices. Do something, or don't do it. Here it was stay or not stay. Her eyes fell on the gun once more. That was what life would become if she stayed here, in the empty city. And it was why so many people had already left. Staying required fighting to keep what she had, and what little there was in the house wasn't worth the cost.

She went into the living room and began sorting through the boxes to find what she'd take with her.

Half an hour later, the truck was loaded. From the driveway, she looked up and down the street, her eyes lingering one last time on Jenny's house, but there was no one there. There was no one anywhere. Everyone was hiding until the nightmare was over, and it was time she did the same. A grey pall of smoke loomed over the city to the south. From its size, an entire block was burning.

"Thank you, Nora," she said, climbing into the truck. "And thank you, Pete." She checked the mirrors, then out of the windows, looking for the dog. Instead, she heard the sharp crack of a rifle. "And thank you, Rufus," she said, and started the engine.

When she left the housing subdivision, this time, she went north.

The cabin was fifty miles across the state line in Michigan, north of Paw Paw, and west of Kalamazoo. She knew the general route well enough: up to Niles, then Dowagiac, Decatur, then through Paw Paw until she saw the farm with the blue water tower. Then it was a right turn. The cabin, and the woodland included in the deed, was off a short track marked with a trio of battered, official-looking signs, warning about landslides. Mr Mathers had put those up to discourage unwanted visitors.

55

Or was it a left turn at the water tower? Worrying about the last few miles could wait until she got there. For now, she had to get more than a few miles from South Bend.

To the east, the St Joseph River was her occasional companion as she drove a straighter path north. The further she travelled, the more confident she was that she'd left just in time, if not a little late. A small house had already burned to the ground, while its neighbour, a far larger, far grander home had a trio of pickup trucks outside. On the back of one stood a woman with a rifle who half-raised her weapon as Olivia stomped on the gas. Something told her those trucks didn't belong to the owners of the home. At other houses, she was sure people were inside. Watching. Waiting until nightfall to either flee or loot, but though she saw an occasional curtain twitch, no doors opened as she drove by, and she saw no reason to slow. Not until Lilac Road became Coop Road as she crossed into Michigan, and then came to the intersection with Bertrand Road, and the barricade.

The road ran west-east, with the barricade on the eastern side blocking the approach to the bridge over the river. A bus was parked diagonally across the road, leaving a car-width's gap. On this side of the bus was a police car, while beyond, she could see a string of cars and small trucks parked along the roadside. In the gap, flagging her down, was a police officer. Seeing the uniform, a bundle of tension finally left her. She'd wondered what had happened to the police, but here they were, on the outskirts of the city. Normality was being restored.

More than that, as he walked towards her truck, she realised she knew the officer. It was the younger cop who'd been outside the hospital. What was his name? Herrera, that was it.

She wound down the window and leaned out. "Is Sergeant Wilgus here?" she asked, before the officer had a chance to speak.

"Sergeant Wilgus?" Herrera repeated, sounding confused.

"You don't remember me? I was at the hospital. The sergeant sent me home to get a few hours sleep. When I went back, it was on fire. Isn't he here? What happened to him?"

Officer Herrera looked at her, then turned to look beyond the bus. There, an officer in the uniform of a state trooper was leaning over the window of a bright pink, mud-splattered runabout.

"You were at the hospital," Herrera said, though without any sign of recognition. "I... yeah, I don't where the sarge is. I haven't seen him since then." He turned around again as a yell came from beyond the bus. The state trooper was ordering the passengers out of the car.

"Is there a plan?" Olivia asked.

"What?" Herrera asked.

"An official plan?" Olivia asked. "I want to help, to be useful. Where's the temporary hospital being set up?"

"What? What hospital?" Herrera said. "There isn't one."

Beyond the bus, the trooper had drawn his gun.

"What's going on?" Olivia asked.

"Go," Herrera said. "Before Vevermee stops you. Turn around and just go. Now."

At the pink car, the trooper fired through the driver's window, before switching aim and firing into the backseat.

"Go!" Herrera said.

But Olivia had already thrown the truck into reverse. She spun backwards, across the intersection, skidding the truck around. She drove east, along Bertrand Road. In the rear view mirror, she thought she saw the trooper striding towards Herrera, but then they were both lost to view. At the first turning, she headed north. When she saw stalled cars ahead of her, she sped up and kept going without stopping, without slowing, driving unfamiliar roads, just to get away.

Keeping to back roads, and avoiding any town large enough to have a name, she drove north and west, wondering what she'd just seen. An execution? A robbery? Why were they stopping people from crossing the river?

The road gave her no answers, and asked very few questions. She saw no people, no livestock, no other traffic, and no more roadblocks, though she saw a few homes which had been hastily barricaded. Passing those at speed, she barely slowed until she came to a station wagon driven off the road. The doors were closed, the front buried in a ditch, but there was movement behind the dirt-flecked windows. She stopped fifty yards beyond the crashed car, picked up the pry-bar and, after the briefest hesitation, the pistol, and got out.

She'd slowed because the station wagon was the same colour as Nora's. But where hers was an ancient relic verging on being an antique, this vehicle was simply old. Two battered brown suitcases dangled over the left side, hanging from the rope which had been holding them to the roof, and which ran through the slightly open passenger windows. But it was the movement which had caught her eye, which had brought her to a stop. A hope, after the police roadblock, after the truck driver, after the hospital, of finding someone else alive. A hope that was dashed as she drew nearer. The figure was moving, but it was no longer alive. A teenager in acid-wash jeans and a blood-drenched hoodie, with blond-tipped hair and gore-flecked teeth, snapped at her as she approached. He was alone in the car. Now. There were… remains on the passenger seat. A woman. A mother? She backed away. The seatbelt held the zombie in place. He was no threat, and she wanted no more violence.

She returned to the truck and drove away.

By the time her headlights shone on the weather-cracked warning signs marking the turn, the shadows had risen to meet the cloak laid by night over the troubled world. The axle rattled a protest as she drove off the road and up the rutted unpaved lane, but she unapologetically drove onward, beyond the blasted stump and around the bend, until she was out of sight from the road. She switched off the engine, and sat, in the dark, listening, looking towards the road for any passing lights.

During her back-and-forth, side-to-side search for the turn, while a guilty sun quickly snuck below the horizon, a few distant pinpricks of light had appeared, marking buildings for her to avoid. Now, in the distance, she saw another, resolving into a pair as the vehicle approached, accompanied by the protesting growl of a stuttering engine. She reached for the bag in which she'd hidden the gun, watching the white lights approach, but not letting go until the red taillights had vanished beyond the trees. Still, she sat, for five minutes more, until she was sure she was truly alone. Gun in hand, with the pry-bar in the bag over her shoulder, and the truck's keys in her pocket, she set off on foot.

The cabin was exactly where she expected it, a dark, and obviously empty, shadow among the settling darkness. It wasn't as if she'd really expected to find Mrs Mathers here, but the smallest part of her had hoped. By feel, she found her way between the two raised-brick vegetable beds, and to the front door. It was padlocked. But the key she'd found in the envelope fitted the sturdy lock perfectly.

She opened the door, stepped inside, and froze. There was barely any light, but something was wrong. *Very* wrong.

She'd been to the cabin twice. Once, on a weekend that had only lasted one night, when Mrs Mathers had wanted to remember the times she'd spent there with her husband. The second time had been to clear it out. Jenny had come with them then, with one of her daughters, Carly. They'd packed almost everything, and taken it back to the garage at Nora's house. Ultimately, most of the boxes had ended up where Olivia had found them, in the den. Except the cabin was clearly full of furniture. Beneath her feet was a rug, not the bare boards she'd swept and scrubbed despite Nora saying there was no point.

Olivia picked her way around the furniture to the light fitting on the wall. A pull of the string, and nothing happened. Of course not, the generator wasn't on. She wished she'd brought a flashlight, a phone, a candle. Candles! Mrs Mathers always kept a stock of them in the cupboard above the sink. Bumping into a chair, then another, then a table, she'd made her way through the living space into the semi-separate kitchenette before she remembered cleaning out that cupboard, too. It wasn't empty now.

The candle was obvious by its shape, as was the box of matches. She lit one, and froze. By the match's flickering light, she could see the rest of the kitchen. The framed prints on the freshly plastered and painted wall. The new-for-the-cabin countertop. The cheap, but matching, kettle, toaster-oven, and microwave. The glass cabinet filled with crockery, all imprinted with a cartoon squirrel-farmer.

The match burned low, singeing her fingers. With a hiss, she waved it out. She lit another, this time lighting the candle. Taking a saucer from the cupboard, she dropped a little wax onto the plate, where it landed on the squirrel's nose, and held the candle there until it remained fixed. By its light, she began a proper search.

An hour later, with three more candles lit, she set a match to the ready-laid fire, collapsed into the armchair, and stared at the flames. Mrs Mathers hadn't just given her a cabin; she'd given her a home, complete with furnishings, with crockery, with soap and toilet paper in the bathroom-annex outside. Most importantly, with food in the kitchen cupboards. Enough food for months. Two. Maybe three. More than long enough to last until the nightmare was over.

Nora's parting gift had saved her life. And if things had been a few inches different, it would have saved Nicole's, too. Quietly, watching the fire, Olivia gave in to grief, weeping until, exhausted, she slept.

Chapter 9 - Win or Lose, You Can't Beat a House
The Cabin, Michigan

According to Mr Mathers, he'd won the cabin in a poker game. According to Mrs Mathers, he'd lost.

Over the years, he'd extended the main room, adding the kitchenette to the northern side, the bedroom to the south. What he'd overlooked, and why it had remained *Mr* Mathers's cabin for the first decade of their married life, was the bathroom. A cement-floored shed had, finally, been built to the north of the cabin, which stored a shower, toilet, and the generator. A complicated valve and handle system theoretically fed greywater from the shower into the toilet cistern, but it had never worked properly. Instead, cistern and washing-water tank alike were filled by hand, usually with water brought from the city, though there was a well another fifty yards into the wood.

Olivia made gathering water her priority for the morning, losing herself in the exercise as she ran through the events of the previous two days. Fear, panic, and shock had tainted her view of it. The news on TV and radio hadn't helped. That state trooper had probably been shooting zombies, not people. Just because she'd not seen the National Guard in South Bend didn't mean they'd been derelict in their duty. It was the same reason there'd been no fire engines at the hospital, and few staff. People had been redeployed to other, larger cities. Or to smaller, more easily controlled towns. Yes, that was probably it.

Probably.

What was undeniable were the undead truck driver and that zombie in the back of the car. The infection had certainly reached Indiana. The radio had said it had already spread across the world. She was inclined to believe it. Yes, she'd made the right choice. Better not to be in South Bend right now.

She hauled up the rope, and decided that tomorrow's task was going to be devising a better way of collecting water. *And filtering it*, she mentally added as she scooped the larger leaves from the bucket before pouring the well-water into the brand-new, bright red, plastic container that had come with a funnel attached.

"It's for gasoline, isn't it?" she murmured to herself. Of course it would be. Which presented another problem. The generator powered the small water-boiler. She hauled the container back up to the concrete-floored annex to inspect the generator.

Staring at the gauge didn't make fuel magically appear in the tank. Nor did it make a full fuel canister magically appear in the corner of the room. The multitude of labels all clearly stated the generator burned gas, just like Pete's truck, but she'd also need that fuel to get back to town when the crisis was over.

Uncertain what to do next, she retreated into the house, put some of the last of the milk into a mug, and had opened the microwave door before remembering there was no power. Sighing, she went back into the main room, laid and lit a fire, then waited for it to take. The milk went into a saucepan, to which she added some of the powdered coffee, all the while thinking of the old but reliable coffee pot she'd liberated from the store.

"It's true, then," she said to the flames. "You really don't know what you've got until it's gone."

The roll of bills she'd taken from the trucker, plus the couple of hundred dollars she'd taken from Pete, amounted to more cash than she'd ever had before. Would anyone be selling gasoline? Except that was the wrong question. Was anyone within driving range still selling it? And would they sell her more than she'd use driving Pete's truck there to get it? Maybe. But in a few days, the generator would have guzzled all she'd bought, and the money would be gone, too. Then she'd have no choice but to rely on the open fire. And rainwater, too, until she'd cleaned out the well. It hadn't rained in a couple of days, though. It hadn't snowed, either.

A stray gust caused the windows to rattle. She pulled the chair a little closer to the flickering flames. The cabin was already close to freezing. More firewood was the answer. At least she had an axe and a saw. She had a chainsaw, too, but that brought her back to her fuel problem. The stack of pre-chopped wood was already considerably diminished. Replenishing it would be her job for the afternoon. After she'd boiled the milk for her coffee.

She stirred the saucepan, and tested the contents. Barely warm. She reached for another log, and paused. When had Mrs Mathers cut the wood? Or had she bought it, pre-cut? But why? Why had Mrs Mathers done any of this? Why set the cabin up like a home?

While waiting on the milk, a slightly more thorough search of the cabin turned up an envelope, containing the title deeds, in Olivia's name, and the details of the realtor who'd sold Nora's house. And that, Olivia thought, was the real point of the furnishings. Mrs Mathers hadn't really expected her to live here, but to sell it, as seen, to some banker or executive who wanted to escape a concierge lifestyle. She didn't know how much the cabin would have fetched, and didn't want to think about it now, but that only left her to think about the hard work in her immediate future.

Calling it *café-au-lait* didn't make the lukewarm milk-coffee taste any better, nor did drinking it make her feel any more refreshed. Leaving the fire burning low, she trekked back to the truck, then down to the road, checking that the vehicle truly was out of sight, but really just putting off the inevitable. She returned to Pete's truck and turned on the radio. The signal struggled to make its way through the trees, but she listened to one crackly station after another, and felt increasingly reassured. The only specifics she heard were that the infection had spread everywhere. But she knew that, first hand. She was far more interested in the talk of deployments, of strategic positioning of troops and police, of call-ups and lockdowns. It was just talk, just rumours, discussion between the lonely DJ and the unresponsive airwaves. A relayed list of official instructions issued by the government would have been preferable, more reassuring, and though it was absent now, it *would* come. The nightmare would soon be over. Maybe in a week. Maybe in a month. But soon.

It took two hours to clean the guttering, and redirect the downpipe into the red-plastic jug. A proper water barrel went onto her mental shopping list. For the rest of the afternoon, her body sawed wood while her brain wondered how she might redirect rainwater directly into the shower's water cistern. At dark, with no answers, blistered hands, and enough wood for a week, she retreated inside.

"There we have it, Nicole," she said as she relit the fire. "I'm crossing off lumberjill and plumber from the list of careers to pursue." She sighed. "Not that I won't still have to learn how to do both jobs if I stay here."

Dinner was pasta cooked in tinned tomatoes. Edible, but thoroughly unappetising. As night drew in, the temperature dropped. The windows rattled. The door shook. She wedged blankets around the frame, and the upturned table against that, telling herself she was simply keeping it closed, knowing she was really adding a barricade of her own against the impossible horrors she'd witnessed in daylight. She added another log to the fire, and spent long minutes debating whether to light a candle as well.

"No," she said. "Better save them."

It would get easier. Maybe. But tomorrow, she'd see about finding some gas. The longer she left it, the less likely she was to find it. And if there really was none to be found, at least then she'd know. Besides, it was that or spend another day sawing wood.

23rd February

Chapter 10 - No One's Special
Michigan

Shivering awake in the freezing dark confirmed two things for Olivia: that Nora had left her the cabin to be sold, not to be lived in, and that electricity was a damn good thing. Wrapped in a nest of blankets, she stirred the saucepan of canned pineapple and dried oats, and wished for fresh pastries. Even stale ones. Bananas. Oranges. Potatoes. Lights. Music. Books. She already missed them all. The future truly wasn't going to be like the past, and certainly not like her daydreams of life at the cabin with Pete, but at least it was nearly spring; things would get easier. She could make them so, in time, and with effort. Well, she had the time and she wasn't afraid of hard work.

By daylight's first glimmer, she trudged down to Pete's truck. The road beyond ran north to south, parallel to and a mile away from the highway. With Kalamazoo fifteen miles to the east, when she came to a westbound turning, she took it. One eye on the odometer, keeping her speed to twenty, she altered her plans. The cabin had seemed remote while she stood on its creaking porch, but it was only a hard day's walk from Kalamazoo. While not as big as South Bend, tens of thousands had called that city home. Any who fled west might spot the smoke from her cabin's fire. Her fingers tapped a frustrated drumroll on the steering wheel. The cabin had seemed so promising. She'd woken up thinking of all the things she had to change, fix, and adapt, but she'd been willing to embrace the challenge. But now, once more, her plans had come crashing down. If it wasn't safe to stay there, she needed the fuel even more, and she needed a destination.

She tried the truck's radio, quickly cycling through the static to the three lonely stations still broadcasting. One DJ was reading the Bible, but he was only up to Exodus. The second was broadcasting the same horror stories and conspiracy theories that had dominated TV, her phone, and the radio since the nightmare began. The third station was more promising, in that it was playing music bracketed by a message that listeners should stay tuned for a government message. After hearing the instruction for the third time, but no government missive, she turned it off.

Ahead, a decrepit sedan was stalled in the middle of an intersection. She slowed, stopping fifty feet further back, just behind a battered sign that pointed north, to Bangor.

"Towns and highways," she said, watching the abandoned car in front. "That's where you find gas stations. Along highways and inside towns. Not in the middle of absolutely nowhere. So, north to Bangor, south to Highway 94, or… or where?"

Her eyes settled on the abandoned car, a grey four-door with mud covering the licence plate and a good portion of the windows. There didn't appear to be any movement inside. Slowly, she climbed out, bringing the pry-bar and the tasselled bag containing the gun. Ten feet from the car, she realised she didn't need the weapon.

The car was occupied by a man her own age, shot in the head. He sprawled on the back seat, still wearing his seatbelt. His hands were tied with rope, secured to the above-door strap with a figure-of-eight knot. She walked around the car, but couldn't find a bullet hole. On a hunch, she tried the passenger door, and found it unlocked. She found the bullet hole in the empty passenger seat next to the corpse. Someone had stood where she was, firing through the open door, killing this man.

"You were infected, weren't you?" she said, turning her head this way and that, looking for a bandage, a wound, but unable to find it. "Must have been. If you'd wanted, you could have untied that rope. Ah, who am I kidding?" She closed the door. "I want you to have been infected, because the alternative is too hideous, but either explanation is still horrific."

She crossed to the driver's door. The keys were still in the ignition. When she tried the engine, it came on. The fuel-needle jumped almost to the halfway mark.

"Bingo."

She switched off the engine. The trunk was empty, except for a bag containing soft toys and board games. That told her a lot about who the car's other occupants had been. Kicking the mud off the licence plates told her they'd come from Ohio, while the maps of Michigan and Ontario told her they'd probably been heading to the bridge, the border, and Canada. She pocketed the keys, but then changed her mind, walked over to the dense row of pines, and hung them on the first high, broken branch she could find.

"Canada? Maybe."

This was how she'd find fuel if she couldn't buy it. And how she'd *have* to find it after spending all her money buying whatever little it was worth. She walked back to the truck, debating Canada. Debating the border. Debating whether to return to the cabin, load up the truck, and simply drive. No, not yet. Better to stick with the plan and work through the alternatives later.

She paused, foot raised. Slowly, she turned back to face the car.

"Of course."

The bag of games and toys had to have been packed by a child. In which case, the dead man was probably the father. His hands were tied. Who tied up a zombie? If he'd been infected, he'd not turned immediately. Some of the radio reports had said as much, that people could be bitten, but not be symptomatic for hours. Since the first symptom was death, she'd ignored it as another piece of speculation. Perhaps there was some truth in it. And if there was, perhaps there was some truth in some of the other wild rumours.

"Not that it helps you now," she said, getting back in the truck. "Right, next stop… Bangor, I guess. Let's see how friendly the neighbours are."

As she drove north towards Bangor, she left the radio on. When she lost the station to static, and as she looked down to retune it, she almost didn't see the white-tailed stag bound across the road. She swerved, but the deer had already bounded into the trees.

Bangor was closed. The houses were dark. Boarded. Not a soul was on the streets. But there were cars in some driveways, and barriers across those yards. Barricades of plank and hoarding, barbed wire and chain link had been strung across doorways and ground floor windows. But where were the people?

Just shy of the train tracks, she found them, guarding the gas station. Ahead, the road crossed a railroad. The crossing was down, but no train was passing. In front, six-foot-high corrugated steel sheets had been run across the gas station forecourt, with *No Fuel Left* painted across them. Behind, and opposite the gas station, on the roof of a three-storey above-store apartment block, stood an obvious sniper holding a rifle. So obvious, Olivia wondered how many better concealed sentries there might be. Her eyes paused on an open window on the top-floor, corner apartment. Was that movement?

Outside the gas station's barricaded perimeter were three more guards. Two men and a woman, all armed with rifles. Or was that a shotgun in the tall woman's hands? They weren't holding them threateningly, except that holding a firearm was a threat all by itself. Stopped near them was an RV. A man and woman had climbed out and were talking with the trio of guards.

Olivia had stopped her truck fifty yards from the RV, too far away to hear what was being said, so she sat, watching, keeping both hands on the wheel. The couple were in their thirties. Late rather than early. He was balding, she gym-thin. Both wore multiple layers beneath coats definitely not thick enough for the weather. If the RV was theirs, they usually vacationed much further south.

The trio with whom they were arguing were a generation apart. A young woman, a middle-aged man, an older man. Three generations of the same family? Maybe. And presumably the same family that owned the gas station. Or perhaps not. She glanced out the window, up at the apartment block. There were two people on the roof now, and a third on the roof of the low-rise bar behind. Whoever these people had been, this was their town, their gas station. From the look of it, they weren't selling. At least not for cash.

She watched the couple argue with the trio, drumming her hands on the wheel, an idea circling her brain. Finally, the couple retreated back to their vehicle.

Olivia waited until the RV had turned a slow circle and driven off before picking up the tasselled shoulder bag, and slowly getting out of her truck. She raised her empty hands, then lowered them as she approached the trio by the gas station.

"Howdy. Guess you're not open," she said in her brightest of friendly tones.

"Nope," the oldest of the two men said. "Town's closed."

"If you're not selling, how about trading?" Olivia asked.

"Nope," the older man said.

"Trading what?" the woman asked. She was younger than Olivia. Out of high school, but only by a couple years. Her hair was short, but styled in that pseudo-scruffy look that had made a comeback over Christmas. She'd even added a little lipstick and a little too much eyeliner. It was the first hint of normality Olivia had seen in days.

"I'll trade anything," Olivia said. "I've got a cabin a day's walk away. And in about a day, I'll be walking everywhere. But if you're not interested in selling anything, I won't use the last of my gas to come back here. I'll look elsewhere."

"Maybe you should," the older man said.

The middle-aged of the trio shook his head. "We don't have much. And we have no gas."

"A radio? Batteries?" Olivia asked. "What about a hand pump and some plastic tubing?"

The middle-aged man nodded. "Maybe. But money's worth nothing."

Olivia nodded. "What about fresh deer?"

The older man grinned. "Now that's always worth something," he said, his icy facade instantly melting.

"Good to know," Olivia said. "A radio, some batteries, a hand pump. Some tubing. Some nails. And a bicycle."

"A bicycle?" the woman asked.

"Like I said, I'll be out of gas soon," Olivia said.

"For a deer?" the older man asked.

"Yep. Fresh killed."

"Sounds like a deal," the older man said.

"I'll be back when I've got it," Olivia said, and returned to her truck.

Driving slowly, eyes on the woodland, and occasionally on the rear view mirror, she headed south. Realistically, she stood more chance of hitting a deer with the truck than with a handgun. Plus, having killed it, she'd need the truck to drive it back to the town. On the other hand, they hadn't been hostile. They'd not tried to rob her. No, she wasn't going to have a deer to trade with them. She did have a cabin full of canned goods. Perhaps they'd accept those. Not for a bicycle, but for a roof. Of course, just because they didn't rob her today didn't mean they wouldn't tomorrow when she returned with a truck full of long-life food.

It was a risk. But it was also an alternative to syphoning what fuel she could find in stalled cars on a drive north, and an alternative to struggling along, alone, in the cabin.

"Yep, this really isn't what we thought it was going to be like, is it, Pete?"

She'd picked a different route back, partly to make sure she wasn't being followed, partly on the lookout for more abandoned cars. Instead, she found the RV. The couple stood outside it. They had been inspecting a tree which had partially fallen across the road, but now they were watching her truck, as were the two other faces peering through the RV's curtained rear window.

As Olivia stopped the truck, the man walked back towards the RV. She could guess what for, so kept a smile on her face as she got out.

"Hiya," she said brightly. "Looks like we're heading the same way. You guys were trying to buy fuel in Bangor, too, right?"

"No one seems to be selling it," the woman said, while the man took another step closer to what was almost certainly a concealed weapon.

"I'm not trying to rob you," Olivia said. "Which, now I hear it, is probably what a road bandit would say. Look, a few days ago, I sold carpets in South Bend. Then I sort of got dragooned into helping out in the hospital until it burned down. Now I'm… I guess I'm trying to decide whether to stay put or drive as far as I can. Olivia," she added. "Olivia Preston."

The woman gave a slow nod. "Naomi Clarke. That's Conrad. You're from South Bend? That's near here, right?"

"About fifty miles south, across the state line. You're from Virginia?" she asked, pointing at the vanity plate.

Naomi nodded. "We wanted to go south, but the traffic on the highway was all going north. Since then—"

"We're keeping to ourselves," Conrad cut in. "We were trying to cross the border. Get to Canada. They said it was shut. Someone blew up the bridge."

"They did? You mean the people in Bangor told you that?" she asked. "I don't know anything about it. I was…" She paused, then smiled at RV's twitching curtain. "We can't do this on our own," she said. "Yesterday, I tried. I've got a cabin near here. My old boss gave it to me. It's secluded, but it's got no power. I spent all of yesterday chopping firewood and hauling water out of the well. Today I'm driving around looking for I don't know what, but I found you. Alone, we won't make it. Together, we might. Why don't we pool resources?"

"You don't know us," Naomi said. "We don't know you."

"Right, but I don't know anyone," Olivia said. "My boss is down in Florida. My boyfriend, well, sort-of-boyfriend, is down in Hawaii, and my best friend was shot, killed, by one of her co-workers the day this all started. I have enough food for me for a couple of months. Between us, I guess it'll stretch a few weeks. We can split the work, share standing watch, or we can share the drive north or west."

"You're offering us a place to stay?" Conrad asked, clearly still suspicious.

"Sure, if you want," Olivia said. "But I'm really suggesting we pool resources and get far away from here. I don't think these woods are going to be remote enough. Canada sounds like a good idea. If we help each other, the journey would be a lot safer." She glanced at the window, where the two children had now pulled the curtain back completely. "Sweet kids."

"Tyler and Robyn," Naomi said.

"What do you get out of this?" Conrad asked, suspicion dripping from every syllable.

"Ultimately, the same as you," Olivia said. "I get to live."

"She's right," Naomi said. "No, Con, she's right. You were saying the same thing yesterday. We need to find people we can trust."

"Cool," Olivia said. She pointed at the tree partially blocking the road. "Since we won't get the RV through there, we'll go back the way we came. Do you have some tubing and an empty container? There's a car not far from here. Abandoned. But there's fuel in it. We can syphon the gas, then go to the cabin. We can eat. Talk. Plan how to get to Canada."

"You lead the way," Conrad said. "We'll follow."

As she reversed, Olivia wondered whether they would follow, and for how far. Conrad was clearly suspicious. She suspected Naomi was, too, but less inclined to show it. For that matter, Olivia was suspicious, but the reality of the last two days was that she wouldn't survive long on her own.

By the time they reached the abandoned car, it appeared as if Conrad had come around to her way of thinking. He climbed out with a fuel can and crowbar in hand. Naomi followed, a length of bright blue plastic hose in hers.

"Stay in the RV, kids," she said, following her husband over to the RV.

"I hid the keys earlier," Olivia said, pointing at the crowbar. "Although I guess I should have realised that wouldn't stop anyone." She retrieved the keys from where she'd hung them on the tree, opened the car, then the fuel cap.

"We need a rag to create a seal around the hose," Naomi said.

"You've done this before?" Olivia asked.

"On the road," Naomi said. "But I learned how during my very-well spent youth in Tennessee. I'll tell you about it later, as long as you promise not to tell the kids."

Olivia smiled. She was going to get on well with these people. As Naomi went back to the RV, Conrad opened the car's door, looking at the dead man before walking a little way towards the trees.

"If this works, I think we should head down to the highway," Olivia said, when Naomi returned. "We're more likely to find abandoned cars there."

"How much fuel would we burn looking?" Naomi asked. "If we're aiming for Canada, better we gather all we need to carry and collect fuel along the way."

"But take the truck and the RV?" Olivia asked.

"A convoy looks more dangerous than a single vehicle," Naomi said.

"Right, yes. Is that another tip from your youth in Tennessee?"

"From—"

But she was interrupted by Conrad. "Did you hear that?" he hissed. "There's something moving in the trees."

"It's the deer," Olivia said. "I saw it earlier." She reached into her bag, drawing her gun. "I might be able to shoot it. Maybe we can trade it with Bangor for a little gas."

"I'll get the shotgun," Naomi said, and hurried back to the RV.

Olivia kept the handgun pointing low as she watched the treeline. Was it worth wasting the fuel to take a dead deer up to Bangor on the off chance they could trade it? Was it worth the bullet?

"It's coming this way," Conrad called. "No, it's not a deer. It's a... hey, are you okay?"

He took a step towards the trees as a blood-soaked figure stepped out. Under five feet tall, it was a boy, not a man. A child. Covered in blood from knee to nose.

"No, Conrad!" Olivia called, but it was too late. The undead child staggered forward and Conrad had automatically reached out to catch him. The zombie tore at the man's arm. Its hands curled around Conrad as the man turned and shook, blood pouring from a vivid gash in his arm, trying to keep the zombie at bay.

Naomi ran forward, shotgun in hand, and so did Olivia, gun raised, but she couldn't get a clear shot. Not until Naomi slammed the stock of her weapon into the zombie-boy's neck. Its mouth lolled open, and Conrad grabbed him, hurling the undead child into the woods. The zombie-child hit a tree with a sodden snap and spray of viscous gore, falling to a heap at its base.

"No," Naomi whispered.

Jagged flashes of white bone stabbed through its clothing as the undead child stretched its broken and twisted limbs. He should have cried. He should have screamed. But the only sound to emerge was a low, whispered hiss.

Olivia raised the gun, and squeezed the trigger. The pistol bucked. Miss. She fired again as the zombie rolled through the mud, squirming to its knees. This time, her bullet found its chest, spraying gore across the trees.

"Sorry," she whispered as the child crawled towards them, teeth snapping, broken arm waving. The third shot was much louder, and came from Naomi's shotgun. The slug smashed into the zombie's head. The remains of the undead child crumpled, finally unmoving.

"Damn it," Conrad hissed.

"Let me see," Naomi said. "Oh, it's not too bad. I'll get the first-aid kit."

"You were bitten," Olivia said, turning to face the man. He clutched his arm, down which blood streamed towards his hand.

"It's fine," he said. "It's not deep."

"It isn't fine," Olivia said, raising her gun. "I'm sorry. I really am. But it isn't fine."

"Relax," Conrad said. "Two days ago, I had to tear a zombie off a guy who wasn't so lucky. Damn thing spat in my face. Didn't get infected then. Won't now."

"Everyone gets infected," Olivia said.

"Not everyone," Naomi said, coming over with a small and half-empty first-aid kit. "Some people are immune. You must have heard them talking about it online, on the radio."

"I... no," she said. "People are really immune?"

"Some people," Conrad said. "Me among them."

Olivia lowered the gun, but only halfway. "How sure are you?"

"Sure enough that I don't want you putting a bullet in my head just yet," Conrad said.

When they got to the turning, and the track leading up to the cabin, the RV, a comfortable hundred yards behind, stopped. Olivia had already turned onto the track. She braked, grabbed the pistol, and got out. Hurrying back to the RV, she expected the worst until the door opened and Conrad stepped out, smiling.

"I still ain't dead," he said. "I wanted to check the ground before we drove up there. Make sure we can turn."

"Good point," Olivia said. "And no, thinking about it, I don't think you would be able to turn the RV. But we don't want to leave it out here on the road."

"Let's take a look," he said.

The children were left in the RV with the shotgun but instructions to slam the horn if there was trouble. Olivia led them up the track, indicating where she'd left the truck the night before, and then on to the cabin.

"There it is," she said. "Not quite a castle, but there's a well, a chimney. There's a toilet that flushes as long as you fill the tank with water."

"It looks nice," Naomi said. "Just the kind of place you were looking for, Conrad."

"I was," he said. "A week ago, I'd have put in an offer. But you're right, it's too close to the town. These woods just aren't remote enough." He rubbed his arm.

"Do you think you can get the RV up here?" Olivia asked.

"I'm not sure," Naomi said. "Maybe if we reversed it, we could get it off the road."

"No," Conrad said. "Not without clearing a lot of the brush. Maybe felling a few of the trees. The branches are too low."

Olivia gave a wan smile. "That's kind of what I figured. So... so I guess we continue, now. Today?"

"South, then west, then north," Naomi said.

"Agreed," Conrad said.

"I'll go gather everything that's worth taking," Olivia said. "Give me half an hour."

"The kids can stretch their legs," Naomi said.

"And use the bathroom," Conrad said.

"It's the blockhouse over there," Olivia said, and went into the cabin.

This time, she saw it differently from yesterday. Even differently from that morning. It was wonderfully twee, and utterly impractical for any real apocalypse. It was a place to escape to, for Mr Mathers to drink and tinker, in the knowledge he had a real house just a car-ride away.

She drew the curtains, but there still wasn't enough light, so she lit a candle, then another, placing them on the fireplace, and a third on the saucer in the kitchen. Opening one cupboard, then another, wistfully wishing she could thank Nora in person.

A furious yell came from outside. Olivia ran to the door. In the clearing, near the annex, Conrad was on all fours. Naomi was scrabbling across the mud, blood seeping through a savage rip in her coat that ran from shoulder, halfway along her back.

Olivia dragged the gun from her bag even as Conrad found his unsteady feet.

"Conrad!" Olivia yelled. "Conrad!"

Naomi turned to look, but Conrad lurched on, towards his wife.

"No one's immune," Olivia said. "No one's special." She fired at the undead Conrad. Her first shot hit his arm. Her second his shoulder, breaking bone and getting the zombie's attention. The third bullet slammed into his temple, ripping through his skull.

"Naomi?" Olivia asked, even as Conrad's corpse collapsed heavily to the mud.

"I know," Naomi said, pushing herself to her feet. "We have to be quick." She began walking towards the RV.

"Where are you going?" Olivia asked.

"To say goodbye to my children," Naomi said. "You'll get them somewhere safe, yes? You promise me? You'll find somewhere safe for them?"

"I do. I will."

"Their aunt is Canada. She works near Medicine Hat. In Alberta. If you can get them to her, she'll take them in. I know she will."

"Of course. Medicine Hat. Sure," Olivia said. Half of her wanted time to slow, for Naomi to have longer with her children. The other half, the part still holding the gun, wanted the confrontation to be over quickly.

At the RV, Naomi stopped by the door. When it began to open, she pushed it closed. "Kids. Your dad and I... we love you very much. We're going to meet you at Aunt Sally's. Okay? Olivia is going to drive you there. We'll meet you there. I love you both, more than anything." She opened her mouth to say more, but the words failed her. "Not out here," Naomi whispered, and walked back through the trees, up the path, and to the cabin. "You'll take them now? Today?"

"Yes," Olivia said.

"Good. They won't hear the shot from inside." She opened the door, and went into the cabin.

"You want me to..." Olivia began, leaving the sentence unfinished as she followed Naomi inside.

"You have to," Naomi said. "I don't want to infect anyone else. Please." She sat in one of the battered chairs.

Olivia raised the gun. But the barrel dropped. "Maybe you *are* immune," she said.

"No one's immune," Naomi said. "It was all myths and lies. Rumours and stories. You can't believe any of it. No one's immune. No one's special. Please." She closed her eyes again.

Olivia raised the gun. Holding the barrel an inch from Naomi's head, she pulled the trigger. The gun clicked. "Sorry. It's jammed."

Naomi let out a sobbing sigh. "Get the shotgun. No, there's no time. Just..." She picked up a candle, then the bottle of lighter fluid from the shelf near the chimney. She squirted some on the floor, then on her shoes. "Just go. Quick. When I turn, I'll drop the candle."

"Wait," Olivia said, but it was too late now. She hurried into the kitchen, grabbing as many of the cans as she could, throwing them into the bag she'd brought from Pete's and which still contained the boxes of cereal. She ran outside. "I'm going to get the other bags."

She ran to the door, out to the track, and down to the RV. She dropped the bag.

"Where's Mom?" Tyler asked. "Where's Dad?"

"They had to help someone," Olivia said. "I'll be back in a moment. I need bags. Bags? Ah." She saw a couple of hold-alls near the door, upturned them, and then ran back up the track towards the cabin. Smoke was already trickling out from under the door. She was too late.

"No one's special. No one's immune," she said. "I'm sorry, Naomi."

But she'd keep her promise. She'd get the children to Canada.

Part 2
A Crazy Thing Called Love

Canada & U.S.A.

27th February

Chapter 11 - Air-Drea
Qualicum Beach Airport, Vancouver Island, Canada

The battered but winterized ambulance sped through the checkpoint outside Nanaimo Airport.

"How far is it to the plane?" Corrie Guinn asked from the paramedic's jump seat.

"About an hour," RCMP Police Constable Jerome MacDonald said. "It's fifty kilometres to Qualicum."

"Bet I can do it in twenty minutes," Andrea MacDonald said from behind the wheel.

"It's not a race!" Jerome said even as the pilot stomped on the accelerator.

"Says who?" Andrea replied. Gravel and grit rattled against the chassis as the wheels carved a path through the semi-frozen slush.

Pete closed his eyes, and held on.

"And you said there are American soldiers at Qualicum?" Corrie asked.

"I said there are crazy Alaskans," Andrea said.

"Four are active-duty soldiers," Jerome said. "The other six are retired or reservists."

"Enthusiastic hobbyists," Andrea added.

Jerome sighed. "They wanted to get back to the U.S. To New York. To go help on the frontline. Came in by helicopter. We took the helicopters to help with the evacuation of Vancouver City. We said we'd find them work, or a flight, and asked them to keep the airport secure."

"Won't have room for all of them, though," Andrea said. "Not in Shqa."

"That's the type of plane?" Pete asked.

"No, it's *her* name. *Shqa'élu.* She's a CL-415 water bomber."

"Why did you name the plane that?"

"I didn't," Andrea said. "Our engineer did. He was from Nanaimo, you know? Um…" She leaned forward, then abruptly spun the wheel to avoid driving over a corpse.

"Whoa!" Jerome said. "Steady!"

"Yeah, he lived somewhere over there," Andrea said blithely while waving to the right with just as much abandon.

"You should slow down," Jerome said.

"I *could* go faster," Andrea said.

"With the same surname, I thought you two were a couple," Corrie said, "but you're not, are you?"

"Us? Ha!" Andrea said, laughing, but still keeping control of the speeding ambulance.

"We're siblings," Jerome said.

"Step," Andrea said. "Which is how come I've got all the looks."

"And I've got all the common sense," Jerome said. "Our parents lived next to each other. Died in a car crash. My aunt adopted us both. Policing's the family business, you see."

"Which is why *I* became a firefighter," Andrea said.

"I don't get it," Pete said.

"Firefighters are one up from police," Andrea said. "You can't put handcuffs on a forest fire."

The highway hugged the coast. To their right lay the bay, close enough to see the white-capped waves. Between and before, and inland, were the quiet homes of the local residents. Very quiet. Far more so even than Nanaimo. Pete leaned forward. "Where is everyone?"

"The town was abandoned days ago," Jerome said.

"Why?" Pete asked. "And what's that smell?" An oily vapour had crept in around the sealed windows. Dark, foetid, unforgivingly pervasive, leaving a metallic aftertaste in his mouth.

"Look to the right," Jerome said. "We'll pass it in a minute."

Three partially burned hulks lay on the beach, the waves lapping at their charred sterns.

"Ferries," Jerome said. "From Vancouver. They approached at night, too close together, too close to shore. One ran aground. The other two ran cables across to stop her listing, but it brought them close enough for the fire to spread to all three. The smoke forced us to evacuate the town, consuming resources that should have helped Vancouver. Plus, without those ferries, getting people out has become far more difficult. You *can* slow down," he added. "No matter how hard you push the accelerator, we won't fly."

"Look at those clouds," Andrea said, waving to the left, turning as she did, at the same time the front wheel slammed into a frost-logged pothole. The ambulance careened left, jumped right, bounced up, and slammed back down. With mud and grit splattering the windshield, she regained control. "Sorry. Sorry. My bad," she said blithely. "But do you see those clouds?"

"I can't see the *road*," Jerome said, leaning forward and switching on the wipers.

"Spoilsport," Andrea said. "Anyway, a storm's coming. Either we want to be on the ground when the storm arrives, above it, or heading away from it. We absolutely do *not* want to be taking off. I guess we should have come here last night. But we're here… now. There. Do you see it?"

Pete could only see mud smeared with the first splashes of rain. Jerome reached across, speeding the wipers up. Ahead, emerging from the growing murk, Pete found the squat tower, then the runway and, on it, a twin engine jet. Sleek white with a green flash on the tail to match the cockpit-surround. There were only eight windows in the cabin, but that was more than enough.

"That's our plane?" he asked.

"That? No way," Andrea said. "That's just a Cessna we found in the hangar. I pushed it outside to make room for *Shqa'élu*. Can't have her sitting outside in the rain."

"She wouldn't have minded," Jerome said. "Of all the planes in the world, *she* doesn't care about getting wet."

"Yeah, but she doesn't like the cold," Andrea said. "She's a summertime plane, you see?"

Pete didn't, but had already learned questions distracted their driver.

"Didn't you say the Alaskan soldiers were on guard here?" Corrie asked.

"They were," Andrea said, finally slowing as they approached the wide-open gates that led to the runway.

"They should be," Jerome said. "I said we'd find them passage east as soon we could."

"Yeah, where are they?" Andrea sped up, driving towards a hangar close to the squat tower. "You two open the doors. Jerome, you uncover the engines. I'll wake her up." With no more warning, she slammed on the brakes.

Pete was thrown forwards and sideways at the same time, jarring arm and chest against the seatbelt while Andrea threw herself out of the driver's door, sprinting over to the hangar.

"Hope she doesn't fly like she drives," Corrie said.

"Oh, she does," Jerome said, opening his door, and following Andrea inside the hangar.

Pete grabbed his pack and the Colt-C7 assault rifle that, like most of his gear, and Corrie's near-matching set, had been a gift from the Canadians. The rest of their supplies had come from the coffin-like containers they'd found aboard Kempton's jet and which they'd unloaded in Nanaimo to make room for the sick children to fly south.

Outside, for a glorious quarter-second, Pete relished the motionless safety of solid ground before the chill wind dragged icy sandpaper over his exposed cheeks. "I'm starting to miss the Australian heat," he said.

"Give me a month, I might re-adjust," Corrie said, and jogged over to the wide hangar doors. She stopped, and shivered, jogging on the spot. "Maybe four months. Can you see the Alaskans?"

But Pete was looking inside. "Is that the plane?" he asked. Through the eight-inch gap in the hangar doors, beyond the pool of icy rain the wind had hurled inside, he saw only one plane. It had to be Andrea's because Jerome was hauling giant blankets away from the engines. And it had to be a plane because it had a cockpit and a turboprop on each of its wings. Bright yellow, except where it was an even brighter red, it had a large, curving, bulbous cabin slung below the cockpit. If planes were birds, then this was a duck. And though he knew the story of how the ugly duckling turned into a swan, somehow he doubted that would happen before take-off.

"The motor's not working on these doors," Corrie said. "We need to push."

"Right. Sure." He added his shoulder to hers. Slowly at first, then faster as momentum built, they slid the gates open, finishing as Jerome slung the engine-coverings inside the odd-shaped plane.

"Where are the soldiers?" Corrie asked as the police officer and pilot joined them.

"Not a clue," Jerome said. "They were here yesterday."

"What do you want to do?" Andrea asked. "We can leave without them, we can wait, or we can go look for them. Your call, but if we don't take off now, we might have to delay until tomorrow."

"Why?" Pete asked.

"She's a summer plane," Andrea said. "Designed to fight forest fires. There's not much call for those during the winter, so she's not rated for these temperatures. She's not rated for night flying, either. We have no way of calling ahead, no way of knowing if the runway will be clear. No way to ask them to turn on the lights. We *can* land on the water, but you really don't want to do that at night. If we leave within the next hour, we'll land before dusk. If we leave it much longer, we'll have to wait until tomorrow. But from how grumpy those clouds look, it might be longer than that."

"Pete?" Corrie said. "It's your call."

He frowned. "We need the soldiers," he said. "I mean… after Broken Hill. But if we don't go now, there's a chance we won't leave. The plane might be needed for something else."

"Wait, there they are!" Corrie said, pointing at the opposite end of the runway where four figures slowly trudged towards them.

"Cool," Andrea said. "I'll wake Shqa up and give her a snack. You'll want to get out the way."

84

Pete walked away from the entrance, out onto the tarmac, waving to the approaching Alaskans. "It'll be good to have the soldiers with us," Pete said. "And good to find out what's happened in Alaska. It can't be so bad if they volunteered to head to New York rather than stay... stay..." He trailed off. The soldiers were waving back. Continuously. Erratically. None carried weapons in their hands, though it looked as if two carried slung rifles. The other two were charred. Burned. As they drew nearer, he better saw the singed rags for what they were. And he saw the figures for who they had been, but who they were no longer.

"They're zombies," Pete whispered.

"I think so," Corrie said. She raised her assault rifle. "Is it just four? Pete? Pete! Is it just four of them?"

"Yes. Yes I think so. I can't see any others. Shall I tell Andrea?"

Behind, there was a bang, a burr, a growl as the plane's engines came to life.

"She'll know what it means when I..." Corrie let her rifle's shot end the sentence for her. The shot was a sharp punctuation to the engines' rising roar, while the sound of the bullet's impact was utterly inaudible. The zombie staggered, turning sideways with the impact against its body armour.

"Missed," Corrie muttered. "Better wait, I suppose. Until they're closer."

Pete half-raised his rifle, then lowered it. He knew he was a terrible shot. His sister wasn't. During her self-imposed exile, she'd guarded and repaired a lonely seven-hundred-kilometre stretch of dingo-fence in the Australian outback, keeping wild dogs away from the sprawling cattle stations. For when the fence broke, she had a rifle, albeit one which fired tranquilliser darts. People were different from dogs, and zombies were different again, but against four slow-moving targets, while armed with military-grade assault rifles, they weren't truly in danger. Not yet.

Corrie fired again. "Damn. It's the cold," she said. "It's just too cold."

"You want me to try?" Pete asked.

"No. No, it's…" Again, she let the rifle finish the sentence. And this time she found her mark. The zombie-soldier fell. "No different from dingoes," she said. "No different at all." She shifted aim to the next soldier, a bearded man in hunting camouflage with a rifle still slung on his shoulder. She fired. The other two, singed civilians in charred denim and scorched winter coats, fell one after the other. "No different at all," she repeated quietly.

"There's more," Pete said. "Two more, coming from the road. But… Jerome's signalling us. He wants us aboard."

"Last chance to change your mind," Corrie said.

"I think we'll be safer aboard than staying here," Pete said.

Corrie lowered her rifle, picked up her pack, and they jogged together, over to the slowly taxiing plane.

The plane's interior was no warmer than the frozen runway. Nor was it any quieter, and it was far less comfortable; the water-bomber wasn't designed for passengers. Andrea waved them into the pair of side-facing jump seats at the back of the cramped cockpit while Jerome secured the door. The plane was already moving as the police officer made his way to the co-pilot's seat. Jerome had barely sat down before Andrea launched the plane into the sky. Pete, not having had time to buckle himself in, was too busy holding on for dear life to worry whether the plane would complete its ascent. But sooner than he'd expected, it began to level off.

He found the buckles and secured himself, slumping against the restraints as, opposite, Corrie gave a rueful shake of her head. Her mouth opened, but he couldn't hear her. He shook his head, and so did she, smiling briefly. Pete closed his eyes. Once again, their plans had changed.

They'd left Australia by accident, having been aboard the plane when the mortars fell nearby. It had been Liu Higson's decision to take off. And it had been her choice to risk the long journey north to Vancouver. On arriving, and meeting the police officer, they'd pitched the idea of travelling to Indiana as a justification for why they were aboard the jet as much as an intended destination. And now, here they were, on their way. But which was most important: searching for Olivia, or completing the

Australian soldiers' mission to discover what was happening in America? For now, he was able to do both. At some point soon, he'd have to pick one, and he knew which it would have to be. But he didn't have to choose yet.

Jerome tapped his shoulder. Pete opened his eyes. The police officer handed him a wired mic-and-headphone set.

"You can hear me?" Andrea said.

"Yep," Pete said.

"I can," Corrie said.

"Cool," Andrea said. "Welcome to Air-Drea flight zero-zero-zero-two. Our next stop is Pine Dock. We've got a flight time of five hours or so, depending on winds. If you have any questions or requests during our flight, please speak to the steward. If you have any regrets, please keep them to yourself. We won't serve food, but we don't have a bathroom, either. There's no inflight movie, but if you ask him nicely, Jerome will do impressions."

"No he won't," Jerome said.

"What about the zombies?" Corrie asked. "Shouldn't we call someone? Let them know?"

"Already done," Andrea said. "We couldn't get a reply while on the ground, but did when we were in the air."

"I think it was the Alaskans," Jerome said.

"Except some of them were civilians," Corrie said. "Wait, this wasn't the first time, was it? There are zombies all over Vancouver Island, aren't there?"

"I'm afraid so," Jerome said.

"But that's not our problem now," Andrea said.

"Andrea," Pete began, "you said this was flight zero-zero-zero-two. Does that make this the second flight the plane's ever made?"

"Ah, no," Andrea said. "It's *my* second time flying her. Counting today."

"Oh."

"The first was when those ferries caught fire," Andrea said. "But I've been co-pilot a ton of times."

"Which isn't the same thing at all," Jerome said.

"Tonight, we're setting down in Pine Dock, on Lake Winnipeg," Andrea said. "If we can't land on the runway, if there's still enough daylight, we'll head for Thunder Bay. If not, we'll have to land on the lake. Either way, we'll land tonight, refuel, and head on to Lake Michigan tomorrow. But we can discuss tomorrow's landing after we have figured out today's. So, tell me again, you're really going after the girl you left behind? That's crazy-romantic. No boyfriend of mine would come halfway around the world looking for me."

"Only because you scare them away after the first date," Jerome said.

"Well, I *know* yours wouldn't come halfway around the couch," Andrea said, "particularly when the hockey is on. So, Pete, tell us about this old-fashioned quest you're on. Was it love at first sight? How crowded was the room when you first saw her, eh?"

"Um… well, it wasn't a room. I guess it was the carpet store. Where I worked. And it wasn't crowded. Our store never was…"

Chapter 12 - Who Cares About Anthrax?
Pine Dock, Manitoba

"There it is," Andrea said, though with a disconcerting degree of uncertainty. "I think."

"We're above Pine Dock?" Corrie asked.

"We should be," Andrea said. "So everyone keep your eyes open. It has to be down there, somewhere."

"We could ask someone to put their lights on," Pete said. The flight had taken longer than expected. Though there was still a glimmer of sun on the horizon, below on the ground, the shadows were slipping into full darkness.

"Is there anything on the radio?" Corrie asked.

"Nothing official," Jerome said after a brief check. "And nothing helpful."

"If we can't find Pine Dock, we'll continue on to Thunder Bay," Andrea said. "We'll land on the lake, taxi up to a jetty, and then walk back to B.C."

"We couldn't take off again?" Corrie asked.

"Oh, sure," Andrea said. "But if we leave Shqa out on the water all night, she'll freeze. But I don't think we'll have to. I see lights ahead!"

"I think it's a runway," Jerome said.

"Of course it is," Andrea said. "A little more faith, eh?"

"But is it Pine Dock?" Corrie asked.

"Let's go see," Andrea said. "Hold on. I'll fly low, check length and condition, and then bring her down."

"Twelve lights, six either side, roughly marking a runway," Jerome said. "Looks like we're the first plane to arrive."

The plane jolted, banking sharply as Andrea brought the aircraft up and around.

"Any zombies?" Pete asked.

"Didn't see any," Jerome said.

"Cool," Andrea said. "Because we're landing."

The plane tilted forward. Pete tried to lose himself in the highlight reel of his past life flashing before his eyes, but he'd seen the show too often during the last few days. He skipped to the end, a countdown of his dumbest mistakes that ended at number two, leaving poll position free for his current undertaking. Trekking across the world after a girl he... he... he still didn't want to use the word. Not yet. Not here. Not until he saw her again because it was all too likely she was—

Before he finished the thought, the plane jolted, the tyres bounced on the runway. The wheels found proper purchase, and Andrea brought the plane to a screaming halt.

"That was—" Pete began, but was cut short by Jerome.

"We've got company!" Jerome called through the headset.

"Zombies?" Corrie asked.

"Soldiers," Jerome said. "Definitely alive, because they're carrying guns."

"That makes a change," Corrie said. "Let's go say hello."

Grateful to stand up, and even more grateful to be out in the bracingly cold air, Pete took a huge lungful before turning his attention to the group running towards them. There were six in total. Judging by their tightly held rifles and slush-stained uniforms, the four bringing up the rear were definitely soldiers. The two people out in front weren't in uniform, but it wasn't simply their casual attire that made him think they were civilians. Nor were they running away from the soldiers. If anything, the military personnel were doing their best to keep up.

They were all probably hoping the plane would take them to safety. In fact... Pete scanned the runway, then the surrounding grounds of the small airfield. The runway had been cleared of ice and snow, and of course, someone had set up the landing lights. They had been expecting a plane, though surely not this one.

The two civilians reached them first. The woman was in her mid-thirties, her black hair streaked with silver in such a neat fashion it must be dyed. The man, despite a hairline in full retreat, was probably a few years younger. Both wore grey and red snow-gear, though his was considerably more stained than hers. And he looked considerably more out of breath, despite his hands being empty, while she carried a heavy metal suitcase and a backpack from which a green neon rope hung, swinging back and forth as she ran.

"Who are you?" the woman demanded, before she'd properly caught her breath. "It doesn't matter. Do you need to refuel?"

"We do, thanks," Andrea said cheerily.

The soldiers staggered to a halt behind her. One stepped forward, a corporal by the chevrons. "Corporal McLean. Who are you?"

"Jerome MacDonald, RCMP. This is Andrea MacDonald, our fire-service pilot. These two are here on a mission from Canberra to find out what's happened to North America."

"Canberra? In Australia?" the corporal asked.

"Catch flies in your own time," the woman snapped. "Get the plane refuelled, and reverse to the other end of the runway. We're going south."

"This is Dr Avalon," the corporal said. "She wants to get to Ottawa."

"We lost communication with Ottawa," Jerome said. "Rumour is that the government's left, and the city was burning. Vancouver is too, but we're putting that blaze out."

"We'd heard about Ottawa," the corporal said. "We tried to tell her. But Vancouver as well?"

"There's rioting, looting, people running scared," Jerome said. "We're evacuating the city and organising the survivors. There's life there, but everything I've heard is that you should stay far, far away from Ottawa."

"I do *not* want to go to Ottawa!" Avalon said. She pointed at the metal case. "I keep telling you that. I need to get *that* to either Winnipeg or Atlanta, and *I* need to get to Pennsylvania. It must, absolutely not, under any circumstances, get anywhere near any population centres."

"Really?" Andrea asked, sounding as much excited as curious. "Why? What's in the case?"

"What's in Pennsylvania?" Corrie asked.

"What's in Atlanta?" Pete asked. "And isn't it a major population centre?"

Dr Avalon gave an enormous, and well practiced, shoulder-slumping sigh of exasperation. "Winnipeg is home to the National Microbiology Laboratory. Atlanta hosts the headquarters of the Centers for Disease Control and Prevention. Both are level-four bio-containment facilities. It doesn't matter to which the samples are taken, but Atlanta is closer to Pennsylvania where Dr Ayers lives. You've heard of her, yes? No? Seriously? And this is why the world is in such a mess. Dr Ayers is the leading expert on rare pathogens. By now, she's almost certainly in Atlanta, but if she's in Pennsylvania, I need to collect her and get her to a lab where she can develop an anti-viral for our new crisis. But I still need to conclude the last crisis, which means getting this case to a level-four facility."

"Oh, you've got to tell us now," Andrea said, her excitement nearly bubbling over. "What's in the case?"

"A variant of anthrax which was frozen in the Arctic tundra for the last twenty thousand years," Dr Avalon said.

"Oh," Andrea said, deflating. "The way you were building it up, I was expecting something a little less end-of-the-worldey. But I can't fly anywhere tonight. Are those hangars empty?"

"She's a strange fish, that doctor," Andrea said to the corporal as they wrapped giant insulating blankets around the engines. The hangar wasn't heated, but it was sheltered from the rising wind. The growing gusts didn't seem to bother Dr Avalon who paced the runway, robotically dialling the same unresponsive numbers on her sat-phone while her assistant, Dr Leo Smilovitz, wearily waited just inside the hangar doors. "A very strange fish. All gills and guts and not enough fins."

"Driven," the corporal said. "And she's been driving me mad for a month."

"You've been with her that long?" Corrie asked.

"Since she broadcast her initial findings worldwide," the corporal said. "Did you miss that?"

"Oh, she's *that* Dr Avalon," Jerome said.

"You know her?" Andrea said. "You didn't say."

"We were briefed about her broadcast," Jerome said. "And told to listen out for anyone discussing this discovery of anthrax."

"Why didn't you say?" Andrea said. "All the times I asked you if anything interesting happened at work, and you only droned on and on about fender benders and snow rage. You were holding out on me, Jer-Jer! So, Corporal, tell me the story. How come you were playing bodyguard, eh?"

"It wasn't a game," Corporal MacLean said. "We were assigned to protect her, the research site, and the samples. After she'd told the world about what she found, hostile actors were expected to attempt seizing a sample. After everything that's happened since, I think we were sent to guard the wrong research site."

"You think that's what caused the zombies?" Andrea said.

The corporal shrugged. "Apparently, it's common to find ancient viruses in the melting permafrost. Anthrax isn't uncommon, and there've been a few deaths related to the release of defrosting pathogens in recent years. Or so Dr Avalon says. What she found up in Nunavut is far worse than anything discovered so far. Dr Smilovitz says it's a far more virulent variant than we're familiar with. Three scientists, collecting core samples, were airlifted to a hospital. Died the next day. That's when she made her broadcast."

"What happened to the research site?" Jerome asked.

"It was sterilised as we left," the corporal said. "But who cares about anthrax, when there's zombies on the loose?"

"And you think that's where the zombies came from?" Andrea asked.

"Me, yes." The corporal seemed wrong-footed by the ever-exuberant pilot. "But Leo doesn't think so. That's Dr Smilovitz. Not if the first outbreak was in New York."

"Who's this other doctor she wanted to see? The one in Pennsylvania?" Corrie asked.

"Ayers? I don't know much about her except she sounds crazier than Avalon. She taught Avalon, before doing something that got her put under house arrest."

"And you've been waiting here for a plane since the outbreak?" Corrie asked.

"We were redirected here before communications were compromised," the corporal said. "Four helicopters, twenty of us, plus pilots and gunners. We had a weapons-free, shoot-to-kill order right here, in Canada. And instructions not to go anywhere more populated."

"I only count two helicopters," Andrea said. "Tell me the others are in a secret underground hangar; it's all that's missing. Oh, don't look at me like that, Jerome. Look at Dr Avalon and tell me she isn't the perfect super-villain?"

"Yeah, that's what we were thinking, until last week," the corporal said. "But no, the other choppers, and the rest of our personnel, went to Thunder Bay. General Yoon put out a broadcast, summoning all troops, of whatever flag, to join her strike force. That's where the others went. And it was the direction we were looking for help to come. We weren't expecting it from out west. And not from as far away as Australia. You've really come from Canberra?"

"There should be some Australian soldiers with us," Corrie said. "But the plane was being shot at, so we took off without them. Me and Pete, we're trying to complete their mission." She tapped the phone she'd taped to the body-armour she'd borrowed in Nanaimo. "We're recording everything. Hopefully that'll help the people in the Pacific plan what to do next."

"I guess it can't hurt," the corporal said. "If you want, I've got some proper bodycams. High-def with a seven-day battery. We had to record everything while on close-protection duties in case of an accident."

"That'd be great, thanks," Corrie said. "What's it like here? How secure is it?"

"You mean Pine Dock? Very secure," the corporal said. "There's about seven hundred civilians in town. Enough food for a month, and enough to spare for another two hundred refugees. If the weather keeps improving, we'll survive. There's good fishing in that lake. But the ammo won't last forever. Nor will the diesel for the generator, the stored food, the medicine. If you want this runway kept open, we'll need to be resupplied."

"Could you take me into the town, to speak to whoever is in charge?" Jerome asked.

"If I could have one of those bodycams, I'd like to come with you," Corrie said. "Pete?"

He looked at the electric lights, then the office. It was the sort of place he might find a coffee pot. "I'm happy to finish off here."

"Cool," Andrea said, dropping the thick insulated blanket. "Give her a bath, too. Corporal, show us the night-life."

Pete sighed. But the hangar was out of the wind, and if there was washing water for the plane, maybe there'd be some to spare for him.

Chapter 13 - Shallow Thoughts
Pine Dock, Manitoba

Pete Guinn tried not to think deep thoughts as he stood by the window in the narrow section of hangar wall that wasn't part of the massive door. Tomorrow had become today. Dawn was close, and his destiny wasn't far behind.

A trio of electric lights appeared as if from nowhere, as their carriers turned an unseen corner. One light broke away, heading his way, while the other two beams continued towards the runway.

"I thought you'd be asleep," Corrie said as she followed her light's beam into the hangar. "This has to be a miracle. Pete Guinn, awake before he has to be."

"I heard metal tumbling and knocking," Pete said. "It was a cat."

"Ah." She opened a small satchel that, like the red and white gloves, scarf, and bobble hat, were new acquisitions. "I have coffee. And I have breakfast."

"You were in town all night?" Pete asked.

"And interviewing all night," Corrie said, tapping the bodycam. "Everyone wanted their story heard. So I listened to them all."

"On that?" he asked.

"And a few phones," she said. "Some people have always lived here, some lived nearby. Some came by boat, some by plane." She pointed at the small planes out on the tarmac which had been pushed out of the hangar to make way for the seaplane.

"I didn't see any boats," Pete said.

"They traded the watercraft with locals who went north to Matheson Island. It sounds like an even more remote place than this. They think there's more people southeast, at Fisher River Cree Nation, but they're getting that third-hand via Matheson Island."

"From people who went there?"

"From shortwave radio," Corrie said. She poured the coffee. "There's supposed to be a shelter-in-place order across all of Canada, but not everyone's obeying it. People are heading to family, to places they went on vacation, and some have ended up here instead. Matheson Island sounds similar to here, though what they said about Fisher River sounds like it's on a much larger scale."

"You mean Fisher River's a place closer to cities?" Pete asked.

"It's closer to towns. I think they said it's about a hundred kilometres southwest, inland from the lake. We can't resupply them all."

"Do we have to? Did they ask for help?"

"The opposite," Corrie said. "They said they'd be okay. Patrols walk the street. People fish. Others are cooking or preserving the perishables. Things are organised, and they wanted me, or whoever sees the recording, to know it. They'll hold on, doing their bit, as long as everyone else, every*where* else, does the same. But if something gives. If something breaks, they have nowhere to run and no way of getting there."

"They're low on gas?" Pete asked.

"Yes, but they're more worried about the diesel for their generators. It's the same at Fisher River and up on Matheson Island. They were about to start taking the aviation fuel. But they won't now. And they've sent word to clear Matheson's runway. It sounds more like a road than a proper landing strip, but it's better than nothing. They'll do what they can to keep the airfields open." She held up her gloved hand. "And they'll share what they've got. And they told me not to worry. Except…"

"Except you are," Pete finished.

"Yeah. I'm worried. Not for now, but for next month. When the diesel runs out, and their choice is between sitting in the dark or taking some of the jet fuel, it's obvious which they'll pick. And when the food is gone, I don't know what they'll do. Leave, if they can. But to go where?"

"I don't know what we can do," Pete said. "I mean, obviously you and me, we can't do anything, but Nanaimo, or Canberra, or Guam, they could send a few crates of food and ammo on the plane each time it sets down, I guess."

"And when the aviation fuel runs out?" Corrie asked. "Except it's not just Pine Dock. There's Matheson Island and Fisher River, too. And there's the people further south of Fisher River. And people further east and west all the way to Nanaimo. What about the places further north? What about the islands in the Pacific? How many places were actually self-sufficient, Pete?"

"I... I don't know."

"Me neither, but I think someone in Canberra does. That's why they wanted to pull back to the coasts and the farms. If we're going to beat this, we need to restore the global supply chains, and that'll be easier if those chains are much shorter."

"You know what? Saving the world is a lot more complicated than I thought," Pete said.

"That's just what I was thinking. It's like running a war, but the zombies aren't our only enemy. The worst of the winter's over. Places like this could survive. They could hold on, but only if they have hope. If they know they aren't alone. If they know help will, one day, come, but without satellites... Oh, it's our own fault. We reached for the stars, and were surprised when our fingers got burned."

Before dawn arrived, Jerome and Andrea returned from their patrol of the runway.

"I'm happy taking off," Andrea said. "Which only leaves the question of where you want me to take you."

"South Bend has an airport," Pete said. "Or there's a runway in Elkhart."

"Indiana? We don't have the range," Andrea said. "Not unless we can guarantee refuelling. Communication is down to radio range. I'm cool searching for places within half our operational radius, but Indiana is way-a-ay beyond that. Lake Michigan okay with you? Don't worry, we've got a dinghy. You can row ashore. Unless you'd rather swim?"

"We'll take the dinghy," Pete said. "Do you have a map? I'm not really familiar with the coast."

Andrea shook her head. "Sorry. Pick a shore, east or west, and we'll have to eyeball a landmark as we approach. Somewhere I can find again, assuming you guys want a pick-up."

"The Michigan shore," Corrie said. "We can make our way from there."

"Cool," Andrea said. "My next question is when do you want that pick-up? We're heading on to Thunder Bay to find General Yoon. If she's in charge, she might have a message for Vancouver. We can leave you a flare, and fly back over the landing site once, maybe twice. So how long do you need?"

"Pete?" Corrie asked.

"I dunno," he said. "I guess a day to get to South Bend. Maybe a day to look for Olivia. A day to get back. But I might need more."

"Three days," Corrie said. "Three days after you drop us off. And if we're not there, we'll find our own way back here. How long before we leave?"

Andrea glanced at the still-dark sky, then the plane. "A half hour."

"Time to find a radio, too, in case the flare doesn't work," Corrie said. "I really don't want to miss our return flight."

She wasn't the only one. As they were pulling the insulating covers off the engine, Dr Smilovitz came over. The man seemed happier than the day before.

"Any chance of a ride to Thunder Bay?" he asked.

"Just for you?" Andrea asked.

He glanced at Dr Avalon, huddled forlornly in a corner of the hangar. "For two."

"Not for your anthrax?" Jerome asked.

"I destroyed it last night," Dr Smilovitz said. "The world's got enough troubles, we don't need to add to them. But with everything going on, I need to get her to wherever there's a working lab."

"Then, good doctor," Andrea said, "your chariot awaits. Just as soon as we drag her outside."

Chapter 14 - Lake Michigan
Point Betsie Lighthouse, Lake Michigan

The seaplane didn't sink when it skimmed across the waves. But, as it slowed, the engines didn't stop. Pete didn't take that as a good sign.

"This is you," Jerome said, hauling himself through to the cabin. With Dr Avalon and Dr Smilovitz in the jump seats, Pete and Corrie had spent the journey in the rear of the plane where there were no seats: only a rail to perch on and straps to cling to.

"Where are we?" Pete asked, grabbing the straps again as the ungainly machine was buffeted by wind and wave alike.

"On Lake Michigan, as promised," Jerome said. "And close to Michigan's shore near an old lighthouse. We spotted it from the air, so we'll be able to find it again. Sorry I can't be more precise."

"We'll see you in three days," Corrie said, grabbing her pack as Pete unhooked the dinghy.

"Rule forty-nine, never go anywhere without an inflatable boat," Pete said, unhooking the deflated square package. "Or am I up to rule fifty?"

"You ready?" Jerome asked, and opened the door before either had a chance to answer.

If getting the door open and inflating the raft while waves washed inside was difficult, getting aboard was next to impossible. With a stumbling leap, Pete fell onto the bright orange inflatable. Corrie, a step behind, slipped, landing only three-quarters on the raft with her leg over the side. As she rolled, Pete tugged, hauling her back onto the violently bobbing craft.

"You need to get away from the plane!" Jerome yelled. "See you in three days, eh?"

"Three days!" Corrie said, shivering.

Prior to inflation, the two oars had been strapped to the top, doubling as handles. Inflated, they'd ended up on the sides of the shallow raft. Pete grabbed an oar, handed it to his sister, took one for himself, extended the collapsible handle, and dug the flat blade into the waves. Water sloshed over the raft's low sides as they slowly rowed away from the plane and towards the ice-bound shore.

Too slowly.

With a roar, the plane lumbered across the lake, impossibly defying the laws of physics by floating, then again by flying, leaving behind a wake, an artificial tide that shunted them shore-wards. On the downside, when the wake met the retreating tide from the shallow beach ahead, a bucket's worth of water sloshed over the craft's shallow sides.

"Keep paddling," Corrie said, a mantra as well as an instruction.

"Mrs Mathers used to say each day's a new lesson if you only pay attention," Pete said as he stabbed the folding paddle into the water. "Today I've learned that I don't like small boats. Or small planes. The jury's still out on boat-planes, but it doesn't look good."

South of the old lighthouse, the stone-flecked, sandy beach was protected by moss-covered groynes toward which they aimed. Ten metres out, Pete's paddle scraped against the bottom, and they had to clamber out into the freezing water. Wading ashore, they dragged the raft up to the nearest of the ancient wooden walls protecting the shore from erosion.

"Ugh," Corrie said, shivering. "You know what we forgot to ask?"

"To pack a towel?" Pete said.

"Yep. I don't know how I forgot that," she said. "Better keep moving, and better we get the raft inside. Is that really a lighthouse?"

Pete turned to look at the white-painted, red-roofed building that was as tall as the three-storey, circular lakeside tower attached to its wing. "Wait! I know this place," he said.

"You've been here?" Corrie asked.

"Not exactly. I was thinking of coming. It's a small museum, but they rent out rooms. Sort of like a small hotel. It's supposed to be one of the... um..."

"What? Tell me."

"One of the best hidden, romantic getaways," he said quickly. "I was... planning ahead. For Olivia. This was before the store got sold. I mean... anyway, yeah, let's get the raft inside."

"Don't think slowly freezing to death will stop me asking questions," Corrie said, as she grabbed a handle. Together they hauled the raft over towards the museum. "You really do love her, don't you?"

"I… yeah, I dunno. It's a possibility."

"Careful, with so much romance falling from your mouth, you might trip," she said.

"No, I mean, all the books, the movies, the songs, they're about eyes meeting across a crowded room, about destiny, about one true love. But real life is different. Messier. More pragmatic. We were both single, and working at the same place, with no one else to date. It was… sometimes it sort of felt inevitable, which is the opposite of love, right? An accidental arrangement."

"You've over-thought it," Corrie said. "You always used to do that. But it sounds like destiny to me. Look, the front door's been broken open. We're not the first to come here. Leave the raft outside."

They dropped the raft, and both unslung the C7 assault rifles they'd brought with them from Nanaimo. Pete even remembered to check the safety, but he left it on as they climbed the steps leading up to the entrance. Fresh splinters showed around the lock, and at the top of the frame, but the door had been pushed closed after it had been forced.

Cautiously, Corrie nudged the door inward. "Hello!" she called, but there was no reply.

Rain had seeped through the gaps in the recently broken frame, mixing with the muddy footprints that led across the vestibule to a reception desk.

Corrie gave a questioning nod to which Pete replied with an indifferent shrug, to which she responded with a puzzled frown.

"We've got to come back in three days," he hissed. "Let's deal with the zombies now."

She gave a rueful shrug and exasperated grin, as if that hadn't been the question she was asking him. But she nodded, and stepped inside.

"Hello!" Corrie called again, but again there was no reply, and certainly no sign of anyone behind the reception desk. The small exhibition room beyond was just as empty, as were the corridors, a small meeting room, the stairwell, and the guest rooms.

"This is the where you wanted to bring Olivia?" Corrie asked, looking around the neat hotel bedroom. "Nice."

"It's a little more... what's the word? Twee. Yeah, that's it. More twee than I was expecting," he said. "Smaller, too."

"It's cosy. Cute. Which means it wouldn't have been the creepy kind of romantic." She shivered. "Good choice." She picked up the small card left on the re-made bed, on top of a small stack of banknotes. "It's an apology for breaking the front door, and payment to replace it. There's over a thousand dollars here."

"That's way too much," Pete said.

"It tells us money's worth no more here than in Broken Hill," Corrie said. "And that we're not going to find anyone here. Not now. You go see if you can find some towels. Some to use now, some for us to take with us. I'm going to find a notepad and pen."

"Why?"

"I want to leave a note with the dinghy about the seaplane returning in three days. If people do come here, and if they take the inflatable to row to Canada, they'll drown. But there's room for a couple more people on the plane in a few days. If we miss our flight, someone else might as well take our seats."

Half an hour after coming ashore, they were ready to leave.

"I'm drier but no warmer," Corrie said, folding the towel as neatly as she could. "You know, I often thought of leaving the outback, and when I did, I didn't think I'd miss the heat. Now it's all I can think of. Oh, how I wish thoughts could make me warm. You didn't see any cars outside?"

"No, I guess whoever came here, when they didn't find a boat, they drove off somewhere else," Pete said, lacing his boots.

"Yeah, probably. Shame. I guess we're on foot. So, which way?"

Pete looked at the map he'd taken from behind the reception desk. "South then east, or east then south to get to the other side of Crystal Lake, then we go south, south, and south some more."

"Then we'll go south from here, too. Then east." Corrie said. "That will feel more like we're heading in the right direction. Yep, we need a car, but we'll find lots along the lake, abandoned on the shore, near where people boarded their boats. That's my theory."

As they walked away from the lighthouse, Pete adjusted his straps. The pack wasn't too uncomfortable, but between the body armour and the rifle slung across his chest, he felt oddly unbalanced. The flashlight, the crowbar, the bayonet, the sidearm in its new holster; he was dressed for war, but still felt like a civilian.

"Without a car, we won't make it back in time for the plane," he said, stating the obvious fear that had been knocking around the back of his mind.

"Nope. But we won't give up," Corrie said. "I'm not saying we'll look forever. In fact, I think we should only look for one day, but if we miss the plane, we'll drive to Minnesota and then up to Pine Dock. We'll figure it out, and you know what? I'm optimistic."

"I'm not. We won't find her."

"I didn't mean about Olivia. If we don't find her, it means she's gone somewhere else, somewhere safer. But I was talking more generally, about the world, about people. It was Dr Avalon's knees that sealed it."

"Her knees? What do you mean?"

"During the flight, they were all I could see," she said. "Her knees and the back of Jerome's head. But her knees didn't move. She wasn't worried about the zombies. Not really. She was annoyed. Frustrated people weren't instantly obeying her, but not scared. That got me thinking about Pine Dock, Nanaimo, and Broken Hill. The small towns, the sparsely populated counties, they'll cope just fine. The cities might be gone for now, but the people have left, or will be rescued, like in Vancouver. It's the people that matter in the long term. They'll make their way to the small towns, and those seem to be coping just fine."

"Yeah, maybe, but what about the outback? Your cabin could be a dictionary definition of a remote place."

"We were unlucky those zombies crashed nearly on our head," she said. "Otherwise we'd still be there. But Michigan and Indiana are mostly small towns. We'll find a sheriff, we'll find the military, we'll find a car, and we'll find Olivia. Then we'll find our way back to Pine Dock, Nanaimo, and Australia. And then, yeah, back to somewhere where a hot day isn't just a memory."

"For now, I'm going to focus on finding a car," Pete said.

Chapter 15 - The Long Walk to Indiana
Michigan

"So that's where the boats are," Corrie said.

They'd only been walking for fifteen minutes, but they had found houses, and they had found boats. A lot of boats. Moored on the inland Lake Crystal. With barely a kilometre between Lake Crystal and Lake Michigan, it was no surprise someone had tried to drag a yacht across land. Tried and failed.

"Do you think other people managed to get a boat all the way to Lake Michigan?" Pete asked, walking slowly around the truly beached craft: a twenty-footer, which had left a red fibreglass stain on the asphalt.

"Probably," Corrie said. "If they had proper towing gear. If they weren't attacked. Must have been a zombie."

"I *hope* she was a zombie," Pete said.

The woman in torn dungarees and a ragged trench-coat had been shot and bludgeoned. Her corpse had been left in the middle of the road, next to the beached and road-ruined yacht.

"Let's keep going," Corrie said, keeping her distance from the boat and her rifle raised as they continued walking.

"I wonder where they went," Pete said.

"Who?" Corrie asked.

"The people who dropped that yacht," Pete said. "This place is remote. Those houses look empty. Summer homes, I guess, though they look too large, but maybe there's a car in one of the garages."

"No, we should keep going," Corrie said. "I think we're being watched."

"You think there are people inside?" Pete asked.

"Someone killed that zombie," Corrie said.

"They'll have seen the plane," Pete said. "Or heard it. Why aren't they coming out to look?"

"Would you? That's your answer. That's where people are. They're hiding. Waiting for the soldiers to turn up, or the radio to broadcast the outbreak is over. Contact with people means trouble of one sort or a worse kind. And they're right. What help can we give them? We can't get everyone onto the plane. Body. Ahead."

Again, it was one of the undead. Hopefully.

The next vehicle they came to was a car, but it was a burned-out pyre. A snaking scorch mark, leading to a discarded fuel can, indicated how the blaze had begun. The blackened skeletons inside explained why. Two were in the backseat, one noticeably smaller than the other.

Corrie shook her head, said nothing, and kept walking.

Five minutes later, they came to another car, a Michigan state-police cruiser, and this one, at first glance, appeared mostly intact. Bullet holes riddled the trunk. Bags filled the backseat. A corpse occupied the front passenger seat. Slumped forward, though still clearly wearing a police uniform.

"The fuel cap's on," Corrie said. "The wheels look okay. The bullets might have hit something, but the only way to find out is to try the engine."

"We'll have to move that body first," Pete said with weary resignation. "But I guess that's better than—"

But even as he spoke, the dead police officer moved. Its shoulders shuddered. The bags shifted, then fell, tumbling aside as the zombie swiped and swatted at the windshield.

"At least we know why the car was abandoned," Pete said. "He's in uniform. Or *it* is. Or he *was*. Whichever, the driver must have ditched the car when the guy turned."

"And if the car was abandoned," Corrie said, "it worked a few days ago."

The zombie-cop shuddered again, trying to turn and twist, hitting its hands against the doors.

"We *need* a car," Corrie said. "You open the door. I'll... I'll do the rest."

Pete nodded, took the crowbar from her, and walked over to the police cruiser as she unslung her rifle. He yanked the unlocked door open as the zombie surged sideways, straining against the seatbelt holding it fast. Pete stepped back while the zombie squirmed and thrashed.

"What are you waiting for?" Pete asked.

"I don't want to get infected blood all over the driver's seat," Corrie said.

"Ah. Understood. Got it," Pete said, drawing the bayonet that, like most of their gear, had been given to them by the Canadians. He swung forward, a lunging swipe that missed the seatbelt. A loose strap from his pack swung within a grasping hand's reach of the zombie, who caught it and tugged. Off balance, Pete staggered sideways.

"I can't get a clear shot!" Corrie said.

Pete twisted and turned, pulling against the tugging zombie, while slashing at the seatbelt. The blade sliced the zombie's nose, fingers, the sweat-stained shirt, then, finally, the seatbelt. The zombie lurched forward, and Pete fell, the creature almost on top, its head by his knees. Pete rolled as the zombie snapped and twisted, turned and thrashed, rolling after him. A loud crack was followed by a deafening silence as Corrie's bullet ended the police officer's inhuman second existence.

"Are you okay?" Corrie asked.

"I guess," Pete said. "Yeah, it didn't bite me. I need more practice at this."

"Here's hoping we never get the chance," Corrie said. "The keys are in the ignition. I guess we could put the towels down on the passenger seat."

"I'd prefer sitting in the back," Pete said. "There's a couple of gas cans in the trunk. One's... Wow. Empty and full of bullet holes. Lucky the car didn't blow up. The other... Double-wow, it didn't get hit. It's nearly full."

"Cool," Corrie said, turning the key. The engine stuttered, before settling into a soft burr. "And this is a quarter full. Let's fill her up. Next stop is the cabin, right? You said that was in Michigan?"

"About fifty miles from South Bend. North of Paw Paw, west of Kalamazoo."

"Good. I think we should hurry."

"Why?" he asked as he climbed in.

"I saw... I'm not sure," she said as she put the car into gear. "A light. A reflection. Something moving. Northwest of the road."

He turned to look, and, just before it was lost to sight, thought he saw a shadow that might be a person. Perhaps it was one of the former passengers of the car. Perhaps it was one of the undead. Perhaps it was both.

Avoiding the highway, they followed a curving Swiss-cheese road that was a gluey mix of crumbling asphalt and flooded potholes, but which abruptly turned to pristine blacktop outside a nearly finished, and utterly empty, new home.

"I think there's someone there," Pete said as they drove by. "Yeah, top floor, by the window."

"We can stop on the way back," Corrie said. "If we come back this way. But we've only got room in the back for three passengers. Four, max. And if we stop now, we might not make it back from South Bend in time for the flight."

"Yeah, no, I don't think they wanted company," Pete said. "I don't even know they were alive."

One road led to another, all roughly leading south, sometimes bracketed by farmland, sometimes bordered by woodland. And in the houses, Pete was sure he saw shadows dance, curtains move, lights dim, and smoke billow. An increasing number of properties had boarded windows and barricaded drives.

"It's weird," he said. "Everyone's staying behind closed doors."

"It's the smart thing to do," Corrie said. "Avoid infection. Avoid trouble. And it means, when the tanks roll in, we'll have people here who can work the farms."

"Work the farms? I guess they'll have to. Spring's coming, isn't it? It was the world's largest food exporter."

"Michigan? It can't have been."

"No, us. America. We were. There was a documentary I saw. Australia must have been a big exporter, too. Weren't you saying there were cattle ranches the size of countries?"

"The size of a small country, sure," she said. "And we… I mean, Australia, was a major exporter of wheat, too. Fresh fruit was speeding up the list."

"I guess you've got to travel to get a handle on how interconnected the world is," Pete said. "When Olivia and I were talking about life after the end of the world— Okay, so it wasn't a real discussion, and it was just as much about watching movies and… and yeah, it was so we had something to talk about. Anyway, we just assumed we'd have food, and that we were waiting for things to get better. But they wouldn't get better on their own."

"That's what they said in Australia. Why they're evacuating the towns and cities."

"Yeah, but if Australia is no longer exporting, if America isn't, then what's it going to be like in the places that relied on that food?"

"Not good," Corrie said. "In some places, things will get worse before they get better. And everywhere will change. But it will end. It will get better."

"It'll take years," Pete said. "Longer than it took the world to get over World War Two, and it'll be a lot different afterward. Yep, reality is not as much fun as fantasy." He mulled that over as they drove by a house in which, this time, he was certain there were people, watching. "There's a truck in front of that house. Two people. With rifles."

"We're not stopping," Corrie said.

"And they're not waving us down," Pete said. "They're not shooting, either. Just watching. Weird." He turned in the seat to look until they'd disappeared beyond the horizon. "Yep, weird. Or maybe it's not. We're in a police car, I guess they were hoping we'd stop, bring them news or something."

"People, ahead," Corrie said.

It wasn't just people, but a fortress.

A neat cluster of houses were divided by the road, surrounded by farmland, and now ringed by barbed wire. The wire stopped where the blacktop began, but the barricade continued in the form of a pair of eighteen-wheelers, parked side on with their rear tyres in the driveways of homes either side of the road.

"No way will we get through," Corrie said, stopping the police cruiser some two hundred yards from the barricade.

On top of the nearest of the two juggernauts stood a sentry with a rifle, next to a chair on which she'd sat until she'd heard the car approach.

"Let's see if she goes to wake up the welcoming committee," Pete said as the sentry climbed down a ladder, and disappeared behind the juggernaut's cab.

"Over there," Corrie said. "The big house on the left. Eight people. No, ten. She must have radioed a warning from the truck's cab."

"Or they all heard our engine," Pete said. "They're well armed. Shall we go say hello?"

"More over to the left," Corrie said. She adjusted the mirror. "There's at least two behind us. I've got a bad feeling about this."

Before Pete could agree, a bullet shattered the driver's-side wing mirror.

"*Very* bad," Corrie said, throwing the car into reverse. A bullet grazed the bodywork, and more hit the road as other guns opened fire.

"They're shooting a cop car!" Pete said.

"Guess so," Corrie said, reversing the car as fast as the engine would allow. "And I don't care if they're sorry when they see our corpses and realise what a mistake they've made."

"No, I mean—" Pete began, but was jolted into silence as Corrie swerved the car hard right and drove onto a tractor's track. "You're leaving the road?"

"Look behind!" she said.

It was the pickup that had been parked outside the property to the north.

A chuntering roar lit up the road behind them, a brief burst barely a second long.

"Machine gun!" Corrie yelled.

But the sound didn't come again. Pete swung in his seat. Behind, through the mud-strewn rear windshield, he could make out a pickup, and someone standing in the truck-bed, braced behind a fixed weapon.

"Tactical," Pete said, as the car swung onto a road heading roughly back the way they'd come. "That's what they call it, don't they? In Africa and places, when they turn a pickup into an armoured car?"

"And I guess they want to save ammo now they've chased us off," Corrie said. "But why were they shooting at cops?"

"Or are we heading into another ambush?" Pete said.

The track met another and she turned south. Another turning, and they met a wider, slightly better repaired road, bracketed by trees.

"I think we're clear," Corrie said. "No more stopping until we reach the cabin."

"Agreed."

Chapter 16 - Bodies in the Woods
Michigan

Finding the correct back road took three tries, but once they had, finding the turning was obvious. Recently broken branches formed a neat trail to the track, as if some large vehicle had torn a path through the overgrown bracken. As Corrie slowed, the headlights glittered off something metallic.

"Wait, stop!" Pete said.

Even before Corrie had killed the engine, Pete had opened the door and flung himself outside. Corrie followed, more slowly, grabbing her rifle before heading after her brother, into the woodland, up to a battered twelfth-hand pickup that was as much repairs as original bodywork.

"It's my truck!" Pete said. He peered through the mud-splattered window before opening the door. "And those are my keys!"

"It must be Olivia," Corrie said. "She must be here."

"No, these are *my* keys. The spare set from my apartment. I gave her the proper set the night I said goodbye to her."

"It must be one of your neighbours, then?" Corrie suggested. "Where's the cabin?"

"Up there," Pete said, pointing, then followed his own finger into the woods.

The track was obvious, as were the muddy footprints leading up to where the cabin had once been. A charred ruin stood in its place. Rain-dampened charcoal added an acidic tang to the air, while the settling mist added a muffling shroud to a scene of utter devastation. The roof had collapsed, as had the wall around the front door, while the southern wall leaned at a precarious angle. The small bathroom-annex was smoke-blackened but intact.

"Where did you keep your spare keys?" Corrie asked, breaking the sepulchral silence.

"In my apartment. But I left my truck at work. I gave Olivia my main set of keys."

"So she'd have taken the truck home for you? Back to your apartment?"

"I guess," he said.

"And a neighbour broke into your place, took your spare keys, and found your address book."

"I don't have an address book, except on my phone."

"Then a scrap of paper where you'd scribbled the address down," Corrie said. "Or did you tell one of your neighbours about this place?"

"I didn't really know them," Pete said. "And I don't think I wrote it down anywhere."

"Well, they found your spare keys, so I'm guessing you did," she said. "And they came here, and they burned the place down. It must have been an accident."

"I suppose," he said.

She turned on her flashlight, and tracked it over the ruin. He'd left his, with his rifle, back in the car. "Stop," he said. "There. Is that...?"

He ran towards the charred timbers, cutting across the light's beam. "It's a body," he said.

She grabbed his arm even as he took another step closer. "Leave it, Pete."

The corpse was partially buried beneath the charred timbers.

"It could be her," he said, shaking himself free. The leaning wall creaked as he hauled at the singed wood covering the body. The charred timbers cracked as he hauled them off the corpse.

"That's enough, Pete," Corrie said. "There's no way anyone could identify that body. She could be anyone."

"It's Olivia," he said. "It could be anyone, yes. But here? With my truck parked there? It has to be her."

"Actually, no," Corrie said. "Look at her hand. That's an engagement ring, and a wedding band. Pete, it's not her."

"Where? Are you sure? Oh. Okay. Yeah."

Corrie grabbed his arm. "Back to the car," she said. "Come on."

"Why?"

"For one thing, because you left your rifle and flashlight there. For another, because there's nothing else to be found here."

"No, there is," he said. "Shine your light there. No, to the left. There. That's... that's a body. A man."

"Or a zombie," Corrie said. "Do you know him?"

"Shot in the head, how could I tell?" he replied. "But no, I don't think so."

"Then let's just go back to the car."

"We have come this far. I can't stop now," he said. "I've got to search."

"Then get your flashlight first," she said.

After an hour, with darkness properly descended, he finally stopped. "Two bodies," he said. "Just two bodies. And neither is hers."

Back near the road, while he examined his truck, she shone her light over the police cruiser.

"Do you see these bullet holes?" Corrie said, shining her light on the police car. "Since that fortified hamlet, we were shot at twice."

"They were hunting rifles, weren't they?" Pete said. "That neat line, that has to be an automatic weapon. Probably that machine gun."

"Right. Probably. But we were shot at twice more. Once from that weird one-storey place set back from the road that had the three-storey tower built where the garage should have been."

"The viewing tower?" Pete said. "That's what I thought it was. For bird watching or something."

"Perfect for a sniper," she said. "And the second time, it was that seemingly empty field. Must have been people who knew the area. They shot at a police cruiser. We weren't stopping, and hadn't even slowed, but they shot at us anyway. That's not good. I don't know what else it means, but from here, if your truck still works, we should drive that. But before we do anything, including working out what we do next, we should wash up as best we can, eat, then keep the lights off until dawn. That's hours away, but that means plenty of time for some other vehicle to drive along that road. If they do, we don't want them spotting a light. Not if, around here, they even shoot at cops."

Ten minutes later, they sat in Pete's truck, in the dark, chewing on ration packs they'd originally found in the coffin-like crates in Lisa Kempton's plane.

"I think that some local came to the cabin," Corrie finally said. "That's who the bodies are. Someone from a nearby farm, maybe. You said this was somewhere your boss owned? Maybe she sold it."

"How'd my truck end up here then?"

"Maybe Olivia left it here," Corrie said. "She had the keys, yes? And the keys for your apartment? And she knew where the cabin was. So maybe that's why she drove here. You said she had a roommate she was close to."

"Nicole, yeah. They're good friends."

"Okay. So they loaded all their food into one car, drove to your place, went inside, took all your food, then the spare keys because they'd lost the originals or just wanted a spare set for safety. They brought both cars here, and found the place had already burned down. Those bodies, I bet they were locals, maybe a neighbour, someone keeping an eye on the place for your old boss."

"Yeah, I guess," Pete said.

"You're sceptical, sure, I get it," Corrie said. "But the key thing is that Olivia isn't here. Her body isn't here. If she was here before the fire, she left. If she came after, there was no reason for her to stay."

"And if she left, she drove," Pete said, cheering as he spotted the faintest glimmer of hope. "Because my truck still works and there's fuel in the tank. And there was crockery and cutlery in the ruin. I know Mrs Mathers had emptied the cabin."

"There, that's proof, then," Corrie said. "Proof that someone else came up here thinking a cabin in woodland would be remote and therefore safe. But it's not that remote. Not really."

"I didn't really think we'd find her here," Pete said. "I mean, I did. I hoped I would. But... that was me thinking the way I did a couple of weeks ago. Now, the new me knows I might have come here, but I wouldn't have stayed."

"No? Where would you have gone? Where would Olivia have gone?"

"Florida," Pete said. "That's where Mrs Mathers was going to retire. She bought a house down there."

"Florida's a long way," Corrie said. "A seriously long way across an entire continent. You'd really go there?"

"I dunno if I would, but Olivia might."

"They shot at a police car," Corrie said. "This little finger on the mitten of Michigan isn't like Canada. We can't expect help from the people barricaded inside their hamlets, and we shouldn't ask for it. The day after tomorrow, we should be back at the lighthouse because if you want to go to Florida, we should see if Canberra will arrange a plane. It's too far to drive."

"No, I get it. And I don't think she'd have gone to Florida. Nicole worked in a grocery store. She stole most of their shopping, so I bet she did that when the news broke. I bet she filled a shopping cart and then filled her car and went back to their apartment. And then they came here. I guess they left in Nicole's car. Yeah, they wouldn't have gone to Florida. Not from here. They'd have gone to Canada. Or they'd have found some abandoned house to hide in, but if they did, we won't find it."

"That does sound like our kind of luck, us looking for her here, and she's already up in Thunder Bay or somewhere," Corrie said.

"Maybe she left a note, though," Pete said. "Not Olivia, but maybe Nicole did. Saying where she'd gone."

"In their apartment? Do you want to go look?"

"Sure. And at Mrs Mathers's old house. It's on the way. Yeah, maybe Olivia would have gone there. It's bigger than her apartment. If nothing else, we'll see what the city is like. That's what we're really doing here, isn't it? Finding out how bad America's got in the last few days." He looked towards the dark shadow of the bullet-riddled police cruiser. "And it's looking pretty bad indeed."

1st March

Chapter 17 - Other People's Expectations
Michigan & Indiana

"Are you awake?" Corrie asked.

"No," Pete said. "But I'm not asleep, either."

Outside, rain pattered against the windscreen. At the edge of the droplets, a faint reflected glimmer offered the promise of an approaching dawn, albeit one which was grim and grey.

"We could try to boil up some water," Corrie said, opening her pack and rooting inside for a couple of the ration packs they'd brought with them. "Although I don't know if I've got any coffee. What's this? Mango and oat. That sounds like cereal."

Pete turned the blue and gold package over in his hands. "It's not the same without a cartoon character on the packet. She must have been planning to market these to campers."

"Kempton? Probably," Corrie said.

"So was she trying to profit from the end of the world? Or only trying to fund her attempt to save it?"

"Both," Corrie said. "With her, there's always more than one motive."

Pete took out his spoon, which was no longer clean, but was still far cleaner than his hands. Like everything that hadn't come from the coffin-like containers, he'd picked it up in Nanaimo, along with a fork and knife, and a set for Corrie, taken from a break-room at the airport.

"This isn't camping, is it?" Pete said. "When Olivia and I talked about coming up here, that's pretty much how we imagined it. Camping, but in a Hollywood kind of way."

"You mean, when you pictured it, you didn't imagine the smell?"

"And the birds were chirruping, the sun was always shining, the ground was a lot less like a swamp. Oh, and without the bodies, of course. Clean spoons, too."

"I know what you mean," Corrie said. "I miss the outback. I miss my cabin. Never imagined I would. There were too many nights I thought of it as a prison, and I was serving a sentence for what I'd done. But it was a sentence in reverse. If I was being punished, everyone else was okay. And now..." She coughed. "Okay, no, we don't have time for that. Are you ready to go?"

"Let me find a tree first," he said.

Ten minutes later, with Corrie behind the wheel, they were driving south.

"I miss the airfield," Pete said, finally breaking the silence.

"In Pine Dock?"

"In Broken Hill. Or Liu's house."

"Being inside, you mean?" she asked.

"No. Somewhere with electricity. Yep, even your cabin. Somewhere you know that, even at the end of the day, you have somewhere with running water and power for a stove. Nope, this isn't the outback. It's colder, for one thing."

"It's not electricity you miss," she said. "You remember how Mick had those rules? They were for the city blokes, the scientists from overseas. Not people who lived in the outback. Because if you lived there, you knew to help one another. You might hate their living guts, but you'd give them a hand because it was, literally, life and death every single day."

"Sounds like that here, now, everywhere," Pete said.

"Except helping each other is the sensible thing to do. The rational thing. The only thing that, long term, will ensure anyone's survival, but if you've only got one crate of beans left in the pantry and a gun on the table, are you going to give a stranger a can of beans or a bullet? That's what you miss. What *I* miss. Normality was when helping someone else rarely imperilled yourself. I think that's why people are hiding. They're still hoping things will return to normal. Hoping someone else will fix this whole mess. Hoping it doesn't get so bad they have to make the hardest choice."

"The people who shot at us weren't hiding. I reckon they've accepted how things are. Or is it that they've decided, not accepted? They've decided things are as bad as they can imagine, not as good as they could be."

"Maybe. It'll be a long time before help reaches here from Nanaimo," Corrie said. "And longer before real help gets there from Canberra. For us, for the here and now, if people are staying inside until their supplies run out, then, in a day, or a week, or a month, things will get a whole lot worse. There's something in the road."

Ahead, a bus lay on its side, and at a shallow angle so it nearly blocked both lanes. The rear window was a holey spider-web. The safety glass had mostly remained intact, but the fractured cobweb was nearly impossible to see through. From the twisted frames, jutting skyward, some of the side windows had been smashed by escaping passengers.

"Hang on, stop," Pete said. "There's someone trying to get out. Someone trapped."

Corrie braked.

The bus's rear window shook. Collapsed, smashing to the roadway. Chunks of shattered glass skittered across the tarmac as a figure crawled out from the trashed vehicle. It was a miracle anyone had survived the crash. Wearing rags as blood-coated as its face. No. It was no miracle. And this was no survivor. Corrie realised the truth before Pete could open his mouth, slamming her foot on the gas and driving partially into the ditch, churning through mud to get beyond the bus, and to a road swarming with the moving, crawling dead.

There were too many for them to have all been passengers. Too many with barely an unbroken limb among them. Unnaturally bent arms crooked upwards, beckoning with crushed hands, while fractured legs and crushed feet pushed at the road, tearing cloth and skin, leaving a bloody trail amid the frozen mud.

Corrie weaved the truck through, and then over, the scores of twisting, pulsating bodies, powdering crushed bones, cracking skulls, and pulverising already broken limbs.

"Yep," she said, when they were finally back onto empty road again. "Yep, I'm changing my mind about one thing. I think that explains why we haven't seen many people. Not on that road."

"And why everyone we did see is staying inside," Pete said, tightening his grip on the rifle.

"Now *that* is a roadblock," Pete said, bringing the truck to a halt a safe distance from the cement and steel barriers ahead. When they'd finally reached roads with which he was more familiar, he'd taken the wheel.

"An official roadblock, originally, anyway," Corrie said. "Two police cruisers, a bus, some riot-fences, and concrete. And that bus is completely blocking the road. But... no, I can't see any people. Where are we?"

"Bertrand Road," Pete said. "That's Coop Road up on the right, just before the bus. Coop Road becomes Lilac Road when it crosses the state line, just down there."

"And Lilac Road is where your boss lived?" Corrie asked.

"Yep," Pete said. "I can't see anyone at the roadblock, can you?"

"They're long gone," Corrie said. "I'm guessing after someone torched that cop car." The police cruiser was identifiable by the light-rack on the roof, but the twisted frame had buckled, letting the doors swing open, revealing the corpse inside. "Hope that body belonged to a zombie. Can you squeeze the truck through?"

"I think so. Looks like the barricade is intended to stop people heading east, across the bridge, and over to Niles. Or was it to stop people coming the other way?"

He restarted the engine and drove forward, weaving through the barricade.

"Don't slow," Corrie said. "Keep driving. That's the smell of death, of decay, I'm sure of it."

Pete needed no more prompting.

"How far is it?" Corrie asked as they drove by one empty house, then another, moving slowly through the clusters of detached, set-back homes with mix-and-match designs that made them neither identical nor entirely unique. A porch from one was replicated on a house three doors down while its windows were replicated on a property nearly opposite.

"It's down here," Pete said. "They bought the house about twenty years ago, I think." He turned onto the side road leading to the small cluster of homes. "Just after they were built. Off-plan. It was the same time they set up the carpet store. It was a used-car lot before…" He trailed into silence as he stopped the truck.

"That's her house?" Corrie asked. "The one with the RV outside?"

"That's Mrs Mathers's place," Pete said. "I don't think she owned an RV, though."

"Looks clear," Corrie said, checking the mirrors, then twisting around to look behind. "Clear. But we should be quick."

Bringing their rifles with them, they climbed out of the car. His boots rang loudly on the ash-coated road. The frost was already melting, turning to dew, mixing with the soot from the wreck of the torched RV, creating a grey slurry drifting towards an already blocked drain. The RV was a large vehicle, but the fire had consumed it so completely, any more detailed description was impossible.

"Body," Corrie said, pointing towards the front of the vehicle.

Glass from the shattered windows crunched beneath his feet. Each step more arduous than the last, Pete walked around the truck, relaxing a fraction as he saw the corpse. Singed, rather than burned, she had been a woman once, a zombie after, and now she was dead twice over, but it wasn't Olivia.

"Don't know who she was," he said.

A gunshot shattered the silence. Pete spun. There was nothing to see, and nothing to hear. The street wasn't just quiet, but artificially still. "I think we're being watched," he said.

"I was just thinking the same thing," Corrie said. "No way everyone's left the city yet. Go check the house. I'll turn the truck around. Shout if you hear anything."

"I won't just shout, I'll shoot," Pete said as he ran up the path.

The front door was locked, and without an inch of give when he gave it a shove. Not wanting to break a bone trying to break it down, he ran to the side gate, and into the once-pristine rear garden. In his mind, it still rang with the laughter from the Fourth of July barbecue, but the lawn was muddy, the beds filled with leaves, and an upturned dog-bowl sat on the back porch.

The kitchen door was unlocked.

"Hello?" he asked, barely louder than a whisper, uncertain he wanted a reply.

Someone had lived here, going by the unwashed bowls by the sink. Next to them was a box of cereal. His heart jumped when he saw the cartoon elf. It was his favourite variety, but the box was empty.

"Hello!" he tried again, louder this time, but still got no reply. With increasing swiftness, he went from empty room to empty room, until he was certain no one was there.

"Anything?" Corrie asked, standing by the truck's open door.

"Nope," he said. "No sign of Mrs Mathers or Olivia. Someone had stayed there. Someone with a dog. Maybe for a night or two. But there was no furniture except some folding chairs. I think Mrs Mathers had moved out. Maybe even sold the place. Before the outbreak, I mean."

"I think we should leave," Corrie said. "I'm certain we're being watched."

Pete got in the driver's seat. "Olivia's apartment," he said.

"I think so," Corrie said. "And then... then I think we need to get out of this city. I'm not saying we're giving up the search," she added quickly. "But I haven't heard a single other vehicle. A noisy engine will attract attention. So, her apartment, then we'll leave the city, and then we'll talk through our plans."

"Sure," he said, knowing what decision they'd reach. He'd already reached it himself, and before he'd left Australia. It was beyond dumb searching for Olivia, but that wasn't the sole purpose of the trip. It wasn't even the main purpose, not anymore. They wanted to know what America was like. And now he knew.

"That's where she lived," Pete said, stopping the truck fifty yards from the front entrance to the apartment block. The trio of upturned cars prevented him from driving nearer.

"Nice place," Corrie said.

"Her apartment's at the back," Pete said. "She doesn't have a river view."

"It's still nice," Corrie said.

"Way better than my—" Pete began but stopped as his eyes caught movement in the rear view mirror. "We've got company."

"People?" Corrie asked, spinning around.

"Yes. No. Zombie. Only one."

"Hmm. Okay, we better get out. Bring the keys, we don't want someone stealing the truck while we're inside."

"You can stay here," Pete said, climbing out. He picked up his rifle, but Corrie had already raised hers, taking aim at the zombie in the torn suit, half a burgundy tie, one brown loafer, and a jagged gash running the length of his face. On either side of the wound, skin peeled away in two nearly-neat sheets that flapped, one over his mouth, one over his eye, until Corrie's bullet slammed into his forehead. The sound of the falling body seemed louder than the shot, but Pete knew the gunshot would carry across the town.

"More will come, won't they?" he said.

"Zombies, or people, or both," Corrie said, eyeing the windows around them. "You've got the keys? Then let's go see if Olivia left a note."

Inside, the entrance lobby was damp, darkly forbidding, decorated with jagged glass from the already broken doors. The stairwell stank of sweat, fear, and urine.

"It's not right," Pete said as they reached the landing, and walked along the dark, dank corridor. "It smells worse than a locker room. Worse than... well, anything I can think of. That's it," he added, pointing at an already broken-open door.

"Careful and slow," Corrie said, stepping in front of her brother, pushing the door open with her rifle.

Inside, their nostrils were assaulted by a different smell. Stronger. Deeper. More pervasive. More permanent. And more familiar, though only over the last few days. In the middle of the floor, between the pushed-back sofa and pushed-aside TV, lay two bodies shrouded in bedsheets.

"Quick," Corrie said, drawing her knife. "Check them. Pete? Pete?" Not waiting to ask a third time, she crossed to the nearest corpse, and cut away the sheet at the face. "Do you know her?"

"It's Nicole," Pete whispered. "That's Olivia's roommate."

Corrie was already cutting the sheet from the other, taller, body.

"I... I don't know him," Pete said.

"Look for a note, something that says where Olivia went," Corrie said, crossing to the bedrooms.

Pete didn't move. Nicole. She'd been dead for days. Her face was sallow. Sunken. Gaunt. Bloodless. Lifeless. Nearly unrecognisable. But in his mind's eye, he could still see her smile. Hear her laugh.

"It's like a changing room floor on Black Friday," Corrie said, coming back into the den. "Pete? Did you find a note?"

"A note?" he asked.

"Someone wrapped those two in sheets," Corrie said. "Someone who cared. It had to be Olivia, so see if she left a note as to where she went."

"There won't be one," he said, after a lacklustre search of the kitchen counter. "Of course there won't. Mrs Mathers is in Florida, and she thinks I'm in Hawaii. Nicole's... gone. Who's she going to leave a note for?"

From outside, muffled by glass, came a gunshot. Then another.

"Time we left," Corrie said. "Anything you want to take?"

"No. Wait, yes." Pete picked took a photograph from the wall in which Olivia and Nicole stood over a five-pint milkshake, trying so hard not to laugh they couldn't keep the straws in their mouths. He'd taken the photograph himself, at a county fair last fall. In the picture, though he hadn't realised it until now, Olivia only had eyes for him. "Just this."

"Where else can we look?" Corrie asked as Pete drove west, threading his truck around the twisted remains of a motorbike.

"Nowhere. Everywhere," Pete said. "I wonder who that guy was. Must have been a friend of Nicole's. But how'd they die? They were shot, but not in the head, so they weren't infected."

"Don't dwell on it," Corrie said. "All that matters is that someone shrouded them in those bed-sheets. It had to be Olivia."

"Right. So she did that, then went to the cabin. And after that… she could have gone anywhere. Absolutely anywhere. We won't find her. Let's head back."

"To the lighthouse? Are you sure?" Corrie asked. "I mean, are you sure you're happy turning around now and heading back to the plane? I don't know what'll happen next, where we'll end up, but I can't imagine we'll ever return here."

"Yeah. It was dumb coming looking for her. But we had to come somewhere." He slowed automatically at the sight of a stop sign, then accelerated through it. "Fire down there. Smoke. Something's burning. Some*where*. No, I'm glad we came. But there wasn't any chance of—"

"Whoa! Stop!" Corrie called.

Pete slammed on the brakes. Ahead, a fawn-coloured dog had darted out into the road, then sprung back to the kerb where it stood, tail wagging, watching them.

"Dogs would be like kangaroos, they can't get infected, right?" Pete said uncertainly.

"I don't know," she said. "But we'll keep our distance. No! There's… it's a boy."

About fourteen, he darted out from an alley to grab the dog's collar. The boy began hauling the dog back towards the alley, but the dog was less eager than the boy to return to cover.

"Wait here," Corrie said. Leaving her rifle, she stepped outside. "Hi!" she called. "G'day. My name's Corrie. Can we help?"

The boy looked at her, and then the truck, and hauled even harder on the dog's collar, but the dog shook and shuddered, tearing himself free. The dog took a step towards the truck, head on one side, almost looking puzzled.

"That's a nice dog," Corrie said. "We're heading up to Canada. If you want, you can come with us. And if you've got friends, family, we've got room in the back of the truck. It'll be safer with us than staying here, I promise."

Another figure stepped out of the alley, this one older. In her late twenties, a baseball hat covered her face, shielding her eyes, while a trailing long coat covered most of the rest of her.

"Where did you get that truck?" she asked in a summer-breeze voice that was, to Pete, as familiar as a dream.

He threw the door open. "Olivia!"

Olivia froze, mouth open, as Pete ran towards her.

"Hey!" the teenage boy called out, dragging a knife from the back of his belt.

The dog growled, leaping in front of Pete.

"Hey, no!" Pete said, staggering to a halt.

"Rufus, down!" Olivia said. "And put that away, Dwayne. It's okay. This is Pete."

"Your Pete?" Dwayne asked.

"*My* Pete," Olivia said. "It is, isn't it? It really is you?" She sidestepped the still suspicious Rufus and threw her arms around Pete, gave him the briefest kiss, then stepped back. "I don't know how. I don't know why. But I want to know, I *do*, just not here, not now. Was that you shooting earlier?"

"Some of it was us, but not all," Corrie said.

"Olivia, this is Corrie. Corrie, Olivia," Pete said.

"Your missing sister? Seriously? You live in Hawaii? I have so many questions, but we truly don't have time."

"Livy, I can hear them!" Dwayne said, his voice ringing with urgent fear.

"I'm ninety percent sure this is a hallucination," Olivia said. "In case it isn't, grab your guns and follow me, quick. Go, Dwayne. Back inside the store."

Boy and dog bounded side-by-side down the narrow alley, stopping by an infinitesimally ajar fire-door. Dwayne pulled out a sharpened chisel and pried the door open. Rufus bounded inside first.

"Why are we hiding?" Corrie asked.

"Go. Inside. Trust me," Olivia said, pushing her, then Pete into the store. She grinned. "Seriously, Pete— No, I can hear them coming. Go. Get in."

She pulled the door closed after them.

They were in a small stockroom. Dark. Dry. The shelves full of coloured paper, pre-packaged glitter, and pre-cut card.

"Dwayne," Olivia said. "Take Rufus. Go wait by the back. Keep watch, okay?"

"What's going on?" Pete asked.

"Shh!" Olivia whispered, lowering her voice. "The short version is that a psycho cop is burning the city to the ground around our ears. We don't have time for the long version." She eased down the crowded corridor leading from the stockroom, through a small office, and paused at the broken door leading to the front of the store.

Pete followed, with Corrie behind him.

Beyond the grimy plate-glass windows, he saw his truck, but nothing else. He was about to ask why they were hiding, when he heard a buzzing whine, growing in volume as a dirt bike shot into view, skidding to a halt by the truck. A man in uniform threw himself off, unslinging a machine pistol. He ran to the truck, laid a hand on the engine, then checked inside before walking, slowly around the vehicle.

"Only one," Olivia whispered, reaching into her coat and withdrawing a small pistol. "On three. Ready?"

Pete glanced at Corrie. She nodded, so he did the same. There was no need to ask *ready for what*, and no time to ask why. Nor was there even time to act. Even as Olivia took a crouching step forward, a second buzzing whine filled the store, a second bike came to a screeching halt outside. Again, the rider was a cop. Or partly dressed as a cop. She wore the coat, but over jeans and boots.

The two police officers conferred. Though Pete couldn't hear what they were saying, it was clear they were discussing the truck with its still-warm engine.

Olivia frowned. Corrie raised two fingers, then three. Olivia shook her head, motioning they should head back through the store, but then grabbed Pete's arm just as he was about to move. She shook her head, raised a finger to her lips, and shook her head again.

Two more vehicles approached. The first, a quad bike, the second, a police cruiser, out of which climbed two people. Again, all were dressed in some form of police uniform, but only the police car's passenger wore a complete set, including tie and hat.

The smartly dressed officer spoke to the first-on-the-scene biker, then snapped his fingers. The car's driver ran to the police car's trunk, retrieved something, and ran back to the officer, holding it out.

Pete squinted, trying to identify the object, realising it was a bottle with a rag in the top just as the cop lit it, and hurled it through the open door of his truck. Flames exploded as the glass broke.

Olivia clamped her hand over Pete's mouth, pushing down on his shoulder as he automatically stood.

"Go," Olivia whispered.

From outside, came another soft crash and just as soft a whoosh as another firebomb ignited. As Pete got level with the stockroom, glass shattered behind them as a third was thrown through the store's window.

He didn't need Corrie's hand at his back to know to run. Dwayne and Rufus already were, sprinting along the alley behind the store, across the road, and to another alley beyond.

A block away, in the kitchen of a mid-row diner, they stopped and concealed themselves behind the metal counter.

"I want to make sure they don't follow us again," Corrie said. "I don't think they saw us. You didn't hear any shooting, did you?"

"No. I don't think so," Pete said.

"No," Corrie said. "Who are they?"

"I'll give you the highlight reel," Olivia said. "Did you see the cop in the shirt and tie?"

"The passenger in the car?"

"His name's Vevermee," Olivia said. "Or I think it is. And he's a state trooper from Michigan. There's another cop, Herrera, who wasn't there, and he might be dead, but he's an officer from South Bend. I think they're the only two real cops in the group. The rest dress as police, but they're just a gang really. Vevermee is burning the city down. I think he is, or was, trying to burn out the infected."

"How many more of them are there?" Corrie asked.

"At least fifty," Olivia said. "They're up at the airport, and they're close to the ruins of Notre Dame."

"The ruins? The university was destroyed?" Pete asked.

"Burned down. By him," Olivia said. "That's why we're trying to get out of here."

"Yeah, the slow way," Dwayne said.

"Precisely," Olivia said. "The slow way. The *safe* way." She shook her head. "I can't believe you came back, Pete. But why?"

"Um… for you, I guess," Pete said. "Sort of."

Olivia laughed. "Seriously? That has to be the most crazy-romantic thing ever, coming all the way from Hawaii after the end of the world."

"Actually, we've come a lot further than that," Corrie said. "From Australia. But there's a boat-plane landing on Lake Michigan tomorrow to take us back to safety. We've got room for six more passengers."

"Counting Rufus, there's seven of us," Olivia said.

"We'll make it work," Corrie said.

"You came from Australia on a boat-plane?" Dwayne asked.

"No, on a jet plane to British Columbia," Pete said. "Lisa Kempton's jet, actually. In British Columbia we met some Canadian police, and they flew us to Lake Michigan. Partly so the jet would airlift some sick children back to Australia, and partly because we're supposed to be finding out what America's like now."

130

"Canadian police?" Dwayne asked. "You mean it's still normal up there?"

"I wouldn't say normal," Corrie said. "It's bad, but not as bad as here. They're evacuating Vancouver City, co-ordinating in the Pacific, and putting people to work on the farms in Australia."

"That's a relief," Olivia said. "It really is. When I tell you what happened here, you'll understand."

"Yeah, but you're not going to do that now, right?" Dwayne asked. "Can't we leave?"

"Not yet," Olivia said. "We can't let him follow. You know, I think he burned down the hospital." She crouched, rose up, and peered at the road, before ducking down. "There's a zombie out there. Not heading towards us. We should stay here a few more minutes. You were driving your truck, so you went to Nora's cabin, right?"

"And to your apartment," Pete said. "We saw the bodies. I saw Nicole."

"Oh. Her death was an accident," Olivia said. "The man with her, the other body, that was Dante. He worked with her at the grocery store. They came home, the day of the outbreak, with this guy, Mack. Dante was already shot. And Mack shot Nicole. I ran for help, straight to the hospital. I sort of ended up working there, until it burned down. I think Vevermee did that. I didn't have my keys, so I went to your place. I had to break into your apartment for the keys to the truck, and, after, I drove up to the cabin."

"There were two bodies," Pete said. "A man in the bushes, and a woman in the cabin. It had burned down."

"Naomi and Conrad," Olivia said, sighing. "They had two kids. Tyler and Robyn. I brought the children here. Found Dwayne and Wayde and their nan. And since then, we've been trying to leave, but we've barely been able to stay hidden from those damn cops. Do you remember when the news carried stories about the long-delayed trial of some far-away and long-ago war criminal? They'd describe atrocities too grim even for Hollywood, and you'd look at the guy's photo and think there was nothing special about him. If you bumped into him on the street, you wouldn't give him a second glance. Vevermee is like that. I first saw him running a barricade north of the city. Stopping cars and…" She stopped, stood, and checked outside. "I'll tell you the rest later. It's raining. They won't be able to follow us. Dwayne, do you remember the way?"

"Of course. Just try to keep up this time."

Chapter 18 - U-Call, We Carry
South Bend

The barbershop wasn't *where* Pete had been expecting, and the woman standing in the shadows wasn't who.

"I know you," Pete said, looking at the old woman holding the shotgun.

"But I don't know you," she said, her hand uncomfortably close to the trigger.

"Yes you *do*, Jenny," Olivia said. "This is Pete."

"Pete? *The* Pete? *Your* Pete?" the old woman asked. "Well, now, isn't that a turn-up for the books?"

"Very old books," Olivia said. "The kind with myths and knights and dragons. He came all the way from Australia to get me."

"Rode in on a white charger, did he?" Jenny asked.

"A truck," Olivia said. "But the cops torched it."

"Of course they did. Devils, the lot of them, wanting to turn our home into hell. Wayde, Dwayne, keep watch at the front. But stay away from that window, you hear? Robyn, Tyler, you help. Listen as much as look, remember? Now, young man, tell me how you came to be here, and what you were doing in Australia because Livy thought you'd gone to Hawaii."

Briefly, Pete and Corrie ran through the explanation, after which Olivia ran through the briefer introductions.

Wayde and Dwayne, twins, were two of Jenny's grandsons. Fourteen years old, they were identical in looks and clothing, and armament. Both carried wickedly long hunting knives in their hands. Their mother had gone to Oregon for a job interview, leaving Jenny to watch the boys in their house a few blocks further west and south. The other two children, Robyn and Tyler, were the children of the couple who'd died at the cabin.

"It's a crying shame you lost your truck," Jenny said. "It'll be a long hike to Michigan."

"Why did you pick this place to hide?" Pete asked.

"Where would a deranged cop not bother looking for people?" Jenny asked. "We were aiming for the mortuary on Napier Street, but this barbershop is as far as we reached."

Olivia glanced over at the children, but they were paying more attention to Rufus than to the street outside, and none at all to the adults. "After Robyn and Tyler's mom and dad died, I drove their RV back to South Bend. I didn't know about Vevermee, you see. Not really. The RV was well supplied, and I figured I could get some diesel from... well, somewhere. I was heading back to what was familiar, I guess. Anyway, we got to Nora's place. It was somewhere I knew. But I saw lights on in Jenny's. There hadn't been any when I went through there the first time."

"I'd gone to get my pills," Jenny said. "Nearly blew Livy's head off before I realised who she was. Thought she was another damn looter. There were a lot of those."

"We joined forces, and nearly joined a convoy. That was before the university was burned down. That's... no. No, I'll tell you about it some other time. After that, we went to the carpet store. But Vevermee followed us there."

"But why did you want to go there?" Pete asked.

"For the tools and the building materials," Olivia said. "We thought we could make a fortress. Somewhere to hide from the undead. There was no food, of course, but there's a lot been left behind by all the people who fled."

"He found us. The demon cop," Jenny said, nearly spitting the words. "Saw the lights, you see. The contractors had left a generator, so we were able to keep the lights on at night. But he found us, and he burned the place down. We tried going east, but he's barricaded the bridges. We're heading south now, keeping to the cover of houses and stores, moving at dawn and dusk, trying to get far enough away we can drive. They look for lights and listen for engines."

"We left some diesel at the carpet store," Olivia said. "That's where Dwayne and I were heading when we heard your truck. I thought we might as well bring it with us. Rufus must have recognised the truck, though I don't know why he likes it so much. I met him near Nora's, just after the outbreak, but he didn't come with me up to the cabin. When we got back to South Bend, in the RV, he was sitting there, as if he was waiting for me."

"He's an odd one," Jenny said. "Acts as if he's the owner and we're his pets. Now, you said a plane will be waiting up at Point Betsie tomorrow? If we can sprint to northern Michigan, we can take a shortcut to Oregon. That's where my daughter is." She gave another nod towards the twins.

"The plane will arrive around lunchtime," Corrie said, "but I don't know for how long it's safe for that boat to bob on the surface of a lake."

"Let's see," Jenny said. "The lighthouse is about two hundred and fifty miles north of here. If we leave at dawn, we'll be there at lunchtime. Depending on the roads. What are they like?"

"We were shot at on the way here, so we'll have to take a different route back," Corrie said. "Although we were driving a police cruiser. Maybe they thought we were with Vevermee."

"He can't have tormented people that far from the city," Olivia said. "Can he?"

"Depends how many people are in his gang," Jenny said. "If we're not on the road at dawn, we won't make it. I don't want to go north, miss the flight, and have to come back anywhere near this city."

"We need a vehicle, and we need to find it now," Corrie said. "And we need to leave now, heading north, or we forget the plane, head west, and make our own way up to Pine Dock."

"West it is," Olivia said. She gave a sigh and a shrug.

"There's the police cruiser up at the cabin," Pete said. "If we could get there, we could drive the rest of the way. Or some of us could."

"The cabin would be a five-day walk for the kids," Corrie said. "Maybe longer."

"There must be plenty of vehicles we can steal," Pete said.

"Of course," Jenny said. "After the hospital burned down, people left. Some had already gone, of course. And after Vevermee started torching more buildings, more people fled. They stole the fuel from the gas stations and gas tanks, and Vevermee's people have been taking what was left behind."

"We need a quiet vehicle," Pete said, slowly. "Something they won't hear coming. Something like... yeah, an electric car. Two cars. Or an electric truck."

"How would we charge it?" Olivia asked.

"You said you had a generator?" Pete asked. "And fuel?"

"Possibly," Olivia said. "We don't know if it's undamaged by the fire, but the generator was kept in a shipping container they'd put outside, in the parking lot, so it might be okay."

"And if we use the diesel to power a generator to charge up an electric truck, we can get away quietly," Pete said, warming to the idea.

"A generator is still an engine," Olivia said. "But I guess we could muffle it. And we'd only need to run it for a few minutes. Enough to charge the truck to get ten miles out of town. Then we could stop, charge it properly. That might work."

"There's a dealership on Michigan Street that sells electric cars," Pete said.

"It's too far from the carpet store," Jenny said. "We'll have to carry the generator to the truck."

"Oh." Pete's bubble of enthusiasm deflated an inch. "The aerospace factory might have something."

"Or they might not," Jenny said. "And if they don't, we'll have to keep moving. A mile at dusk, another at dawn."

Pete's bubble burst.

"There were a couple of handcarts at the carpet store," Olivia said. "Little flat trolleys the construction crew were using. We can get the generator onto one of those, and move it a bit, maybe half a mile. So where could we reach? The museum? No."

"The railroad?" Jenny suggested.

"No, got it!" Pete said, nearly jumping with renewed enthusiasm. "The moving people. Oh, what's their name? The people with the ads on all the benches."

"You mean *U-call, we carry*?" Olivia asked. "They have electric trucks?"

"Yeah, remember last year?" Pete said. "They were doing that deal, hire an electric van, get it half price. You said that was still twice the price of using the work truck. These were vans, but there'd be enough room for us and a small generator."

"And it's close?" Corrie asked.

"LaSalle Park. Like, five blocks east of the carpet store."

"Then we have a plan," Jenny said. "Good. So, what do we need to do first?"

Chapter 19 - One Dream at a Time
South Bend, Indiana

"You really came all the way back for me," Olivia said as they gathered their gear. "Who does that? In real life, I mean? In fiction, sure, all the time. But in history? Wow. I think it's a first."

"Yeah… um… well," Pete stammered over the hard-to-find words. "I guess it's the first zombie outbreak in history, that's why."

"Here's hoping there won't be a second," Olivia said. She grinned. "Thank you, Pete."

"Thank me when we're on the plane. Better yet, thank me when we're down in Australia grumbling about how hot it is."

"No, I'll thank you now, because no matter what happens, *no* matter, you risked everything, and you didn't have to."

"I… well…" he stammered, increasingly uncertain what to say. He knew precisely what he *wanted* to say, but the setting was wrong. "Just wait until you see Corrie's cabin in the outback. You'll change your mind then."

"I won't." She picked up her pack. "Though I've had enough of cabins. It wasn't anything like we imagined it would be, living in Nora's old cabin. It took me one day chopping logs and hauling water to realise that it just isn't the life for me. Maybe if I hadn't been alone, it'd have been easier, but it'd be better still in a house with running water."

"Tell me about it," Pete said. "I think that's got to be rule fifty-two."

"You're writing rules?"

"They're not mine. Well, they sort of are. There was this guy down in Australia—"

"We're ready," Corrie said.

"I'll tell you about it later," Pete said.

Counting Rufus, four of them were going on the mission, leaving Jenny to watch the children. Pete took the lead, guessing at a route he only vaguely remembered, and that from the seat of his truck. Corrie and Olivia followed, with the dog padding back and forth, sometimes keeping pace with Olivia, sometimes darting ahead, sometimes falling back to bring up the rear.

Avoiding the roads, they kept to alleys, moving slowly so they could listen, slowing even more at each distant creak, crack, or crash. When Rufus froze, baring his teeth in a silent snarl, they all raised their weapons: rifles for Pete and Corrie, and a shotgun for Olivia. A clatter came from the road ahead, but the corrugated fencing on either side of the alley made it impossible to identify the cause of the commotion.

A figure staggered across the alley's mouth. Pete almost breathed a sigh of relief when he saw it was a zombie. Dripping brown gore from the stump of its arm, with a kitchen knife embedded in its shoulder, another in its chest, it was obviously undead.

Pete let a hand fall from his rifle, reaching for the bayonet at his belt, but Olivia grabbed his arm. She shook her head as the zombie staggered on, passing the alley mouth and continuing along the sidewalk. The monstrous shadow hadn't heard them. An invisible clock ticked in his head while they stood, listening, waiting for the undead creature to venture beyond hearing.

After what had to be at least two minutes, but which felt closer to two years, Rufus padded in front of them, stopping eight paces ahead. The dog turned and gave them a *hurry-up* look. The humans gave each other a *what-else-are-we-waiting-for* shrug, and followed the dog down the alley. At the road, they sprinted across and into an industrial parking lot, taking shelter behind a stalled eighteen-wheeler whose container doors had been ripped off. They now lay, chains still attached, ten feet away, while the cardboard boxes in the back had been slashed open.

"We lost too much time," Pete whispered. "Next time, we should kill the zombie."

"Not until we've left South Bend," Olivia whispered back. "Vevermee burns the bodies of the dead, zombie and living alike. If we left a dead zombie, he'd know it was you, because he surely knows your truck didn't drive here by itself."

"Fair point."

"The fuel cap's been removed," Corrie whispered. "They drained the tank."

"Told you," Olivia said. "Where next? We're close, aren't we?"

"I think it's on the other side of that fence," Pete said.

It was. And it was deserted. Like in the industrial lot next door, the vehicles' fuel tanks had been drained. But the two electric vans were still parked on their stands, cables snaking to the boxy electrical outlet.

The keys were easy to find, in a prefab office decorated with health and safety signs. From the gaps in the fob-rack, five vehicles were missing.

"Here goes nothing," Olivia said, opening the first van's door and putting the key in the ignition. "Bingo. There's some charge in the battery." She spoke in a whisper, but it was still louder than the van's quiet hum.

"How much?" Corrie asked.

"Forty-three miles," Olivia said, pointing to the digital display. "I don't know how accurate that is, but it's more than enough to get us out of the city. How fast can these vans go, do you think?"

"Faster than a quad bike, not as fast as a police cruiser," Corrie said. "But if we leave at dusk, then hide tonight, and set off again before dawn, they won't find us. So we'll leave tonight, one way or another. How far away is the generator?"

"Just a couple of blocks," Pete said.

"Then I'll get Jenny and the kids," Corrie said. "You two see if the generator is intact. If it's hard to move, we can give you a hand. If it's a ruin, we'll drive back to the cabin, or as close as we can get. A couple of us can walk from wherever we break down, get the police cruiser, drive it back to the van, and we can figure out the rest when we're there."

"Do you remember the way?" Olivia asked.

"No worries. A city is a lot harder to get lost in than the bush," Corrie said. "And I'll take Rufus. What do you say, sport? Will you lead me back to the kids?"

"That's new," Pete whispered, as he took in his old place of work.

"The zombie?" Olivia whispered back.

"The sign. That's the worst bad-taste joke this planet's ever heard."

Across the wooden hoarding, made slightly illegible by blood, bullet holes, and the fire which had devastated the interior, had been painted: *Claverton Construction. Rebuilding the World, One Dream At a Time.*

"Really?" Olivia asked. "Ironic, yes, but why is it in bad taste? No, explain later. That zombie's not moving."

The zombie lurked in front of the quarter-collapsed doors, leaning forward, head bowed, shoulders curled, one hand dangling low, the other just a stump, dripping dark gore onto the ashes around its shoeless feet. The zombie wore the luminous-lime and bedazzled-brown uniform of the burger ranch franchise near the airport. But for the undead fry-slinger to still be wearing the clothes, the woman couldn't have gone home after the outbreak. Had she hidden in the restaurant for a week, living on par-cooked beef patties and increasingly stale buns? Pete hoped not. He hoped she'd come from much further away. Even New York, though that was impossibly far. Anywhere but a few blocks away from the place he'd eaten many lunches, and far too many dinners.

The doors, giant wooden gates, had been painted to blend with the hoarding, and were wide enough for construction vehicles to enter. They hung loose, sagging inward, their upper hinges broken. Only the lower set now kept them upright, and only a long chain, partially visible through the foot-wide gap where the gates should have met, held them closed.

"I can't see any others," Olivia whispered. "But she's not moving. We'll have to kill her. No shooting."

"No shooting? No worries," Pete said. He drew the bayonet while Olivia withdrew a crowbar from her pack.

"Ready?" she asked.

"Never," he said. "But yeah, let's take it down."

Running in an instinctive half crouch, he dashed across the road, with Olivia two arm's lengths away. The zombie heard them, jerking its head to the left, twisting as it rose from its slumped crouch. Its arms rose. Its fingers twitched. Its stump waved, spraying flecks of gore towards them as its feet shot forward, seeming to leave its knees behind. The zombie staggered, falling forwards more than walking, lurching on towards Pete.

He tried to ignore the unblinking eyes, the mud-matted brown hair, the flag tattoo that ran up above the collar and which was now missing half the stars where the skin had been ripped away. He knew her. And he knew the flag was covering another tattoo, inked in haste two years and two boyfriends ago.

He raised the bayonet, ready to plunge it into her eye just as she tumbled. Olivia straightened, the crowbar having smashed through the zombie's knees, raising the tool above her head, and slamming it down, once, on the creature's skull.

"I'll never get used to this," she said, exhaling hard.

"Yeah, me neither."

Leaving the zombie where it had fallen, they squelched through the ash and rainwater puddles, squeezed under the chain, and entered the ruins.

All his happy memories were dashed when he saw what had become of the place he'd wasted so many busy, and far more idle, hours with Olivia. The construction crew had torn out most of that with which he'd been familiar, and the fire had ruined what remained.

"What was it Mrs Mathers used to say about regret?" he asked.

"Which time?" Olivia asked, heading to the shipping container in the corner, now partially covered with fallen timbers. "She had a lot of sayings. Do you mean how you should keep your regrets for the grave, since they'll be all you'll have to keep you warm?"

"She said that?" Pete asked. "That's pretty dark for her."

"Yeah, she was a young goth in an old woman's body," Olivia said. "*Is.* She's still alive."

Pete grabbed a two-by-four and used it to lever clear a charred stack of four-by-eights. "I've been doing that, too. Assuming everyone's dead. They're not. You prove that."

"*We* prove that," she said.

The thin timbers of the collapsed hoarding, though charred, weren't heavy. Dragging the last clear, Pete hauled the door open. "There are rags in here," he said.

"Clothes," Olivia said. "But really, they're camouflage. It was Jenny's idea," she added, hauling the smoke-stained rags clear. From beneath, she pulled out a nylon zip-bag. "Here. Soap and detergent. We stashed it here. You see, we thought looters might come, but we didn't think they'd search through our dirty laundry. We didn't think they'd burn the place down, either. Who does that? Ah. Perfect." She tore away the last of the blankets, revealing a small generator, sitting on a wooden pallet. "Looks okay, right?"

"It's smaller than I was expecting," Pete said. "But I guess we don't need much power from it. How do we know if it still works?"

"By turning it on," Olivia said. "But I don't think we should do that here."

"Agreed. Where's the diesel?"

"Stashed over by the contractors' portable john," she said, "I'll go fetch it if you get the hand-truck. It's out in the lot, near the old delivery entrance."

Ten minutes later, they had the small generator, and a far smaller container of diesel on the handcart, and next to the chained gate. Olivia tugged at the chain still holding the gate closed.

"We hung the key on that nail," she said, pointing to an empty nail embedded in a pole close to the gate.

It took longer to find than it had to retrieve the handcart, diesel, and generator. Olivia paused before putting it into the lock.

"What is it?" Pete asked.

"I'm now worried the entire gate will collapse if I undo the chain," she said. "Maybe push the generator back a—"

She stopped speaking, then raised a warning hand.

Outside, on the street, the high-pitched burr grew in volume, resolving into an approaching engine that came to a dead stop outside.

Pete hadn't moved, and Olivia hadn't lowered her hand. Both remained frozen, looking out through the charred gaps in the fence.

A dirt bike had halted outside. The rider was alone and dressed like a cop. In his hands was a distinctly illegal machine pistol. But he didn't have it raised. Slowly, the cop walked along the road, towards the charred ruins, though not towards the gate. The cop paused a few metres from the dead zombie, looked down, then up, around, turning slowly until his back was to the gate.

Olivia reached for her shotgun.

Pete shook his head, and held out his rifle while, with his free hand, he unbuttoned his holster.

Olivia frowned.

Pete nodded frantically, and mouthed, "*Trust me.*"

Olivia took the rifle.

Pete drew the pistol he'd taken from the assassin in the Australian diner. From the pouch intended for a spare magazine, he withdrew the assassin's suppressor.

Olivia nodded, her jaw tightening as she understood. Slowly, not moving anything but her arms, she raised the rifle, aiming it as much at the wooden gate as the cop outside. As quietly as he could, Pete slowly screwed the suppressor onto the pistol.

Outside, the police officer was walking a curving arc, a few metres from the dead zombie. Pete understood why just as the cop froze and bent down. The man had been looking for recent footprints among the ash and mud, and he'd found them. He turned, this time half-raising the machine pistol as he looked at the gate.

Pete raised his arm, but couldn't get a clear shot, not from where he stood. He was too far from the gate. Too far from the gaps in the wood. But if he moved, he'd certainly make some noise.

A sharp squawk came from the bike: the cop's walkie-talkie. The officer turned towards it, and Pete stepped forward. Beneath his feet, wood creaked and charcoaled timber cracked. The cop turned as Pete pushed the gun-barrel forward, between two of the warped timbers. The cop must have seen Pete because he began raising his machine pistol, but Pete fired first. Six shots into chest and arms and face as the cop fell.

Olivia was already undoing the chain. Rifle raised, she ran onto the street.

"He's dead," she said. "And alone."

The walkie-talkie squawked again.

"Let's go," she said.

"Yeah," Pete muttered. He glanced again at the assassin's gun, which he'd just used to assassinate someone himself. But there would be time enough to dwell on it later. He hoped there would be time.

Chapter 20 - Escaping the Past
Indiana and Michigan

The hand-truck's small wheels weren't designed for long distances, or for travelling through unevenly paved alleyways, littered with mud, recent debris, and the partially decayed detritus dumped by the nearby businesses. Having to pause at each creaking crash in case it was one of the undead, and freezing whenever they heard a distant engine buzz then fade, they were unable to pick up any momentum. By the time they reached the haulage depot, Pete's hand was blistered and his back was sore. Rufus yipped his approval as they dragged the generator inside, while Jenny closed the door behind them.

"You got here before us," Olivia said.

"Of course we did," Jenny said. "Did you have any trouble?"

"Yes," Olivia said. "One zombie. One cop. We killed both, but you can hear them driving around. I think they're looking for the cop we shot. He must have been on patrol, but we shot him just before he could radio in."

"Good, then we have time," Jenny said. "And we're leaving just in time, too. Had to deal with two of the monsters myself."

"The cops?" Pete asked.

"The other monsters," Jenny said. "There are more of them around than before. Now, get yourselves inside, and that generator up and into the van."

Corrie was dismantling the charging station, with Tyler and Dwayne holding it steady. Robyn and Wayde were emptying the back of the van.

"Wayde, find us two planks," Jenny said. "Long enough to use as a ramp. Help him, Robyn. Good girl."

"What are you doing, Corrie?" Pete asked.

"Vans like this don't have a two-pin plug," Corrie said. "Easier we bring the whole thing with us, and I'll figure out how to connect it all when we're a little less pressed for time. Just as soon as I dislodge this recalcitrant bolt." She braced the wrench, stood, stepped back, and kicked. The wrench went flying, skittering across the hard concrete floor.

"Cool," Tyler said.

"And that's how you undo a bolt," Corrie said. "Go see if you can find the wrench for me."

Olivia smiled. "That's the first thing he's said since… since the cabin," she whispered.

"Perfect," Jenny said, as Tyler and Robyn returned. "Now you can give Pete a hand getting it aboard."

Twenty minutes later, they were ready to go.

"So when do we leave?" Pete asked.

"Not just yet. A bit closer to dusk," Jenny said. "In the dark, we'll see their headlights, we'll hear them, but they won't hear us."

All four stood by the doors, watching outside, listening to the buzz of the bikes. It was obvious the cops were searching the city. What Pete couldn't tell was whether the bikers were searching for their missing comrade, or searching for the people who'd killed him.

"We'll go due west," Olivia said. "That's the quickest way out of the city."

"But then north," Corrie said. "We have to. Not just to catch the plane, but if we can't get the charging station or generator to work, we'll need that cop car. Jenny, you said you've been to Point Betsie?"

"I have," Jenny said.

"So you know the way?" Corrie asked.

"Yes," Jenny said, "but I'll be the one staying behind. I know what you're suggesting, and I'll have none of it. You and me, Ms Guinn, if it comes to that, we'll walk."

"If anyone's staying behind, it'll be us," Olivia said.

"It will not, and I will not be argued with, young lady," Jenny said with matronly sternness. "You two will take the children to the plane, and then you'll come back, aboard that plane, and with enough gasoline to drive to Nora's cabin where you'll collect Ms Guinn and myself. Understood?"

"Yes, Jenny," Olivia said, giving a shrug.

A buzz in the distance grew louder, nearer. Much nearer. But even as they raised their weapons, it began to fade. The silence stretched, and so did the tension, until it was thinner than their patience.

"They've gone," Olivia said. "Whether they're looking for us or not, they're not looking around here. I say we leave."

The van had been designed more for deliveries than moving house, even small homes like Pete's. More familiar with which roads to avoid, Olivia drove while Corrie rode assault-rifle in the passenger seat. Pete, Jenny, Rufus, and the children were crammed in the back. There were no windows, but lining the van's sides were brackets to which cargo could be secured. To those, they'd knotted blankets which gave them something to grab as the van swerved left and right with violent irregularity. With an unnaturally quiet engine, the bump and scrape of every collision was magnified tenfold.

"Just a trash can," Jenny would say, her voice calm and almost soothing. "Just a side mirror, that's all."

But there were just so many collisions. One after another, with barely time to brace between impacts. Pete was certain the van wouldn't stay on the road for long. Some collisions were soft, followed by a rocking bump, which had to mark an impact with one of the undead. But as gruesome as that was, as terrifying as their ignorance in the confined, windowless space, they were moving forward and at speed.

"Should have thought of a way to signal to them in the cab," Pete said.

"And what would you want to tell them?" Jenny asked.

"That we're still alive," Dwayne said.

"And we'd like to stay that way, please," Wayde added.

"Hush, you two," Jenny said. "This is more comfortable than that roller coaster you made me suffer through last summer. Twice, I'll add. If I could put up with that, you can put up with this."

Robyn had gone as quiet as her brother, and he'd turned as pale as flour. Even Rufus whined unhappily as he sprawled, legs splayed, his nails screeching against the metal floor as they swerved left, then right, then left again.

"Why don't you tell us a story, Pete?" Jenny said. "Tell us about Canada."

"Sure. Yeah, why not," Pete said. "But let me start at the beginning. And that's Australia, and Corrie's little cabin in the outback. It's a place so hot that cheese would melt. And the spiders, they're small but—"

A narrow beam of light speared through the van's wall. His brain registered the sound of the metal tearing a second later as a second bullet ripped a hole in the vehicle's side.

"They found us!" Dwayne yelled.

"Lie flat!" Jenny said.

Pete could hear it now, the sound of an engine. But it sounded normal. Like a car, not a dirt bike. A third bullet pierced the van's walls, while another ricocheted off the thicker metal near the hinges.

The van began to pick up speed, accelerating fast, but it wouldn't be fast enough, certainly not when they reached the open road beyond the city.

Pete picked up the rifle, and crawled on hands and knees to the door.

"What are you doing?" Jenny demanded.

"Shooting back," Pete said. "It might slow them down."

He reached up, pulled the latch, and the door flew open, slamming back against the van's side. In turn, he slipped, nearly falling out of the door, but landed on one knee. Something cracked, and he hoped it wasn't him, as he raised the rifle, firing a wild and un-aimed shot.

He dropped down, crawling forward, leaning against the edge of the open door, assessing his target. They were being chased by a police car with two people inside. Driver, and a passenger with a handgun, which was being wildly fired out the window. Pete fired, but it did no good. He didn't know if the bullet had hit anything, but the car kept on coming. Accelerating. The buildings on either side of them were low, spaced out. They were nearing the city limits, and so running out of side roads to swerve down. He flipped the switch, and fired on fully automatic.

Spider-web cracks danced across the cruiser's windshield. Pete wasn't sure if he'd hit either of their pursuers, but the car slowed. Stopped.

"That's it!" he yelled. "We got 'em."

"Nan?" Wayde asked, his voice tremulous.

Pete turned. Jenny was clutching her shoulder.

"I'm fine. Don't worry about me," she said, jerking her chin towards the still-open door. "Worry about them."

Pete turned. A quad bike had pulled out onto the road, a dirt bike riding level, the rider barely holding on with one hand as he raised a machine pistol, spraying the electric van with half a magazine.

"Hell, no!" Pete barked, firing back.

The quad bike erupted in a blossom of fire, a volcanic explosion that threw the rider from the dirt bike, and Pete back against the van's wall. Baffled, he stared at the flames spreading across the road.

"What did I just hit?" Pete asked. "Whatever it is, we'll get away now, Jenny." He turned. Jenny was motionless, her eyes open, but unseeing. "Jenny?" Letting go of the rifle, he scrabbled over to her. He'd thought she'd only been shot in the shoulder, but there was a second bullet wound in her chest.

"The children are safe," Olivia said, as she and Pete stood over Jenny's body. After the van had stopped, they had carried Jenny to a small cluster of trees near the roadside. "The children are safe, Jenny. Thanks to you. And we'll keep them safe. I promise. Thank you."

They stepped back. Pete waited for Olivia to turn around before he did the same, following her back to the van.

"It must have been the rider of the dirt bike who shot her," Pete said. "But he died in the explosion. I still don't know what caused it."

"The flamethrower," Olivia said. "Vevermee had a flamethrower. Must have got it from a farm. I hope that's where he found it."

"A flamethrower?" Pete shook his head.

"I wish I could have buried her," Olivia said. "But there's no time."

Corrie finished her inspection, then walked back around to the cab in which Wayde and Dwayne now sat.

"How's the van?" Pete asked.

"It'll be fine," Corrie said. "I think we can make another fifteen miles before we have to charge the battery. You better drive, Olivia. The twins can ride up front, and I'll ride in the back."

Pete looked back towards South Bend, the city he'd called home. The city he'd left, and never imagined he'd see again. He almost wished he hadn't. But he was leaving with Olivia. Unbelievably. As the result of one accident after another, they were together. Which raised the question of where they would go now.

Part 3
The War for Humanity

Canada

Chapter 21 - A Canadian Quarantine
Lake Michigan

"Welcome back, Romeo. I knew you'd make it," Andrea said, helping Pete up from the dinghy onto the bobbing seaplane.

"She did not," Jerome said. "She was sure you were dead."

"Hey, no fair. I'm nothing but romantic," Andrea said. "And you found Juliet."

"Her name's Olivia," Jerome said.

"Spoilsport," Andrea said. "Let go of the dinghy, Pete. We're crammed tighter than crabs in a bucket."

Pete was the last aboard the plane. "You've added seats," he said.

"Welcome to Air-Drea, delivering mail and people since the apocalypse began," Andrea said, as Jerome secured the door. "Hi," she said, loudly as she made her way back along the aisle to the cockpit. "Welcome aboard Air-Drea flight zero-zero-zero-six. Flight time to Thunder Bay is only a few hours, so we won't be serving food. For entertainment, Constable MacDonald can serenade you with his favourite songs from his least favourite musicals. But if you ask him nicely, I'm sure he'll stop."

"We made it," Pete said, taking the free seat next to Olivia, opposite Corrie and Rufus. "We actually made it. And we made it back to the plane in time."

"And there *is* an actual plane," Olivia said.

"You thought I was making it up?"

"I worried that my subconscious was making *you* up," Olivia said. "But it's real. You're real. And we're *really* getting out of here."

Further conversation was paused as the engine's whine grew to a roar, and the boat-plane lumbered through the waves. Rufus whimpered. Olivia closed her eyes, and Pete smiled.

The previous evening, they'd driven north until the van's battery was nearly drained. Stopping at a farmhouse foreclosed on months before the outbreak, they'd spent a tense hour watching Corrie jury-rig the mains-powered charging station to the generator. An even tenser hour followed as they'd waited for the digital range-meter in the truck's cab to reveal they'd reach the lighthouse. By the time it did, night had descended, and they were forced to spend a miserably cold night in the farmhouse. Despite having a generator and an inch of spare diesel, they were unable to turn on a light in case Vevermee, or his people, were hunting for them nearby. Instead, they sat together in the dark, mourning the death of Jenny and so many others.

But it had been an uneventful night. So, too, had been the morning's drive north. There were zombies in the fields, and shadows in the woodland, but no danger on the road.

They'd taken a different route back, avoiding the roads on which Pete and Corrie had been shot at, stopping only once to discuss whether to travel to any of the hamlets and houses where they'd seen people on their journey south. They'd decided no. The plane would already be packed, and they didn't want to risk being shot at again.

At the lighthouse, they'd been both disappointed and relieved to find no refugees waiting for the seaplane. Nor had anyone been there in the last few days. If people hiding nearby had seen them arrive, no one had ventured out to investigate.

There was nothing but relief when the yellow and red water bomber had appeared overhead. Getting aboard, in the overloaded dinghy, had renewed the tension, but it was seeping away now the plane was airborne.

Pete had done it. He'd actually, somehow, done it. He'd made it to South Bend and out again. For the woman he… yeah, it had to be love.

She was looking at him and smiling. He really did like her smile.

"We actually made it," Pete whispered.

Olivia took his hand. "Nice job, Romeo," she whispered back.

He grinned, until his eyes fell on Dwayne and Wayde, both downcast and quiet, emotionally exhausted like Tyler and Robyn. The children had been through so much in such a short space of time. But they were safe.

They were alive, and they would have the opportunity to grieve and, one day, recover.

Jerome appeared in the cockpit, and beckoned them both up to the front.

"Answer me this," Andrea said, after he and Olivia had donned the mic-and-headphones sets. "How can *Romeo and Juliet* be the greatest love story ever told if they die at the end, eh? That's been bugging me since we dropped you off."

"It really has," Jerome said. "She's talked about little else."

"I guess it says something about the romance stories Shakespeare read," Olivia said. "And a lot more about his idea of a good date."

"That's what *I* said," Andrea said. "She's a keeper, Pete."

"Glad you approve. This is flight zero-zero-zero-six?" Pete asked. "You've been busy the last few days."

"From here to Thunder Bay was flight three," Andrea said, explaining her arbitrary numbering system. "From there to Nanaimo via Pine Dock was four. Back to Thunder Bay was five, making this number six."

"You went back to B.C.?" Pete asked. "How is it?"

"It could be a lot worse," Andrea said. "The quality of the nightlife has gone seriously downhill, but there are people there."

"They're retaking Vancouver City," Jerome said. "Refugees are being organised into soldiers and construction crew. The people who aren't fighting are building defences. Street by street, block by block, they're clearing the city, bringing back order, control. The news of a Pacific Alliance is spreading, and calm's going with it."

"Cool," Pete said. "Have more Australians arrived?"

"Nope," Andrea said. "And your jet wasn't due back until a couple of hours after we left. The idea of an alliance is bringing calm. But the refugees are bringing zombies. It's going to get messy, but then it'll get better."

"Is there any news about Alberta?" Olivia asked. "Specifically a place called Medicine Cap?"

"Do you mean Medicine Hat?" Jerome said. "There's no news. Nothing specific that I've heard."

"We could pass over it on our way to Vancouver," Andrea said. "If you know how to parachute, I'll drop you off."

"Tyler and Robyn have an aunt there," Olivia said. "That's where they were trying to reach."

"They're Canadian?" Jerome asked.

"I guess they are now," Olivia said.

"And the other two?" Jerome asked.

"Step-siblings," Olivia said quickly. "Which makes them Canadian, too, right?"

"Borders and nationalities don't matter anymore," Jerome said. "We'll help them whatever, but they'd be safer coming with us to Vancouver."

"Safer than staying in Thunder Bay," Andrea said. "That place has gone super-military. I heard they'd conscripted the geese into the air force."

"Unless you want to take them with you to Australia," Jerome said, ignoring the pilot. "I assume that's where you're going now?"

"I… I guess so," Pete said. "We haven't… I mean, we haven't really talked about it. But we should report back in."

"You won't get a seat on the jet," Jerome said. "There was a long list of sick but treatable children awaiting airlift to a functioning hospital. People need a reason to fight, to work, to struggle. For now, saving the children is providing it."

"But there'll be more planes by now," Andrea said. "More jets. I'm sure of it. We're getting close. You better take your seats."

Thankfully, the plane landed on a runway rather than the sea, and at an airport where it wasn't the only plane. Helicopters and fighter jets waited on stand, though there appeared to be no civilian aircraft. As he clambered down the steps, after Corrie and Jerome, Pete saw what appeared to be a welcome party, two of whom he recognised. Dr Avalon and Dr Smilovitz stood next to a uniformed soldier and two other civilians. Smilovitz waved. Avalon scowled as she slowly coiled a neon green rope. The other two civilians grabbed bags from the towering stack behind them and stepped forward before the soldier motioned them back.

As a ground crew ran over to refuel the plane, the private came forward to meet them.

"Constable MacDonald?" the private asked. She was tall, but slightly overweight for a soldier, with longer hair than was usual, and which, oddly, appeared dyed at the tips. "Are these the Australians?" she asked.

"More or less," Corrie said.

"I have four more passengers for you," the private said, turning back to Jerome. "You're to refuel and return to British Columbia immediately." She pulled out a trio of letters. "Those are your orders, and dispatches for the officer in charge."

"In Nanaimo?" Jerome asked.

"In Guam," the private said. "That's where the scientist wants to go." She jerked a thumb at Dr Avalon.

"What about the children?" Corrie asked.

"What children?" the private asked.

"We've got four child-refugees. Canadians," Jerome said. "Trying to get to their family in Alberta."

The private shrugged. "My orders are that Dr Avalon gets on that plane. She needs to get to a lab. *We* need her in a lab, and a better equipped facility than we've got here." She gave a shake of her head. "That woman..."

"We'll give up our seats," Corrie said. "Pete, me, Olivia, and Rufus. You'd have room then?"

Jerome eyed the scientists. "I think we'd have space, but weight would still be an issue. Do they need those bags?"

"I'll speak to them," the private said.

"And I better speak to Olivia," Pete said.

But she didn't object. "Let me just say goodbye to the children," she said.

"I'll be back in a couple of days," Andrea said. "I promise you a ride then."

"Wait, hang on," Pete said. "You better take this." He unclipped the bodycam he'd picked up at Pine Dock. "It stopped working days ago, but it might have something useful on it for Canberra or whoever."

"I'll make sure they get it," Andrea said. She took Corrie's as well.

Pete, Olivia, Corrie, and Rufus joined the private while the scientists boarded the plane. The ungainly duck lumbered around, and barely twenty minutes after it had landed, it was back in the air.

"Lacoona," the private said. "Jan Lacoona, my name. What's your dog's?"

"Rufus," Olivia said. "But he's not really mine. He's very much his own."

"He'll have to join you in quarantine," the private said.

"Quarantine?" Pete asked.

"Yep, it's standard procedure," Lacoona said. "Every newcomer has to go through a twenty-four-hour quarantine. I s'pose I should have made those kids go through it." She shrugged. "Not my problem now. It's over here."

She led them to a hangar, recently painted red and white, where plastic sheeting had been run across the quarter-open, wing-width doors. Outside, metal riot-barriers created four arm's-width lanes. The private ignored those and went to the pedestrian entrance, holding the door open for them as they entered.

"Where is everyone?" Olivia asked, looking around the cavernous space.

Immediately in front of the main doors were rows of desks, most folding, none matching. Behind them were another set of waist-high barriers that seemed to filter people towards the edge of the hangar and an above-head-height curtain. From the crudely rigged pipes, the curtains concealed showers. Beyond those were more barriers, though this time with only two exits. One led to what resembled a departure lounge. The other exit led to three prefab-offices, the size of shipping containers, and with covered windows.

"Everyone else?" Lacoona asked. "They've already been processed."

"I mean… I suppose I'm asking about the planes, the refugees," Olivia said. "Did you get many through here? By air?"

"Oh, originally, during the first few days," the private said. "But that's stopped now. People still drift in by road or rail, but not by air. Not really by boat, either. Satellites are down. Telephone's mostly dead, except the new lines the general is laying. Radio works, but only short range. If you're a pilot with a working plane, why would you come here? And if you weren't familiar with the airport, how would you find it? You're the first people who've arrived by air since yesterday. And that was the first since the rush ended." Her eyes fell on the rifles Pete and Corrie carried. "Okay, there's two ways this can go. You need to go in, strip, and I need to confirm you haven't been bitten. You've got to shower. Then wait. I'll get you some new clothes, and there's some bleach for cleaning any of your gear you don't want incinerated. Then I'll get you some food. You stay here tonight. Tomorrow, you'll be let go. Are you okay with that? Because the alternative is I go tell the captain, and he tells General Yoon, and you don't want to get on the wrong side of her."

"This isn't our first quarantine," Pete said.

"Modesty, it's the first casualty of the apocalypse," Corrie said.

"Not the first," Olivia said. "But yeah, that's fine."

"Good. Then you can keep your weapons, and..." She looked at the dog. "He'll have to be washed, too."

"Good. Fine. Perfect," the private said after the most perfunctory of intimate examinations. "Showers are there. I'll get the captain."

"She didn't give us the clean clothes," Corrie said, as the private hurried out of the cavernous hangar.

"Maybe they're here, somewhere," Olivia said. "Rufus, find clothes."

The dog tilted his head to the side, but didn't rise from his haunches.

"It was worth a try," Olivia said.

"How'd you end up with a dog?" Pete asked, quickly redressing as much due to the chill as to awkward embarrassment.

"Oh, he sort of found me," Olivia said. "Then left me again. He didn't want to come with me first time I left South Bend, but he was waiting when I got back. I'm surprised he came with us this time. Surprised, but glad. We want clothes, right? It'll be easier if we split up."

Once again, she was avoiding discussing the details of what had happened during the last week, but Pete didn't press. Instead, he mooched his way around the cavernous hangar. Above, the expansive ceiling with its dark overhead lights gave him a sense of the square footage. On the ground, with shoulder-high partitions dividing the space into rooms and corridors, it seemed far larger. As illumination came entirely from wall lamps, recently bolted to the walls, the partitions cast deep shadows, making a search even more difficult until he struck on the obvious solution of pushing the partitions over.

Refugees, arriving by air, would have been led to a row of desks. Probably where their names and details were taken. From there, they were funnelled through the partitions to the showers, which was as much an opportunity to disarm people as to check whether they'd been bitten. Then they'd entered the main part of the hangar, which was filled with worn chairs and limp folding beds, except for an even more depressing corner filled with beanbags, mats, and soft toys.

That wasn't as depressing as the corner with the prefab container-sized rooms. They'd been painted white and adorned with red crosses, but that didn't disguise their purpose, nor could the thick layer of bleach entirely hide the smell of death. Inside each were hospital beds fitted with restraints. In the floor, beneath the beds, were bullet holes. He didn't count how many, but made his way back out into the hangar, shivering, but not because of the cold.

Back near the entrance, Rufus sat beneath the table, a glum look on his face.

"You and me both, buddy," Pete said, taking a chair. A few minutes later, Olivia drifted over, Corrie a few steps behind.

"I couldn't find clothes," Olivia said. "I guess people took their bags with them when they left."

"I found a few books," Corrie said. "You have a choice between regency romance or a western crime-thriller."

"Did you see the cabins?" Pete asked.

"And the bullet holes," Olivia said. "But there *is* electricity here. I'd rate it three stars. Three and a half if the showers work."

Rufus sat up, turning around to face the door just before a soldier entered.

It wasn't the private, but an exhausted officer fraying at the edges. His eyes were bloodshot, sunken, ringed by dark shadows. His shoulders had a near-permanent slump. His hand was steady, balanced on his holster, the other clutching the strap of a slim shoulder bag.

"Still alive. Good," he said, letting go of his gun. "I'm Captain Crawford. Currently in charge of the military contingent until General Yoon returns. You're the Australians?"

"Sort of," Corrie said.

"Meaning?" Crawford asked, sitting at the desk. He took out a small audio recorder, then a notepad and pen.

"We came here on a mission for Canberra, yes," Corrie said.

"To Indiana," Crawford said. "Yes, I know the broad strokes. I'd like the fine details."

So they told him, as he made notes.

"Vevermee was a United States police officer?" Crawford asked when they thought they'd finished.

"A state trooper, I think," Olivia said. "From Michigan."

"And the people with him were all police officers?" Crawford asked.

"No. They were wearing uniform, but I don't think they were cops," Olivia said. "Not all of them."

"I will ask the commissioner," Crawford said. "He'll ask his officers, see if we can find anyone who knows the name."

"Can't you look it up on a database?" Pete asked.

"It was stored in the cloud," Crawford said. "Everything. Every blessed useful thing was stored online. The data centres have been powered down to preserve the information therein." He shook his head in disgust. "Was there anything else?"

"Only that we need some new clothes, and some food," Corrie said.

"Ask the private," the captain said. "Good day."

"Now there's a man who needs a vacation," Olivia said.

"Or an assistant," Corrie said. "I guess we wait for the private. So, who wants the romance, because I think I'd prefer the thriller."

"Definitely romance," Olivia said. "Pete and I can share."

But Private Lacoona returned before they'd read more than a page.

"Uniforms," she said, dropping the stack on the table. "And I've got dinner outside. Things got busy there for a moment."

"Why? Did something happen?" Corrie asked.

"People arrived," Lacoona said.

"I didn't hear a plane," Pete said.

"No, it was a road convoy," Lacoona said. "They should have gone through quarantine further east, but they didn't, so we're all running around with bees in our boots. General Yoon being away doesn't help." She shrugged. "But even if we're making up the rules as we go along, we're making them work. I'll get your dinner."

It was a U.S. military, beef stew MRE, but one each. She'd brought four.

"We got these from a quartermaster, one of yours," Lacoona said. "From the U.S., I mean. He came up here with about two tons of them in the back of a semi. Now there's a story, remind me to tell you about it. Listen, you're going to stay in here, right? You won't sneak off, eh?"

"Nope."

She grinned. "Then I'll see you in the morning."

"No flights at night, I guess," Pete said, as they watched the private leave.

"Off on a romantic tryst of her own, I'd say," Olivia said.

"Speaking of which," Corrie said. "I'm going to find a quiet corner to read my book. I'll see you in the morning."

"That was nice of her," Olivia said when she and Pete were alone, "but this place doesn't exactly ooze romance. We forgot them, you know?"

"Who?" he asked.

"Books," Olivia said. "Back in the store, when we were planning how we'd live in that cabin, we forgot books. And a solar-powered reading light. Or a little wind turbine. We forgot electricity. But also how dark it can get at night without lights. It took me about a day to realise I was so

162

far out of my depth I was wading in seaweed. It's why I was glad to meet Naomi and Conrad, to take the risk and hope they weren't psychos."

"They were Robyn and Tyler's mom and dad, right?" Pete asked.

"Yeah, I don't want to think about that. Not now. Tell me more about Australia."

"I think I've told you everything," he said. "Wait, no, did I tell you about Matilda?"

"Who's she?"

"Corrie's best friend. The first thing you need to know, she's very hairy…"

Chapter 22 - A Change of Direction
Thunder Bay

The screech of a departing fighter jet was louder than any alarm clock, but Pete was already awake. It was difficult to sleep in the quarantine zone when, for company, they had the ghosts of those recent denizens whose fate was memorialised by the bullet holes in the shipping container's floor. By the time he'd dragged a table over to the side-window, three planes had vanished into the grey morning's gloom.

"Can you see anything?" Olivia asked, having followed him over.

"Just rain," Pete said.

"That beats snow," Olivia said. She shivered. "I didn't think anywhere could be colder than that cabin, but this hangar managed it. I cannot *wait* until we get to Australia."

"You say that now," Pete said. "I got heatstroke walking from the plane to the terminal building."

"No fooling, you got heatstroke?"

"Yep. According to Mick Dodson, who might have been exaggerating, but not by much."

"He's the doctor with all the rules? Tell me about him again."

"I only met him a few times," Pete said. "But Corrie knows him well."

"Let's go ask her," Olivia said.

If sleeping had been difficult, reconnecting with Olivia was as difficult in the hangar as it had been the previous night, hiding in the Michigan farm. Something had happened to her in South Bend, something she didn't yet want to talk about, but which was a shadowy chaperone, looming over every conversation.

"You three still here?" Private Lacoona called out. "I see *you* are. Good boy," she added as Rufus bounded over to her, wagging his tail as he fixed his eyes on the bag. "Yep, you can drop the glad-to-see-you act, I know you're really only after breakfast."

"Where were those planes going?" Corrie asked.

"Taking reconnaissance photographs of South Bend," the private said.

"You're going back there?" Olivia asked.

"Not me," the private said.

"But maybe us," Corrie said. "If they want to go back there, they'll ask us to go with them."

"In the army, they don't *ask*," Lacoona said. She left. Time marched on.

Two of the three fighter jets returned, bringing a storm with them. Rain hammered down, hard enough to find a gap high up in the hangar's roof. They looked for a bucket, settling on a black garbage can, and then watched the rain pounding the runway, wandering if they'd been forgotten. Noon came. The rain eased. Finally, Captain Crawford returned, buttoned up in a thick raincoat.

"Your quarantine's over," he said from the doorway, turning around before the words were out of his mouth.

"Wait, um, sir," Corrie said. "What do we do now? Where do we go?"

"You wait for orders, like we all do," Crawford said. He unstiffened a fraction. "We lost the hard-line with General Yoon last night. I sent the fighter planes to make contact."

"You mean the plane that hasn't returned?" Olivia asked.

"*Yet*," Crawford said. "It hasn't returned *yet*."

"I thought the jets had flown to South Bend," Corrie said.

"The other two, yes. They were on a reconnaissance mission at the request of the commissioner," Crawford said. "He doesn't want someone like Vevermee in control of a city."

"The commissioner? Who's that?" Corrie asked.

"The commissioner of police," Crawford said. He glanced at his watch. "I can't waste any more time. The hundreds who arrived by road are due to leave quarantine in an hour."

"What do we do now?" Corrie asked. "Where do we go?"

"You wait," Crawford said. "A team might be sent to South Bend. If so, you'll be part of it. Australia might send orders for you, and if not, we'll find you work. There's always more than enough to go around."

"We should wait here?" Olivia asked.

"No. Go to the donut shop on Arthur Street. Ask for the police commissioner. He'll find you somewhere to sleep."

"Where's Arthur Street?" Pete asked.

Crawford sighed with weary exasperation. "North of the airport is the Neebing River. East is Highway 61. Everything between is our green zone. The donut shop is where Highway 61 meets Arthur Street."

"I thought he was joking about the donut shop," Pete said.

The Tim Hortons' signage had been partly covered with a sheet on which *RCMP* and *Police* had been recently painted. Inside, sadly, there was no sign of either coffee or donuts, but there were plenty of police. One had her head buried in a reassuringly thick stack of paperwork. Another, in a corner, was taking a statement from a pair of teenagers. A third was listening to a pair of younger children while making notes on a map, but a fourth officer was staring at them. Old enough to have more white hair than grey, he wore a bright red Mountie's dress uniform coat, polished black shoes, and creased, gold-striped blue trousers.

"You're the Australians," he said.

"Sort of, but we're Americans really," Pete said. "How did you recognise us?"

"You're travelling with a dog," the Mountie said. "Not many people are, these days. I'm Superintendent Clive Peterson, formerly retired, currently commissioner of police until someone more senior is found. I wanted to speak to you, but you came here. Was there a reason why?"

"We were looking for somewhere to sleep," Corrie said. "And somewhere to wait until we know whether we're returning to South Bend."

"Interesting, because that's exactly the place I wished to discuss with you," Peterson said. "I'd like to know a bit more about..." He paused, held up a finger, then reached for a neat stack of notebooks, quickly flipping through the pages until he found the entry. "Vevermee. Is that how you pronounce it?"

"Then you only need to speak to me," Olivia said hurriedly. "I was there. I lived through it. They didn't see much. Go and get some food, Pete. I'll catch up."

"I don't mind—" Pete began but his sister cut him off.

"Is there somewhere we can wait, sir? And sleep?" Corrie asked. "Maybe buy a coffee."

"Nowhere is selling anything," Peterson said. "But there's still some space at the Marshall Hotel. They'll give you a meal, and I'll come find you if I have questions."

"And bodycams," Corrie asked. "Do you know where we can find some of those?"

"What for?" Peterson asked.

"We flew here from Australia to find out what had happened in North America," Corrie said. "We recorded footage in Michigan and Indiana. But I'd like to record some interviews with people here, too. Find out what they saw and where they saw it."

"You recorded footage of Indiana? Could I see it?" Peterson asked.

"Sorry," Corrie said. "We gave it to Officer MacDonald to take back to British Columbia and then send on to Canberra."

"Pity," Peterson said. "But there should be a record of all that's occurred." He tapped his stack of notebooks. "And I've been creating one, but I like how you think. The police station burned down a few nights ago, hence our current accommodation, but everything we salvaged is in the stockroom. You're welcome to some cameras but I'd like a copy of whatever you record for my own records."

"Olivia doesn't want you to know what happened," Corrie said as she, Rufus, and Pete walked away from the coffee shop. "Not yet. Telling you makes it real in a way telling a stranger doesn't."

"Yeah, I think I get it," Pete said. They stepped back from the edge of the sidewalk as a fuel tanker, followed by a pair of halftracks, rumbled eastwards. In the turret of each halftrack stood a scruffily dressed but

167

heavily armed soldier. "And I know not to make this about me," he added. "It's just that we *actually* got here from Australia. I *actually* found her, and we escaped from South Bend, but instead of getting a happily-ever-after ending, we're in limbo. It's not Olivia's fault. It's not mine. It's just the way the world is now, and it just sucks."

"You're looking at it all wrong, Pete. You rescued the girl from a fire-breathing ogre, and now you need a new quest. And since I think that's the hotel, I'll task you to find us some rooms. I'm going to speak to those soldiers." She tapped the bodycam they'd found in the donut-cop-shop stockroom.

"Why?"

"For one thing, they look as uncomfortable in uniform as us," Corrie said. "For another, that barbershop actually looks open. I don't know what they'll accept for currency, but I could do with a trim."

The hotel didn't have any empty rooms, but it did have an empty gym, which Pete was given, along with the promise of a few sheets and mattresses. But not even that was free. Money was worth no more in Thunder Bay than in Broken Hill, but the kitchen was understaffed, while the overworked cook, Renatta LeMouk, was handing out meals nearly as fast as they could be eaten.

"Two Michelin stars," she muttered, as Pete scrubbed pans. "I had *two* Michelin stars and now I'm making tray-bake lasagne."

And she was making a lot of it. Through the swing doors, as they opened for the empty trays to come in, the full to go out, Pete saw glimpses of the packed dining room. The tables were arranged in regimented lines, while a long line had formed by the door. An old man dressed in tails and a bow tie was acting as maître d'. As soon as someone finished, the old man ushered a new diner to their seat, prompting the finished soldier to stand and bus their plate to the long racks near the door. From there, an exhausted teenager with blaring headphones propped on her blonde-frosted hair, dragged the cart inside, and then loaded the dishwasher.

Her name was Christina, but Pete got that from the chef, not from the young woman who didn't even bother asking Pete his name. As the chef was only interested in complaining and cooking, Pete concentrated on scrubbing the giant metal trays.

Though she was not in uniform, he got the impression that Christina, like him, had been drafted into this work. So too had the chef. LeMouk was another refugee who'd found safety and hoped for a hot meal. Having made the ill-advised comment that she could prepare a better meal than she'd been given, she'd been drafted into the kitchen. The maître d' was actually the hotel's owner, and was willing to talk, but the constant stream of customers kept him too busy to share more than a few words.

Those customers, or diners since no money exchanged hands, each wore a uniform. Not always Canadian, and not all were military. Some were in neatly pressed hunting gear, who must be retired and recalled locals. Others, wearing nondescript tactical gear, he pegged as Special Forces, but whose? From among them he caught snippets of conversation in English, Spanish, Arabic, and what he was reasonably certain was French. But there were other languages, too. Were these not-so-recent immigrants, vacationing foreign military personnel stranded in Canada, or had they been recently deployed as part of some co-ordinated effort?

"Hey, no! No dogs in here!" the chef said.

"Sorry," Olivia said. "I was looking for him."

"Well, he's working," LeMouk said. "You can work, too. But *that* can not come in here."

"He's a *he*, not a *that*," Olivia said.

The exhausted mask Christina had been wearing fell from her eyes as she knelt by Rufus. "You're a nice dog. A friendly dog. Like my dog."

"And he can't come in here. Not in a kitchen," the chef called.

"The children would like to see him," Christina said. "I can take him there. If he likes children?"

"He does," Olivia said.

"As long as he isn't here," the chef said. "And you, whoever you are —"

"Olivia."

"You can load the dishwasher."

They worked. They scrubbed. They loaded and cleaned. There wasn't time to talk, but in an odd way, Pete relaxed and Olivia seemed to brighten. Working together again wasn't quite like old times, but it did suggest better times ahead.

When the rush finally ended, Olivia and Pete got the last third of the tray-bake all to themselves, and were kicked out of the kitchen while the chef began swearing her way around the remaining ingredients.

"Welcome to the army," Olivia said. "As jobs go, it's a bit too much like restaurant work for me."

Pete picked his words with care. "Everything okay with… I mean… Look, I know you don't want to talk about what happened. That's cool. I get it."

"No, you don't," Olivia said, giving a wan smile. "You can't, unless I tell you what happened. And I will. It's just… You coming all this way, looking for me, it's my very own fairy tale. Telling you about Notre Dame will destroy it, and right now, I want to cling on to the fantasy just a little bit longer."

"Did the cop tell you anything about what's going on here?" Pete asked. "I didn't get much out of the cook. Well, you met her yourself. But the closest I've seen that compares was Broken Hill."

"Broken Hill was like this? Cool. That *is* good news," she said. "Peterson told me a little, but he wanted to listen rather than talk. Thunder Bay isn't just a military hub, it's the capital now. Ottawa's a nightmare of fires and zombies and trapped civilians."

"It sounds like Vancouver," Pete said.

"And Toronto and Detroit, and every other city," Olivia said. "Anyone who is, or was, military is being drafted into General Yoon's army. She's in charge. Not just of the army, but all of Canada from what the commissioner was saying. There's some politicians in Nova Scotia, and a couple here, even a governor. I didn't think Canada had those, so maybe he's one of ours, but the general is running things."

"And she's out east somewhere?"

170

"Securing the farmland, apparently," Olivia said. "A lot of American armoured units made it across the border somehow. Tanks and helicopters, and that's what she's commandeered. Everyone else, the people who were here and the refugees who come through, are being sent to build forts around towns and hamlets and intersections. I think they're trying to push the frontline closer to the border and then beyond."

"That's good," Pete said. "What happens to the other refugees? The ones who aren't soldiers?"

"Unless they're farmers, or have some specific specialist knowledge, everyone is now a soldier."

"Ah. Yeah, I thought so."

"But the old, the injured, the children, they're being sent to a couple of islands of the coast. McKellar Island and... and... I forget the other one. They're turning those into farms, too, but an island needs fewer defences. They're going to secure more farmland here and across the border. The *old* border. That's how he described it. All across the American Plains. Everything between the mountains, north of the desert and south of the ice, will become one giant farm."

"Wow."

"It's... ambitious," she said. "I guess that's a good thing. But is it too ambitious? They're worried about food, fuel, ammo, and every other type of supply. The hospital is full. They've turned a school into an overflow-jail, and that's full, too. They think it'll get easier now most of the quarantine is taking place further east and west and south, but it still seems..." She sighed. "You know that expression, a little knowledge is a dangerous thing? I wish I hadn't asked him." She raised the empty tray. "Do you want to see if we can get some more?"

As if on cue, a barrage of clashing pans, punctuated by a thesaurus of synonymic swearing, erupted from the kitchen.

"How about we go find Rufus," Pete said.

4th March

Chapter 23 - Apocalyptic Dating
Thunder Bay

"Why are people staring?" Pete asked as he and Olivia strolled through the streets bustling with uniforms, busy with military vehicles, bristling with the weapons everyone now carried.

"It's because soldiers don't usually hold hands," Olivia said, gripping his more tightly.

Even though they were nearly bumping shoulders with the passing soldiers, and knocking elbows against the slowly moving line of half-tracks and trucks, they were experiencing wonderfully more solitude than they'd had the night before. They'd had to share the hotel's gym with a squad of firefighters who'd escaped the nightmare of Detroit and a chaotically circuitous journey north. When they learned that Corrie was collecting the stories of how people had escaped the outbreak, they'd wanted to share theirs. But their grim tale had made for a sombre evening and sleepless night.

Dawn had arrived bright and sunny, with even a hint of warmth in the early morning rays. Going in search of breakfast, they'd found the octogenarian maître d' on duty at the door, the chef in the kitchens, and themselves quickly assigned to serving duties. The young woman, Christina, made the briefest of appearances, but only long enough to grab a bowl which she scurried away with.

Serving became clearing, which became washing up. When the rush was over, Olivia had led Pete outside by the hand, and not let go of it since.

"I'm giving the hotel two stars," Olivia said. "We got a shower this morning, and we got fed, but I don't like sharing a room with other guests. And their policy on dogs is absurd." Not allowed in the kitchen, Rufus had joined Corrie as she collected interviews with the refugee-soldiers.

"I'd give it one star," Pete said. "The shower was cold."

"Hmm, that's true. But there was hot water in the kitchens."

"Tell me about it. I've never done so much washing up in my life."

She patted his hand. "Get used to it, mister, because I was thinking that there is *some* electricity at the moment. To some places. Somehow. Wonderfully. Gloriously. Thankfully, the lights are still on. But though there was hot water in the kitchens, there wasn't in the gym's locker room. I think they're restricting its use."

"Hot water?"

"Electricity. What kind of power station did they have here? Are they running low on coal or gas?"

"I thought it was all hydroelectric in Canada," Pete said.

"It can't be *all* hydroelectric, can it?" she asked. "We should find someone who knows. But not today. Or maybe we shouldn't ask since we can't do anything about it. A little knowledge really is a dangerous thing, isn't it? Maybe I'll be happier living in ignorance. But we have to expect the electricity to be cut, that's what I'm saying. Not forever, and maybe not everywhere. But some times, some places. Not today, though. So, what would you like to do? We worked last night. We worked this morning. I don't know how it goes in the military, but I think we're entitled to a few hours off."

"We should have a date. A proper one," Pete said. "Or as proper as we can find, at least until someone yells us into doing some more work."

"I like how you think. But it's too early for the movies. Too early for lunch, too, and I don't want to spend the afternoon scrubbing more pans, not when we'll probably do that most of the evening. Do you think they have museums here? We could break in if it's not open. Or maybe go ask the commissioner for permission first. I think he'd say yes."

"I thought we could go to the ornamental gardens," Pete said. "I found a brochure at the hotel. The pictures made it look like a quiet place."

"Oh, that sounds perfect," Olivia said as they had to step back, hugging the wall as a double row of trucks rolled down the street. Aboard

173

were soldiers in a mismatched collection of uniforms, though all clutched identical C7 assault rifles.

"I wonder where they're going," Olivia said.

"No," Pete said decisively, leading her on. "Let's not think about it. Because now, we're on a date. Our first date."

"You're not counting last night?"

"With those firefighters talking about fighting zombies street-by-street in Detroit? Definitely not."

"Fair point," she said. "And Michigan doesn't count either. Call me old-fashioned, but it's not a date when you keep one hand on a loaded rifle. What's wrong?"

"Nothing. But I think the short cut leads us up there, through a golf course. Did I tell you about the golf course in Australia? It's where we found the bodies of the pilots."

"You didn't go into any detail," she said. "And I don't think you should. We can go another way."

"There's too many trucks," Pete said. "Too many soldiers, which means officers, which means, sooner or later, they'll give us a job to do. No, we'll go through the golf course. It's fine. I'm just being irrational."

"Easily done at the moment," she said. "Ever since the news first broke, I've had this nagging voice telling me superstition is suddenly important."

"Right? Me too! It's like there's a string of rituals that could ward off the zombies, if only I knew them."

"You're getting that from a movie," she said.

"I am?"

"The one with the helicopter rescue at the beginning. With the guy who was in the movie about the lighthouse and the woman who was in that thing about witches."

"That's not very helpful."

"It wasn't a very good movie," she said.

They strolled across the lawn.

"I wonder what happened to them, the actors," he said.

"Same as everyone else," she said. "I wouldn't want to be in L.A. with desert and mountains and sea surrounding you. No, I'm glad I'm here. A soldier. Which is probably not as good as working in a care home in Florida."

"What do you mean? I wouldn't want to be down in Florida either."

"No, I suppose you're right. Can you hear that?"

It was the sound of vehicles, but not traffic. This was something deeper, far louder, a crunching, clattering, growling rattle of industrial machinery. Another few metres and they reached the crest of the rolling greens. Before them, yellow-coloured, mud-covered construction machines were ripping apart the verdant links.

"They're prepping farmland," Pete said. "So much for our date."

"No, I think… Let's go and take a closer look, because I don't think they're making fields. Look at those cranes. I think those are going to be giant greenhouses."

"Can I help you?" a towering, barrel-chested soldier asked as they approached. Mud covered most of his uniform except the three stripes, which were suspiciously clean.

"No, sergeant," Olivia said. "We're on a date."

"A what?" he demanded.

"A date," she said.

"A date? Think you're a joker, eh?" the sergeant said, his voice dripping with disapproval.

"We worked the kitchens last night," Olivia said, "*and* this morning, and now our shift's over, so we came to the ornamental gardens on a date. Life goes on, sergeant. Even in a crisis."

The sergeant's lips twitched as his brain searched for a vaguely reasonable objection, before settling into a thin smile. "The ornamental gardens are off limits. So is the golf course. You want a date, go have it elsewhere."

"He doesn't approve of romance," Olivia said, as they walked away, angling towards a recently rutted path that, in turn, led towards the entrance.

"He's the kind of soldier who disapproves of children," Pete said. "Bet he thinks all babies should be born in uniform."

"Babies? Now that's definitely *not* first-date talk," Olivia said.

"I... um... oh, sorry."

"I'm kidding," Olivia said, taking his arm. "And who cares what the sergeant thinks? Who cares what anyone thinks? We're all in this together now. Everyone alive. We're all saving the world, one day at a time, and we've done our bit for today, so why shouldn't we..." She trailed into silence.

Ahead, emerging from a two-metre-deep trench, a steel lattice was being constructed. In the trench were a gang of civilian workers.

"It's him," Olivia whispered. "It's Mack."

"Who's who?" Pete asked, looking at the crowd of construction crew.

"That's him," Olivia said, and without any further warning, stormed forward "Hey! Hey, Mack!" she called, pointing at the crowd who turned to look at the approaching, angry soldier.

Before Olivia had managed another five metres, one of the mud-coated labourers pointed back at Olivia, and yelled. "That's her! That's the murderer. She's the killer. She's one I was telling you about."

Olivia stopped in her tracks. "What?"

"She's crazy," Mack said. "She killed my girlfriend. Killed my bro."

"Nicole wasn't your girlfriend," Olivia said, wrong-footed.

"See?" Mack said, turning to the crowd. "Oh, sure. It was an accident. The gun went off. But only because she was acting like a lunatic. Completely off her head. Totally loco."

"I... No." Olivia turned to Pete. "That's Mack."

"Who killed Nicole?" Pete asked.

"*She* killed her," Mack said. "She killed Nicole and Dante. We had food. We had a plan. We could have made it. All of us. But she lost it, and they died. I almost died, too. Barely got out of South Bend alive. Look," he added, raising his hands. "The past is the past, right? What's done is done. I forgive you."

Pete had left his rifle with Corrie, who'd said she'd find someone who knew how to clean it, but he had his sidearm, and so, still, did Olivia, now

176

secured in a professional holster attached to her belt. Her fingers fumbled as she undid the button.

"Whoa! No," Pete said grabbing her hand. "Don't."

"Who said you could stop work?" the sergeant bawled, storming over. "Get back to it!"

"He killed my best friend," Olivia said.

"She killed my girlfriend," Mack said.

"Hand off your weapon, soldier," the sergeant said. "And you better explain."

"Sure. Fine," Olivia said, shaking Pete's arm free. "But I'll explain it to Commissioner Peterson because I'm filing charges."

Two hours later, Pete and Olivia sat in a booth in the donut-cop-shop, waiting for Peterson to return. She'd stormed across the town, back to the green zone, and to the temporary police station, Pete struggling to keep up. She'd informed the commissioner about Mack being a labourer at the ornamental gardens, and insisted she be allowed to press charges. The police officer had taken the briefest of statements, then left, leaving Pete and Olivia alone.

"What happened in South Bend?" Pete asked. "It wasn't just that Mack shot Nicole. Something else happened. Something at the university."

"Sort of. I mean, yes," she said. "Yes it did. But… it's complicated."

"Tell me," Pete said. "I think this is one of those things you'll have to tell me sooner or later."

Olivia sighed. "Yeah, maybe. Okay, you know how I told you about going up to the cabin, meeting Naomi and Conrad? How they died, and I ended up driving their RV, with Tyler and Robyn aboard, back to South Bend? It was the day after. That's when it happened."

177

24th February

Chapter 24 - The Destruction of Notre Dame
South Bend

It was still less than a week since the televised horrors of Manhattan had upended her world, but Olivia had already forgotten how comfortable, and comforting, a real bed could be. Though she was reluctant to get up, Rufus was sitting at the bedside, licking her hand for attention.

"Is it morning?" she asked.

Rufus yipped.

"Don't get snippy with me, mister," she said, to which Rufus replied with another enthusiastic bark.

Yesterday she'd met Tyler and Robyn, and their parents, Naomi and Conrad. It was only one day since the two adults had died, leaving her with the responsibility for their children. One day since the cabin had burned down. It already seemed like a distant memory.

She'd driven the RV back to South Bend, aiming for Nora's house because it was familiar and had running water. The drive had been fraught at the time, but in hindsight, without incident. On arriving, they'd retreated inside. She'd barely begun to wonder what next when she'd spotted the light moving around the house opposite, belonging to Jenny. Inside, she'd found the twins, Dwayne and Wayde. And she'd found Rufus. Rather, Dwayne and Wayde had found Rufus hanging around outside Nora's house.

Now they were hiding in a different property, three blocks to the south. A house with real beds and a solid roof. Sadly, there was no power and no running water. Not anymore.

"And there you are," Jenny said, scolding her for the benefit of the children as Olivia entered the kitchen. "The last up, and we've all been awake for hours. You can help me with the washing up. Kids, we need some bags. Dwayne, Wayde, off you go. Tyler, Robyn, go on. Did you sleep well?" she added, turning to Olivia.

"It was wonderful sleeping in a real bed," Olivia said, adding, when the children were out of earshot, "but I suppose I shouldn't get too used to it. And it's even more wonderful waking up in a house full of friendly faces."

"And if I'd known it was you traipsing in and out of Nora's with that dog, I'd have said hello. I thought you were just another looter. And a nasty one, to leave her dog behind when she fled."

"Rufus didn't seem to want to come," Olivia said.

"Oh, he's a strange one, that mutt, and no mistake," Jenny said. "He has a will of his own, and a plan to match."

"At least one of us has a plan, then," Olivia said, as she attacked the plate of eggs. "These are perfect."

"They're not. They were supposed to be waffles," Jenny said wistfully. "No power, you see. I made do with the barbecue grill. The waffles were a disaster, but Marge liked her eggs, so we've got plenty of those."

"Marge? Did she own this house?"

"Marge Robinson," Jenny said. "We played bridge together. Do you know how?"

"Sorry. I can just about manage blackjack."

"I'll teach you," Jenny said.

"What happened to Marge?" Olivia asked.

"That is a very good question," Jenny said. "But her daughter has a chicken farm just east of Teegarden. She'll have gone there."

"Maybe we should, too," Olivia said.

"I considered it," Jenny said. "But no, it's not far enough away. This is going to be the last journey. Wherever we end up, that's where we'll stay. A chicken farm slap bang in the middle of America doesn't appeal. No, we should go west. To Oregon if we can, Canada if we must. We'll know how far we can reach once we know what state the roads are in."

Olivia nodded. "Then we'll take the RV, but we need diesel."

"We might be okay for food," Jenny said, opening the pantry. "Marge always did insist on overstocking."

"Then I'll go back to the RV to get the keys," Olivia said. "I left them there last night, and that's just the kind of vehicle someone might steal."

"The children can pack the food," Jenny said. "I'll come with you."

"To make sure I don't leave?"

"To make sure we *both* get back," Jenny said.

Leaving Rufus to watch the children, and Dwayne watching the windows, they left by the garden door. Jenny had her shotgun. Olivia had her crowbar, with the handgun once again in the tasselled shoulder bag. It was supremely less convenient than a holster. To her mind, it was less threatening, too. After her run-in at the fortified gas station in Bangor, where she'd arrived just after the RV, she knew that most people were terrified. Just like her. Appearances might not matter to the undead, but looking peaceful to strangers might save her some grief.

They walked briskly the short distance, with Jenny keeping her eyes ahead while Olivia looked around, watching the houses, looking for signs of life. Of movement. There was none. Not until they reached the RV.

Olivia grabbed Jenny's arm, moving to the partial cover of a white picket fence shaded by a towering green ash.

"That's Marge Robinson," Jenny whispered, using the shotgun to point at the zombie leaning against the RV's engine.

Dressed in sweatpants, trainers, and a tight-fitting ski-suit that had been ripped to shreds on the left side. Over Marge's right shoulder hung a heavy-duty leather bag that had survived the mauling she must have received from the zombie that had infected her.

Jenny lowered her shotgun. "Are we alone, dear?" she whispered.

"Utterly," Olivia said, sparing a quick glance around, but her ears heard nothing. No birds. No cats. No people. Just the wind whistling in the trees, and the zombie clawing at the RV's paintwork.

"Quietly, then," Jenny said, and pulled a large wrench from her bag.

It wasn't the most obvious tool to use as a weapon, but it was no worse than Olivia's pry-bar. A forgotten memory surfaced, of a blistering Tuesday last summer, when the store was as empty as their appointment book. She and Pete had watched Romero movies on a tablet propped against the register, discussing apocalyptic weapons. Spears were their favourite. After guns.

She shook her head, clearing it, and focused on Marge Robinson. What she and Pete hadn't discussed, and what she and Jenny should certainly at least have addressed, was precisely how to attack this zombie. Before, with the undead trucker, and with Conrad, the fight had begun before she'd had time to think. Jenny solved the dilemma by whistling.

Marge spun around, her arms moving as if they were on string. Her neck jerked, her teeth snapped. Her hand scraped and scratched against the paintwork, tearing flecks free.

Jenny hesitated.

Marge didn't.

The zombie lurched forward, arms punching out, grasping and reaching. Jenny stepped back. Olivia swung the crowbar two-handed. Carbon steel slammed into bone, snapping Marge's arm. The zombie didn't notice, still snapping and swiping as it spun forty degrees. Jenny swung her wrench, breaking the zombie's other arm while Olivia stepped to the right, changing her angle, swinging low, this time cleaving the crowbar down on the zombie's leg. Again, bone snapped. This time, Marge toppled. Sprawling to the ground, she began crawling and rolling, thrashing her broken limbs until Olivia stabbed the crowbar's chisel-tip through her eye.

"It was harder than I thought," Jenny said.

"That was your... your first zombie?"

"First time killing someone I knew," Jenny said.

"A reply which begs a question or three," Olivia said, though she didn't ask them. "The RV looks okay. Tyres are fine." She stepped back, then bent down, careful not to touch the asphalt where the zombie's blood had oozed. "No damage underneath."

She went to the cab and tried the ignition. The lights flashed, the needles danced. "Looks fine," she said.

"Then we have wheels," Jenny said. "Ah, it's a shame. Poor old Marge." She gave a sigh, then seemed to shrug off the horror. "How much fuel is left?"

"Ten miles, give or take," Olivia said.

"The university had a groundskeeper's compound near the stadium," Jenny said. "Carly broke in there once."

"That's what she went to prison for?" Olivia asked.

"No, that was for doing it a second time. First time was a prank. Second time was a robbery."

"Ah."

"But it was a long time ago," Jenny said. "She's a different woman now. A grown woman with two kids, who should, by rights, be with her."

"You said she was in Oregon?"

"At a job interview. Hence why I had Dwayne and Wayde. She got the job, too. Not that it matters now. The boys think she'll return. I think they're right, but that doesn't mean we can stay here, waiting for her. We can get the diesel from Notre Dame."

"They had a pump?"

"They had a roadblock of tractors," Jenny said. "About twenty of them, I think. That was a while ago, of course, and their tanks will hardly be full, but it'll be enough for us to make a start. Now, tell me, how are you on a bicycle?"

The bicycles, two of them, came from Marge's garage, which was festooned with barely used exercise equipment and hobby-sport paraphernalia.

"Bit of a hoarder, was our Marge," Jenny said as they wheeled the bikes out onto the road. "Liked to try things, but never found her passion. Dwayne, you keep an eye on the others. And you keep an eye on that dog. If he seems nervous, that means trouble. We'll be back in two hours. Olivia, give him the keys."

"To the RV? Do you know how to drive?" Olivia asked.

Dwayne gave an exasperated roll of his eyes.

"He knows how to crash, but he won't do that again. If we're not back by morning, you know what to do," Jenny said as Olivia handed the boy the keys.

Cycling felt safer than walking, though not nearly as safe as driving, and far from as secure as staying inside. Again, on the ride south through the city, she was sure she saw movement behind windows, shadows moving through backyards, but it was only when they reached the bridge that she saw a zombie, partially trapped beneath an upturned car, waving at them as they cycled on.

They didn't make it to the university because a barricade had been thrown up outside, on East Angela Boulevard. On top, a woman with a hunting rifle stood sentry, though she barely paid them any attention. Below was a giant of a young man with the physique of two defensive tackles crammed into one body. He held an improvised plough made of a ten-foot V of corrugated fencing to which a sawn-off flagpole had been added as a handle. Prior to their appearance, he'd been clearing the undead corpses from the road. At least three were tumbled at the base of his plough. Perhaps four. There were too many heads and too few limbs to get a proper count.

"Good morning," Jenny said cheerfully, as if the corpses, weapons, and barricades were an entirely everyday sight. "Never has the sight of a rifle been so welcome."

The young man nodded, while the armed sentry ignored them. It was an older man who spoke. "Jenny? Jenny O'Dwyer?" He emerged from behind the barricade, a shovel in hand, a holster on his belt. About forty, he had a hipster's beard and a lumberjack's dress sense, and a physique halfway between the two.

"Marv?" Jenny said. "It's odd to see you not in a tie, and not on my screen."

"Glad you made it," Marv said.

"You know each other?" Olivia asked, then paused, in partial recognition. "Do I know you?"

"From TV," Jenny said.

"I did a bit of commentating when I wasn't coaching," Marv said.

"And he was a boyfriend of Carly's before she met Trent. Marv Wainwright, this is Olivia Preston. Are you in charge here?"

Marv shrugged. "Hard to say."

"He's the coach," the muscled young man said.

"Things are fluid," Marv said. "You better come in."

"We're not alone," Jenny said. "Well, we are, but we've got Carly's kids, and a couple others we acquired over the last few days."

"Where are they?" Marv asked.

"The other side of the river, and to the north, near my old house," Jenny said.

"I see. Still, better we talk over here so we leave a clear line of fire in case more arrive." He waved his hand at the corpses as he led them through a gate in the container-and-fence barrier that had been thrown up on the road. "We tried to turn Notre Dame into a fortress," Marv explained. "But we assumed— I assumed that the government would arrive. Clearly, they've gone to help somewhere else, and we're beyond the limit of what we can achieve here."

"You're leaving?" Olivia asked.

"We are," Marv said. "There are zombies in town. Each time we shoot one, more arrive. Then there're the damn fires. No matter how many we put out, more start. I guess people left their stoves on, though how that would start a fire since the power was cut, I don't know. That was the clincher, the power going down. It proved that wherever the government's chosen to save, it isn't here."

"Where are you going?" Jenny asked.

"Wisconsin, to start with," Marv said. "We'll make plans after that, depending on what we find. Maybe continue west. Maybe cross the border. We're leaving tomorrow."

"Do you have diesel?" Jenny asked.

"Plenty. Not much gas."

"We've got an RV," Olivia said. "But we don't have much fuel."

"And there's six of you?" Marv asked.

"Plus a dog. Four children," Jenny said. "We have room for more, if that's what you're asking."

"It is. Albie! You drove your pa's combine-trailer, yes?"

The wall of human muscle nodded. "Yep."

"Think you can drive an RV?"

Albie gave a shrug.

"I don't know if he'll fit in the seat," Jenny said.

"I don't think he'll fit through the door," Olivia said.

"I can keep it on the road," Albie said, his voice as deep as a double bass, with as melodious an undertone. "I can keep anything on the road."

"Then you're very welcome," Olivia said. "Cool. Great. This is… this is all great."

"It certainly is," Jenny said. "Do you want us to drive here tomorrow?"

"If you can wait a few hours, I'll get you some fuel," Marv said.

"I don't like leaving the children alone that long," Jenny said. "And we have some supplies we could move up to the RV. If we do that, and if Livy comes back here later, could she bring the diesel?"

"Albie can carry it," Marv said.

Albie nodded. "As far as you need."

"Livy will be back in a couple of hours, then. Livy?"

"Hmm? Oh… sure," Olivia said.

"What is it?" Jenny asked.

"Nothing," Olivia said. "I just thought I saw… but it was no one. Nothing. It doesn't matter." Behind the barricade, she thought she'd seen someone she knew. A man in a sports jacket and baseball cap, carrying a shovel, who'd been strolling towards the barricade, but then turned and walked away in the opposite direction. As he had, he'd tilted the hat and she'd seen his face. It couldn't be. Surely not. Not here. Not Morgan Mack, the man who'd shot Nicole.

"Are you okay, Livy?" Jenny asked.

"I'm seeing ghosts," Olivia said. "Someone I used to know."

"Not a friend, I take it?" Jenny asked.

"Not exactly," Olivia said. Before she could say any more, a mechanical rumble filled the air, followed by a sharp whistle as the sentry pointed south.

"More arrivals," Marv said. "Maybe it's the government."

He went back to the road to meet them. Jenny and Olivia followed, but only to the edge of the wire cage doing service as a door.

The road convoy certainly looked official. Two police cars were led by a pair of odd-looking motorcycle outriders, with a quad bike bringing up the rear. Marv walked out onto the road to meet them, Albie a protective four steps behind.

They weren't police motorcycles, Olivia realised, just as the vehicles stopped. No, they were just ordinary dirt bikes. And were the bikers cops? They had police motorbike helmets and windbreakers, but both were wearing jeans. Well, of course they were, she realised. It wasn't as if any drycleaners were still open.

The driver of the lead car was dressed in police uniform, though it was fraying and stained. The passenger, though, was immaculate. He adjusted his hat, then his belt, and slowly sauntered towards Marv.

Olivia frowned. There was something about him. Something… She looked back at the driver, then the immaculate officer.

"Oh, no," she whispered.

"What?" Jenny asked.

"It might be nothing, but I'm certain I know those two. The younger one, the driver, his name is Herrera. The other is Vevermee, I think."

"And that's bad?" Jenny asked.

But Vevermee answered that himself. He'd stopped ten yards from Marv, with his hand on his belt, threateningly close to his holster.

"It's good to see you," Marv said. "We've been waiting for the government."

"You in charge here, boy?" Vevermee drawled in an accent and tone that surely had to be copied from a movie because Olivia had never heard a person speak like that in real life.

Albie tensed, his shirt rippling as his muscles moved to get out of each other's way.

"Yes," Marv said slowly. "Yes, I'm in charge."

"This is an illegal assembly," Vevermee said. "As per orders from the governor, you're to return to your homes."

"The governor is still alive?" Marv asked.

"Return to your homes, await further instructions," Vevermee said. "And before you go, I want a list of everyone who's here."

186

"That'll take time," Marv said. "There's a lot of us."

"You haven't been keeping records?" Vevermee asked.

"Didn't seem much point," Marv said. "But we'll disperse. I'll go spread the word."

"Sir, hostiles," Herrera called, and pointed down the road to a pair of zombies lurching towards them.

Vevermee eyed Marv up and down once again, then spun on his heel. He strode to his police cruiser, opened the back seat, and reached inside. Oddly, he came out holding not a rifle, but a heavy padded metal pack which he hauled onto his back. Olivia's first thought was disinfectant. That, after the zombies were killed, the cop planned to spray the street. It was a notion dispelled when the pilot-light at the tip of the torch-gun ignited. Vevermee strode down the street, as the undead lurched towards him.

Despite the mud covering them nearly head to toe, there was no disguising these woken dead were young. Barely older than Robyn. Still children. Still deadly monsters, a walking horror from the worst nightmares.

Fifty yards away, Vevermee raised the flamethrower's torch-gun and fired, spraying one creature and then the other with liquid fire. He began at the feet, moving the jet of flame upwards to legs, torso, head, before pivoting across to the second zombie, and coating her, head to chest to legs. But the zombies didn't stop. They didn't scream. Their clothing popped. Their skin sizzled. Their bones cracked, and they walked on, inhuman torches.

All the while, the officers on the dirt bikes, and the officer from the rear car, watched Albie and Marv. Only Herrera watched his boss, but Olivia couldn't see his expression. Was he impressed? Was he horrified?

At ten yards, the first of the flaming zombies collapsed. On the ground, rolling, twitching, the zombie finally appeared to be acting normally. At five yards, the other zombie fell.

"I want everyone gone from here within the hour," Vevermee said. "You remain here," he added, addressing Marv, before slowly striding back to his car. He extinguished the flame-thrower's pilot light and handed the rig to Herrera before getting into the driver's side. He barely waited for Herrera to get in before starting the engine. The cars reversed around the still writhing, still burning zombies, driving away, the dirt bikes following in their wake.

"He's no cop," Jenny said.

"Not anymore," Marv echoed. "We're leaving now. No point waiting until morning. You said you have enough diesel for a few miles? I'll get you a few more cans. We'll give you the rest later. Albie, those two cans in the shed. Quick."

With surprising speed, the young man sprinted for the shed.

"The rendezvous is the cemetery on Edison Road," Marv said. "Do you know it?"

"Too well," Jenny said.

Albie ran back as fast as he'd gone, a fuel can in each massive hand. "You want me to go with them, Coach?" he asked.

"Can you make it on your own?" Marv asked.

"I'm not as feeble as that, not yet," Jenny said severely.

"Because I could do with Albie's help for now," Marv said. "We'll see you at the cemetery."

Without another word, Marv hurried away, with Albie on his heels.

"That was—" Olivia began.

"Talk later," Jenny said, hefting a fuel can. "Think later. Act now."

Balancing the fuel while cycling and watching for the undead, Olivia barely noticed the roads they travelled as they cycled back to the house. The journey seemed to take no time, though they'd been gone long enough for the children to fill all the bags they'd been able to find.

"There's still more, Nana," Dwayne said. "More clothes. More food. More batteries. More—"

"And more to be found in other houses," Jenny said. "But you did a good job, all of you. We're leaving now. We met an old friend at the university, and he's leading a convoy out of South Bend. We're going with him, and we're going now. Grab a bag. No more than you can carry, Dwayne, and you certainly can't carry three."

Five minutes later, Olivia was leading the way, Rufus at her side, Wayde a step behind, pushing her bicycle onto which they'd slung as many bags as it could feasibly take.

One block away from the RV, the city shuddered as a dull and distant explosion shook the sky. A narrow column of smoke rose to the southeast. A second explosion, louder, flatter, longer, followed it. The smoke rose to a billowing cloud.

"A fuel tanker," Jenny hissed.

"You think that was the university?" Olivia asked.

"I worry it might have been," Jenny said. "Boys, get those bags off the bike. Livy, you cycle south, find out what happened. We'll wait in my house. I don't want to drive to the cemetery if we're the only people going to be there."

"Got it," Olivia said, grabbed the bike, and began cycling frantically south. A third explosion, softer than the previous two, but still loud enough to hear, echoed across the city. Olivia tried to cycle faster, but was already going flat out.

She heard the screams first. Then the gunshots. Zombies. It had to be. Zombies were heading toward the sound of the explosion, picking off the injured and disorientated. But when she drew close enough to see the barricade, she saw something worse. She jumped from the bike, but had the presence of mind to grab it before it fell, laying it quietly down next to her as she took shelter behind the neatly sculpted hedge bordering a college-adjacent house. In front of the barricade were the people dressed as cops. She recognised the police cruiser Herrera had driven, and which Vevermee had ridden. With it were two dirt bikes, and two multi-wheeled armoured cars that must have been military surplus before the police department had purchased them.

Vevermee stood, hands on hips, in front of the armoured car. She counted twelve others, all wearing some pieces of police gear. Half were watching the road. The other half watched the prisoners.

There were five of those, kneeling, with their hands cuffed behind their backs, attached to the now buckled fence. Marv was in the middle, Albie next to him, the woman who'd been on sentry duty on the other side. The other two, Olivia didn't recognise. Behind the prisoners, smoke and screams rose to the sky as the university burned, but she couldn't see any more survivors. No, there was one! Someone was running out of the smoke. A figure in a baseball cap and sports coat. Guns were raised until Vevermee yelled a command to lower them.

The figure slowed from a run to a saunter, walking around the prisoners, and over to Vevermee. There he gave a sloppy salute before taking off his cap. This time, Olivia was sure. It *was* Mack.

Mack handed something to Vevermee, though Olivia couldn't see what. A shot rang out as one of the police sentries fired. All of the guards turned to look, but Vevermee didn't. He reached into a pocket, and pulled something out. When Olivia saw the small flame, she realised it was a lighter. Vevermee tossed it onto the road. A burst of flames licked upwards, turning into a smoking trail, quickly dancing towards the prisoners. They screamed, and their screams only grew worse as the fuel-trail burned closer, quickly reaching them. Already doused in fuel, they erupted into human candles. Olivia froze, unable to move for a long second as the screams grew worse.

She reached for the bag in which she kept the gun, drawing it, but Vevermee and the others were already boarding their vehicles. As for the prisoners, there was nothing she could do for them. Not now.

Chapter 25 - Justice Delayed
Thunder Bay

"That's what happened," Olivia said. "Afterwards, I went back to Jenny and the kids. We decided to wait until night, leave a few hours before dawn, and look for more diesel along the way. But Vevermee was hunting for people, survivors from the university. One of the dirt bikes drove down the street. They saw the RV. Saw Marge's body. The rider threw a Molotov cocktail into the cab before driving off."

"Why would anyone do that?" Pete asked.

"It's beyond my understanding," Olivia said. "As is Mack. I'm sure it was him, there, at the university. And I think... okay, so I don't know for certain, but I think he caused the explosion at the university. And before you ask me why he did it, give me another explanation for why Vevermee didn't shoot him."

"I can't," Pete said. "And I believe you. There was nothing you could do. You couldn't have stopped them."

"Oh, I know," Olivia said. "I was too far away, and too uncertain a shot to even give the prisoners a quick death. But there's a difference between achieving something and doing something, you know? It's why I went back to my apartment. I thought Mack might be there, or hanging around nearby. Of course, he wasn't. If he had been, I... I don't know. But sometimes, even if you're not going to achieve anything but death, you should try."

"You'd have been killed. The children would have died."

"Maybe. Or maybe not. You'd have still come to South Bend, so who knows. I... I'm not going to justify what I did, or didn't do. And I'm not looking for absolution. It's... in that moment, I saw how much the world had changed, and I'm not prepared to stand for it. I'm not going to let that be the way the world *is*. That's what I'm saying. No, firing off a few shots wouldn't have achieved anything, but that doesn't mean I shouldn't have tried. And next time, I will."

It was another hour before Commissioner Peterson returned, and with Captain Crawford in tow.

"Have you arrested him?" Olivia asked.

"No," the commissioner said. He sat, heavily. Crawford slumped into a chair at the next booth over.

"What do you mean, no?" Olivia asked. "I want to press charges. I want Mack arrested for murder."

"I'm truly sorry about your friend," Peterson said. "But there's no evidence. It's your word against his."

"But he's lying. When we got here, I told you everything. I told you how he was working for Vevermee. Don't you believe me?"

"I do," Peterson said. "But even by your own admission, your friend's death was accidental."

"The guns Mack brought to my apartment were taken from a police officer," Olivia said. "Mack stole them. That's a crime."

"Jurisdiction," Crawford said. "We don't have it."

"That can't matter now," Pete said.

"We don't have evidence," Crawford said. "And his friends saw you. He *has* friends."

"I don't... why does that matter?" Olivia asked.

"I mean you can't go and take matters into your own hands," Crawford said. "You do that, it *will* be murder."

"I wasn't... I don't... I *want* justice," Olivia said. "You think I want to kill him?"

"I'm saying you shouldn't try," Crawford said.

"So that's it? He's being let go and I'm being warned off? He was with Vevermee, you know?"

"And he admitted something of that," Peterson said. "After the death of your roommate, he went looking for police, but the officers he found were killers. He said he fled as soon as he realised, and is citing his presence here, now, as proof."

"So is that it?" Olivia asked.

"He's being sent away as part of a group of reinforcements to a front-line fort," Crawford said. "Odds are he'll be dead by the end of the month."

"We sent a team of Special Forces to South Bend this morning," Peterson said. "US Rangers. They are going to scout Lansing and Detroit in preparation for the General's southward push. But first, they're going to deal with Vevermee, Herrera, and any other villain they find in the city. I'll look carefully at the evidence they bring back, and I'll know where to find Mr Mack if there's a reckoning to be had."

"Assuming he's still alive," Crawford added.

"You've already sent soldiers to South Bend?" Pete asked. "Does that mean we don't need to go back there?"

Before Peterson could answer, the door opened. Rufus bounded in and over to Olivia. More slowly, Corrie entered, Jerome MacDonald a step behind.

"Jerome! You're back," Pete said.

"I have a message for the general," Jerome said.

"And she's not here, so you better give it to me," Crawford said.

Jerome handed it to the commissioner, who read it first, then handed it to Crawford.

"You know what it says, Constable?" Peterson asked.

"Yes, sir," Jerome said. "They made me memorise it. *The sun rises over Denver.* I don't know what it means, though."

"It's an old Cold War code," Peterson said. "And it is merely a confirmation of what we already suspected. Who was there when you were told?"

"Admiral Carol Larkin, she says she's the Prime Minister now, and a guy who said he was the Governor of Oregon. There were others there. Spooks and spies."

"And CIA, I expect," Peterson said. "They didn't send any with you?"

"They said they'd dispatched their own team."

"And do you have orders for these three from Australia?" Peterson asked.

"No, just a message to say their mission has been endorsed."

"We need to get this message to the general," Crawford said. "Shall we send the constable?"

"We can't risk that plane near the front," Peterson said. "Another Black Hawk arrived this morning. We can send the message aboard the helicopter; if the weather remains favourable, it has the range. But we'd better send a backup team by road." He smiled and looked at Olivia. "You can drive, can't you?"

With instructions to report to the motor pool in thirty minutes, they were dismissed. In the few hours they'd been inside, bruised purple clouds had swarmed the horizon.

"Looks like rain," Jerome said, zipping his coat up. "I better hurry."

"How are the kids?" Olivia asked.

"They're staying with my aunt," Jerome said. "Don't worry about them. There's nowhere safer they could be."

"You're going back to Nanaimo now?" Corrie asked.

"Yes, but I'll go to the hospital first. If you three aren't coming with us, we've got space for passengers."

"How are things in Vancouver?" Pete asked.

"They could be worse," Jerome said. "We're ferrying over work gangs to secure the waterfront. But I think…" He glanced around, then shrugged as if it didn't matter if his words were overheard. "When all the trapped survivors have been rescued, I think we'll abandon the city."

"That doesn't sound good," Pete said.

"We don't have the ammo, the fuel," Jerome said. "And what does the city have for us? Islands and small towns are the future. But it might change again. Britain has a vaccine."

"Really?" Pete asked.

"So the rumour goes," Jerome said. "I think Dr Avalon has gone to work on it."

"To Britain?"

"No, to Australia. She left by ship. A vaccine could change everything, if it's real. If it works. We've just got to hold on. Are you still recording footage as you go?"

"Yep," Corrie said.

"Keep doing it. In a few years, when this is over, the horror will fade from people's memories. We can't let it be forgotten."

"And Canberra wished us luck?" Pete asked.

"Liu Higson said a message had come from the government, from..." He took out a notebook. "She made me write it down. From Anna Dodson."

"Mick's daughter?" Corrie asked.

"She's a friend?" Jerome asked.

"Sort of," Corrie said. "She's a politician. I'm friends with her father."

"She thanks you for your efforts and wants you to continue. She wishes you luck. Liu added a note of her own, wishing they'd sent you some SAS, but things are bad in Australia, too. But you know what I think? If the worst isn't over, it will be soon. Here's the hospital. Until next time."

"Until next time," Corrie echoed.

A used-auto dealership had been commandeered for use as a motor pool, with most of its stock having been replaced by partially disassembled military vehicles. But standing next to one was a familiar face.

"Private Lacoona!" Corrie said. "You've been moved from quarantine duty?"

"And I got a promotion. Corporal Lacoona, at your service."

"Congrats," Pete said. "Are you running the motor-pool now?"

"Nope. I'm waiting for you," Lacoona said, holding up a small bag. "The commissioner gave me the dispatches for General Yoon. You three are the drivers, and I'm the guide. Sorry. You four. Didn't see you there, boy. How are you?" She bent to tousle Rufus's fur. "Four seems like overkill, though. We're going to be crowded."

"They want us out of town," Olivia said.

"Really, why?" Lacoona asked. "Oh, you've got to tell me, but while we drive. We're going to Wawa, and that's about five hundred kilometres away, near Lake Superior."

"Lake Superior? Close to the bridge and border with Michigan?" Olivia asked.

"The bridge at Sault Ste. Marie is gone," Lacoona said.

"That's what I heard," Olivia said. "Was it you? Or us? The general, I mean."

"I don't think so," Lacoona said. "General Yoon took responsibility, but I think it was accidental. Done in panic. Closing the border there didn't help because millions of refugees came through Detroit. I heard a battalion of engineers have built a temporary crossing over the Soo Locks at Sault Ste. Marie, but I don't think rumours are any more reliable now we don't have phones than when we did."

"If it's five hundred kilometres, we'll be lucky to get there tonight," Pete said.

"We'll be lucky to get there tomorrow," Lacoona said. "And I don't know whether the general is still there, but Wawa was where the fighter jets saw her last. They've been using them to fly reconnaissance."

"And you can tell us about that as we drive," Corrie said. "So, how about we find a car?"

"It's got four wheels, so it must be a car," Olivia said, as they walked around the TAPV.

"The mechanic said it was a Tactical Armoured Patrol Vehicle," Corrie said.

"I can see the armour, and I suppose we're the patrol, but I'm feeling light on tactics," Lacoona said. "Does anyone think they can drive it?"

Corrie climbed up the step, opened the driver's door, and peered at the controls. "I think so."

"They didn't teach you how to drive these when you joined up?" Pete asked.

"I'm a schoolteacher," Corporal Lacoona said. "Or I was until a week ago. I taught Clive's grandchildren. The commissioner. But they've moved the children over to the islands. And they have plenty of older teachers, and older grandparents who can cover a semester of lessons. The rest of us have been conscripted. Clive offered to deputise me. But what do I know about law and order? But police, soldiers, it's all the same now, isn't it? Are you sure you can drive this?"

"There's one way to find out," Corrie said. "Besides, it's this, or that tank. You taught in Thunder Bay?"

"Oh, sure. But I know the way. We have to put these on the truck." She handed a pair of flags to Pete. One bore the red maple leaf of Canada, the other was the Stars and Stripes. Both were rigid, small, and easily attached to the rear of the armoured car.

"Why the American flag?" Pete asked.

"I didn't ask," Lacoona said. "I know enough about the military that you're never supposed to."

"Do you know what the message is?" Pete asked.

"I do," Lacoona said. "Do you know what it means?"

"I was going to ask you that next," Pete said.

"Clive knows," Lacoona said. "But he wouldn't tell me. We'll find out when we get there, eh?" She pulled out a thin cloth chevron. "So, last question, do any of you know how to sew?"

Chapter 26 - Three Women, a Man, and Their Dog
Thunder Bay to Nipigong

Getting spare fuel for the TAPV took two minutes. Getting ammo necessitated returning to the commissioner for authorisation. Having no spare shells for Olivia's shotgun, the armourer gave her an assault rifle instead. Getting food, after queuing for an hour in an unmoving line, required returning to the hotel and begging it from the eternally grumpy chef. Finally getting out of Thunder Bay took just as frustratingly long, as the small city's roads were clogged with foot traffic.

"Thunder Bay is bigger than I thought," Olivia said, the sheer number of passers-by bringing her out of the dark mood which had settled after the confrontation with Mack.

"These people? Oh, they're all refugees," Lacoona said. "I s'pose we should stop calling them that. Farmers, I s'pose that's what they are now."

Mud-covered, exhausted, and empty-handed except for an occasional small bag, they filtered through the roadblocks, then spread out across the road as they continued on to their night's rest in a multi-occupancy hotel room, or overcrowded house. A few others still laboured at the roadside, digging up a verge or front yard. Others, covered in as much grease as mud, worked on turning roadblocks into the barricades going up at nearly every intersection.

"Each block's becoming a mini-fortress," Pete said.

Rufus yipped his agreement.

"The fences are too high," Corrie whispered.

"What's that?" Lacoona asked.

"The fences," Corrie said. "They've dug up the yards for planting, then built fences around them, but the fences are too high. The sun won't get in."

"You're a gardener?" Lacoona asked.

"No, but I am an expert on fences. I used to maintain the dingo fence in New South Wales, to keep the wild dogs out of the farmland."

"You should tell Clive when we get back," Lacoona said. "He'll put you in charge. Seriously. No one knows what they're doing here. How could we? Who could think something like this would ever happen? Oh, sure, you worry about a disaster, but it'll never happen before the day after tomorrow, so there's always time to prepare. But how can you prepare for this?"

"Exactly my thoughts," Corrie said.

They reached another roadblock, and had to stop while the gates were opened. The guards, three of them, armed with hunting rifles, were all in their seventies. Perhaps they'd been soldiers once, but they weren't now. They weren't police, either, despite the windbreakers they wore. They didn't ask to see papers or I.D., but waved the TAPV through with a nod of mutual appreciation.

From the weary conscript-labourers trudging bed-ward after a backbreaking shift they received a different look: pity mixed with gratitude that they were going to bed rather than the out into the nightmare dangers beyond Thunder Bay's half-built walls.

Finally they reached the northeastern edge of the city, and the last of the new logging camps, where the old forest was being torn aside to make way for farmland. On Highway 17, vehicles had been pushed to the roadside, and often into the woodland on either side. Some had scratches. Some bore dents. Others were riddled with bullet holes. Most had open fuel caps suggesting someone had come along after they were abandoned to salvage any remaining fuel. A few were burned wrecks, marking the pyres where the infected had been aboard.

"We should have gone shopping," Olivia said.

"Oh, no stores have been open for days," Lacoona said.

"I guess I should have said looting," Olivia said, opening the bag and quickly sorting through it. "You see all those open fuel caps of the cars we're passing?"

"Someone's taken the gas," Pete said.

"Yes, but why leave a car out here, so far from Thunder Bay?" Olivia said. "I assume that's where they were heading. They must have run out of fuel. Maybe not all of them, but a lot. Someone came along later to take whatever was left. And there are so many vehicles, it had to be someone official."

"The general," Lacoona said. "I bet it was her. I didn't hear about it, but who would say they spent an afternoon stealing what was left in other people's cars? But why did that make you think of looting?"

"It just struck me that nothing is going to be made anymore," Olivia said. "Everything we don't have, we'll have to do without, and we have hardly anything here. A small first-aid kit, some ammo, enough food for a few days, but there's no stove. No utensils. A water bottle, and no coffee. A few tools, but no rope. No compass."

"I have one," Corrie said.

"That's something," Olivia said. "And we have a sewing kit, but no clothes. I suppose..." She trailed off.

"What?" Pete asked.

Olivia shook her head, then shrugged, deciding that there was no harm in sharing. "It's not just how quickly things change, but how often. I'd just gotten my head around the idea of the outbreak and working in the hospital when that burned down. I had *not* gotten used to life in the cabin before I had to return to the city. I was on the run there, playing foster-mom to a bunch of kids when you arrived, and now I'm... here. It's a whirlwind, that's all."

"You worked in a hospital?" Lacoona asked.

"I was only helping out," Olivia said.

"What was it like? Or would you prefer not discussing it?"

Olivia glanced out the window, then back at the corporal. "No, it's fine. And it was chaotic. Far worse than Thunder Bay."

She talked as they drove, while outside the number of abandoned vehicles thinned.

At a southerly road signposted for Pass Lake and Sleeping Giant National Park, the abandoned vehicles had been dragged together to form a wall around a solitary truck stop. Above it, on a small crane, hung a maple-leaf flag. Standing on the door of an upturned minivan, a uniformed sentry raised a hand as they drove by. It would have been reassuring if, on the other side of the road, a trio in heavy-duty hazmat clothing weren't dragging corpses over to a smouldering fire.

It was a grim sight to keep them thoughtful as they turned northeast, venturing inland. To Pete, it suggested what they'd seen in Indiana and Michigan were truer representations of how the world now was than Nanaimo or Thunder Bay. But which would become a template for the future? Mulling that over kept him occupied until the thought was driven from his mind by the cows.

Occasional small fields, belonging to equally small farms, were bracketed by equally small pockets of ancient arboreal forest. Among the waterlogged winter grass, and between the trees, marched and munched scores of cows. Hundreds. Thousands. The further they drove, the higher Pete revised his estimate.

Parked on the road, and in the fields, were livestock transports guarded by armed sentries, who must also have been the vehicle's drivers. None offered a greeting to the passing TAPV beyond a relieved relaxation when it became clear the army vehicle wasn't going to stop.

"The plates on that transporter were from Wisconsin," Pete said.

"I'm guessing the cows are, too," Olivia said.

"They're Holsteins," Lacoona said. "Dairy cows. This must have been what they were talking about."

"Who was talking?" Olivia asked.

"Oh, I overheard Captain Crawford discussing it with a couple of farmers," Lacoona said. "Someone pitched the idea to the general a week ago. They'd been a farmer before enlisting in the U.S. army. They knew where the cows were, and said they should bring them north, but I didn't think it was this many."

"They went south to steal the cows?" Pete asked.

"Or to save them," Olivia said.

There were so many. And so many transporters. Hundreds, and so perhaps twice that number of people.

Pete grinned.

"What's funny?" Olivia asked.

"Oh, it's not funny," he said. "But if the general can organise all of that, I've got hope for the future."

They continued beyond the last of the transporters, and then beyond the last of the stray cows that wandered alone through the trees, nibbling at the frost-tipped grass. The road continued, and so did they, as the sun dipped towards the horizon.

"We'll have to stop soon," Lacoona said.

"Any idea where?" Corrie asked. "No. Warm your hands, we've got trouble ahead."

Even as Pete leaned sideways to peer out the windscreen, Corrie braked.

Rufus growled a protest as he was thrown from his perch.

"You and me both, buddy," Pete muttered, rubbing his knees. He frowned, again looking ahead, again looking for the danger, but all he could see was a car. The ocean-blue four-door had stalled in the middle of the road. There was mud on the tyres and fender, but otherwise nothing remarkable about it. The doors were closed. The windows were unbroken. Pete let his gaze roam beyond the vehicle, settling on the large house on the northern side of the road. Or was it a small farmhouse? The main building was a two-storey, white-trimmed, wood-clad, with an upper-floor balcony built over the front door, creating a sheltered porch. To one side was a double garage, and to the other a barn, again both of the same white-trimmed, wooden style. Behind the building, the ancient forests, which bracketed the house's flanks, turned to cleared grassland, but there was no livestock. It was the same with the land on the other side of the road. A section of woodland had been cleared a few seasons ago, left to grass, but with no sign of livestock. Had it been cleared simply so the owner of the house had a view?

Rufus gave a low, warning growl.

"Is there only one?" Olivia asked.

"Check behind us," Corrie said. "But I think so."

Pete turned back to the car. This time he saw it because, now, it waved. It was the wrong verb to describe the languid, beckoning curl of its hands.

The zombie was trapped beneath the front wheel of the car, its head beating slowly against the road.

"I think it… it must have… it must have clogged the axle," Corrie said, struggling to find an antiseptically bloodless form of words.

"It shouldn't be here," Lacoona said. "This is the area the general cleared. The cows must be part of the reason why. We're about fifteen kilometres from Nipigong, and that's supposed to be a supply hub for communities in the north as well as for the frontline."

"Well, it's definitely here," Pete said.

"I mean this is a well-travelled road," Lacoona said. "That car has to have stopped recently. But that doesn't explain how the zombie ended up there."

"Let's go ask," Corrie said. "Eyes bright, safeties off. Pete, have you still got that suppressor?"

"For the pistol, sure."

He glanced at the house, which still appeared dark, then up and down the road before finally getting out. "Rufus?"

The dog jumped down, circling the TAPV while continuously looking at the trapped zombie. Pete did the same, though he included the house in his continuous inspection. The car had been abandoned after colliding with the zombie. If the driver had taken shelter, it would have been in the house, but it appeared utterly empty. And why hadn't the driver killed the zombie?

The air was cold, the wind brisk, creating a low whispering susurrus among the trees. The hairs rose on the back of his neck as he walked slowly towards the car. Olivia came to join him from the other side of the TAPV. Lacoona stood facing the way they'd come, leaving Corrie behind the wheel as Pete paced forward, suppressed pistol in hand, his attention increasingly focused on the trapped zombie. He raised the handgun, bracing his right hand with his left.

"Uniform," Olivia whispered.

Pete blinked. He'd not noticed at first. But, yes, the zombie wore a uniform. A complete set, at least as far as he could tell with one wheel parked on its back, another on its left ankle. Its right leg kicked weakly while its right hand reached up towards the humans. It was almost as if it was asking for help. Almost, except there was nothing but death in its eyes, and even worse in the snapping mouth. Pete fired. The bullet whispered from the gun, entering the creature's skull. The sound of the soft impact was immediately lost behind the muffled thud as the bullet slammed into the hardtop beneath.

"Only one," Pete whispered, and the wind seemed to catch his words, echoing them in a rising whisper.

"Pete, the house," Olivia whispered. "The balcony."

He turned to look. There was someone there. Not on the balcony itself, but standing behind the French doors. He wasn't undead, not unless zombies had upped their table manners. With a bowl in one hand, a fork in the other, he was methodically eating while watching the new arrivals watching him.

"He must think we're soldiers," Pete said.

"We should go say hello," Olivia said. "Ask him what happened. "Ask him…" She paused, stopped, and looked around. She'd walked as far as the edge of the road and the beginning of the poorly paved drive leading up to the house.

Pete stopped next to her, turning around himself. "What is it?"

All he could hear was the sound of the wind through the trees, except… Except the trees were mostly leafless, and around the house, they'd been trimmed. The sound was far closer. Far lower. Far wetter. He looked down, jumping back, just as Olivia fired.

At the side of the road, separating it from the large house, was a drainage ditch. Partially overgrown further along the road, it had been cleared near the driveway where a narrow-gapped metal grid had been laid over it. From beneath came a wet, soft, squelching whisper as the zombie crawled through the deep mud. Olivia's rifle cracked loudly. The bullet softly slapped into the boggy morass near the creature's head, but not near enough. The zombie crawled on, somehow finally managing to get a knee beneath its body. Dripping wet mud, seeping black pus from dozens of slashing knife wounds, it stood. Its shoulder slammed into the edge of the metal grating, leaving a sodden patch of cloth and skin behind.

Olivia fired again and this time, from less than three metres distance, she hit. The sound of the corpse splashing into the swampy murk was lost beneath another gunshot. Pete spun towards the TAPV, but it wasn't Corrie or Lacoona who'd fired. It was the man in the house. He'd opened the balcony doors, and with what looked like a hunting rifle, he'd fired towards the field on the other side of the road.

"The car!" Olivia said. "Quick. The roof. Rufus, heel!"

Still unclear why, Pete ran back over to it, following her lead. Bracing a foot on the wheel arch, he clambered up onto the car, and then its roof. And then he saw them. Zombies. In uniform. Crawling across the cleared ground.

"Rufus!" Olivia called. The dog was still circling the car. "Rufus, please!" Finally, the dog bounded up onto the roof. Pete kneeled, grabbing the dog's collar.

"There's got to be at least ten. Why?" Olivia asked. She raised the rifle, and lowered it again. "How?"

A shot came, this time from the TAPV as Corrie fired from the vehicle's turret. Another shot came, this time from the house.

Pete half raised the pistol, while Olivia crouched, tracking her rifle left and right, but neither fired. As soon as a zombie reached the road, Corrie, or the man in the house, and sometimes both, shot the creature. All the undead wore uniform. They'd all had their legs crushed.

"I think that's it," Olivia finally said.

"Clear!" Corrie called.

"He could have warned us," Pete said, letting go of Rufus's collar. The dog gave a frustrated shake. "That guy in the house, he could have given us a heads-up."

Even as he turned back to the house, a scream ululated from the balcony, ending as abruptly as it had begun. There was no sign of the man.

"Quick!" Olivia said, a step before Pete. Both jumped down, sprinting for the house, and its front door. Rufus quickly overtook them.

There was no way it would open without a sledgehammer. Cement had oozed around the hinges, and set hard. It was the same at the ground-floor window. But through a scratched inch of glass, he could see stacked furniture dripping with cement.

"Back door!" Pete yelled, sprinting onto the bare-earth yard. At least they knew why the man hadn't dealt with the zombie beneath the car. With the vehicle in the way, he'd not had a shot from his window. Cemented into his house, he'd been unable to leave.

"Careful, Pete!" Olivia yelled, a step behind.

The back door had a cat flap. Once. Not anymore. The plastic frame had been ripped free, leaving fresh splinters and a hole large enough for a figure to crawl through. Assuming, of course, the figure didn't mind ripping its skin on the fractured wood, dislocating a bone or two as it contorted its way inside. And of course, a zombie wouldn't even notice such painful discomfort.

"I don't think I'd fit," Olivia said. "You certainly wouldn't." Rufus took a cautious sniff, then backed away. "And he doesn't want to."

From the road came a mechanical growl. By the time they'd dashed back to the front of the house, they saw Corrie drive the TAPV off the road, into the yard, and right up to the edge of the house, swerving at the last minute to bring it broadside-on to the house, and only a metre from the wall. Lacoona was already in the turret. She clambered the rest of the way up and out, and jumped, grabbing onto the edge of the balcony, hauling herself up, getting a knee onto the balcony rail before pausing.

"What is it?" Olivia called.

For the longest second, Lacoona didn't move. She knelt, staring into the room beyond. "Dead," she called, and lowered herself back down, swinging by her hands until, with a nimble leap, and a half-turn in mid-air, she landed on the TAPV's roof. "Go," she called. "They're dead."

The muscular tyres churned deep furrows in the mud as Corrie reversed back onto the road. With as much attention on the house, at least until they reached the deep drainage ditch, Pete and Olivia followed.

"What did you see?" Pete asked.

"Zombies," Lacoona said. "At least five. He's dead. The man in the window."

"Should we…" Olivia turned back to the house. "We should see if there's anyone else in there."

"They would've have called out," Lacoona said. "Or screamed."

"They might not have," Olivia said.

Lacoona shook her head. "We just don't have time. Nipigong is only fifteen kilometres away. If it's fallen, all the cattle are in danger. Have you seen what zombies do to livestock? They rip them apart."

"She's right," Corrie said. "We've got to raise the alarm."

Nipigong wasn't a city, but a fortified town, lit up brighter than Christmas with searchlights and spot-lamps, and with a pair of tanks parked on either side of the approach road.

They had to explain the situation three times. First to a sergeant aboard a tank, then to a captain who'd been dragged from a post-office command post, and then to a civilian who seemed to outrank everyone. But within ten minutes, the sergeant, his tank, and two of the trucks crammed with soldiers were speeding south. Pete and the others weren't sent with them, but told to park the TAPV where the tank had been positioned, and wait for further instructions.

"Zombies don't run," Corrie said.

"Yeah, I hope not," Lacoona said.

"I mean we've got some time before danger comes, so why don't we see if we can find some food. Olivia, Pete, can you watch the road?"

"Sure, but can you see if you can find some cereal?" Pete said.

"You're still addicted to that?" Olivia asked as Corrie and Lacoona made their way inside the barricade.

"It was the sight of all those cows," Pete said. "Made me think of milk, and that made me think of cereal. Something with marshmallows and chocolate."

"Milkshake," she said. "That's what I'd go for. But I'd keep the marshmallows and chocolate. And I'd settle for just the chocolate." She sighed. "You know the sad part?"

"That it's going to be years before we see those in the stores?" Pete asked.

"No, that I've had worse dates than this," she said.

"Dates?" he asked.

"Don't you remember? Earlier, after we finished washing dishes in the hotel, you said we should go on a date."

"Oh, yeah. That seems... that was only this morning?"

"It does seem like a lifetime ago, doesn't it?" she said.

"I'm not calling this our date," Pete said.

"That's not how it works," Olivia said. "Good or bad, it counts. I didn't make the rules."

"I wonder who did. You've really been on worse?"

"You know what they say," she said. "It's the company that counts."

Chapter 27 - Evacuation
Nipigong to Marathon

One of the trucks, which had driven west with the tank, returned after an hour, though with only a driver and one soldier aboard. The tank and the other truck had continued back to the dairy herd.

The fort spent the night on a tensely vertiginous high alert. But though the alarm was frequently raised, it always proved to be false. Before dawn, led by the remaining tank, an eight-vehicle convoy was ready to journey west to help protect the herd, but there was as much concern about what lay to the east as this new danger behind their lines.

As she'd advanced eastward, General Yoon had repurposed existing telephone wires into a new and dedicated hard-line, but the connection had failed an hour before the TAPV had arrived at the fort. With the timing worryingly coincidental, the decision was made to send another convoy east. Most of the better-repaired vehicles had already gone west. An armoured personnel carrier, a hastily repaired armoured car old enough to be a museum piece, and three fire-service vehicles with so many dents even a scrap yard wouldn't take them were all that were left. The TAPV brought up the rear, Lacoona driving as the lead APC set a ferocious pace.

After a few miles of veering left then swerving right, Pete closed his eyes, already feeling road-sick. Though it had been cold during the night, it hadn't been cold enough for ice. The road was damp, not slick, but littered with debris. It was better, he decided, to think of it as debris rather than bodies, particularly now that so many limbs had been torn from torsos, so much flesh had been crushed, and bones pulverised by the passage of many large vehicles. Tanks, he supposed. The general's *army*. On its *advance*. He'd not given much thought to that until now. They were at war, with which, despite the handful of skirmishes over the last few days, he was only familiar as a couch-bound spectator. Thousands had died on this stretch of road. And it was with the frequent thud and soft bump he finally realised how many more would have to die before peace returned.

The undead weren't uniformly littered along the road, but clustered a few miles apart, and always close to where a junkyard of cars and trucks had been shunted to the verge. Ploughing aside broken exhausts and crushed fenders, crunching over broken windscreens as well as the remains of the undead, Pete found himself remembering the outback and the nightmare drive from the plane to Corrie's cabin. Perhaps this *was* a form of warfare with which he was familiar.

The convoy halted at Terrace Bay, an indecently peaceful hamlet, where boats fished on the lake, while washing was being optimistically hung on the line. That a lot of the gear was camouflage, and the lines were being hung in yards already dug over, gave a hint that the new normality had taken hold. But clearly, the resident-soldiers had no recent trouble from the undead.

Leaving the captain to organise a better defence of the town, and carrying a new dispatch for the general, they continued east, alone except for Lake Superior to the south for company.

At the outskirts of Marathon, on the eastern edge of Lake Superior, they stopped to refuel the truck and themselves, but they didn't enter the hamlet that was already crammed to the rafters. Refugees were arriving, more by the hour, sent by the general, and apparently awaiting a ferry to take them to Thunder Bay.

"Had you heard anything about a ferry?" Corporal Lacoona asked as they drove away, continuing inland.

"I was going to ask you that," Corrie said. "You mean you hadn't?"

"Clive allocated me to work the quarantine at the airport to keep me out of trouble," Lacoona said. "Obviously, this was before we knew how bad it could get at the airport. Considering how bad it got at the quarantine centre by the rail yard, maybe he knew what he was doing. But after the first rush of planes, there wasn't much to do. We had fighter jets coming in, of course, and they were flying survey missions."

"Like to South Bend?" Olivia asked.

"Exactly," Lacoona said. "So if they were going to send a ferry from Thunder Bay to Marathon, they'd have flown a survey mission first."

"Are there ferries in Thunder Bay?" Olivia asked.

"Oh, sure," Lacoona said. "But I didn't hear anyone saying they would be used for a rescue mission."

She might not have, but others had. An hour later, and ten kilometres south of White River, they had to pull off the road onto a logging track, to let a convoy pass. Coaches. Buses. Trucks. Cars. All had a recently painted red cross on the side. Some so recent, they'd begun driving before it had time to dry, leaving a drip-drag trail across the chassis, bearing far too close a resemblance to blood to offer reassurance.

Pete had counted twenty-seven vehicles before a white pickup detached itself, pulling over and off the road to stop in front of their TAPV. A maple-leaf flag flew on the roof, while two dozen empty stretchers were stacked in the truck bed, held in place by a web of nylon washing lines and electrical tape.

Neither driver nor passenger were in uniform, though both were armed. The driver had a hunting rifle he grabbed the moment the car came to rest, and which he held at the ready as he scanned the trees. The passenger had a holster at her belt, but she left it there as she walked, wearily, around the truck and over to the TAPV.

"Dr Lutz," she said. "Have you come from Marathon?"

"We came *through* Marathon," Lacoona said. "But we came *from* Thunder Bay. Jan Lacoona. Hi."

Lutz nodded. "The ferries have arrived, then?"

"Ah, no," Lacoona said. "Not an hour ago. We've driven overland. Set off yesterday. The first we heard of a ferry was when we drove through Marathon. We're bringing messages from Thunder Bay to Wawa. Are these more passengers?"

"The old. The sick. The far-too-young to be anywhere near the frontline," Lutz said "General Yoon said there'd be a ferry. You're going to Wawa? You can tell the general. Excuse me."

She got back in her truck. The driver did the same, giving a nod before returning to the still passing convoy. All four stood, watching the road until the vehicles were gone, leaving only fumes as a reminder of their presence.

"No birds," Pete said. "There should be birds. Weird. What?" he added, realising the three women all wore a pensive frown. "What did I miss?"

"They think there's a hospital in Thunder Bay," Corrie said.

"Isn't there one?" Pete asked, turning to the corporal.

"Sure," Lacoona said. "But it's not geared up for a ferry full of patients."

"And there's no ferry," Olivia added. "But there are zombies near Nipigong."

"You mean we should have warned them?" Pete asked.

"You saw the driver," Olivia said. "They know to watch for zombies."

"I still don't get the problem," Pete said.

"They expect a ferry in Marathon and a hospital in Thunder Bay," Corrie said. "And if there isn't, if there's a problem, they expect someone to call. The satellites are down. The radio waves are clogged, and reception around here wouldn't be great. With power blackouts, there are no repeater stations, comms would be very limited, and reception somewhere so wooded would be difficult enough normally. The general was repurposing old telephone lines into a new network, and that broke yesterday. But that also tells us the old system doesn't work. But people instinctively assume instant communication. Sure, consciously they know phones don't work now. Subconsciously, they don't. Which, Pete, means that things are bad out here and likely to get a lot worse."

"I still don't..." Pete began.

"They're evacuating the people who can't fight," Olivia said.

"Oh." And then Pete truly understood. "This really is a war, isn't it?"

Chapter 28 - The War for Wawa
Wawa

When they stopped to empty a fuel can into the TAPV's tank, they heard a rolling thunder, too regular to be natural. They listened until they were sure they'd all heard it, and certain that it came from ahead.

Ten kilometres on, buttoned up inside the TAPV, they didn't hear the helicopter, but Olivia saw it, hovering in the distance ahead of them before it darted ground-ward, disappearing behind the trees.

"Was it shot down?" Pete asked, peering into the distance.

"I don't see any smoke," Corrie said.

"Landing," Lacoona said. "We'll reach the airport before we reach the town. That's where it was going, eh?"

But when they reached the airport, it was in time to see the helicopter departing again. A low chain-link fence ringed the airfield, though with a recently dug ditch between it and the roadside. Nearby, freshly cut and trimmed tree trunks suggested that the construction of a sturdier defence had been recently interrupted. Behind the gated road entrance, two tanks stood on guard. In front of the gate stood one sentry, while another sat. His leg was bandaged, and he had a crutch close to the hand that wasn't holding his assault rifle.

"We bring a message for General Yoon from Captain Crawford in Thunder Bay," Lacoona said.

"You just missed her," the seated sentry called out. He jerked a thumb at the disappearing helicopter. "The colonel will take the message. He's in the tourist information office, across the road. You better bring your transport inside."

"Are you expecting trouble?" Corrie asked.

"After zombies, I'm expecting anything," the soldier said. He gave a nod, and his comrade hauled the gate back, allowing them to drive the TAPV inside. Lacoona stopped it near the tanks.

213

"If I can borrow Rufus," Corrie said, "I'll see what those mechanics have to say."

"Mechanics?" Pete asked.

She pointed to the soldiers by the tanks. Pete looked at them again, this time properly. They weren't the tanks' crews as he'd first thought, but mechanics repairing two broken machines.

Lacoona, Pete, and Olivia left the TAPV, and his sister and Rufus, and headed back through the gate and across the road to a cluster of low buildings, one of which was clearly marked as a tourist information office. Another of the walking wounded, this woman with a bandage on the arm not holding the shotgun, stood guard over the entrance.

The interior had been stripped down to the carpet. Folding tables had been brought in and covered in old-fashioned fixed-line telephones. Wires ran from those to an even older switchboard over which a trio of engineers sweated. There were screens, too. A few military-grade laptops, a lot more civilian models so brand-new they still had the protective screen covers in place. But the computers were dark, except for a multi-screen bank in the far corner; four screens high, four screens wide, and no two screens the same size or model, attached to a bolt-and-bracket rig. Hunched over a keyboard in front, a uniformed operator muttered into a handset. Behind him sat a man in a wheelchair.

"Excuse me, um... sir?" Lacoona asked, uncertainly. The man in the wheelchair wore a dress uniform, and even Pete knew the shoulder-badge indicated an officer, but he understood Lacoona's hesitancy. The man was sick. Very sick. The jacket hung limp on his frail frame. Attached to the back of the wheelchair was a drip from which a tube ran to his arm. His head was bald. Not shaved, but utterly bald, while his skin was shiny and taut.

"And you are?" the officer asked.

"Private— I mean, Corporal Lacoona. From Thunder Bay."

"You're a new recruit?" the officer asked.

"A week ago, I was," Lacoona said. "Sir, we were looking for the colonel, the general's second in command."

"Colonel Montoya. That's me. And these are the Australians? I was told there were four of you."

"Yes, sir," Pete said. "But my sister is speaking to the mechanics repairing the tanks."

"You knew we were coming, sir?" Olivia asked.

"Indeed," Montoya said. "A helicopter arrived last night from Thunder Bay. None of you sound Australian."

"I'm from Thunder Bay," Lacoona said. "I was a teacher a month ago. It's these two who're here from the Pacific."

"Ah," Montoya said. He turned his attention back to the screens. "But these two don't sound Australian, either."

"We're from Indiana, and were only supposed to be the local guides," Pete said. "But the plane had to depart before the soldiers arrived, so we're trying to complete the soldiers' mission for them. That's why my sister's speaking to the mechanics. She's gathering information on where and how the outbreak began."

"And that's important to Canberra? Why?" the colonel asked.

"Honestly, sir, I don't know if it is," Pete said. "We're just gathering information in the hope it might help stop this nightmare."

"Nothing can stop it now," the officer said. "We must ride it. Subdue it. Survive it. But yes, who knows what will help us in that goal?"

"If a helicopter arrived," Lacoona said, "does that mean Thunder Bay *is* sending a ferry? We came across some refugees in Marathon, and a road convoy heading there."

"Yes, Thunder Bay knows. The civilians are being evacuated."

"Sir?" the soldier in front of the screens said, raising a hand. The colonel eased his wheelchair forward as the operator conferred with him.

They hadn't been needed. The message had got through by other means. Pete supposed that was something he'd have to get used to in the military.

"Are those zombies?" Olivia asked, pointing at the bank of monitors.

Pete focused on the screens. He'd been looking at them, but not seeing what they showed.

In the central and largest screen, a mob lurched out of the trees towards the camera. In irregular ranks, a hundred zombies wide and at least ten deep, they staggered across a wide field, trampling a three-wire fence into the mud. Some wore uniform, some were dressed as civilians. Some were too covered in dirt or soot to tell. Pushing. Scrumming. Knocking one another over, and trampling each other into the once-fertile soil, they advanced until the camera jerked. The screen lost focus for a second, before resolving on a wide gap in the advancing line. Mud, mixed with blood and bone, fell like rain.

"That's what a Leopard can do," the colonel said.

"Abrams, sir," the operator said. "That's the major."

"Is it? One of yours, then," he added, turning to Olivia and Pete. Silently, another hole was punched through the line, at an angle to the first, ripping asunder the foremost four rows.

"And that was one of ours, sir," the operator said.

"The zombies are attacking us, here?" Olivia asked.

"No," the colonel said. "We're attacking them. Cotton, bring up the aerial view."

The image changed, showing a top-down view. At the edge of the screen were trees, but the battlefield had been chosen as the cleared ground where two massive firebreaks met. In the centre of the broad clearing were seven tanks, slowly advancing in a V-formation. Two different types of tanks. Assuming the major was in command, and in the lead tank, that made the first three U.S. Abrams, while the other four were Canadian Leopards. One by one they fired, a barrage of seven shells, all aimed at different points along the advancing line. A line that was far wider than the tank's-eye view had suggested.

The zombies fell like dominoes. Hundreds died in that barrage alone. Hundreds more were ripped asunder in the next. Added to the thousands of corpses littering the mud, but discounting those corpses still crawling on towards the shelling, thousands were dead. And yet more still came.

"They're going to be surrounded," Pete whispered.

"Yes," the colonel said.

"They have to retreat," Pete said.

"No," the colonel said. "There will be no retreat from here. Only advance. Only—" He coughed, dragging a handkerchief from his pocket to cover his mouth. Specks of blood were left on the white cotton square before he returned it to his pocket. "Just watch."

Without sound, it somehow felt more real. The tanks maintained their methodical barrage even as the undead advanced. Olivia took Pete's hand. He gripped hers tightly as the undead advanced to within fifty metres of the lead tank. Forty. Thirty. And then they fell.

"Machine gun," the colonel muttered, as the zombies danced and spun, toppling one after another. But as soon as the macabre dance began, it ended. The undead continued their advance. This time, they didn't fall.

"Are they out of ammo?" Pete asked.

"This is phase two," the colonel said.

The tanks had stopped firing. Their cannons and machine guns remained silent as the undead reached the vehicles but then, weirdly, seemed to keep going.

"Show them," the colonel said, his words trailing into a whispering cough.

"This is footage from a different drone," the operator said, changing the image on the central screen to show an aerial view from behind the tanks, and the advancing undead. The image swung left and right as the small machine was buffeted by the winds.

Behind the tanks were three, massive, caterpillar-tracked yellow machines.

"What are they?" Olivia asked.

"Crane platforms," the operator said. "Aboard are our snipers."

They couldn't see the shots fired, but they saw the undead fall. One by one, as they made their way beyond the buttoned-up tanks.

"How... how are they doing it?" Pete asked. "Why aren't the zombies attacking the tanks?"

"Music," the operator said.

"Excuse me," the colonel said, and wheeled himself slowly around.

"Do you want a—" Olivia began, but the colonel waved away her help, as he wheeled himself towards the signposted washroom on the other side of the room.

"Cancer," the operator muttered, when the colonel had gone. "It's terminal. He refuses to die. And that's how we'll win. Yeah, you missed the big show, the helicopters flew in first, luring in the undead, bringing them to the killing ground, five miles outside town. The tanks fired first, then the machine guns, now the snipers."

"And they're on crane platforms?" Olivia asked.

"And other construction equipment," the operator said, waving a hand at the other screens. "Anything with a stable base, taller than an outstretched arm's reach, and which can take a beating. We've tried it before on a smaller scale, but nothing like this. It's the forests. Trees provide them with cover, neutralising the effectiveness of air power. We have to lure them out, lure them away from a population hub. The colonel didn't think the firebreaks would give us enough ground to manoeuvre, but it's working."

"Firebreaks?" Olivia asked. She turned to the other screens and pointed to the screen in the top left. "Those are different tanks. How many... how big is the army? How big is the battle?"

"We're engaged on..." He glanced at the screens, then a clipboard in front of him. "Seventeen positive contacts. All similar. All forces are holding the line. Most of our troops, the newer recruits, are being kept in reserve. They're guarding the approach to the town just north of here and the highway five miles to the south."

Pete tried to do the calculation, and simply came up with *a lot*. Both of soldiers, and tanks, but more of the undead. "Where did the zombies come from?" he asked.

"Ottawa," the operator said. "Maybe Montreal. Maybe from across the border. This is the first wave. They're swarming."

"Swarming?" Olivia asked.

"It's what the general calls it," the colonel said, wheeling himself back from the washroom. "They swarm. Gather. We think it's sound. One hears a sound and heads towards it. So does another. Another. They reach a critical mass where they're louder than the surroundings. They start moving and keep going. We got reports yesterday that it was coming. We were expecting to fight it further east. But here is where the war began. Here is where fear ended."

"Sir, the drone's out of fuel," the operator said. "I'm bringing her back. And the general wants to speak to you."

Olivia jerked her head towards the doors. Pete followed her back outside. Above, dark clouds were gathering.

"There's an army. An actual army, actually fighting," Pete said. "What? You look… I was going to say worried, but that's become everyone's base-state."

"They're evacuating refugees," she said, "and building a wall, or at least a defensive line, while trying to secure farmland, and fight a war. And they're trying to create an army at the same time, getting all these different soldiers to work together. Not just soldiers, not really. It's…"

"A lot?" Pete finished. "But it has to be done."

"Oh, I know," Olivia said. "But I'm shocked by the scale of it."

"They knew we were coming," Pete said. "We could have stayed in Thunder Bay."

"Welcome to the army," Olivia said. "Welcome to our new lives."

"Each day there's something new to get used to," Pete said.

"Like finding food when we can," Olivia said. "Because there's a hungry army out there, about to return."

Before they could take another step, though, a shot rang out. Loud. Clear. Close. Another followed, and then a fully automatic staccato. Pete ran, Olivia close behind.

A beat-up shocking-pink city-car had come to a halt on the airport's approach road. Somehow the zombies had got there first. The mangled remains of a uniformed zombie was curved around the passenger-side wheel, legs and lower chest a bloody ruin, but its hands still clawed at the paintwork, reached for the passengers inside. That creature, gorily lodged during what must have been an attempt to run it down, had immobilised the car. The second zombie was beating its hands against the driver-side door. A third was down, dead, shot by the injured sentry who was now limping towards the car.

Behind them, Corrie and half the mechanics were tugging at the clearly stuck gate while Rufus snapped and barked in a frustration Pete echoed.

"Driver!" Olivia called, claiming her target as they overtook the slowly limping sentry.

"Passenger side," Pete called back.

Ten metres from the car, Olivia slowed her run to a walk as she raised her rifle. Pete raised his own, but loped on another step before firing his weapon. Two shots, from near point-blank range, and both hit. One in the shoulder, but one in the head. A single shot came from his right as Olivia fired, and her target fell. Pete grinned. The nightmare was over.

"Thank you," the driver said, as she opened the door. She wore uniform. Not military. Not police. Not even firefighter or nursing. It was an airline's outfit, and matched that of the woman in the backseat, though the five children crammed into the car were dressed in the usual collection of whatever had been quickly found.

"Whoa, no!" Olivia said, pushing the door closed. "More coming. More are coming." She breathed out. "Stay inside until we say it's safe. Pete, the roof!"

"The roof?" he asked, because as far as he could see, the road behind the car was empty.

He felt a tight pressure around his ankle. Looking down, he saw a hand with peeling, burn-blistered skin curled around his boot. Before he could call out in warning or surprise, the hand pulled, tugging him off his feet. He fell, hitting the asphalt heavily and hard as the zombie tugged again, dragging him across the road as it, in turn, dragged itself up his leg. Its mouth snapped and bit at air as Pete thrashed his legs, trying to free himself, trying to keep it from biting him.

Olivia's boot smashed into its jaw. "No way," she hissed. "Not my boyfriend, you don't." She kicked again, stamped on its shoulder, pinning it. From point-blank, she fired the rifle. The bullet slammed through its skull, into the road beneath. "The roof, Pete," she said, helping him up, then pushing him up onto the car. "You okay?"

"Yeah. Bruised. My self-confidence took a bit of a hit, but..." Then he saw them. The *real* danger. Traipsing towards the airport from the east. In the trees. At least twenty. The nearest only ten metres away.

Olivia fired.

Pete reached for his rifle and realised it was on the ground, where he'd fallen. He thought of jumping down to get it, but a rumble distracted him. At the airport, by the entrance, a tank advanced. Corrie and the mechanics, now armed, rode on the armoured machine. But far closer, he saw the limping soldier, still gamely plodding towards danger. And behind the soldier were the undead. The nearest zombie was five metres from the limping soldier, and gaining ground.

Pete jumped down, running faster than he'd run since high school, but it wouldn't be fast enough. The soldier, already battling against pain, was so focused on reaching the car, he hadn't realised the zombie was just behind, nor that there were two more, just behind that first creature. Pete ran. The tank advanced. The soldier limped. No one was quick enough.

The zombie lurched forward in a falling dive where both of its out-flung arms slammed into the soldier's injured leg. The man screamed as he fell, turning, twisting, trying to bring his gun to bear, but when he fired, just after he hit the ground, the bullet went wide, disappearing into the trees. Yelling and screaming, he rolled onto his back, firing again, but now the shots were too high, whistling over the zombie's head as it bit down, ripping at the man's ankle. He screamed again. But Pete had reached him.

Pete grabbed the zombie's neck. Beneath his fingers, the flesh was a stomach-churning patchwork of tissue-soft and rock-hard, breaking and tearing as he ripped the zombie from the soldier. The creature twisted and bucked as Pete hurled it sideways. Somehow, that resulted in the zombie finding its feet. It staggered back a step before lurching forwards. Now Pete screamed as he wrestled with the button on his holster, but his fingers were too covered in gore. He dragged his bayonet free instead. The zombie lurched on, less than a metre away, oozing pus from ragged tears in the skin of its neck, spitting and hissing as its mouth snapped down on splintered teeth. Pete plunged his bayonet forward into a sightless eye, releasing the knife as the zombie collapsed.

221

Pete hauled the soldier up. "The tank!" he yelled. It was closer, and getting closer still, but there were two zombies between them and it. No, five, as another three lurched out of the trees. Then four as one was shot by someone on the tank. Three.

A bundle of golden fur bounded forward, leaping from the tank, sprinting across the ground, barrelling into the legs of the nearest zombie, knocking it from its feet as Pete carried the bleeding soldier to the tank. People followed Rufus down, Corrie and a mechanic. With the mechanic on the other side of the injured guard, Corrie providing covering fire, and Rufus snapping and snarling in the direction of the nearest enemy, they ran on until they reached the tank.

Hands reached down, wondrously warm and alive. They hauled the injured soldier up, then Pete, the mechanic, and then Corrie. Rufus turned tail and bounded down the highway, darting through and around the dozens of the undead who'd reached the road behind Pete. There, in the distance, further away than he'd imagined, was the car. On the roof, alone, stood Olivia, firing into the undead. Not alone. Rufus leaped onto the roof of the car, but there was little comfort in that.

"You okay?" Corrie asked, as the tank rumbled on, crushing the undead as it rolled towards the stalled car.

"Ask me again in a couple of hours," Pete said. His hand shook as he reached, again, for his holstered pistol. He gripped his wrist, and tried to push fear away.

As guns barked, the tank rumbled onward, slowing as it neared the car, but not stopping until it had bumped into the smaller vehicle. Even as the car creaked in protest, Pete jumped down to its roof.

"So that's what it takes to get you to go for a run," Olivia said, lowering her rifle now that others had joined the battle. "Let's get these people onto the tank."

"Windshield or door?" Pete asked.

Olivia nodded towards the trees. "Either, but do it quick."

The zombies near the car were dead, but coming through the trees were dozens more. Olivia ejected her empty magazine, reloading as Pete jumped down, opening the passenger door.

As the car's occupants scrambled up onto the tank, he looked to the trees, and wished he hadn't. They were full of the undead. Despite how many had been shot. Despite how many were being shot every second, more came. For all the tank's formidable armour, its weapons remained silent because the ammunition had been removed while it was under repair. Most of the mechanics had now formed a kneeling ring on the armour, firing at the undead approaching from the treeline. One of the car's passengers had joined them, a hunting rifle in her hands. Pete climbed back up onto the car, then onto the tank, Olivia a step behind, and Rufus, leaping up last, a half step behind her.

"Are we retreating?" Pete asked.

"Negative," one of the mechanics said. "The general's orders. We're to hold the enemy south of the airport until reinforcements arrive."

From where? How long would that be? He wanted to ask those questions and a dozen more, but doubted the mechanic would know the answer. Now that the man had started firing again, he doubted he'd be able to hear. As the tank began rumbling backwards, he could barely hear his own thoughts. Rufus nuzzled closer, seemingly disconcerted by the loud noise. A noise loud enough to lure the undead.

His hands still shook, but he freed the pistol, holding it ready, waiting for the moment the undead came within range.

Instead, above, he heard a different sound. Music, barely audible over the beat of a helicopter's rotors and the grind of the tank's tracks. Not Wagner, but something incongruously cheery that was drowned by the far faster beat of a Gatling gun ripping into the trees. The machine gun roared. Bark flew. Bone broke. Branches snapped. Limbs were torn from their sockets. A second machine gun on a second helicopter joined the first. Then a third, a fourth, a fifth, hovering above the trees, laying down fire. The machine gun in the first helicopter went silent. The chopper buzzed low, hovering over the road. At two metres from the ground, people jumped out. Led by a short woman in a long leather trench-coat wielding a pistol in both hands, four soldiers followed. Five in total. Only five. All armed, but so few. Even as these newcomers ran to the abandoned car, the helicopter shot back into the sky, circling east until the machine gunner had a clear angle on the trees. It was the second helicopter's turn to come in low, to disgorge its passengers who joined the defensive line around the stalled car. The tank driver changed gears and directions, shifting from a slow reverse to just-as-slow an advance, halting the tank a metre from the car just as the third helicopter unloaded its handful of crew.

It wouldn't be enough. Two of the helicopters, empty of ammo and passengers, turned towards the airport. Hopefully to get more reinforcements. And hopefully they wouldn't need to refuel first. But it still wouldn't be enough.

Olivia, next to him, had stopped firing. "Out," she mouthed.

Pete reached into his pouch, pulling out his one, solitary, spare magazine, and handed it to her. She smiled and reloaded.

No, it wouldn't be enough. The undead still came on. Less numerous than before, but there were still hundreds. And everyone would soon be out of ammo. They'd retreat to the airfield, he supposed. And then...

The sound of the tank's engine changed. Except it wasn't the vehicle on which he was perched. It came from along the road. At top speed, tearing up the highway, raced a pair of tanks. One Canadian Leopard and one American Abrams. And behind came dozens more. Reinforcements had arrived. And perhaps *they* would be enough.

Chapter 29 - The Wages of Courage
Wawa

"You and me both, buddy," Pete said as he and a wearily wary Rufus picked their way through the corpses, over to where Olivia stood by a tank.

"I offered to bandage his leg," Olivia said, indicating the wounded gate-guard. He was sitting on the hood of the battered pink car, talking softly with the woman in the trench coat. "He said there was no point."

"He was bitten?" Pete asked.

"Yep."

"You see the woman in the trench coat speaking to him?" Pete said. "She's General Yoon."

"She is?" Olivia asked.

The general had grey hair cropped close to her head, on which a bald patch formed a neat Y over what had to be a scar.

"And you know the four guys who got out of the helicopter with her?" Pete asked. "Those are her staff officers. One's Canadian Army. One's Air Force. One's French. I think he's a sailor. That guy with the turban, he's Indian. I mean actually in the Indian Army. They were at a conference when this began. Did you know the military had conferences? It's weird, isn't it? Thinking of them in some airport hotel drinking cheap coffee and stale donuts, and talking about weapons and war."

"I bet they get better catering than we did at those carpet trade shows," Olivia said.

Rufus yipped.

"Hey," Corrie said, coming over. "Spare ammo. Here." She handed them a magazine each. "I was speaking to those flight attendants," she continued. "They flew here from Pittsburgh. Tried to land on a road, and ended with their plane partly in a field, partly in a lake, about an hour north. There were more passengers aboard. More kids."

"We should tell the general," Pete said, pointing to where she was still talking to the injured gate-guard.

As they approached, the general patted the injured gate-guard's arm, stepped back, and, in one fluid movement, drew and fired her pistol. The man slumped forward, almost falling before the turbaned officer caught him, and carefully laid him on the ground.

"What…" Pete stammered.

The general turned around, seeing the trio for the first time. "It was at his request," she said. "He was bitten. He would have turned. I gave him the option of waiting. He requested a more peaceful end."

"You…" Pete began again.

"No one is special," the general said, her voice as cold and firm as diamond. "A swift end is the one kindness we must all hope for, and which we expect everyone else to offer. You are the Americans now working for the Australians?"

"Yes, ma'am," Corrie said. "Ma'am, the flight attendants, the passengers in the car, they flew here. Crashed their plane to the north. There were passengers aboard. Children. They're—"

General Yoon cut her off. "Colonel Singh, speak to the refugees, prepare an extraction team." She turned back to Corrie. "You have the orders in writing? From Guam?"

"The colonel has them. At the airfield," Corrie said.

"Then we must fetch them," the general said. "Trowbridge insisted on having the written order. Verbal confirmation wasn't enough for him." She shook her head and turned to her staff. "Major, deploy the drones. Flush the enemy out of the trees and re-secure the road."

Trailing after the general, they walked back up the road. Lacoona was on guard at the airport gate, alone. The colonel and the operator were both still in the tourist-information-military-command-centre, though the colonel appeared to be struggling to keep his eyes open. The general took the written message they had brought from Thunder Bay, and which Jerome MacDonald had brought from Nanaimo.

"This is it?" the general asked.

226

"Yes, ma'am," Corrie said. "Is there a problem?"

The general turned the letter over. "For me, no. Trowbridge might think differently. Or Ms Winters might. She was expecting something more official." The general refolded the paper. "It will do. We will make this work. Come. You will want to witness this."

"Where are we going, ma'am?" Olivia asked.

"I sent a helicopter to Thunder Bay last night," the general said. "We need ferries to evacuate the civilians. For the last three days, we've been dragooning them into the army, or to build and then defend roadside forts. Having reached the end of the easy advance, the refugees must be transported behind the lines where they can be trained or put to work in the fields. The helicopter returned with verbal confirmation of the message, and the information that you were bringing the original by road. You came from Australia? Tell me about it."

They ran through the now familiar summary of what they'd seen and how they'd ended up on the flight to Nanaimo.

"You witnessed our battle from the control room?" the general asked as they approached the edge of the town proper. "Then you saw my tactics? You can tell them that in Australia. You *must* tell them. We face an enemy that will not retreat, that will not surrender, but nor can it attack us at long range. The reports I've received of efforts overseas, the rumours I heard, suggest we are, collectively, being lulled into a complacent defence. This will not bring victory. Nor will retreat. We must lure the enemy to us. Let them get close, and kill them close. Every bullet counts because the factories are behind enemy lines. You must tell Australia I need bullets. I need fuel. I need them to produce food, to secure the Pacific oilfields. I will provide them with refugees, with workers."

"You want to evacuate Canada?" Olivia asked.

"Initially, I wish to evacuate the cities of North and South America," the general said. "Removing the civilians removes the potential for them to be infected."

Which wasn't really an answer, and nor did it explain where they were going. Pete wasn't too bothered, since he'd just realised something else: the general had implied she wanted them to tell people in Australia what

227

they'd seen. *Tell* them. In person. He didn't smile. After the mercy-execution of the gate-guard, he wasn't sure he ever would again, but he did let himself relax a fraction at the thought they might soon be leaving the frontline.

At the beginning of the town of Wawa, a kilometre north of the airport, there were a reassuring number of uniforms, though most of the guards standing on the newly built ramparts didn't look like soldiers. There were too many paunches, too many beards, too much long hair. Too much fear in the eyes of those standing on the uneven walls made of upturned flatbeds, planking, and prefab plasterboard. Outside were coils of razor wire, barbed wire, and sharpened metal poles. It didn't look sturdy. It didn't look secure. Not considering what they'd just witnessed. He shuddered.

"There is no safety in defence," the general said as if reading his mind, angling across the road towards an old garage just outside the walls. "You saw our enemy's numbers? They will not tire. They will not retreat. That is why we must attack. Did you see the mobile fighting platforms?"

"The crane-bases on caterpillar tracks?" Corrie asked. "We saw the camera footage."

"Height offers protection," the general said. "They can't climb. They can't run. And if we attack, they won't be able to mass together. If we break them now, we will be victorious by the year's end. Tell them that in Australia. And tell them I need equipment. I need ammunition. I need Australia to become the factory of the world. And I need proper communications. But first I need Benton. Benton! Delores! Where are you, woman?" The general's voice rose as she picked up her pace, storming into the garage's lot. There were no barriers or barricades here, just a single guard standing in the turret of an armoured car Pete would have called a tank except it had wheels rather than treads, four on either side.

"She's below, ma'am," the sentry said, saluting, before he ducked inside, bellowing. "Your Honour! The general wants you!"

A hatch opened, and a grease-stained face peered out. "Jill?"

"You're wanted, Delores," General Yoon said.

"Trowbridge?" Delores Benton asked.

"Yes," the general said.

"Do I have time to change?" Benton asked, crawling out of the tank. She was covered in grease except the parts covered in oil. "Damn thing should have been in a museum."

"We make history today, Delores. So yes, you must change. Five minutes, see it's no longer."

Benton gave the old APC a swipe with the wrench, then trudged inside.

"She's a judge?" Corrie asked. "Or is she a mechanic?"

"A judge foremost," the general said. "Though we have little use for those now. Restoration was a hobby of hers. We found eight Coyotes, these armoured vehicles, awaiting decommissioning. Through prayer and luck, we got them this far, but spit and sweat won't get them much further. Tell them that, that we are re-commissioning museum pieces."

Pete and Olivia shared a look, still unsure what was going on.

"Ma'am, where exactly are we going? What does that message mean?" Olivia asked.

"The sun rises in Denver," the general said, leading them over to the barricade. A gap between two upturned trucks turned out to be a door, through which they stepped. The general gave a salute to the civilians in uniform. "Carry on." And did the same herself, walking up the road, and into the town. "Yes, the sun rises in Denver, but the question we must ask ourselves is where will it set?"

The reason for the convoy, the ferries, the order not to retreat, all became obvious as they followed the general through the town. Wawa was full. Behind every secured window faces peered at them. Some faces were old. Some were very young. Few were in between. In every doorway a civilian-soldier stood guard. And those guards, too, were either old, young, or injured.

Crude chimneys jutted from holes in the brick and plasterwork, funnelling grey soot skywards. And now he was looking for it, Pete realised there were no electric lights. Of course it was daytime, but there was no sound of electricity either. No fans whirred, no music played, no heaters hummed, no illuminated signs blinked their wares. But there had been power at the airport. Clearly, as in Thunder Bay, electricity was restricted and rationed.

The general led them to a police station. Outside, three flags fluttered gently in the cool breeze: two Canadian maple leafs, and one Stars and Stripes. In front of the doors stood two uniformed officers. Both in the bright red dress jackets of the RCMP, rather than military.

"Lower our flags," General Yoon said.

One of the Mounties ran over to the flagpole while the other opened the door. Inside were more guards, but these weren't police. Two men and two women, dressed in tactical gear with body armour over full combat uniform worn with such ease as to make Pete, in his borrowed uniform, feel like a fraud. They jumped to attention as the general entered.

"At ease," the general said. "You'll want to watch this. Remember this. To tell your fellow nationals. Today we make history, for your country, yes, but also for the entire continent. The entire world."

The soldiers grinned, though they said nothing, while the general walked further into the bullpen. Those four soldiers weren't the only people present. A larger group had taken over a trio of desks in the middle of the bullpen, while near the back, a woman sat in front of a closed door. Wearing tan-coloured hiking gear, thick black boots, and a red scarf tied around her neck, she jumped up as the general approached, and knocked on the door.

It opened. Another woman came out, closing the door behind her. She was the strangest-looking person Pete had seen in days, but simply because she was dressed normally. Or what had been normal before the outbreak, in a pantsuit and heels, but also with a red scarf around her neck.

"General. Was your action a success?" the suited woman asked.

"Ms Winters, we have taken the first steps on the road to victory. It's time you walked a few of those steps yourself. Here." General Yoon held out the message that had been flown in to Thunder Bay. "This is the official confirmation, signed by the admiral in charge of the Pacific fleet, countersigned by your ambassador to Beijing and the governors of Guam and Hawaii."

Winters took the piece of paper, but only gave it the briefest of indifferent glances. "It is important things are done correctly," she said.

"Agreed," Yoon said, matching her frosty tone icicle-for-icicle. "The judge is on her way."

Winters's eyes roamed across Pete, Corrie, and Olivia, before settling on Rufus. "Canadian soldiers are allowed pets?" she asked.

"He's trained for sniffing out terrorists hiding in caves," General Yoon said instantly. "It makes him an expert at finding undesirables." The general pointed at the door. "Is he ready?"

"Hoyle, get Trowbridge," Winters said.

The woman who'd been sitting guard outside the office door nodded, and entered the office.

Pete slotted the pieces together. A judge. A police station. Soldiers standing guard. Presumably all for a trial with one obvious ending. What was the name they'd mentioned? Trowbridge? He didn't recognise it. Nor did he recognise the face, either, when the man emerged from the office.

Short. Balding. Overweight. Over fifty. Badly shaved, with his face a mixture of nicks and missed bristles. Wearing a tie that was askew and too loose. Sweating, despite the cold. Blinking in the dim lamplight. Scared, yes, but he didn't look like a prisoner. His hands were clasped together, gripping one another tightly as if he had nothing left to cling to but himself. But, oddly, Yoon snapped to attention, saluting as he approached.

"Mr Trowbridge, sir," Yoon said. "Confirmation has been received from your Pacific fleet. The sun rises in Denver. You are the senior surviving member of the cabinet, and the most senior survivor in the line of succession. Sir, you *are* the President of the United States."

Trowbridge blinked. Winters sighed. But it was Olivia who spoke. "You mean President Grant Maxwell is dead?" she asked.

Winters raised an eyebrow, while Hoyle smirked. But before anyone could reply, Judge Benton entered, in clean robes, but still smelling of oil.

"Let's get this done, shall we?" Yoon said. "In the open air, perhaps."

"Is that safe?" Trowbridge asked, his voice quavering.

"Yes, sir," Yoon said. "I guarantee it."

"Do you recognise him?" Pete whispered as they trailed outside, very much the last and least important of the group.

"I know the name," Olivia hissed back. "He was secretary for housing. Don't you remember him? Ten years ago, he was in Congress. He switched parties after he lost his seat, ran for governor, and lost. But then he set up that charity, housing former gang members."

Despite the judge's best efforts to inject some solemnity into the proceedings, the ceremony was brief and perfunctory.

After it was over, Yoon turned to Trowbridge. "Mr President, I have three helicopters on the ground, ready to take you west. From Vancouver, you can be taken to Guam, from where you can co-ordinate your nation's part in the war effort."

"No," Winters said, not bothering to even look at Trowbridge, let alone consult him.

"You mean to stay here?" Yoon asked, also ignoring the newly sworn-in president. "I cannot guarantee his safety."

"His safety is not your concern," Winters said. "Considering what befell the vice president, we will drive rather than fly."

"Drive to Vancouver? That would be considerably slower, considerably more dangerous," Yoon said.

"There are other contingencies in place," Winters said.

"Such as?" Yoon asked.

"I'm so sorry, General," Winters said, "but you don't have clearance."

Yoon clearly didn't care. "As you wish. Mr President." She saluted, and stormed off.

Winters smiled, and went back inside. Her deputy, the woman called Hoyle, took the newly-sworn-in president's arm and led him after her. The mixed group of soldiers followed. Pete watched them go, thinking maybe his earlier assumption wasn't entirely wrong; Trowbridge looked more like a prisoner than a leader.

"That was something for the memoirs," Judge Benton said cheerily. "Nice dog. A Great Dane, yes? I had one like him when I was much younger."

"He's really the president?" Pete asked.

"He is," Judge Benton said. "The last time we worried about an invasion of Canada, it was by your people. More recently there were concerns about a Soviet invasion of your country. And it was from that time, that code, the sun rises in Denver, comes. The assumption was of an invasion from the south, and another in Alaska, but it was also assumed that Washington would be attacked."

"With nuclear bombs?" Olivia asked.

"No, these plans come from a time before then. In the event of an invasion that cannot be immediately repulsed, and where our allies have been neutralised, a joint command shall be established in the North American continent. Civilians, where possible, shall be evacuated from the combat zone, thus reducing the number of hostages and slave workers. Slaves? Yes, these were very old plans, but they were correct in one thing. They assumed the crisis would begin in the United States. In Washington, rather than New York, but it makes little difference. The nuclear arms race brought very different concerns, and so these older plans were shelved, and became nothing more than training exercises at the war college, or so Jill tells me. General Yoon," she clarified.

As interested as Pete was in how judge and general had become friends, he was more interested in something else the general had said. "The vice president is dead?"

"Yes," Judge Benton said. "The U.S. chain of succession has been broken. There is no way of knowing who has survived, or which official has seniority. One day there might be a challenge to Trowbridge, but on that day, I shall rejoice, for it will mean that we've drawn back from the brink."

"And you're really a judge?" Olivia asked. "And a mechanic?"

"I find engines relaxing," Benton said. "After spending my days sitting in judgement over the most depraved examples of our species, I find cogs and gears gratifyingly explicable. You came from Guam, how is it?"

"Not from Guam, from Australia," Corrie said, and ran through the well-practiced story. "And here, what is it like?"

"Pandemonium," Benton said. "Have you read Milton? Looking about me, I wish I had not."

"The general is building an army?" Corrie asked.

"Yes, but slowly," Benton said. "She has gathered all military units that made it north of the border. It is a small force, as of yet. More units are being created from among the refugees. Mobile castles are being created from construction equipment. Fields are being formed on land that was once ancient woodland. Our world is changing, and we must change, too, because in that lies our salvation. Speaking of changing, I must get out of these robes and back to my engines."

Chapter 30 - Presidents and Prisoners
Wawa

"We just met the president," Olivia said.

"*A* president," Pete said. "But I don't know why we were there."

"General Yoon was making a point, but I'm not sure to whom," Corrie said. "Guam, I suppose. Or Australia. If I had to put money on it, she doesn't think we need politicians right now."

"I agree with her," Olivia said.

"How do you think the Veep died?" Pete asked. "That woman, Winters, said it was the reason why they wanted to fly."

"It's something to ask the judge," Olivia said. "She seemed chatty, anyway. But the V.P. is dead. And we have a new president. Or America does. Which brings me to the more pressing question of what the three of us do now."

Rufus yipped.

"The four of us," Olivia said.

"We find food, a shower, a bed, some clean clothes, and not necessarily in that order," Corrie said. "And I'd like to get some more information on this Trowbridge guy and the people with him. If we're supposed to report what we saw to Canberra or Guam, I'd like more facts and less opinion."

"*That's* what we should do," Olivia said. "We'll become journalists. No, think about it, no one else is doing it. And the general actually wants us to. The woman in charge of this part of Canada actually wants *us* to tell people what we saw, right? Besides, there should be a record of moments like the general's victory and the swearing in of a new president."

"What about the execution of the infected?" Pete asked. "Because that's something we should be talking about."

"Yes, that too," Olivia said. "Maybe especially that. Clearly, General Yoon had done it before. Would people want to discuss it? Would they even want to think about it? Maybe not now. Not yet. But it shouldn't be hidden or forgotten. Somehow, we're at the centre of events, and with access to the high command in the Pacific and North America. We have a duty to record everything, and one day, report it."

"I'll vote for that," Corrie said. "We'll set up a news agency. Pete?"

"I dunno. I thought we could head back to Vancouver, and then Australia. I kinda like the idea of getting out of here." He looked down at Rufus. "Two to one. It's down to you, Rufus. Rufus? Who's a good boy? Come here, boy!" He knelt as he spoke.

Rufus took one look at his beckoning hand, and padded over to Olivia. She laughed.

Pete sighed. "Serves me right, I guess. Three to one. Journalists it is. We'll need cameras, right? I'll see if they have any more bodycams at that police station. Maybe see if I can speak to Trowbridge."

"I'll head up to the airport and borrow a laptop for storage," Corrie said. "And maybe even a drone."

"I'll see if I can find us some more food and ammo," Olivia said. "Whatever happens, I've got a feeling we're going to need it. Meet back here in an hour?"

Pete strolled back towards the police station. Rufus, for reasons of his own, ambled along at his side.

"Do you think this is a good idea?" Pete asked the dog. "On the one hand, I like the idea of taking back a little control of my life. Battles like we fought outside the airport could happen anywhere, anytime. The zombies won't stop if we stick a camera in their faces. We'll be on the frontline, so we'll be soldiers carrying cameras as well as weapons. So are we really in control of our future, or are we just kidding ourselves?"

Rufus yipped.

"Yep. That's what I thought."

The two Mounties were no longer outside the police station, though the U.S. flag still flew above. Inside, the booking hall was deserted, as was the bullpen behind. The office where Trowbridge had lurked, and which Hoyle had guarded, was open and empty.

Uncertain where to go, Pete tried a door behind the booking desk. With no power to the police station, the keypads were inoperative, and the electro-magnetic locks had disconnected. An old-fashioned bolt held the doors closed, but the key remained in the lock.

"What happened to the prisoners?" Pete murmured, his voice low.

He turned onto an empty corridor, uncertain where he was going, and feeling increasingly like a trespasser. The police station wasn't large, but nor was it signposted. If you were authorised to be there, you were expected to know your way around. He took a random turn, then another. The third brought him to a barred holding cell. There was a key in the lock, but a trio of close-wrapped chains and padlocks seemed to be doing the lion's share of securing the door. None of those had a key in the lock. Inside the cell, a figure lay on a bench with her face to the wall and her back to him.

Pete backed up a step, not wanting to disturb her, but Rufus had other ideas. He bounded to the cage, raised a paw, and pushed at the lowest of the chains. The coiled metal clinked. The woman stirred, rolled over, and swung herself up.

"Ah," Lisa Kempton said. "Do I have visitors?" An eyebrow arched in puzzlement that was only a fraction of the stunned disbelief Pete felt. "Mr Guinn?" she said softly. "Of all the people in the world, I can say you are not whom I expected." She walked over to the bars, looking up and down the corridor to confirm they were alone. "And you have a friend, I see. Wonderful. We should all be so fortunate."

"Ms Kempton?" Pete said. "Why are you here?"

"Shouldn't I be the one asking you that question?" she replied.

"We flew here," Pete said. "Well, to Vancouver. We're gathering information on what things are like in America. For the Australian government."

"You and your sister?" she asked.

"Yes."

"Good. And you gave her the message? She completed the task?" Kempton asked.

"What? Oh. Yeah, sure," Pete said. He'd nearly forgotten that he'd been despatched to Australia to give his sister a phone. On the call, his sister had been given instructions to activate some code. He was still a little hazy about why, except it was connected to the collapse of satellite communications and aimed at preventing a pre-emptive nuclear war. "But you knew she activated the code, right?" he said. "And that code, it was just a con, a distraction?"

"Things have become a little complicated, as you can see," Kempton said, tapping the bars. She bent down. "And what is your name?" she asked.

"Rufus," Pete said, after he remembered the dog was unlikely to answer for himself.

"Everyone needs a friend, don't they, Rufus? And it is good to see you again, Mr Guinn. However, I would suggest you leave before anyone finds you down here."

"What are *you* doing down here?" he asked. "And locked up?"

"Reaping what I sowed," Kempton asked. "It is a small comfort to know that Corrie is safe. And yourself, of course. A larger comfort comes from knowing Tamika is far, far away. What can you tell me about my pilots, Jackson and Rampton?"

"Sorry, they're dead. Tortured. Murdered. I think Jackson was a spy for the cartel, but they were both murdered."

"I see. Thank you. Now, please go, before you land yourself in further trouble."

"But how come you're here? Is Trowbridge holding you prisoner?" he asked.

Before Kempton could answer, the door opened and the woman who'd been guarding Trowbridge's door, Hoyle, entered. Now she wore body armour and carried a shotgun.

"What are you doing here?" Hoyle demanded.

"Looking for bodycams," Pete said quickly. "For General Yoon. Why's she locked up?"

Hoyle shook her head. "Get outta here," she growled, half raising the shotgun.

"Yeah, I was going anyway," Pete muttered. He threw Kempton a glance, but said nothing, and nor did she. Pete made his way outside, Rufus at his heels.

"Lisa Kempton," he finally said, when he stood close to the lonely flag fluttering from the pole. "Okay, Rufus, any ideas why she's being held prisoner? No, me neither. I think we better go find Olivia and Corrie."

Chapter 31 - Determining a Just Cause
Lake Wawa

"Are you sure it was Lisa Kempton?" Corrie asked. A cold wind whipped across the lake, snatching away their muted conversation. Having found them both, Pete had looked for somewhere secluded to talk, opting for an empty beach overlooking the lake.

"I spoke to her," Pete said. "So yeah, I'm sure."

"Why were they holding her prisoner?" Olivia asked. "Or, seeing as the *they* in question is the President of the United States, maybe we shouldn't be asking *any* questions."

"He's not *my* president," Pete said.

"And he's certainly not mine," Corrie said. "But the general recognises Trowbridge as president, and she's probably the biggest authority that exists in Canada. Maybe she's the most powerful authority this side of Guam."

"And there's the CIA," Olivia added. "We spoke to some of the Canadian sentries, and boy did they want to speak back. Winters freaks them out. They say she's CIA. Hoyle is, too. Or NSA, or something like that. They arrived with the prisoner, though the Canadians didn't know who she was. Those four soldiers who were just inside the door, the four who actually looked like they *were* soldiers, they're U.S. Marines the general assigned as a presidential protection detail. Everyone else is CIA."

"Tell me about the cell," Corrie said.

"What? Oh, it's just a police cell," Pete said.

"Spoken worryingly like someone familiar with them," Olivia said.

"I mean it's a holding cell, with open bars," Pete said. "The electricity to the station has been cut so the electric locks don't work. This cell, it was held closed with a trio of chains and padlocks."

"Huh. And there was no guard?" Corrie asked.

"Not really, but that woman who was guarding Trowbridge, she found me talking to Kempton and threw me out."

"Did she ask what you were doing?" Corrie asked.

"I said I was looking for bodycams," Pete said.

"But she wasn't actually guarding Kempton?" Corrie asked.

"Why does it matter?" Olivia asked.

"I'm just building up a picture," Corrie said. She breathed out. "Okay. You two should go speak to the judge. She seemed approachable. See if she knows why Kempton is being held prisoner, or where she was captured, and why. Don't say that we know her. We're journalists now. Tell her that's why you're asking."

"What are you going to do?" Pete asked.

"If I can, without being caught, I'm going to speak to Kempton," Corrie said. "If I can't..." She shook her head. "Meet back here in an hour."

"I thought we were leaving the past behind when we left Australia," Pete said, as he and Olivia walked through the town. The faces were gone from the windows, though the sentries were still present at the doors, and it still had the air of a town ready to burst.

"Presidents, billionaires, the CIA? It makes you glad when it's just zombies to be dealt with," Olivia said.

When they reached the judge's garage, they found a dozen tanks there, all newly returned from the battlefield, and the judge too busy to talk. Soon, so were they: holding, bracing, carrying during a frantically frenetic hour that ended with ten tanks back on the road and two stripped for parts. When the war machines were thundering towards the new frontline, they looked again for the judge, only to find she'd gone to shower and sleep, and so they returned to the beach.

They weren't the only people there. The soldiers, returning from their victory in the forest, had descended on the beach. Sunset wasn't far off, and the temperature was still closer to winter than spring, let alone summer, but some soldiers were swimming. A few more splashed in the shallows, bathing, or washing their gear. Someone, from somewhere, had found a bright yellow inflatable dinghy. Though anchored to the shore by a long length of rope, the craft now bobbed on the evening tide. Two people were aboard, fishing. In the trees, birds cawed, but wisely stayed away from the fires. Around those, people sat, watching, thinking, remembering, except around the largest blaze, where they were talking to Corrie. They were taking it in turns, addressing the phone on which she was recording.

Quietly, Olivia and Pete approached, and found they weren't listening to a soldier's account of today's battle, but his recollection of the day he'd returned home after the outbreak. Having been trapped at work, a government office in Ottawa he cleaned, he'd finally returned home only to find his family gone. He'd been looking for them ever since.

Rufus padded over to the fire, and provided a distraction long enough for Corrie to slip away.

"Everyone's keen to talk anyway," Corrie said, tagging the clip she'd just recorded before slipping the phone into her pocket.

"Where'd you get the phone?" Olivia asked.

"Oh, one of the tank drivers is collecting them," Corrie said. "He's putting together a database of every song ever made with a plan of launching a streaming service just as soon as normality is restored. I got ten phones from him, and a promise he'll store all the clips I record if I promise to use his music service on our radio station."

"What radio station?" Olivia asked.

"I might have implied we're going to launch one," Corrie said. "Just as soon as things settle down."

"You're telling me there are people who still think it will?" Olivia asked. "I'm not saying I don't like the idea. I think... yeah, I could see myself as a D.J."

"I don't know if it ever will settle down," Corrie said. "But it might settle into a new normal. Did you see the judge?"

"Saw her, yes," Olivia said. "Spoke to her, no. She was too busy repairing the returning tanks. What about you did— Wait, is that still recording?"

Corrie checked the phone. "No. And no, I didn't see Kempton. She was gone. They all were."

"You mean Trowbridge and Winters?" Olivia asked.

"Yep," Corrie said. "I looked in the cell to see if Kempton had left a note for us, but no."

"Huh. That's a shame," Pete said.

"You looked *inside* the cell?" Olivia asked. "Do you mean you picked the locks?"

Corrie shrugged. "I blew the cylinders in the lock-barrel. It's quicker than picking a lock."

"If she'd been there, were you going to break her out?" Olivia asked.

Corrie pressed the phone's power key again, triple-checking it was no longer recording before answering. "Yes. Winters, and Trowbridge and Kempton, are driving to Vancouver Island where a plane will transport them to Guam. Maybe that'll be Liu's jet, or maybe that'll be waiting on the runway, in which case they are bound to ask how Kempton's private jet is now part of our fleet. Even if they don't see the plane, in Guam they'll ask about comms and transport links, and they'll learn about Liu and the plane, and about us. They'll want to ask us questions. Canberra won't refuse. Nor will the general, or whoever's running Canada. At which point, we'll be in as much trouble as Kempton."

"Ah," Pete said. "Oh." His shoulders slumped. "So... I mean..." He gave up.

"So if she escaped, we'd be safe," Olivia asked. "And by we, I really mean Pete."

"Partly," Corrie said. "But it's also the cartel. Tess Qwong will deal with the gangsters we left behind in Broken Hill, but they never had much of an operation down in Australia. Here, it was different. They're a group that revels in chaos. Forget Trowbridge. Forget that it's pretty damn obvious the new U.S. government is going to be run by Winters and the CIA. The cartel has an entire continent as their playground. Kempton knows who they are, *where* they are. She could have slowed them down. I wonder if that's what she was doing when they caught her."

"Where *did* they catch her?" Pete asked. "And how did Trowbridge end up in Canada?"

243

"I don't know why," Corrie said. "But I can guess where. Kempton was building a radio telescope a few hundred kilometres north of here."

"The ten billion dollar telescope?" Olivia asked. "That's here?"

"You've heard of it?" Pete asked.

"I'd heard of it even before she bought the carpet store," Olivia said. "It was all over the news."

"The ten billion price tag included the cost of some new satellites, which is why I paid attention," Corrie said. "Or as much attention as could be paid out in the bush."

"You mean it wasn't actually a telescope?" Pete asked. "It had something to do with that code, and stopping a nuclear war?"

"I don't think construction had begun," Corrie said. "But maybe Kempton had people there she thought she could trust. Since she got caught, it hardly matters now."

"You should have told us," Pete said.

"About the telescope?" Corrie asked.

"I mean that you were going to try to break her out of jail," Pete said.

"So you could help, or so you could stop me?" Corrie asked.

"I… yeah, I don't know," Pete said.

"The CIA won't want cartel thugs running loose over America any more than we do," Olivia said. "And they're better placed to do something about it than Kempton. In the long run, I think this has worked out for the best."

"Leaving us to do what?" Pete asked.

Corrie fished out a pair of phones. "Leaving us to let other people talk, and in return, get a fish supper."

Chapter 32 - Unhappy Endings
Wawa

"I was looking for you lot last night," Judge Benton said, wiping her grease-stained hands on an equally greasy rag. "I had three bunks and a nice basket waiting." She pointed towards the dark office at the back of the workshop.

"Sorry," Olivia said. "We got talking to some tank drivers up by the lake about the battle. When it got dark, we stuck with them, and did a stint on guard duty to the north. Do you know where we can find Corporal Lacoona?"

"*Sergeant* Lacoona," the judge said. "And she left, about an hour before dawn."

"She's already gone?" Pete asked.

"Back to Marathon with the next batch of refugees for the ferry," the judge said. "You've missed your ride. And let me save you the trouble of asking if I have a vehicle to spare, because every last one is playing ambulance. All being well, they, and the other vehicles down in Marathon, will return here tomorrow. Until then, if you want to get back to Australia, it'll be on foot."

"Actually, we had a different idea," Corrie said. "We wanted Corporal, I mean *Sergeant* Lacoona, to take a message back to Thunder Bay for us, to be sent on to Canberra, but we didn't want to go with her. We *would* like some paint if you can spare it."

"Paint? Help yourself to any you can find," Benton said, waving at the shelves. "What for?"

"I'll show you," Corrie said. She crossed to the shelves bracketed to the wall, quickly scanning them until she found a small jar of white primer and a rag to use as a brush. "Perfect. Pete, you first."

A minute later, she'd painted a word on the front and back of his body armour.

"Press?" Benton asked. "You've appointed yourselves as journalists?"

"It's shorter than camera crew," Olivia said. "And aren't we all self-appointed now?"

"Not all of us," Judge Benton said. "I was very *definitely* appointed. I remember the ceremony quite clearly."

"Fair dinkum," Corrie said. "But you've acquired the status of Canada's, maybe the world's, most senior judge because there's no one else. There don't seem to be any other journalists. Not here, or in Thunder Bay, or Nanaimo, South Bend, or even Broken Hill. Nowhere we've travelled."

"There's no news outlets, either," the judge said. "Not unless you count a few remote radio stations broadcasting conspiracy theories and warnings to stay away. Of course, if they really wanted people to stay away, they'd stop broadcasting. How do you intend to disseminate the news you're creating?"

"We haven't figured that out yet," Olivia said. "But there should be a record of all of this. Trowbridge, the general, the battle, the war, you, us. All of this is history, and I want there to be a future, a time when we look back at this past and are thankful it's no longer the present."

"Now that's a notion I can get my head around and my shoulder behind," the judge said. "I'll officially authorise you, for all that's worth. I take it that means you want to come with us today, rather than wait for the next convoy back to Marathon?"

"Go with you where?" Olivia asked.

"To continue the war," the judge said.

Half an hour later, they were ready to leave. Corrie had been recruited as the judge's driver, with Pete and Olivia following behind. With only a single APC at their backs, they were travelling aboard two tow trucks at the very rear of the convoy. Far ahead were the tanks and construction equipment turned into mobile fighting platforms. And far, far ahead were the helicopters, scouting for the next battlefield.

Due to the sheer size of the advancing column, different vehicles had been given different routes and waypoints. Theirs, and the judge's, were

North Bay, and then Whitney, some eight hundred kilometres east-southeast. But everyone's final destination was similarly vague. They were aiming for the Saint Lawrence. Where, precisely, and whether it was closer to Quebec or Toronto, depended as much on the undead as the living. Ultimately, the river would become a defensive line. The cities would be evacuated, while the towns would be fortified, the civilians enlisted and prepared for an assault south to liberate the United States.

"This isn't bad," Pete said.

"A drive through Canada? I can think of worse ways to spend the day." Olivia grinned. "Am I being super-naive, or does it really seem like the worst is over?"

"The war's only just begun, hasn't it?" Pete said.

"It's not really a war, though," Olivia said. "I mean, yes, there'll be fighting and danger, but it's mostly logistics." She pulled out a road map, turning to the back, which had a miniature map of Canada. "Secure Quebec, Montreal, Ottawa, Toronto, then Detroit. Then we sweep across Michigan and Indiana, curving back up towards the border."

"The *old* border," Pete said. "You notice how that's what the judge called it."

"Hey, if she wants to call this an invasion, I'm fine with that," Olivia said. "We can worry about a Canadian land-grab after we've dealt with the zombies. I suppose we'll be heading back through South Bend."

"Are you okay with that?" Pete asked.

"It doesn't really matter if I'm not," Olivia said. "But I'm travelling with an army this time. I wish the plans were a bit more developed after we reach Indiana. I suppose they can't be until they know how many troops can be gathered in Nova Scotia and British Columbia, and whether those planes can be salvaged."

"That's something good that came out of yesterday," Pete said. "Those flight attendants telling us about all those hundreds of planes in Atlanta."

"There'll be other airports like that," Olivia said. "And if we can get the planes, and secure the runways, we can fly the troops in from British Columbia. From the Pacific. From Australia. That's what I mean, it feels like we're at a turning point."

"Yeah, but we're not actually taking back the cities," Pete said. "We're just trying to get the civilians out. Did you notice that? And did you notice the plan is to take control of the Great Plains? There's no plan for retaking the East Coast, or California, Texas, or most of the South."

"Because it's not a plan to save America," Olivia said. "Secure the farmland, secure the people, and then send them overseas. The general isn't just talking about survival, she's trying to save the entire world."

"And that's why you're optimistic? This army is big, sure, but it's not big enough to take one city, let alone an entire continent."

"Most of a continent," Olivia said. "And only by area, but it won't just be the general. It'll be everywhere else. I know the U.S. is a mess. But even if Winters and the CIA are now in charge, that's better than chaos. There'll be other people like the general, all over the world. Like in Australia, right? And the Pacific. We're not doing this alone. That's why I'm... no, I won't say optimistic. Not exactly. Everything has been so bleak over the last few weeks. Each day, things got worse. But I think, now, they're going to get better."

It was nearing midday when the tow truck in front abruptly swerved, and just as abruptly braked.

Olivia jumped out before Pete had stopped. A second later, rifle in hand, he was following her over to the truck. The door opened, and Rufus jumped down, angrily shaking his coat as he turned a quick circle.

"It's fine," Corrie said waving her hands as, behind them, the soldiers in the APC also jumped down. "Just a flat."

The tow truck's front right tyre had blown.

"I should have thought of this," the judge said, eyeing the three spares balanced in the back, secured to the truck's tow cable. "I planned for us having to repair the military vehicles, not each other."

"The tyres won't fit?" Pete asked.

"Far too large," the judge said. "Same as the tyres you've got. The spares for the civilian vehicles are on the flatbed up ahead."

They all turned to stare at the empty road.

"We could tow one truck with the other?" Pete said.

"Which would defeat the point of having the tow trucks in the first place," the judge said. "And we can't afford to leave one of these behind. It's not just the tyres. I've got the actuators aboard. We'll have to go ahead, get a spare, and come back. Pile in, then," she added, making for the second tow truck. "Wait, no, that won't work. If we've got to tow someone else, further ahead, we can't leave their passengers by the roadside, and there's no space in the APC. I should have considered this."

"But people would be safe in a vehicle," Olivia said. "We can wait here. It's only for a few hours, and it seems quiet enough. If we have to, we'll hide inside."

"Fine, yes, good," the judge said. "I'm sorry about this. But I'll be back soon. Or someone will. Before nightfall. Almost certainly. But… ah… yes. Sergeant, do you have the spare machine gun? And the ammunition? In case we're not back before dark."

Pete took the machine gun uncertainly, but before he could ask how to operate it, the judge had boarded the APC. The soldiers climbed aboard, and before Pete could properly frame the question, they'd driven off.

"Nightfall," he said, glancing up at the sky. Clouds were slowly gathering, but it didn't feel like rain. Not yet. "At least there are no zombies," he said. "Why do you think he gave us this machine gun?"

"In case more zombies follow the sound of the engines to the road, and so are now behind us," Corrie said.

"*More* zombies?" Pete asked. "I didn't see any."

"You didn't see the corpses by the roadside?" Corrie asked. "Must have been killed by people further ahead in the column."

"Oh," Pete said. "Right." He carried the machine gun over to the tow truck. "I think I might wait inside the cab. What do you say, Rufus?"

But the dog was staring at the trees.

"What is it, Rufus?" Olivia asked. She sniffed. "Is that smoke?"

"Wood smoke? From a campfire?" Corrie asked.

"Maybe from a cooking fire," Olivia said. "What do you say, Pete?"

"You mean do I think we should walk randomly through this forest? Yeah, no."

"There's a track up there," Olivia said. "A logging track, I suppose."

"It's just wood smoke," Corrie said, walking back to the tow truck. She leaned up, peering at the gear inside. "So, either it's a campfire, or it's a forest fire. Yep, thought I saw one." She jumped back down, but now holding a fire extinguisher.

"I don't think that'd put out a forest fire," Pete said.

"Nope," Corrie said. "But if that's what's burning, the extinguisher will help us get back to the road. We'd need to get out of here, on foot, and the firebreak is about five kilometres back that way. But I don't think it *is* a forest fire. I think it's a cook-fire. Rufus?"

Rufus fell into step next to Corrie as she walked towards the overgrown track.

Pete sighed.

"Oh, don't be so glum," Olivia said. "Think of this as a news story."

"A forest fire?" Pete asked.

"No, a city guy fighting a forest fire with a fire extinguisher. I bet that would make some of the Canadians smile."

"You're not helping, Livy," he said.

From the frost-coated tyre marks and snapped low branches, someone had recently driven down the track, though it was in such bad repair, it couldn't have had much traffic since the summer. When Pete saw the rickety cabin, he revised his opinion. Few people had been this way since the turn of the millennium.

The house itself, a compact two-storey chalet, would have been at home in any suburb, and looked out of place here in the woods. For fifty metres around the house, the ground had been partially cleared, and long ago. Trees had been felled, though their stumps remained, and around them, grass had been left to grow. In the very recent past, someone had inexpertly hacked furrows in the frozen soil. The pick they'd used had been left discarded in the dirt. The smoke tumbling from the tall metal chimney bolted to the side of the house said the wannabe-farmer hadn't fled far.

"Hiya? Anyone home?" Olivia called. No reply came. The smoke trail came from a thin metal chimney bolted to the side of the house, emerging from the wall in the upper floor.

"We best ring the bell," Pete said.

"I'll keep watch," Corrie said. "Something's spooked Rufus."

"I always wanted a garden like this," Olivia said as they walked over to the small house.

"You mean full of tree stumps?" Pete said.

"Like how this place will be after another month of work," Olivia said. "I never understood the point of lawns. I wanted a garden for growing food."

"Maybe somewhere not as remote as this," Pete said. "I want people around me. Now more than ever."

"Me, too," Olivia said. "So somewhere like this, but in town? I like how you described Broken Hill, but Thunder Bay wouldn't be too bad. Definitely not South Bend."

"Nope. Not South Bend," Pete agreed. "The door's blocked. And the windows are all covered."

"There must be a way in, though," Olivia said. Slowly, they walked the house's perimeter, keeping close to the wall as they tried to peer through the covered windows. Beneath their feet, the ground was made uneven by the discarded dirt from the shallow trenches dug for vegetable plots.

Pondering where the seeds would come from, and so whether the work was a wasted effort, Pete barely noticed that the footing beneath his feet had changed. He checked the nearest window, but like the others, it was sealed. Wood had been nailed to the outside, but through the gaps he could see more wood piled inside. Furniture, he supposed, haphazardly stacked to offer equally haphazard protection.

"Yeah, I'm changing my mind," Pete said, rapping the wall with his fist. He turned around. "I know why I first liked this place. I think I know why you did, too. It's because—"

Even as he spoke, the ground gave way. Pete fell through the thin glass skylight, which had been covered in a loose layer of soil above rusting chicken wire and rotting planks. But his fall was short, and broken by something soft.

"I'm okay!" he called, but a second too soon.

The object that had cushioned his impact began to squirm. Roll. Turn. Twist. Reaching out with its undead hands to claw at his webbing, his coat, his legs.

"Zombies!" he yelled, trying to roll his way free, lashing out blindly in the near darkness. Fragments of glass from the broken skylight bit into his flesh as he found his way to his knees. More slashed against his wrist. No, not glass. Fingernails belonging to a five-foot-tall, undead girl in stained dungarees.

Pete pulled his hand back and the zombie came with it, bucking her head forward to bite his forearm. He slammed his palm into her forehead. A jolt of pain shot up his arm, but he loosened the girl's grip. Another blow, and he loosened her bite, freeing his arm. He pushed her away, and reached for his belt.

His vision was clearing and so was the air. The dust and dirt disturbed during the fall was settling, allowing the forest-filtered light to illuminate the dank subterranean chamber. And the first thing he saw was Olivia, down in the basement, only two metres away, stabbing her bayonet into a zombie's eye.

"The rack, Pete!" she yelled. "Pete, can you hear me, the rack! Move to the rack!"

His brain cleared slower than his vision as Olivia grabbed a broken shovel, swinging the rusting and bent blade into a head already matted with blood and dirt.

There was more than one zombie in the cellar. More than three. More than he could quickly count when all he could see were blood-stained hands clawing and reaching for them.

"Pete!" Olivia yelled again, and he realised she'd been yelling for some time. Long enough for Rufus to hear. The dog leaped down through the broken hole, snarling and snapping at the zombies. The undead child dived at Rufus, clawing at his coat before the dog curled, rolled, and bounded across the room, barrelling into an old woman in an equally old leather apron.

Before Pete saw the dog get free, hands clawed at his back. He spun, raising his empty fists. Inches away, sagging jowls flapped as the undead mouth snapped. Dentures clicked as they rattled against the rotting gums. Instinctively, he punched his open palm into the jaw, wincing at the pain while the dentures flew out, pinwheeling across the room. He kicked, a wild stomp that slammed into the zombie's leg. The bones of the old man had been brittle before he'd been infected, and cracked louder than a bullet as the zombie fell.

No, it *was* a bullet. Corrie had fired from the hole down which he and Olivia had fallen.

"The rack!" Olivia called again, running to the row of metal shelves leaning against the wall. Pete grabbed the other end.

"No," Olivia said, pushing him back against the wall. "Stay there. Corrie, can you get them?"

"No worries," Corrie said, and fired a shot.

"Aren't we getting out of here?" Pete asked, his words a plaintive yell.

"The chains, Pete," Olivia said, matter of fact and calm. "Don't you see them? They're chained. The zombies are all chained. We're safe here. I dropped my gun. And my knife. And that shovel."

Corrie fired as Pete reached for his belt, and drew his sidearm. He didn't bother attaching the suppressor. As he raised his hand, his wrist sent a painful protest echoed by his back, his leg, all of which served to clear his mind as he aimed at the old woman in the leather apron. He fired, again and again until the zombie collapsed. He shifted aim to the teenager in the dungarees. He hesitated. Corrie didn't. She fired. The zombie died.

"Are you clear?" Corrie called.

"No movement," Olivia said. "Yeah, they're all dead." She picked her way over the corpses and retrieved her rifle, though she left the bayonet where it was embedded in the fallen zombie's eye.

"Hold on," Corrie called. "I think there's a rope in the truck."

"We'll try the stairs," Olivia called back. "Are you okay, Pete?"

"Shaken, that's all," he said, trying to ignore the growing ache in his wrist.

The stairs were in the cellar's far corner, steep, old, and hugging the wall, leading to a hatch that was closed but ominously unlocked.

Slowly, with Olivia aiming her rifle upwards, Pete pushed the hatch open, but there was no one there. No one alive, nor undead.

The man, no older than Pete, was slumped in a chair, a gun on the floor, a bullet in his head.

"Why?" Pete muttered. "Why chain up the people?"

"He thought he was special," Olivia said. "Look at his wrist. He was bitten. He realised he wasn't. Realised he'd turn into the same thing as his family. This must have been their cabin in the woods. Their family retreat. Their vacation home. And this is where they came. Like I did, I suppose. Running from the horror, but you can't, can you? You can't escape something like this by running. He didn't learn it, though. He chained them up. Downstairs. And then he was bitten. He killed himself, but he should have killed them first. He thought he was special, and then he gave up."

"Olivia," Pete said slowly, holding out his bleeding wrist. "I was bitten."

"Me, too," she said.

Chapter 33 - Last Dates
Highway 144

"Hold still while I clean the wound," Corrie said.

"It doesn't matter," Pete said.

"Shut up, it might," Corrie said.

"It won't," Pete said, but let his sister tie a bandage around his arm.

"No one's special," Olivia said.

"No," Corrie said. "Before you say any more, no. No way."

"You have to," Olivia said.

"We stopped a nuclear war," Corrie said. "We survived the outbreak. We escaped the outback. We escaped from the cartel. After all these years apart, I got to see my brother again, and then we found a way to get to the middle of a different continent to rescue the girl he loves. You can't die like this."

"I think Rufus is hurt," Olivia whispered. "Can you take a look?"

She sat next to Pete, on the edge of the tow truck, where they'd retreated after leaving the cabin. "Want to go back and burn the place down?" she asked.

"Nope," Pete said. "Not really."

"Yeah, I don't think it'd make me feel much better. How long do we have?"

"Eight hours, I think," Pete said. "Or less. But no more than eight."

"We die first, right?" Olivia asked. "That's something. We won't be us when we... we..."

"Yeah, no. I don't know," Pete said. "How's Rufus?"

Corrie shrugged. "Needs stitches, I think. Might be able to make do with glue."

"But he'll be okay?" Olivia asked. "He won't turn?"

"I don't think so," Corrie said.

"Good. Good," Olivia said. "He was super-brave. He deserves to live."

Pete sighed, biting down on the wave of despair. *Everyone* deserved to live.

An engine's growl jerked him to his feet. As he stood, he found his limbs stiff. It was the first sign of his impending death. The virus spreading through his system. And the speed with which he'd responded to the sound, that was like the undead too, wasn't it?

An APC rolled to a stop, two spare tyres strapped to the roof just behind the machine gun mount. The judge jumped out.

"I brought you an extra spare to go with the spare," she began, but her improvised ditty trailed to silence as she saw their expressions, the bandages, the blood. "What happened?"

"Zombies," Olivia said slowly. "There's a house through the trees. Someone couldn't kill their zombie-family, so chained them in the basement. We fell in. We dealt with the zombies, though. They're dead."

"You were bitten?" the judge asked.

"Me and Pete," Olivia said.

"I'm sorry," Judge Benton said. "I truly am."

The driver had climbed out of the armoured car, and now reached inside the cab for his rifle.

"We should go for a walk," Benton said. "Just the three of us."

"No," Corrie said. "If it has to be done, it'll be done by me."

"It *will* have to be done," the judge said. "And you don't want this on your conscience."

Realisation of what they were talking about hit Pete like an anvil. "I... I don't know, Corrie," he began.

"*I* do," Corrie said. "You're my brother. She's... she's family. I know what has to be done, and I'll do it when the time comes, but it hasn't come yet."

The judge shrugged. "Give them the tyres," she said to the driver. "We brought you two. There's a fort ahead, but it's deserted. It shouldn't be, but everyone's gone. We're continuing east. Catch up, or head back to Wawa. Thank you for all you've done," she added, then got back into the APC. With no more fanfare, and leaving the two spare tyres on the road, the APC reversed, and drove off.

Pete sighed. "And it was looking to be such a nice day."

"It still is," Olivia said. "Look, Corrie, you don't need to wait."

"I do," she said. "For after, but let's not talk about it."

"And I don't want to wait here," Olivia said. "Let's change the tyre, head to the town and find a sofa. You get sick first, don't you? You get sick. You die. You come back. And I don't feel sick yet. Do you, Pete?"

He shrugged, not wanting to lie. Not wanting to admit the truth.

It wasn't a town, just a crossroads hamlet, partly burned to the ground, and ringed by a partially built palisade. Trees had been felled and stripped of their branches. The trunks had been dragged to the edge of a deep-dug trench, where a garden-excavator sat next to a flatbed on which was a small crane. The discarded branches had been dragged into dense piles on either side of the road, and then set on fire. Beyond the trench, the fires seemed to have spread to a cluster of small homes, but not to a small diner and gas station.

Corrie stopped the armoured car on the forecourt. The diner had been recently looted. The plate glass window was intact, but the kitchen was empty.

"This will do," Olivia said, looping a chain around the fire door. She gave it a shove. "That will hold. Um... I'm going to say goodbye to you now, Corrie. Thanks for coming to rescue me. And thank you for saving Dwayne and Wayde, and Tyler and Robyn. They're alive thanks to you, to us. Keep an eye on Rufus, and take care."

"I can wait here," Corrie said.

Olivia shook her head. "The plate glass window at the front looks strong, but it won't stop a bullet fired from outside."

Pete nodded. "You don't need to be here for this," he said. "Thank you. For everything. For running away. For helping me come back. Remember rule one."

"Remember rule two," Corrie said. "And..." She shook her head. "Strewth, Pete, this isn't how it should end."

"I know," he said.

Corrie nodded, stepped forward as if to hug her brother, then turned and left.

Pete sat at a table close to the window. "This sucks," he said.

"Yep," Olivia said, slipping into the chair opposite. "Sorry, Pete."

"Hey, it's not your fault," he said.

"No, I mean I'm sorry, but this has to go down as the worst date in history."

"Ah. Yeah." He smiled. "Yeah, very *Romeo and Juliet.*"

"Andrea was right," she said. "That play has a real sad ending."

They both sighed, met each other's eyes, and looked away.

Pete searched for something to say. Something to discuss. But his mind just filled with an image of a gravestone. "This is depressing."

"Tell me about it," she said.

"And there's not even any food here. I mean, by rights, we should get a last meal."

"I think I've got a ration pack in my bag," she said.

"Yeah, no one on death row ever asked for one of those," he said. "I'm kinda looking at the general in a different light, you know?"

"You mean her… how she… how she shot people who were infected?"

"So people's friends and family didn't have to do it," he said. "I guess, now that everyone's been conscripted, a lot of people are serving with their family. It's a kindness, isn't it? Not so much for the infected, but so the living will hate her rather than themselves."

"That's true. And, hey, that's something. I got to meet your family," she said. "Corrie's nice. I like her."

"Your parents are dead, aren't they?"

Olivia frowned. "That was a lie. It was simpler than the truth. My dad… I don't know where he is, not for years. He's probably dead. My mom is, or was, in prison. She burned down a church."

"Oh."

"I was seventeen. I set out on my own. There was a job at a care home that offered a room to sleep in when you worked nights. So I took that, showered and washed there. Worked every night I could, every shift. When I wasn't working nights, I slept in my car until I could afford rent."

"Wow. That sounds…"

"As bad as your childhood, but let's not keep score. Everyone gets hard times, that's what I think. Our hard times were right at the beginning, so I thought my future would be easy. Okay, cards on the table." She spread her hands across the Formica table top. "I've got a confession to make."

"That doesn't sound good."

"I was going to quit," she said. "Technically, I hadn't started, but I wasn't going to work for Kempton. You had the dream job so I had to quit."

"Why? I don't get it."

"Because I wanted to go out with you," she said. "It wouldn't have worked if I'd stayed at the carpet store and you were my boss."

"Because of the money?"

"Not really," she said. "But you wouldn't have been working in South Bend. You'd have been in Detroit or Chicago or somewhere. We'd have hardly seen each other. You'd've been doing all these cool new things, and had all these exciting new stories to tell whenever we met. And me? I'd have been doing the exact same thing we've both done these last couple of years. I'd have grown resentful, and you'd have grown bored, and we'd both have gotten lonely with all that time apart. So I was going to quit, and follow you to whichever big city you went. I'd have gotten some minimum wage job doing whatever, and I'd have given our relationship a try."

"Seriously? You'd have given everything up?"

"What did I really have in South Bend? Nicole was coming with me. We were doing a sort-of *Thelma and Louise* thing. Although I guess that has as sad an ending as *Romeo and Juliet*, and a pretty sad beginning, so maybe it's not a good metaphor. But me following you, that wouldn't have worked either. Not with you in the executive job, and me waiting tables. I was looking for something different, and circling the answer, but Nora had already worked it out. I would have moved down to Florida, close to her, and worked in a care home. Managing it, hopefully. Eventually."

"Oh." Pete ran through that. "Yeah, I don't get it. You knew the relationship wouldn't work, but you still wanted to give up everything to try, even though you'd already made up your mind to go down to Florida. That's not very... I mean, it's not like you, throwing your life away to chase after a guy."

"Which isn't why I was doing it," Olivia said. "I liked you, Pete. I still do."

"Thanks."

She grinned. "I didn't want any regrets," she said. "I didn't want to look back on *us* when I was old and wrinkly, on a relationship that never was, and wonder what-if. I needed... not a job, but a life. I guess, in my heart, I knew I'd end up working in a care home because it's the job I disliked the least. And there were some parts I even enjoyed and found truly fulfilling. Nora had worked it out, so it must have been totally obvious. But I had to be sure because there would be no running away again. No changing my mind. It would be my life, my future, good *and* bad, forever. And so I didn't want to spend it wistfully regretting what might have been, but which almost certainly never could."

"I... yeah, I sort of understand," he said. "I mean, kinda. I had a few nights where I was wondering what next. Since the promotion, I mean. I was trying not to think about it. But it was this nagging question at the end of the fantasy. I'd spent a long time dreaming of having enough money to get the nice apartment with the big TV, the decent car, and everything else, but since I'd never imagined I'd get it, I didn't really think about what I'd do after. What else I wanted. What I needed. I was just enjoying the moment."

"I get that," she said.

"And it was all a lie," Pete said. "There wasn't a job. I mean, I don't know what would have happened if there hadn't been the outbreak, but I doubt I'd have ended up selling carpets for Kempton."

Olivia laughed. "You know what? After all my planning, turns out I have one huge regret."

"You do?"

"I love you, Pete. It's taken the end of the world for me to realise, but I do. I really do."

"I love you, too."

"Yeah, I kinda guessed that when you travelled halfway around the world through a demonic warzone to come rescue me."

He grinned. "So what's your regret?"

"That I didn't say it until we're both dying," she said.

"Yep. That sucks. But hey, you got those children to safety," he said. "That's got to count for something."

"And you brought news of the Pacific Alliance to Canada," she said. "Giving people hope like that, it might have saved the entire world."

"Or some of it."

"Yeah."

An uncomfortable silence settled, redolent of the unspoken words and companionable silences it would take a lifetime together to share.

"Too much time is spent talking about first dates," Pete said. "No one ever talks about last dates."

"Now that's *too* dark," she said. She grinned. "But it'd make for a great self-help book. Wait, did you hear that?"

"What?"

She stood and walked to the wide plate glass window. "I thought I heard… there!"

This time, he heard it too. "Shooting," he said.

"Corrie," she said.

A third and fourth shot had shaken the chill air before they'd opened the door. Outside, it was only after they'd sprinted beyond the tow truck that Pete remembered his rifle was inside. So was Olivia's. And the machine gun the judge had left with them back on the road. They had their handguns and not much else, but they didn't turn back because a trio of gunshots rang out, not far to the north.

Beyond an ash-filled block filled with the charred timbers of four houses that had burned to the ground, they saw Corrie in the upper floor window of a soot-stained house. Immediately below her, a red-tiled porch shielded her view of the cluster of zombies beating their fists against the smoke-blackened front door. More undead were gathered by the windows, the walls. Ten at least.

Corrie fired, shooting a zombie in the leg: an undead man in pre-torn jeans and a skimpy polo shirt utterly unsuited for the weather, or the decade. But the zombie was on the driveway, close to the ground-floor window, not by the front door. Worse, as it tried to put weight on its now broken leg, it toppled forward, staggering forward, arms outstretched, until it smashed into the window.

Glass broke, but with a dull, shattering crack. Someone, presumably the house's former owner, had barricaded the window. Time-poor, they'd chosen the expedient of using a tall bookshelf. Improperly anchored, the shelves rocked, and toppled into the room as the zombie tore its flesh punching through the glass remaining in the frame.

"Buy me five minutes!" Olivia said, and dashed off down the street before Pete could ask what for or how.

The obvious answer was with the handgun. He drew it, braced his feet, aimed at the rearmost of the zombies by the front door. The figure's floral shirt had been torn, exposing bare arms covered in gore, its white sweatpants covered in blood. Its scalp dripped black pus from where clumps of brown hair had been ripped away. And as it turned around, Pete saw the open mouth filled with broken teeth.

He pulled the trigger. Nothing happened except that the zombie completed its turn, taking one step, then another, towards him. He pulled the trigger again. Still nothing happened. He checked the safety. It was off, and the zombie had managed another two lurching footsteps.

It was only then he thought to check the magazine. It was empty. He'd fired his last bullet in the cellar where he'd been infected and not realised. Not remembered. Not known. Now it was too late.

He had no spare mag. He had no knife at his belt. He had no weapon. But the hamlet's transformation into a fort had been well begun before its occupants had fled. On the lawn of the neighbouring house, two spades and a pick leaned against a wheelbarrow filled with soil from a half-dug well. Pete grabbed a spade for a weapon, and stepped forward to meet the advancing zombie.

"Hoy! Oy! Hey, you!" he yelled.

"Step back, Pete!" Corrie yelled. "I've got the shot!"

But Pete didn't hear her.

Channelling all his anger, his frustration, his misery, his pain, he swung low, aiming at the gore-soaked zombie's legs, hacking the tool into sinew and muscle. The zombie's outstretched hand swiped out as it fell, its nails clawing against Pete's palm. But he didn't care. You could only die once.

He grinned as he dragged the spade back, and punched it down onto the now fallen zombie's skull. "You can only die once!" he yelled, charging at the crowd of zombies beating at the door. Swinging low, left to right, he cleaved the spade through one leg before thick muscle brought it to a halt deep within the creature's calf. He yanked the spade free, stepping back a pace before punching it forward, into the zombie's open mouth. Another step back and he swung again. This time high. This time right to left. This time into the side of a zombie's face. Teeth flew as its jaw disintegrated, but again, he had to step back.

His charge had failed, but his attack hadn't. The undead were lurching towards him. Only three were left by the door now. The others were coming on, towards him. Too many to fight, though that didn't stop him swinging again. At a thigh exposed beneath a torn ankle-length skirt, smashing the hip, then into the outstretched many-ringed hand reaching out, clawing at him. Gold glistened, and jewels glinted as that hand curled around the spade, gripping, tugging downwards, pulling him off balance and the spade from his grasp.

Twisting as he fell, he nearly rolled straight into the partially dug well. A pivot and pirouette he'd never managed on the football field and he leaped over the hole, landing on the mound of loose soil on the other side. Grabbing the other abandoned spade, he straightened in time to see the bejewelled zombie lurch after him, and fall down into the hole.

"Should have looked where you were going!" he gleefully yelled, raising the spade. Three more of the oncoming undead were heading towards the hole, but there were others on each side who'd miss it. Three to the left, two to the right, the others too far away to be sure, with three more still by the house. One to the right as Corrie fired. Then only two on the left, with another zombie walking straight into the hole, landing with a bone-cracking thud on the already downed zombie.

He raised the spade. A twinge from his arm, and another from his leg told him he'd run as far as he was going to. This was where he'd make his stand. He braced his feet, waiting for death.

Behind him came a mechanical roar, followed by a thudding silence as the speeding tow truck slammed to a halt. Instinctively, he turned and saw Olivia jumping out, the large machine gun in her arms.

"Down!" she yelled, as she braced the weapon on the truck's hood. So he did, diving forward, hugging the dirt, as she opened fire.

It sounded like a waterfall just overhead, a rain of nails hurled by a hurricane, and doing as much damage. It lasted forever. It was over in seconds. He rolled to his feet. Two of the zombies were trying to do the same, but the others, including those by the house, were dead.

Pete slowly walked over to the nearest of the crawling undead. It had taken a dozen bullets in its chest, and enough in one of its legs to leave it hanging by a sinew. He slammed the spade down on its skull. The other zombie was… he tried not to look at her small frame, before finishing her with as much dignity as haste allowed.

A clatter of wood came from inside. Then breaking glass. A gunshot. Then more falling wood. Pete was already walking over to the house when Corrie appeared, coming around the side.

"How many are left?" she asked, glancing behind her.

"Just the two in the hole," Pete said.

"Watch behind," Corrie said. "I think I got them all, but there's always more." She walked over to the hole, and fired down at the trapped undead.

Pete, eyes as much on the house as on where he put his feet, walked slowly backwards, back to the road where Olivia was peering at the machine gun.

"I think it's jammed."

"Let me take a look," Corrie said.

"But they'd have heard that, right?" Olivia asked. "They'd have heard the machine gun."

"Who?" Pete asked.

"The zombies," Olivia said. "Every zombie within a mile. Two miles. Four. However far the sound travelled. And they follow sound, don't they? So they'll be coming. All of them."

"I guess so," Pete said, walking over to the cab to retrieve his rifle. He ejected the magazine, checking there were bullets loaded in it. "Yep, I guess they will."

"Here," Corrie said, placing the machine gun back on the truck's hood. "Try it now."

"I'll wait for the undead," Olivia said, shaking her arms. "Wow. The recoil on that is something else."

"You're bleeding," Corrie said.

"It doesn't matter," Pete said.

Corrie took the small med-kit, and tore open one of the last of the sterile wipes. "I think it does. Right up until it doesn't."

He shrugged, indifferent. He understood why it mattered to his sister, but it truly didn't matter to him. Not now.

"Weird," Olivia said after a few minutes. "We should have seen some more by now. Those can't have been the only ones here."

"I think they were," Corrie said slowly.

"Where did they come from?" Olivia asked.

"Do you see over there, the house with the open door?" Corrie said. "I thought the buildings that had been torched were those with the infected inside. I assumed that the general had searched all the other buildings. Clearly not."

"And all these zombies were inside that house?" Pete asked. "Why?"

265

"Let's go take a look," Olivia said. "Because I really don't think any more are coming."

Twenty seconds later, they were running back outside, and over to the cover of the tow truck.

"That's what I think it was, right?" Pete asked. "Taped to the wall."

"Yeah, that was a bomb," Corrie said. "Probably a mining explosive, set to a remote detonator."

"Did you see the speakers?" Olivia asked.

"I only saw the explosive," Pete said.

"I think they used the speakers, and music, to lure the zombies into the house so they could blow them up."

"Burn them down, I think," Corrie said. "It would explain all the other burned buildings."

"Right, so let me get this straight," Pete said. "The general had some people turning this place into a fort. They began, but didn't finish, because the zombies turned up. Some of the houses were burned down. Some weren't. That explosive didn't go off." He frowned. "Yeah, that doesn't make sense. Wouldn't the general have searched this place? Or the judge."

"I think this place was abandoned before the general's army came through here," Olivia said. "As to why the general didn't search it, building to building, why would she? They're trying to reach Ottawa."

"Yeah, but why..." Pete frowned. "I mean, why would anyone want to lure zombies inside a house so they could blow them up? Or burn them down? Why not finish building the wall? Why not run? It's weird, right? What do you think, Corrie?"

"How are you two feeling?" Corrie asked.

"Tired," Pete said.

"Ditto," Olivia said. "But fine."

"Good, because I have two questions I want answered. How did the zombies get here? Is everywhere nearby like this? And where did the people go after the explosive failed to go off?"

"That's three questions," Pete said.

"No, that's just the first question," Corrie said. "The second is whether there are more zombies buried in the burned ruins. We've got a couple of hours before dark. Want to go check it out?"

But there weren't any bodies in the other ruins. Nor did any more emerge through the trees before darkness descended.

"Weird," Corrie said. "They lured them to a house, tried to burn them down, but didn't. But they did manage to burn down half the other houses."

But Pete didn't care. The day, and his life, had caught up with him. Beyond exhausted, dead tired, he decided it was time to, finally, sleep.

Chapter 34 - Second Chances
Whitney, Ontario

Pete was woken by a nuzzling against his leg. He opened his eyes to see an impatient Rufus desperate for his attention.

"I'm awake," he said. "What? Wait. I'm awake? I'm alive? I'm *alive!*"

He looked at his hands, his arms, and tugged at the skin on his face before noticing Olivia, sitting at the end of the sofa, watching him.

"You're alive," she said. "And so am I."

"That's impossible," Pete said.

"And yet undeniable," she said. "I love you."

"I love you, too," he said, though automatically as his brain processed the impossibly glorious truth. "Did we not get bitten?"

"I know *I* did," she said. "I love you."

"You said that."

"I know. But I like saying it. I like being *able* to say. I'm alive. You're alive. We *are* alive, Pete!" She grinned, but Rufus interrupted her with a bark. "I think he wants a tree."

Outside, the stars were fading as the promise of dawn swept in over the horizon. The air felt cold, but the glistening dew wasn't frozen. Spring had woken from its long winter slumber, and with it came the promise of a new year. A hope for the future matched by the song in his heart.

"We're alive," he whispered.

"Yep," she said. "Feels great, doesn't it."

"But how?" he asked. "We were bitten. I know I was."

"I think we're immune," Olivia said.

"No one's immune," Pete said. "No one's special. It's one of the rules."

"Then you'll need a new rule," she said. "Conrad thought he was immune. He wasn't, but he said there were rumours on the—"

Footsteps crunching on the soft leaves made them spin around, but it was only Corrie, except she had her rifle raised.

"It's okay," Pete said.

"You're still…" Corrie trailed into silence.

"We're still us," Olivia said. "And still alive. We think we're immune."

"No one's immune," Corrie said.

"I just said that," Pete said. "And yet, here we are. Rule fifty… which one was it? Well, either way, the next rule is that some people *are* special."

"Jenny heard some rumours," Olivia said. "And so had Conrad and Naomi. With most viruses, some people are immune."

Corrie lowered the rifle. "There are other explanations. You could be carriers. Or you could be having a delayed response. Or, somehow, you didn't get infected. It doesn't mean you're immune."

"I'm not saying we go find a zombie to put it to the test," Olivia said. "But I'm not going to spend another minute here fretting that I might turn any second."

"No, you're right," Corrie said. "We've got to get back to the general. We've got to tell her, and tell her to stop shooting everyone who gets bitten."

Twenty minutes later, they were in the tow truck, and on the road, driving south, with Corrie at the wheel, and Pete with his head by the open window, enjoying the cold breeze.

Only when Rufus whimpered a frozen protest did Pete wind the window back up. "Where are we going?" he asked.

"Whitney," Corrie said. "That's where the rendezvous is supposed to be."

"Wouldn't Wawa still be closer?" Pete asked.

"But it's the general who needs to know," Corrie said. "She can issue an order, or…" She trailed off.

"Or what?" Pete asked.

"Exactly what I'm wondering," Corrie said.

"You mean there's nothing she can do?" Olivia asked. "Or that she might even already know."

"I don't think she knows," Corrie said slowly. "But maybe she does. No. No, she can't, because she'd realise news like this will get out soon. It'll spread fast, and then everything will change. Get more difficult. We'll have to leave guards with the injured. But she does *need* to know. Everyone does. Whether it brings comfort or false hope, they should know, which means telling her first."

Pete closed his eyes, leaning back against the headrest. He slept.

And was woken when the tow truck braked. Not hard, but quickly as Corrie pulled the vehicle to the side of the road.

"Why are we stopping?" Pete asked, seeing the answer even as he spoke. A convoy approached. Riding up the hill below them were dozens of buses and vans. There wasn't a single military vehicle among them, but each flew a flag. Among the forest of maple leafs glinted a few white stars, offset by an occasional tricolour.

The lead vehicle, a four-door truck, came to a halt in front of them. The driver disembarked, waving the following bus onward. Wearing a plaid shirt and jeans, a holster at his waist, a week of stubble on his chin, and a badge on a chain around his neck, he ambled over to the tow truck, but took a step back when he saw their bloody uniforms.

"I know you," Olivia said. "Sergeant Wilgus! From South Bend."

"I'm sorry," he said, puzzled. "You have the advantage of me."

"We met at the hospital," Olivia said. "I went there the night the outbreak began. My roommate had died, so I went to the hospital, and was helping out there. You sent me home. When I got back, the hospital had burned down."

Wilgus nodded slowly. "I remember now. Yes. First a nurse and now a soldier. Or does that say 'Press' on your body armour?"

Olivia looked down. "I forgot about that. Yes, we're sort of the press corps and messengers for the general."

"General Yoon?" Wilgus asked.

"You've met her?" Olivia asked.

"She sent these people to the rear," Wilgus said. "They're supposed to retrain and properly equip."

"They're all soldiers?" Pete asked, pointing at the convoy slowly rumbling by.

"They will be," Wilgus said.

"They're not all from South Bend, then? What happened at the hospital?" Olivia asked.

"It burned down," Wilgus said. "I'm sure it was arson. We got everyone out that we could. Loaded them into ambulances, and we drove. East, basically. Then north. We drove and we fought." He shrugged. "Same as everyone else. But it's good to see you made it. I was going to requisition your tow truck, but it sounds like you need it. Good luck. I hope to see you around."

"At the front, I guess," Olivia said. "Wait," she added.

"Yes?" Wilgus asked.

"No, nothing," Olivia said. "Just, good luck."

Wilgus nodded, got back in his truck, and pulled out to join the rear of the column.

"Good thing we're wearing the uniforms," Pete said.

"Good thing Olivia knew him," Corrie said. "You didn't want to ask him about Vevermee?"

"I thought about it," Olivia said. "But it seems like ancient history now. You know what we should have asked, though? Where the frontline is."

"Wherever it is," Corrie said, walking back to the truck, "it'll have moved by the time we get there."

Whitney wasn't the town Pete had been expecting, but another small hamlet being turned into a timber fort with the materials everywhere available. Outside the small conurbation, a wooden barricade ran across the road. There was no sentry or guard, but there were a group of eight foresters, carrying as many chainsaws as rifles, who'd stopped their felling as the tow truck approached.

"G'day," Corrie called out. "We're looking for General Yoon."

"Then you want to keep looking another day east," the sentry called back. "Maybe in Ottawa. Maybe beyond."

"Who's in charge here?" Corrie asked.

"That'd be the judge," the sentry said.

"Judge Benton?" Olivia asked.

"Yep."

She was easy to find; they just followed the sound of hammering until, when they drew nearer, they were able to zero in on the swearing. An old auto-garage had been turned into a tank triage centre. Eight of the mammoth machines sat in the lot, their mechanical guts in view. Assistants, in the odd mix of civilian, hunting, and military gear that was becoming humanity's new uniform, were hurriedly erecting plastic-sheet canopies to keep away the beginning of a rain shower. Judge Benton herself was elbow-deep in an engine, drenched in oil, and cursing a blue streak that was on the verge of turning crimson before she noticed the tow truck. She stood, slowly walking over as Corrie climbed out of the driver's seat. When she saw Pete and Corrie, the judge stopped.

"You're not dead," she finally said. "Weren't you bitten?"

"We think we're immune," Olivia said. "We absolutely were bitten, but here we are. Clearly not dead. Certainly not undead."

"No one's immune," the judge said.

Around them, the assistants putting up canopies around the disassembled machines paused, looking at the newcomers with understandable interest.

"And yet, here we are," Olivia said. "In South Bend, I heard rumours. And there were some online."

The judge nodded. "You better come with me." She raised an oily hand, pointing at her team of assistants, then pointed skywards. They hurried back to work, though while talking in confused excitement.

"I see," the judge said, pacing the office as they finished recounting the brief story. "Immunity? Natural immunity, one assumes. I suppose it is theoretically possible. However, I would advise you both to exercise caution."

"In who we tell, you mean?" Pete asked.

272

"No, in how you act. It is just as likely that, somehow, you weren't infected, that you two aren't special, but there was something different about your attackers."

"You mean that the zombies aren't as infectious as they once were?" Olivia asked.

"Oh, trust me, they still are," the judge said. "I'll put in a call, pass this up to the general, and see what Jill wants to do. I suspect it will be to send you to a laboratory for testing, but we'll wait and see."

"Is she here?" Corrie asked.

"I'm not sure where she is," the judge said. "Other than it'll be the very front line. You've heard the saying by von Moltke that plans never survive contact with the enemy? We have a new one. They don't survive contact with the refugees. There have been far more than we were expecting. Too many to send back behind the lines. We've added thousands more professional military personnel to our ranks, but we lack the equipment for them." She waved a hand at the disassembled tanks beyond the window. "For now, we're regrouping, creating a defensive line while Jill advances towards the Saint Lawrence."

The call was made, a coded instruction for the general to call the judge back.

"And now we wait," Benton said. "So, tell me, do any of you know what a regulator looks like?"

When the reply from the general came, it wasn't in code.

"You're correct," Judge Benton said.

"About what?" Pete asked, turning from the road he, Olivia, and Corrie had been detailed to guard.

"You're immune," the judge said. She screwed up her face. "Well, no. Strictly speaking, you're correct in that some people do appear to be immune, and the balance of probabilities suggests this is the case with you."

"You mean there are others?" Olivia asked.

"The general's received word of a case in Halifax, Nova Scotia," the judge said. "And there is a possible case in Thunder Bay. The message came in the open, not in code, meaning Jill wants everyone to know that it is a possibility, and she's altered our rules of engagement accordingly. But she also wanted to stress there are four confirmed cases out of the entire populations of Canada, the U.S., and Australia."

"Oh. I hadn't thought of it like that," Pete said.

The judge shrugged. "It's good news for some, which is better than bad news for all. Speaking of bad news, for now, you're stuck here. The general doesn't want you at the front until she's had it confirmed that Dr Avalon doesn't need to prod and poke you in the lab."

"I don't think I'd call being kept away from the frontlines bad news," Olivia said.

The judge nodded. "Spoken like an experienced soldier," she said, and turned to head back to her garage.

"Sorry, Your Honour?" Corrie said. "Can I ask something?"

"Call me Delores. What is it?"

"The orders came from General Yoon, but what did President Trowbridge say?"

"There's been no word from him. No sign, either." The judge shrugged. "Does it matter?"

"Absolutely not," Corrie said.

Chapter 35 - Unwanted Visitors
Whitney

Pete yawned, shivered, and forced himself out of the chair and over to the window. The street outside, bathed in generator-powered spotlights, remained quiet and empty. He'd hear trouble before he saw it, of course, and it was more likely to come from inside than out. He turned around, glancing along the motel's hallway at the locked bedrooms.

The convoy had arrived after dark. Four cars, one minibus, one battered school bus. Twelve adults, and twenty children, had disregarded the order to shelter in place, though they claimed not to have been aware of it. The partial remains of a zombie lodged in the school bus's fender had prompted the judge to quarantine them all for the night. Subsequently, Pete's plans for a quiet evening with Olivia doing absolutely nothing had become quiet sentry duty where he'd *hoped* to do nothing. And he hadn't. He'd sat, paced, and dozed in the chair, rifle on the desk, waiting for a dawn which had almost arrived.

Outside, he saw the judge walk from the small house she was using as a command post to the restaurant they were using as their communal dining hall. It was time to check on the recent arrivals.

"Time to get up!" he called, knocking on the first door, pitching his voice loud enough to carry the length of the hallway. He didn't open the door, however, leaving that to the room's solitary occupant, assuming they were still alive. Knocking on one door after another, he moved along the hall, reaching the end as the first door opened. An old man stepped out, nodded to Pete, but then waited for the door opposite to open. The man relaxed as he saw the young boy who, in turn, gave a shrug.

"Where's breakfast?" the boy asked.

"No one's infected," Corrie said.

The judge shook her head. "As far as we know. We assumed people turned within eight hours, but we also assumed everyone who was bitten was infected."

"We need a radio station," Corrie said.

"For broadcasting your news?" the judge asked.

"To tell people to stay inside," Corrie said. "And to tell those who can't where they should go, where they should avoid."

"I'd like to know that, too," the judge said. "But yes, I see your point. A radio station would be useful as we advance southward. I shall put it to Jill. And speaking of the marvels of technology, we had a phone call this morning, and a message to expect a fuel delivery."

"For the tanks?" Pete asked.

"Indeed," the judge said. "Though we still await their crew and munitions. Fuel was easier to locate. But order is being slowly restored. Supply chains are being re-established. Let me get these people fed, and I'll see who among them we can get to stand guard."

"And where do you want us?" Olivia asked.

"Building the walls for the guards to stand behind," Benton said.

"There's warmth in the sun," Pete said, pacing across the bridge. "And fish in the river."

"Do you want to try to catch them?" Olivia asked. "And pass me that wrench, the bracket, a couple of bolts. The hammer, too. And some nails."

He brought over the entire toolbox. "Need a hand?" he asked for the third time.

"In a moment," she said, fastening the bracket beneath the ledge she'd attached to the broad plank wall covering one half of the road. The other half was sealed with a garage door to which rollers had been added so, in theory, it could open outwards. "There," she said. "Try that. See if it takes your weight."

With a measure of trepidation, he clambered up, bouncing gently on the balls of his feet.

"Cool," Olivia said. "Now, jump."

"I'm happy standing."

"Spoilsport," she said.

A mostly blue butterfly landed on the garage-door-gate, then fluttered across the bridge, disappearing over the side. "Blue and yellow," he said.

"What is?"

"That butterfly," Pete said. "If Trowbridge is out of contact, that means he's dead, isn't he?"

"I suppose," Olivia said.

"And so is Lisa Kempton."

"Probably," Olivia said. "Does it matter? So many people we knew far better are certainly dead."

"But it means we don't need to worry about the CIA asking about why Lisa Kempton's jet is playing ferry between the hemispheres, or about Corrie, or me. We're immune, and we're alive, and we've escaped the past."

"I guess we have," Olivia said. She grinned. "Oh, and it's such a nice day, too. You can really believe summer is on its way. So, do you want to go fishing?"

"I've never tried it," he said. "You?"

"I never caught anything, but yes, twice. I bet you could find a fishing rod somewhere in town. Only one of us needs to be on guard. We could take it in turns."

"No, I'm cool. I like the company up here."

In the distance came the buzz of a chainsaw. A creak was followed by a sharp crack as another tree was felled.

"It's the calm in the middle of the storm," Olivia said, her smile fading slightly.

"So what's coming is going to be as bad as what went before?"

"Or as hard," she said. "As difficult. But if we're in the middle, we're approaching the end."

"Speaking of approaching," Pete said, climbing up to the gantry. "Is that... that is! That's an engine."

It was a big one. A fuel tanker was barrelling along the road. Battered and bullet-scarred, mud-flecked and gore-splattered, the windscreen was obscured with blood and worse. The vehicle came to a hissing halt fifty metres from the barricade.

"Keep your rifle close," Olivia whispered. "I've got a bad feeling about this."

The driver's door opened, and a young woman jumped out, wearing a neon-green coat and hat. Another woman jumped out of the passenger side, wearing a matching coat, nearly matching hat, and carrying a shotgun. Neither were soldiers. Neither were yet twenty.

Pete frowned. "Wait, I know her. I know the driver."

"You do?" Olivia asked.

"From Thunder Bay," Pete said. "Don't you remember? She was working in the hotel kitchens. Christina something."

Pete slid the garage door-gate open, and walked along the road to where Christina and her near-identically dressed passenger had stopped, in front of their battered cab.

"Heya," Pete said cheerily. "Small world, right?"

Christina frowned.

"The hotel," Pete said. "In Thunder Bay. We both were working in the kitchens. I don't think we were properly introduced."

"Chrissie M," Christina said.

"And I'm Chrissie K," the other young woman added.

"You're both called Christina?" Olivia asked. "Well, that's a coincidence, isn't it?"

The two young women shrugged in near synchronicity.

"How did you happen to be out here?" Pete asked.

"We're hauling fuel," Chrissie M said.

"For the war effort," Chrissie K said.

"We're soldiers," Chrissie M said.

"Everyone is," Chrissie K said.

"You're not dressed like soldiers," Olivia said.

"The zombies don't care what we wear," Chrissie M said.

"So why should we?" Chrissie K said.

Pete couldn't decide if they were finishing each other's sentences, or refusing to let the other have the last word, though trying to keep up was giving him a pain behind his right eye.

"We better get the tanker inside," Olivia said.

"There's another tanker," Chrissie M said.

"The truck blew a tyre," Chrissie K said.

"We left it with the sergeant," Chrissie M said.

"Further up the road," Chrissie K said.

"Then we definitely better get this tanker inside, and then go get the judge," Olivia said.

"That's the diesel I was waiting on," the judge said. "The other tanker is gasoline."

"Is this for the tanks?" Pete asked.

"For the attack on Toronto," the judge said.

"I thought we were attacking Ottawa," Pete said.

"At the moment, yes. By the time we get the troops, and the ammunition, the front will have moved, divided, some going north, but these tanks will join those who turn south."

"It's happening fast, then?" Olivia said.

"It is," the judge said, though an edge of uncertainty had crept into her voice. "The enemy doesn't stop, doesn't sleep, so neither can we. The longer we delay, the less food we have, the more of our number, around the world, will become the enemy, but… yes, I think Jill's putting everything into this assault. Whether it's too much or not enough, we won't know until we succeed or fail. Nevertheless, we need the tanker, and it's currently stranded to the west. About fifty kilometres away, according to those two Christinas. The punctures are on the cab's driving-wheels. Detach the rig from the tanker, and take it to get the gasoline tanker."

"I've never driven anything that big," Olivia said.

"One of the rules of the outback," Corrie said. "Be able to drive anything. If there's an accident, you need to be able to get the vehicle off the road, or back to a diesel stop."

"I guess that's a rule that goes double for everywhere nowadays," Pete said.

"Rufus, sit down," Olivia said, pulling the dog back from the window. "I think he's had enough of driving."

"Or he just wants to see some more of Canada," Pete said. "I get that. I think I like it here."

"It's the trees, isn't it?" Olivia said.

"The outback, those open spaces, it seemed so vast," Pete said. "The trees are... comforting. So tall and old, so densely packed. It gives a different perspective on the flow of time. Like, it's a reminder the cities were built, so we can build them again."

"That's almost poetic," Corrie said.

"Yeah," Olivia said. "You really are in a good mood today."

"Here's hoping it— Zombie!"

"Seen it," Corrie said, though she didn't slow as the ragged creature seemed to drift onto the road. It wore a long and trailing dress, which utterly covered its feet and legs. Pete automatically thought *wedding dress*, but this was blue, not white. And it wasn't a dress. It was a sheet. A shroud in which the corpse had been laid out before it had come back to life. The zombie flowed onto the road, but Corrie didn't swerve until the last second, clipping the creature with the edge of the cab, sending it flying back into the undergrowth, and the sheet up into the air.

"I wasn't trying to hit it," Corrie said.

"We'll get it on the way back," Olivia said.

Pete nodded, his good mood now on ice.

The odometer climbed the kilometres. The road curved southward, but if it hadn't been for the compass on the dash, he'd not have realised.

"Are we going the right way?" he finally asked.

"Assuming we're heading to the smoke," Corrie said.

"Where?"

"Look between the trees," Corrie said. "Above them. There! No, it's gone."

"There," Olivia said. "Do you see?"

"It's only a thin plume," Pete said. "That's too small to be a gas tanker. Right?"

"Definitely," Olivia said, but he heard the uncertainty in her reply. "Probably a cooking fire. The soldiers are keeping themselves warm and fed while they wait."

From the signage as they drew nearer to the smoke, Pete expected a roadside truck stop, perhaps a gas station, but what they found was more like a motel. The kerbside billboard advertised rooms for rent, kayaks for hire, and food for sale, with the note about gas way down at the bottom. The main building was a sprawling many-roomed restaurant. From the vast size of the parking lot outside, it was a popular haunt for tourists and the handful of locals. The gas pump, nestled in one corner, hung loose, and clearly wasn't the source of the fire. Nor was the broken-down fuel tanker, still on the road. The smoke rose from a broad fire burning perilously close to the stalled tanker, where a road-adjacent shed merrily burned. Dotted near it, on the building side, were other pockets of burning fuel. Eight, Pete counted. The same number as the undead gathered around the single-storey row of chalets.

No, *nine* small blazes. A burning rag tumbled through the air from the open ground-floor window of one of the low homes. The bottle, made invisible by the flame's bright glow, missed all of the undead, and smashed on the well-maintained blacktop. The fumes erupted upwards and quickly subsided, leaving another burning puddle on the lot's asphalt.

"They must be out of ammo," Corrie said, already reaching for the door. They jumped out.

All hopes of the undead being distracted by the sound of the juggernaut's engine had been dashed by the explosion of the breaking bottle and evaporated as quickly as the fumes. But the soldiers weren't out of ammo. A burst of automatic fire erupted from the broken window.

"Pete, Livy, watch the rear," Corrie said. "Rufus, watch the zombies. Stay!" she added as the dog paced a cautious step towards the undead. "Watch from here."

She raised her rifle and fired.

281

Pete turned a full circle, walking out towards the road. Where had the zombies come from? He turned back towards the chalets, and realised that two of the creatures wore uniforms. Some of them had to be the guard accompanying the fuel.

Between the gunfire from the cabin and from Corrie, with the undead turning between the two sources of sound and death, the skirmish was over so quickly it barely deserved the name.

"Coming in!" Corrie yelled after the last of the standing undead had fallen. She walked slowly towards the chalets. "Watch the road, the rear," she added to Olivia and Pete, while Rufus fell in close to her legs.

Even as woman and dog carefully picked their way around the burning pools, the door to a cabin opened. The door to the second cabin opened a moment later. Survivors came out. Soldiers. Not two groups, just two people, one from each cabin, both in uniform. From the first, a man with a rag-stoppered bottle in one hand, a lighter in the other. From the second, a soldier with a rifle held awkwardly in the hand not dripping blood.

"Does that say 'Press' on your body armour?" the injured soldier asked. "Never imagined I'd be glad to see a journalist."

The other man put the bottle down on the ground, and the lighter back in his pocket. Pete turned back to the road, scanning for approaching undead, turning a slow arc that ended when he turned towards Olivia. She'd frozen, rigid, her mouth open in horror.

Pete spun back to face the soldiers, and in time to see the second man draw his sidearm and shoot his injured comrade in the head.

"Why'd you do that?" Corrie demanded, raising her rifle.

"Relax," the soldier said, holstering his pistol. "He was bitten. Infected. Better he die without realising."

No, Pete thought as he took another step forward. This man wasn't a soldier. Despite the uniform. Despite the sergeant's stripes. This man was very definitely a civilian. One he knew. One Olivia knew, too. One Olivia had recognised because she was now striding across the parking lot.

"Mack," she said.

"Oh. You," Mack said, frowning. "You're still alive, are you?"

"This is Morgan Mack," Pete said to Corrie.

"Since when are you a sergeant?" Olivia asked.

"Since when are you press?" Mack replied.

Pete thought Olivia was going to shout at Mack. Charge at him. Even, maybe, shoot him. But she didn't. She just stopped, a dozen paces away. Rufus padded over, eyes on Mack, teeth bared, but not quite growling.

"What?" Mack asked. "You're not still mad about Thunder Bay?"

Olivia shook her head. "We've got to get your tanker onto the back of our rig. Is everyone else here dead?"

"Infected," Mack said. "There was a whole nest of them in that motel. I think there are still some in there." He turned around and picked up the glass bottle. And now, with his back turned, Olivia charged.

She dived forward, rifle swinging, aiming low, knocking Mack's legs out from beneath him. The man sprawled to the ground, trying to roll, but he was slower than Olivia. She pushed her rifle's butt against his throat, not hard, but with enough force to stop Mack from squirming.

"Hey! You can't kill me!" he protested. "That'd be murder!"

"Look at your arm, Mack," Olivia said. "Look at your arm." She stepped back, flipping her rifle to hold it by the grip, the barrel pointing at Mack as he raised his arm to his eyes.

Pete saw the blood, the gash, the bite marks on the man's wrist.

Mack swore, closed his eyes. "It's nothing," he said.

"Pete, go swap out the rig," Olivia said. "Corrie, show him how."

"Livy," Pete began.

"No. I've got this," Olivia said. "Orders are to stop shooting the infected-living because some people are immune, Mack. So let's see if that's you. It might have been him, that soldier you just shot."

"Pete, come on," Corrie said. She took her brother's arm, and tugged with enough force to make him turn.

"We shouldn't leave them," Pete said.

"Yes we should," Corrie said. "Trust me."

Each time he began to turn around, Corrie tugged on his arm. Increasingly frustrated, he was about to shake her off when, behind, there came a single gunshot. He tore himself free from Corrie and spun around. Mack was nothing but another corpse among so many.

"He turned," Olivia said simply. She knelt down, and quickly searched the dead man's pockets. "That's not what I was expecting to find, but maybe it should have been." She held up a small black rectangle.

"What is it?" Pete asked.

"A remote detonator," Corrie said. "I think we should leave the rest of the cabins alone. I'll check the tanker while you get the rig closer."

"You remember the hamlet, the night after we were bitten?" Pete asked. "That can't have been him who placed the explosives, could it?"

"I'm absolutely certain he was responsible for Notre Dame," Olivia said. She shrugged. "But what does it matter? He can't hurt anyone anymore."

Part 4
The World on Fire

Canada

Chapter 36 - Prometheus
Whitney, Ontario

"Not bad," Olivia said, dumping another load of trimmed branches among the trees.

"It's not good, though," Pete said. "It's still more like an obstacle course than a barricade."

"Yeah, but give us another week," Olivia said. She stretched.

"Assuming we're still here in a week's time," Pete said.

"True," Olivia said. "And that's exactly why we should build our defences like this. With the frontline always moving, and with us soon to move after it, we don't have time to dig deep foundations and towering walls. No, we just need a barrier sturdy enough to slow the zombies until we can deal with them. And this will do for that."

Pete surveyed their morning's work. The goal was to finish clearing the woodland around the hamlet. Eventually the stumps would be removed, the land ploughed and planted; a ditch would be dug, a crane built, and the trunks planted in a neat palisade. Eventually. For now, they were creating a wall of horizontal logs, with stacks of brush and branches filling the gaps between the trees they'd not felled. Against people, it wouldn't be much protection. Against zombies? He hoped he'd never find out.

That morning, just after dawn, a battered TAPV and two overloaded SUVs had arrived with twenty soldiers aboard. Though not all had served with armour before the outbreak, all *had* served, and they were the tanks' new crew. Almost as soon as they'd arrived, the tanks the judge had repaired had rolled west.

"Maybe we should have volunteered," Pete said.

"For what?"

"To go with the tanks," Pete said.

"We'd have been in the way," Olivia said. "We go where the judge goes, and if she's been left here rather than sent to the front, maybe they've got enough proper mechanics now. Proper soldiers, too. Give me a hand with this tree trunk."

He grabbed hold of the rope and hauled the trunk into place, then helped shift the pile of cut branches. It was muscle-burning work, but deeply satisfying.

Olivia whistled. Pete reached for his slung rifle, but saw she was pointing towards the hamlet. Rufus was bounding towards them, the two Christinas following at a more sedate pace.

"We bring lunch," Chrissie M said.

"Or breakfast," Chrissie K said.

"Or brunch?" Pete asked.

"Who cares, I'm famished," Olivia said.

Rufus yipped his agreement.

"We *did* feed him," Chrissie M said uncertainly.

"A lot," Chrissie K added apologetically.

"He knows to stock up in the good times," Olivia said. "Any word on the radio, or the phone?"

The two women glanced at each other, as if uncertain who should go first.

"It's gone weird," Chrissie M said.

"The radio or the phone?" Olivia asked.

"Both," Chrissie M said. "The phone only connects to the next bastion west, and the radio is mostly static."

"The judge will be happy she's got something to fix," Pete said. He opened the lid of the plastic container, releasing a waft of steam. "Potatoes in… is that soup?"

"Stew," Chrissie M said apologetically.

"And it's good," Chrissie K said defensively.

"I'm not complaining," Pete said. "It's been a long time since I saw potatoes."

"It's only three weeks," Olivia said.

"It feels like longer," Pete said. "A *lot* longer. Do you think we could plant some?"

"Not after they've been cooked," Olivia said, taking a plastic box from the Christinas.

"You know what I mean," Pete said. "Is this good land for growing potatoes? We'd have to pull up those tree stumps. Shame the tanks are gone. They'd be perfect for that."

An odd sound filled the air, growing in volume from a distant hum to an everywhere-buzz. Pete turned towards the approach road before he thought of looking upward. A fighter jet, trailing a spreading plume of smoke, stuttered across the sky until it seemed to break apart. A dart shot upward from the plane, from which a parachute emerged, caught the wind, and slowed the descent of the ejector seat. The plane, however, drifted downward, tumbling, falling, until it disappeared among the distant trees.

"I'll get some wheels," Olivia said. "Christina, watch that parachute. Pete, get the judge."

Five minutes later, two vehicles bounced along the road, heading west, towards the now lost parachute. In front, aboard a battered RCMP four-wheeler the judge had been repairing, were the Christinas and Benton. Behind came Pete, Corrie, Olivia, and Rufus, in the TAPV that had arrived with the tank crews earlier that morning. Tape-V would be a better name for the vehicle, Pete decided, since half the interior seemed to be held together with electrical tape and dime-store glue.

Ahead, the four-by-four swerved left, pulling off the road onto a logging trail.

"Hold on," Corrie said, dragging the TAPV after them.

After five hundred metres, when the trail met a firebreak, the truck stopped.

There was no sign of the pilot.

"It came down here," Chrissie M said. "I'm sure it did."

"I'm certain it did," Chrissie K added, though her tone was unsure.

The trees were far from silent. Leaves rustled. Birds chirruped. Insects buzzed in a sunbeam warm enough to make Pete think spring really had arrived. But there was no sign of the pilot or the crashed plane.

"Find the pilot," Olivia said to Rufus. "Go on!"

The dog looked at her, the woods, then her again, before taking a tentative step towards the trees. A cautious sniff was followed by a more certain bound into the woodland.

"Christina, Christina, watch the road," Benton said, already hurrying after the dog.

They didn't have far to run. Rufus found the crashed pilot at the edge of a sloping clearing, barely two hundred metres from the road. The parachute had caught in the trees during the descent, then torn, leaving the pilot to plummet the last dozen metres to the ground.

"Can you hear me, son?" Benton asked, checking for a pulse. "Have you got a first-aid kit?" she added, turning to Corrie.

The pilot reached out, gripping the judge's hand. "I need to get a message to Benton. Judge Benton."

"That's me," Benton asked.

"I found you?" the pilot asked.

"You did," the judge said.

"The general… the general sent me. Told me to find you. Last message. Warn the judge."

"Warn me of what?" Benton asked.

"Mushroom clouds," the pilot said. "Ottawa. Montreal. They're gone."

Benton swallowed. "And the general?"

"I was flying air patrol. Saw the clouds. Got a message. Last message from anyone. Warn you. Warn the judge. She says you're in charge. Says…" The words trailed to silence.

"Is he dead?" Olivia asked.

"Unconscious," the judge said. "Help me carry him back to the car."

"Mushroom clouds mean nuclear bombs, don't they?" Olivia asked.

"Yep," Benton said. "So, help me move him."

"It won't only be Ottawa and Montreal," Corrie said, as they strapped together a pair of long branches into a stretcher.

"Before the plane was spotted in the sky, we lost communications," the judge said. "The hard line failed beyond the next fort. The radio is nothing but static. I think you're correct. I think this is more than just our corner of Canada."

"I thought phone lines were designed to survive a nuclear blast," Pete said as they hauled the pilot back to the trucks.

"Nothing survives the blast," Corrie said. "But the copper wires will survive an EMP. The switchboards and exchanges won't."

"Okay, but why bomb Ottawa or Montreal?" Olivia asked.

It was a question echoed by the Christinas as they laid the dying pilot in the back of the truck.

"Either it was a rogue nation, conducting a terrorist attack," the judge said, "which is unlikely. Or it was an accident. Someone was trying to kill the largest concentration of zombies possible. On some satellite image, they saw the undead the general had gathered."

"No," Corrie said, and Pete had to agree. "No, sorry, Your Honour. The military satellites are down, which means no guidance systems, and almost certainly no surveillance. The missiles were fired blind, on a mathematical trajectory calculated in a bunker on the other side of the planet. They weren't aiming for Ottawa or Montreal or the general. Perhaps they were aiming for New York, but wherever they hit wasn't the original target. That means only one thing for certain, that these weren't the only missiles that were fired."

"Does that mean—" Chrissie M began, but the judge held up her hand.

"No, that is logical," Benton said. "We must assume that you're correct, and that New York was the logical target. We need to organise a retreat from the Saint Lawrence to Wawa, or even Thunder Bay. To Nanaimo if necessary."

"They need to be warned," Corrie said. "We'll go. We'll go now. Tell them you're coming. Tell them to get ready, and get ready to send help."

The judge nodded. "But tell them to send no one until I send word. Until we know how bad this is, how many there are to be saved..." She trailed off, shaking her head.

"Act now, think later," Olivia said, walking over to the TAPV. To the back were strapped six fuel cans, left there by the tank crew. She loosened the webbing enough to raise one a few inches and give it a shake. "Nearly full," she said.

"You have ammo? Food?" Benton asked.

"Here," Chrissie M said, opening the other Christina's pack. "The lunch for the other sentries."

Pete took the still warm plastic boxes of potato stew. "That'll see us to Wawa."

The judge nodded. "And if..." She shook her head. "Tell them... no. Whoever launched these missiles, they must have been aiming at New York. They *must* have been. We'll retreat to the Great Lakes, away from the fallout, all the way to British Columbia if necessary, where we can be resupplied from the Pacific. Make sure they know what's happened, then tell them to prepare, and tell them to get word to the Pacific to send help."

Chapter 37 - Revelation
Ontario

"Do you know the way?" Pete asked, as the TAPV rattled along the road.

"West," Corrie said, tapping the compass.

"It says we're heading south," Olivia said.

"Yep," Corrie said. "But I think… yes, ahead. There's a firebreak. We'll take that west as far as we can."

"Down a firebreak?" Pete asked.

"The maintenance vehicles would have driven along it," Corrie said.

In better weather, Pete thought, but he didn't say it aloud. His doubts were far bigger than the route they were taking. Silence reigned for a dozen rattling miles. Even Rufus was subdued as they bounced along the ruler-straight trail. Pete didn't need to ask to know that the pilot's words were replaying on a loop in everyone's minds.

"How much food and ammo do we actually have?" Olivia finally asked.

"Six small containers of the potato soup," Pete said, leaping at the task, anything to distract from the sheer enormity of the new horror visited upon them. "I've got two of Kempton's ration pouches, too. The mango curry ones which are… well, there's a reason we haven't eaten them yet. Ammo, I've got three magazines."

"Four," Corrie said, without taking her hands from the wheel or eyes from the road.

"Two and a half," Olivia said. "And two spare for the pistol."

"Water," Corrie said. "That's more important."

"Just my water bottle," Olivia said.

"The same," Pete said.

"I've got three spare," Corrie said. "Outback habit," she added. "And how much fuel?"

"Six containers, and those are about five gallons each, right?" Olivia said. "So, what do you think the fuel efficiency of this TAPV is?"

"We'll reach Thunder Bay," Corrie said. She glanced at the dash. "Probably. But Wawa, certainly."

"Good. Cool. Fine," Olivia said, leaning back in the seat.

"But probably not until tomorrow," Corrie added. "We can't go any faster than this, and we can't drive along a firebreak at night."

"Maybe we'll reach a road soon," Pete said, but without much confidence. On their journey eastward from Wawa, despite taking the most direct roads, they'd still followed a circuitous route.

"Would rainwater be safe to drink?" Olivia asked.

"Today? Probably. Tomorrow? Possibly not," Corrie said.

"Right. Fine. And river water?" Olivia asked.

"Not after tomorrow's rain," Corrie said.

"We need a Geiger counter, "Olivia said.

"And to find a river quickly," Pete said. "Get as much water as we can."

"If we find a river, we'll have to turn back," Corrie said. "They won't have built a bridge for a firebreak."

"Right. No."

Silence settled again, as their minds independently buzzed, circling the new reality.

"Corrie?" Pete said. "Back in Australia, you said Lisa Kempton—"

"Yes," Corrie cut him off.

"What?" Olivia asked.

"Yes to it all," Corrie said. "This is the nuclear war that Kempton was trying to stop. Not in the targets. I honestly can't imagine why anyone would consider the cities along the Saint Lawrence as strategically important. The code I created to hijack the satellites, it was to stop this, or something very like it."

"It can't be," Olivia said. "I mean... no. It can't be. You said... no. I thought you said that some politicians were working with the cartel. Why would they start a nuclear war now? How would they do it without any satellite communications?"

"Exactly," Corrie said. "That was us. Me. Kempton. The code I wrote, years ago, was destined to shut down satellite communications, including the missile guidance systems. That was the goal, of course. The aim. But... I can't believe we were so stupid. Kempton, me, all of us."

"What do you mean?" Pete asked.

"Kempton wanted a way of pulling the plug on the guidance systems as a brute-force way of stopping a nuclear conflict if all other methods failed. But she envisaged it being preceded by coups, with there being enough honest politicians, dutiful generals, and thoughtful soldiers left that, after the first wave failed, the second wouldn't be launched. She didn't plan for the undead, for the chaos it brought. Nor did she realise, without comms, there was no way of stopping any plans that were in progress. She was worried this was coming. That's why she had Rampton and Jackson, and you, Pete, sent down to Australia. She could have found someone else to activate my code. I wasn't necessary for this part of her plan, but she wanted to exile and expose the traitors in her midst. The plans were in motion, but if it hadn't been for the undead, they could have been halted."

"You mean that in some missile silo in—" Olivia began, and then stopped. "Wait. We fired first, didn't we? That's what you're saying. America fired first, and the missiles that hit Canada were retaliation?"

"Almost certainly, yes," Corrie said. "Part of a plan set weeks ago."

"And if it hadn't been for the undead," Olivia continued, "the commander of a missile silo in Omaha might have queried the orders. The same, maybe, for someone in Siberia. But with the undead roaming the streets, maybe they thought it was part of the battle plan to defeat the zombies?"

"Right. Exactly," Corrie said. "At any other time, cutting comms would have given them pause. Maybe even only long enough to ask who was responsible. But Kempton didn't plan for the undead."

"We fired first," Olivia whispered. "They hit Canada, so where did we hit? Sweden? Denmark?"

"Korea?" Pete asked. "What if the Pacific was attacked, too?"

Once again, the silence returned, deeper and even more pensive than before.

The firebreak led to a logging trail, which became a road, and as that began curving, they rattled onto another firebreak, and so continued mostly west. Even when they found another road, Pete didn't bother trying to locate it on a map. They drove up a shallow hill, down a steeper incline, and up a taller crest where the trees had been cleared around a lookout point. Space had been cleared for cars to park, while some lumber had been cut into shallow benches, on the back of which rusting metal signs reminded visitors to take their litter home. There were no other amenities, and no other vehicles stopped there, but the elevation provided them with a perfect view of the mushroom cloud.

"Where is it?" Olivia whispered. "Is that Wawa?"

"It's too far to the east and south," Corrie said. "Did anyone see a flash when we were in the trees?" She peered at the map. "I have no idea. It's nowhere. They dropped a bomb on nowhere."

"Except it's close to Wawa," Pete said. "And Sault Ste. Marie and the border with Michigan. That would be worth targeting, destroying, wouldn't it? Tactically, I mean."

"Anyone retreating from the Saint Lawrence will drive straight into it," Olivia said. "We should go back and warn them."

"It'll take days for the judge to gather the remains of the general's army," Corrie said. "And during that time, they'll shelter from the fallout. It's those closer to the blast I would worry about. They can't help the judge, but the judge can't help them, and neither can we."

"Do you mean you want to give up on Wawa?" Olivia asked.

Corrie turned to face the road. "I don't know. Maybe."

"We should go to Thunder Bay," Pete said decisively. "That's what the judge said, and we might reach there tomorrow evening. We can send a message to Nanaimo by plane, and maybe fly back to the judge as well. Planes, yeah," he said, warming to the idea. "That's got to be the answer. Thunder Bay."

"Zombie," Olivia said, pointing in the rear view mirror. The creature was slowly lumbering up the hillside behind them.

"Save the ammo," Corrie said, putting the TAPV into gear. "We'll need it."

When they came to a logging trail, wider than most, Corrie turned off the road. They were heading north now, but no one said anything. No one had said anything since they'd driven away from the mushroom cloud.

Trail, firebreak, road, and finally Corrie pulled in.

"Is something wrong?" Olivia asked.

"I just wanted a minute," Corrie said. "A minute to breathe the air."

"Is that a good idea?" Pete asked. "I mean, with the mushroom cloud so close." He frowned. "And how come we're still able to drive? Aren't nuclear bombs supposed to fry anything electrical?"

"Military vehicles are shielded against EMPs," Corrie said, getting out and taking a deep lungful of air. "And fallout isn't a problem for hours. Days, depending on the winds. And depending on where the bombs fell."

Pete and Olivia followed her outside, standing on the roadside, protectively close to the TAPV, tentatively stretching while Rufus bounded into the trees. The dog sprinted back almost immediately.

"What is it, boy?" Olivia asked, as all three reached for the weapons. "Zombies?"

Rufus yipped, circling around the truck before settling by the door.

"Want to go investigate?" Pete asked.

"Not really," Corrie said.

"Hello!" Olivia called. "Anyone there?"

No reply emerged from the forest.

"Probably just a stag," Corrie said.

"Or a bear," Pete said. "Speaking of which, it's getting dark. We're going to need somewhere to sleep tonight. I don't think we can drive along those trails after dark."

"Or these roads," Olivia said. "You want to look for a motel?"

"Or a cabin," Pete said.

"Or a river," Corrie said. "Next one we see, we stop."

"You want me to drive for a bit?" Pete asked.

"Sure, yeah," Corrie said. "Although…" She peered along the road, at the trees, turning back to the TAPV just as Pete heard it: an engine.

A very civilian, very muddy, grey four-door sped along the road, clocking at least sixty which only increased as the vehicle drew near the TAPV. The car sped onward, still accelerating, leaving dust behind and Rufus huffily growling.

"Our guns must have scared them off," Pete said, seeking a charitable explanation.

"They thought we'd broken down," Corrie said. "And were worried the three armed soldiers would requisition their car."

"But their car still works," Olivia said. "So wherever it came from was beyond the EMP. Which means, I think, that no bombs fell to the west."

Corrie shrugged, but didn't answer.

One kilometre and four minutes later, the vehicle-column of refugees appeared. Travelling in the same direction as the grey car, they sped by, mostly in the other lane. A few were driving the wrong direction in the wrong lane, and hurriedly pulled in when they spotted the TAPV. A recklessly veering matte-red convertible caused Pete to swerve off the road and onto the beginning of a track. Trucks. Buses. Vans. Cars. The convoy seemed to go on forever. They were all civilian vehicles. All packed with people and possessions, but it was only the passengers who stared at the army vehicle now stopped on the roadside.

"I suppose we'll wait until they pass," Pete said. "Unless you want to try to flag one down?"

"We'd get flattened," Olivia said. "Where are they coming from? Or is that the wrong question?"

"Are they fleeing another bomb, you mean?" Corrie asked. "Or are they fleeing the undead?"

Even as they waited, and as Pete lost count of the number of vehicles in the convoy, a truck appeared on the road, coming the other direction, the way the TAPV had been travelling. An ambulance came behind, then another truck, and then a column of cars. Soon the sound of honking horns and screeching brakes wrecked the forest's silence as the two columns came within inches of disaster.

"It's too soon for them to have come from the Saint Lawrence, right?" Olivia asked.

"By at least a day," Corrie said.

Pete threw the truck into reverse.

"You're not driving out there?" Olivia asked.

"Nope," he said, turning the TAPV. "But I don't want to sit here until dark, or until a crash makes us play ambulance. Not when there are plenty of real ambulances out there on the road."

In a dead-end clearing at the end of a track they'd thought would lead to a road, they found a cabin one storm away from being a ruin. Though it was deserted now, they weren't the property's first arrivals since the outbreak. Two of the previous occupants were buried in neat graves dug beneath a towering maple.

"There's no one here," Corrie said, coming out from the small cabin. "Whoever dug those graves tidied up before they left, and took the food with them. We won't get much further before dark. Do we stop for the night, or keep going?"

"I'd like to keep going," Olivia said. "But we can't. If we crash, the message will never get through."

"Then I guess we're stopping," Corrie said. "I'll start a fire."

At least the forest provided them with plenty to burn in the small iron stove that was the cabin's only method of heating and cooking. After carrying in a third armful of reasonably dry and thoroughly dead wood, Pete collapsed onto a high-backed chair with tufts of stuffing erupting from the crudely stitched seat. It was still more comfortable than the TAPV.

"Nuclear bombs," he murmured.

"If it weren't for the zombies, I might be shocked," Olivia said. "But I just don't have any surprise left in me."

298

"We have a problem," Corrie said, entering the cabin and closing the door behind her.

"Zombies?" Pete asked.

"It's the fuel," Corrie said. "Only two of the containers we're carrying have any in them."

"Oh. I thought... sorry," Olivia said. "My fault. I should have checked them all."

"None of us checked," Corrie said. "We're all to blame. Or none of us are."

"How much do we have left? How far can we reach?" Pete asked.

"Four or five hundred kilometres," Corrie said. "That's on roads. Off road, less."

"We could get back to the judge, then?" Pete asked. "Go back, refuel. Start again. We should have brought more ammo with us anyway. And food. And water. And everything else."

"We'd lose an entire day," Olivia said.

"Can we reach Thunder Bay?" Pete asked.

"No. But we might reach Wawa," Corrie said.

"But the bomb was dropped close to Wawa," Olivia said. "I wonder if that was where those refugees were escaping, and where the others were heading. Because that's a possibility, isn't it? That more bombs were dropped elsewhere. What was the name of the lakeside town where the ferry was supposed to come?"

"Marathon," Corrie said.

"We should aim for that," Olivia said. "We could catch the ferry to Thunder Bay. Or at least get them to take a message."

Corrie unfolded the map she'd brought from the TAPV. "Other refugees will have arrived before us," she said. "Is going there the best way we can help?"

"Where else could we go?" Pete asked.

Corrie held out the map. "We're north of Wawa. I'm not sure how far north, not exactly, but there's one place we might find more fuel. We can't be far from where Kempton was building that telescope."

"Where you think the CIA caught her?" Olivia asked. "You actually want to go there?"

"Not really," Corrie said. "But they were bringing supplies and materials in on the old rail-freight line. I don't know if that's the same one that's marked on this map, but the railroad runs almost to Lake Winnipeg."

"To Pine Dock, you mean?" Pete asked.

"I think so," Corrie said, peering at the map. "I mean, no. Not to Pine Dock. I think the railroad runs close to the eastern shore of Lake Winnipeg. We'd still have to find a way around the lake to get to Pine Dock, but there were other groups, other communities, holding on up there."

"You want us to drive along the railroad?" Olivia asked.

"We got lucky today with the trails and firebreaks and roads," Corrie said. "But those refugees we saw, they'll just be the start. There'll be more over the coming days. The roads are going to be clogged."

"That still doesn't solve our lack of fuel," Pete said. "You think we can find more at the telescope?"

"It was a construction site, so probably," Corrie said. "But I thought we could look along the railroad. Steal it from a locomotive, or loot it from a depot."

"We won't find it in a gas station, that's for sure," Olivia said. "The general can't have left much on her way east, and those refugees will take the rest. A railroad? Yeah, okay. Maybe. Pete, what do you think?"

He shrugged, doing his best to hide his real feelings. "Why not," he said. But what he thought was that it didn't matter. Wawa, Thunder Bay, Pine Dock, Nanaimo. Wherever they went, wherever they reached, news of the nuclear war would travel ahead of them. By the time it reached Guam or Australia, even if help was available, it would arrive far, far too late.

Chapter 38 - If Not Us Then Who?
Ontario

"It shouldn't be such a beautiful morning," Pete said. He'd woken last, come outside, and found Olivia on the small veranda, watching dawn dance through the trees.

"No it shouldn't," Olivia said. "I'm glad it is, I wouldn't want to force our way down firebreaks in the rain." She handed him her water bottle. "That said, we could do with some rain later, assuming it isn't glowing."

"Are we wasting our time?" Pete asked. "It feels like we are. Even if we get a message to Australia, what will they be able to do? Aren't we just looking for an excuse to run away?"

"You'd prefer running towards a mushroom cloud?" Olivia asked.

"Motivation is important," Corrie said, appearing from around the side of the small cabin. "We're trying to save more than just ourselves. In doing so, we're trying to survive, but that's the by-product rather than the purpose. Besides, what else can we do? We can't stay here, so we can either go back or go on."

Pete mulled that over as they gathered their gear and headed over to the TAPV.

"Planes might work," he said, holding the door open for a reluctant Rufus who was enjoying a last minute dash after solitary bees. "If we can get a whole load of 747s to land in Thunder Bay, we could airlift everyone out. But there's the EMPs, aren't there? Maybe the planes won't be able to fly. And there needs to be somewhere to airlift them to."

"Australia," Corrie said. "That's what I'll assume until we're proved wrong. And yes, planes would be the answer. For Thunder Bay, and the Saint Lawrence. To take people out, and bring supplies in. Just like the plan was before. Despite the nuclear bombs, the war is still on. The zombies must still be defeated. But the frontline has changed, that's all."

They followed the dead-end track back to the trail, and then to a road, and onward. When they saw a house with figures in the open doorway, Olivia slowed.

"No. Zombies," Corrie said. "They're zombies. Keep driving."

"Are you sure?" Olivia asked. "There could be living people inside."

"Not in there," Corrie said. "Not this time."

Olivia didn't slow, and Pete didn't ask how Corrie could be so sure. A few miles on, they were overtaken by a trio of motorbikes, on which were five people who studiously avoided making eye contact with the military vehicle as they darted ahead.

Two kilometres later, they were forced to stop. The motorbikes had made it around the upturned truck, but the TAPV wouldn't. The juggernaut had skewed off the road, and upturned, as had its wide trailer on which it had been carrying massive blue-plastic barrels. They'd survived the crash intact but some recent travellers had ripped open one. Finding only paint inside, they'd tipped the barrel onto the roadway.

"We've got a tow cable," Olivia suggested.

"It'll take too long," Corrie said, an edge of agitation in her voice. "It's already been nearly a day."

"Then back to the trails and firebreaks it is," Olivia said.

They reversed back to the first, a recently well-driven logging trail that took them nearly due north before they reached a road, this one leading vaguely westward.

Pete didn't want to give voice to his feelings, but he guessed Corrie and Olivia must feel the same way, too. They were too late. If a billionaire with all her resources had failed to stop a nuclear war, what chance did they have of salvaging anything afterward?

"There's people ahead," Olivia said. "Waving. I think they've broken down."

"We better stop," Corrie said.

"Oh, that's odd. Now he's waving us on," Olivia said. "Weird. A moment ago he wanted us to stop, now he doesn't."

Pete leaned forward, his despair momentarily banished back to its depths. Ahead, yes, there were two young men by the roadside, and two cars, both with their hoods up, parked on the verge. One of the roadside-men had stepped back onto the verge while the other vigorously motioned the TAPV onward.

"They realised we're in a military vehicle," Pete said. "That's why they're waving us on."

"You mean they're bandits?" Corrie asked. "Already? But I think you're right."

"Do we stop?" Olivia asked, already slowing.

"Stop and do what?" Corrie asked.

"Something," Pete said. "Anything. If not us, then who?"

"Fair dinkum," Corrie said. "Olivia, stay behind the wheel. Pete, go up top. We'll do *something*, but we won't do anything stupid."

"More stupid than this?" Olivia asked, bringing the vehicle to a halt fifty metres from the two cars.

Pete opened the hatch to the machine gun mount, taking his rifle with him. Two men were by the roadside. Stubbled rather than bearded, and probably younger than him. There were other figures, too, in the shadows, and he couldn't make out how many. But there were only two cars, so no more than eight.

"G'day," Corrie called out, having climbed out. Rufus jumped out after her, taking a cautious step towards the strangers before stiffening. "Do you need a hand? A tow? A ride?"

The two men turned to each other, and then to the trees, just as uncertain how to proceed.

"We're okay," one of the men said, the closer of the two, wearing an insulated vest over what looked like a white dress shirt in dire need of a wash.

"You heard about the mushroom clouds?" Corrie asked.

"We did," the man said, after another a hesitant glance at the trees.

Corrie turned back to the TAPV. "Okay, guys, what do you want to do?" Before waiting for an answer, she peered along the road.

Pete heard it, too. Engines. A lot of them. Advancing fast.

It was a civilian convoy, mostly consisting of vans and small trucks, onto each of which had been hastily painted a red cross. The first four vehicles drove on, but the fifth, a postal delivery van, stopped in front of the TAPV.

The passenger climbed out. A bearded man in a plaid shirt, jeans, with a holster at his belt, a shotgun in his hands, and a badge around his neck.

"Sergeant Wilgus!" Olivia said, in a snap of recognition as she jumped out. On the roadside, the would-be bandits looked even more confused than ever.

The van's passenger, Sergeant Wilgus, frowned, then grinned in recognition. "It's the press corps!" he said. "Talk about a small world. Where are you heading?"

"Good question," Olivia said. "Originally, we were trying to get to Wawa, or Thunder Bay, but we're trying to get word to the Pacific. Did you... did you hear about the nuclear bombs?"

"We did," Wilgus said. "But you don't want to go to Wawa. We're evacuating. Pulling back to Thunder Bay. Picking up whomever we can from the forts, and warning the rest. We're telling them to head for Thunder Bay or Nova Scotia."

Corrie frowned. "Nova Scotia? But we came from the east. Bombs fell on Ottawa and Montreal. We're trying to get a message to Thunder Bay, or to the Pacific. To anyone. To everyone. A warning. We think the general is dead. Judge Benton is now in charge. She plans to pull everyone back to the Great Lakes."

"Ottawa and Montreal?" Wilgus asked, clearly shocked. "We thought it was just the lake."

"The lake? Which lake?" Corrie asked.

"Lake Superior," Wilgus said. "Close to the shore with Michigan. On the western side of the lake, that's where the bomb fell. You say two others fell on Ottawa and Montreal?"

"The lake must have been the mushroom cloud we saw yesterday," Pete said.

"Yesterday? You've been driving east?" Wilgus asked. He turned to look in the direction the convoy was driving. "And you saw a mushroom cloud?"

"It was in the distance, and it can't have been Lake Superior," Corrie said. "We've been driving by compass when we can, and off road when we must, but it can't have been the same cloud you saw."

"We assumed there were more," Wilgus said. "But... but assumptions kill cops. That's something my training officer taught me."

"But you're evacuating people to Thunder Bay?" Olivia asked.

"From where they'll be sent east or west," Wilgus said. "That's Crawford's plan. Go west, or go east. Nova Scotia or British Columbia. But we thought the banks of the Saint Lawrence had been secured by General Yoon."

"Captain Crawford?" Corrie asked. "He's in charge?"

Wilgus pointed at the column, which had continued on without him. "And I better catch up and warn him."

"Wait," Olivia said. "Those people there, by the road. You better take them with you. I think they were about to try to rob us."

"No problem," Wilgus said. He waved a hand at the truck which had stopped behind him. "New recruits!" he called and waved towards the roadside. A trio of soldiers jumped out and jogged over to the increasingly shocked would-be bandits. "What about you?" Wilgus asked. "Are you still going to Thunder Bay?"

"There's no point, is there?" Olivia said. "Can you spare us some diesel?"

"How much?" Wilgus asked.

"Enough for us to get to Vancouver Island," Olivia said. "There was talk of an airlift, to bring in troops to support the general. We could use those planes to get people out."

"I'd heard about that. They said to keep the runway clear. Never saw the first plane, though. You'd drive all the way to British Columbia?"

"This is too big for us to solve here," Olivia said. "But what else can we do?"

Wilgus nodded. "I don't know if I can spare you that much fuel, but I'll give you all I can."

The two bandits, and their two comrades who'd been hiding in the tree, were hustled into the back of the truck. Wilgus gave them the spare fuel, and then re-joined the column driving west.

"We're not alone," Pete said. "For a minute there, I forgot that we're not the only people left in the world. So we're going to British Columbia?"

"Pine Dock first, I think," Corrie said. "It's only the message that has to get to Vancouver Island."

"A message about planes," Pete said. "Assuming there still are any that can fly."

Chapter 39 - Beginnings and Endings
Kowkash

After they left Sergeant Wilgus and his convoy, they drove by a remote home with people watching from the windows. They didn't stop, though they debated whether they should have until they reached another house, again with a living human watching from the window. Again, they didn't stop. Again, they debated whether they should. The third house had zombies outside, with the windows and doors all broken. Again, they didn't stop. This time there was no debate.

The decision to head north, pick up the railroad, and then follow it west, was an easy one since no one had an alternative suggestion, and the railroad was easy to find. Though a rattling ride when the occasionally steep embankment forced them to drive along the tracks, at least they had solitude.

"What happens when a nuclear bomb is dropped on a lake?" Pete asked. "The water becomes radioactive, right, and the water that's vaporised becomes rain?"

"It's the wrong question," Corrie said. "The right question is how many other bombs were dropped."

"No, I was thinking about the general's plan," Pete said. "To turn the centre of America into a giant farm to feed the world as we fought the zombies. If the rainwater is radioactive, if the ground water is contaminated, the crops will die."

"That's why they're pulling back to British Columbia and Nova Scotia," Corrie said.

"Not Nova Scotia," Pete said. "Not anymore. And is it British Columbia, or just Vancouver Island?" But it was a question none of them could answer.

The lonely railroad offered few distractions from their grim thoughts. The isolated houses and infrequent small hamlets through which they travelled appeared deserted, both of people, and the undead. The vastness beyond was just as unforgiving. Just as empty of life. Pete turned his gaze from the tracks to the trees, and then to the sky, hoping to spot a bird, a bee, anything that might confirm they weren't the last beings alive. But, instead, he saw something utterly out of place in the rural woodland.

"Is that a crane?" he asked, peering forward.

"Nope. Three cranes," Olivia said.

Far taller than the trees, two were painted blue and one a yellow that might be charitably described as gold. They loomed above the ancient pines, less than a mile further along the tracks.

"It's Kempton's telescope," Corrie said. "That was Kowkash back down the tracks."

"When?" Pete asked. "You mean that siding was the town?"

"I don't think it's a town," Corrie said.

"And I don't think this is a telescope," Olivia said.

As they drew nearer, it became clear the cranes weren't as large as they'd first appeared. They still loomed over the massive pines, but a wide swathe of woodland had been cleared and levelled around them.

"This doesn't look like a telescope," Pete said. "It's more like a railroad junction."

The rail line split into five sets of tracks. The outermost each had at two sidings, with a further branch line leading to the north. Even more rails were placed in two-metre high stacks beneath the cranes. Lining either side of the newly laid tracks, and sometimes dotted between, were prefab huts, all sky blue or golden yellow, complete with guttering, and a forest of signage. Some of the huts on the forest-facing southern side were double-wide, made of two joined together, with curtains hanging on the windows, a porch over the door, and a plank sidewalk ringing the outside. From how the porch was painted white, and the sidewalk was unseasoned, that was the relatively recent work of whoever had been stationed at the construction site over the winter.

"It *is* a railroad junction," Pete said as the TAPV idled at the edge of the site. "She wasn't building a telescope after all."

"No, she was," Corrie said. "But it would have taken a decade to finish. They had to build the junction so they could bring in the equipment and materials to build a train line up to the site before they could even lay the foundations."

"Why?" Olivia whispered. "Ten billion dollars. That's what the news report said. But why? Why here? I bet there was another reason."

"Do you really think this is where they caught her?" Pete asked. "How would she have gotten here? How would they?"

"Yeah, I don't know," Corrie said. "When looking at the map, it made sense, but looking at this place, I'm not sure. There's no locomotive."

"Should there be?" Pete asked.

"Probably," Corrie said. "For shunting the construction equipment around after it arrived. And there's no people. Whoever hung the curtains in that cabin's window, they've left. I guess by train. Probably after the outbreak. I don't think we'll find any more diesel here."

"Do we need it?" Olivia asked.

"If we have to keep going west after we reach Pine Dock, maybe," Corrie said. "And we do need food and water."

Cautiously, Pete opened the door. Before he could climb out, Rufus jumped over him and outside, circling the TAPV before giving a satisfied bark.

"He seems happy enough," Corrie said. "I suppose it's too far from anywhere for any zombies to be nearby. I'll fill up the truck if you two want to look for some food."

With Rufus happily bounding back and forth at their side, Pete and Olivia picked their way over the newly laid train tracks, and towards the forest-facing cabins with the curtains and wooden boardwalk.

"Footprints," Pete said, pointing down at the muddy track, half-filled with water.

"Must have belonged to someone in the construction crew," Olivia said.

"I can't smell smoke, though," Pete said. "And if you were stuck out here, after the end of the world, you'd light a fire, wouldn't you?"

"I think I'd leave," Olivia said. "It'd be like the cabin in Michigan, but worse. More remote, so safer in that respect. But whoever was stranded here after the outbreak had been living here before. Probably on a shift system, one week on, one off, here to supervise the unloading of materials for construction in the spring. But even with a porch and sidewalk and curtains, this can't have been a fun place to live. And after the outbreak, they'd have wanted to return to their families."

"Just before they used so much diesel they wouldn't get their locomotive to... to wherever," Pete said. "You think they left after the outbreak, then?"

"About a week after, I guess," she said. "After the relief shift didn't arrive, and so when it was clear things weren't going to get back to normal."

Neat pre-printed signs, in English and French, adorned each cabin, though the words bore little relation to what was inside. The double-long cabin with an extended awning over an equally long porch wasn't a canteen and first-aid post, but a storage room filled with sacks of sand and neat stacks of track-ties. Conversely, the smaller cabin marked as a store had been turned into a two-room bunkhouse, with curtains on the recently added windows, foam panelling to provide insulation, and a neat chimney affixed to the wall.

"Two people remained to watch the site over winter," Olivia said. "From how the beds are neatly made, I think they left soon after the outbreak. So soon, they thought things would get back to normal, and they might want their old jobs back."

"There's nothing useful in the cupboards," Pete said. "Two beds. No chairs. A stove, but no cooking utensils. No sink. I guess we'll find that somewhere else."

They went back outside and continued along the warped wooden boards to the next cabin, another store. After that, the boardwalk ended, and they were back to walking in the mud as they picked their way around a stack of rails next to a swathe of levelled ground on which, presumably, it was intended they be laid.

"Maybe this is the answer," Olivia said.

"Hmm? For us? If we're living somewhere this remote, my vote's for a cabin in the outback."

"No, we could use the railroad to evacuate the survivors from the Saint Lawrence," she said. "And use the tracks to move them wherever we need to afterwards. It won't be easy, but if the planes were all damaged by an EMP or knocked out of the sky, we need an alternative. We can still get through this, all of us. We can still stop the undead. We just have to think differently, that's all."

"Pull them back to Pine Dock or somewhere, build the forts along the train tracks," Pete said, trying to warm to the idea. "Yeah, maybe."

"Yeah," she echoed. "Maybe. We'll try two more cabins, then head back. That large one first?"

Beyond the levelled ground was another neat row of recently decorated cabins. The first was another pair of single units, joined together. Steel trim covered the seam, from which oxidised orange streaks now spread onto the chipped blue walls. The plastic secondary glazing was another on-site addition, with more steel trim holding the almost-transparent sheet in place. Floral print curtains hung, closed, inside. A mostly metal porch stood above the door, next to a distinctly uncomfortable looking metal bench.

Pete pushed the door open.

It was gloomy inside, though not dark, and there was enough light to see the tools. Neat rows of picks, shovels, levers, spades, rakes, and spanners dominated one half of the pair of cabins. On one wall hung hard hats, on the other was a shelving unit with neat steel boxes of pins and bolts. Whoever had been responsible for these stores had also used the cabin as an office. One they'd made comfortable. A sink had been bolted to one wall, a small kettle and coffee pot on the metal worktop next to it. A rug covered the floor beneath the table, with another beneath the trio of folding chairs.

But what struck Pete most, and what had hit him the moment he'd entered the cabin, was the smell of decay. What had hit him second was the sight of the bodies. There were four in total. Two sat in the chairs, two lay on the rug. Two men, two women, all in military fatigues and body armour. All had been shot multiple times.

Rufus gave a soulful whine.

Olivia stepped forward, letting the door swing shut, cutting out the principal source of light. But the sudden gloom made it easier to see the light piercing through the bullet holes in the wall behind the table. Dozens of them. Pete turned around to check behind, but no, there were none in the opposite wall.

"They were shot from here," he said, his voice sombrely quiet. "From the doorway."

"They're not zombies," Olivia said, taking a step forward. "Or were they?"

"Bitten, maybe, but not turned," Pete said.

"No, I don't think so," she said, taking another step forward. She knelt. "No, this woman wasn't shot in the head. So... if she was infected, she'd have turned, yes? Or no?"

"I'm not sure," Pete said. "Maybe she was like us, immune."

"Maybe," Olivia said. "Wait, hang on." She leaned forward, gently rolling the dead woman onto her back. "I know her."

"You do?"

"And so do you," Olivia said. "Come here. Have a look."

Reluctantly, he did. "No, I don't think so."

"What about the others, do you recognise them?" she asked.

"Well, there's no way anyone would recognise *him*," Pete said, indicating the man who'd taken at least two bullets to the back of his head. He swallowed hard, turning away from the gory mess, looking instead at the man on the floor, then the woman slumped in the chair. "I... no. I don't think so."

"They were in Wawa," Olivia said. "With Trowbridge. These are the U.S. Marines the general gave Trowbridge as a protection detail."

"Are you sure?"

"She reminded me a little of a cheerleader in high school," Olivia said, indicating the dead Marine at her feet. "I don't *think* it's her." She reached down to find the Marine's dog tags. "Ramirez. No. It's not her."

"Their weapons are missing," Pete said. "Taken after they were shot, I guess. If it was before, if they were prisoners, they'd be tied up, right?"

"Maybe," Olivia said, looking around. "I don't think they knew they were in danger. Those two on the floor, I guess they were sitting and had time to stand, but death had to have been unexpected."

"Kempton," Pete said. "It has to be. Or her people. She… somehow, she persuaded Trowbridge to come here, where she knew she had people waiting, people who then killed the Marines."

"Could be," Olivia said. "So where's Trowbridge? Where are the other bodies? Or were the Marines sent here alone?"

"We're not going to find the answers standing here, are we?" Pete said. "So I guess the question is whether we want to look for them outside, or just keep driving?"

Near the door, where he'd stayed since entering, Rufus gave a now familiar, low growl. Outside came a soft squelch. A shadow moved across the window.

Olivia raised her rifle, then paused. She pointed to Pete's belt, at the suppressed pistol.

Pete nodded what he thought was understanding: a zombie was outside, and they needed to kill it quietly. But they also needed to preserve ammunition. He reached for the nearest tool, a spade, carefully lifting it from the rack.

Olivia shook her head.

Pete raised the spade, holding it at head-height in front of the door.

Again, Olivia shook her head, but holding her rifle with one hand, she reached for the door handle with the other. Giving a pronounced nod of her head, exaggeratedly mouthing the words, she counted to three, and pulled the door open.

Pete saw the eyes first, the gun second, and froze. The figure on the other side of the door was alive. Wearing a ski mask and body armour over hunting gear. She stood in the muddy track, two metres from the cabin, feet pointing towards the railroad, as had been the machine pistol in her hands, until the door had opened. Now it pivoted with her as she turned towards them.

Rufus bounded forward, charging at the woman. She stepped sideways, but not fast enough. Not faster than Olivia's bullet which slammed into her cheek, and up into her brain.

"It was her or you," Olivia whispered. "I just hope—"

But before she could finish, another shot sounded. And then a barrage of gunfire returned, all coming from the direction of the TAPV.

"Think later, act now," Olivia said.

Their boots kicked up a rain of mud as they sprinted towards the gunfire. Only when they were close enough to hear bullets ricochet off the stack of un-placed rails ahead of them did they slow. And only when they'd reached the stack did Pete think to check behind them. But no one was there, and their frantic dash had provided ample opportunity to be mown down.

"They're between us and your sister," Olivia said as another bullet smacked into the stack of steel. "It's Corrie's bullets hitting these tracks. We're in exactly the wrong place." She peered around the corner, crouching, then standing, then ducked back into cover. "There are two of them. But if we shoot, we might hit Corrie, and if we leave cover, she might hit us."

Pete looked around and behind, and saw inspiration. "Got it," he said. "I'll get them to move."

"How?" Olivia asked.

But Pete was already running. Rufus bounded along at his side, but then veered leftward, disappearing behind a pair of cabins stacked one on top of the other. A metal staircase provided access to the topmost cabin, and would provide a perfect vantage point, but Pete knew he wasn't a good enough shot to play sniper. He ducked behind a small excavator with a broken pneumatic arm.

He'd been hoping the vehicle might work, that the sound of it might provide enough of a distraction, but the cover had been removed from the control box, and the wires hung loose from where someone else had abandoned a futile repair. Instead, he unslung his rifle.

In Whitney, he'd spent an hour practicing, expending the one hundred bullets Judge Benton felt could be spared. His skill level still tended to *shooting-towards* rather than *shooting-at*, but that was all he'd need. From behind the excavator, he could see both of the enemy. Two men. Crouched at either end of a long pile of concrete sleepers. One had a machine pistol, the other a rifle. Possibly automatic, though he was firing single shots. Why were they waiting?

Pete aimed the barrel at the back of the man with the machine pistol.

They were waiting for the woman with the machine pistol who Olivia had shot to sneak around the back of the TAPV. That was it.

He breathed out.

Who were they? The thought made him pause. But only for a heartbeat. They were the people shooting at his sister. He fired.

From the way the man jerked and spun, the bullets had hit. From the way he pivoted, spraying bullets from his machine pistol, Pete had hit his bulletproof vest.

Pete ducked back behind the excavator, counted to three, and was about to spin around and fire another shot when Rufus barked. Pete looked left and right for the dog, but couldn't see him. Then Pete looked up, and into the barrel of a gun.

The man stood at the top of the stairs above Pete, on the landing just by the door to the upper-storey cabin. Pete had been right, it was the perfect place for a sniper. This one had been waiting until Pete saw him. Then he smiled.

Rufus barked again. Pete caught the flash of fur as the dog bounded up the steps. The sniper half turned, and so was caught off balance as Rufus charged into him. Dog and sniper hit the thin rail around the landing's edge. Momentum caused Rufus to bounce back and skitter down the metal stairs, while it caused the sniper to trip, topple, fall, landing heavily in the mud with a dull crack of breaking bone. But that didn't slow him.

The sniper threw himself sideways, scything his leg out, knocking Pete down. Pete lost hold of the rifle. When he scrabbled upright, the weapon was out of reach. The sniper grinned. His face was streaked in mud, his left arm hung limp, but his right reached for a long knife at his belt. The wickedly curved blade was no one's standard issue, and met no government's regulations. It wasn't a hunter's tool, nor even an assassin's blade. It was a killer's toy, and from the way the blade danced, this killer had played the game often.

"I'm waiting," the man said.

Pete glanced at the rifle, but he wouldn't reach it in time. He reached for his belt, drawing his own knife.

The killer's grin grew wider until, again, a dart of fur bounded out of the shadows. This time the killer caught sight of the dog, managing to step sideways as Rufus skidded across the mud.

Pete, taking advantage of the distraction, dived forward, stabbing the knife forward. The killer sensed the movement, turning again, this time into the blade.

The knife slid into the man's throat as if it were paper, lodging even as the man's eyes went wide. The killer dropped his own blade as he reached his one working hand up to clutch the wound, already pouring blood. Pete stepped back, and again, as the killer stepped after him, but the dying man only managed three paces before collapsing to his knees, then the mud, pulsing blood onto the already disturbed ground.

Rufus yipped, bringing Pete back to himself, to the moment, and the still real danger, only then realising the gunfire had ceased. He grabbed his fallen rifle and looked towards the TAPV, and saw the other two shooters were dead.

"Four of them?" Pete asked, picking his way across the bullet-flecked mud, towards Olivia and Corrie, standing near one of the corpses by the stacked railroad sleepers.

"Four?" Olivia asked. "What happened to you?"

Pete looked at the blood. "It's not mine. I guess I'm asking... actually, I don't really know what I'm asking."

"It happened after I'd finished refuelling," Corrie said. "I heard a shot, turned around, saw them, and took cover. They fired first."

"The first shot was me," Olivia said. "A woman in a ski mask, outside a cabin where we found the bodies of the dead Marines that the general sent to guard Trowbridge."

Corrie blinked, slowly processing the news. "The Marines?"

"Murdered," Pete said. "Shot. Not infected."

"Probably," Olivia clarified.

Corrie knelt and pulled the ski mask from the face of the dead man at her feet. "Do you recognise him?"

"No," Pete said.

"No," Olivia said. "Should I?"

"I don't know," Corrie said. "I don't recognise him, but I wonder..." She checked his left arm, then his right, pulling back the sleeve with a hiss of resigned triumph. "A branch with three leaves."

"What does that mean?" Olivia asked.

"The cartel," Pete said. "Like in Australia. The people who were after Kempton down there. Right?" he added, hoping that Corrie would tell him he was wrong.

"Right," Corrie said. "We can be grateful they were only gangsters and not trained soldiers."

"The cartel are here?" Olivia asked.

Corrie stood. "The Marines are here, and they're dead? What about Trowbridge?"

"We didn't see any other bodies," Olivia said. "Just those four Marines."

"Then the cartel have Trowbridge," Corrie said. "Maybe the CIA people, too. Unless they're dead."

"And Kempton," Pete said.

"And her," Corrie said.

"It was Winters giving the orders, not Trowbridge," Olivia said. "Not that it matters."

"They were trying *not* to hit the TAPV," Corrie said. "I think they wanted to steal it, so they could drive out of here."

317

"Meaning they're alone and without transport?" Olivia asked.

"I think so," Corrie said.

"But you want to make sure?" Olivia asked.

"Not really," Corrie said. "I'd like to just drive away and never look back, but when we get wherever we're going, unless Trowbridge is there, they'll send people to look for him. Even now. Even after a nuclear apocalypse. They *will* send a team to find the president. We should confirm he's not here."

"By looking in the other cabins for bodies?" Pete asked.

"Those cartel people weren't staying in these cabins," Olivia said. "Where those trees are cleared, there, to the north, does that lead to where the actual observatory was being built?"

"Probably," Corrie said. "And it's the right direction for the gangsters to have come from." She glanced up at the cranes. "And if there were more here, if there were sentries up there, they'd have made their move."

"And so would the zombies," Olivia said. "One hour, no more. One hour, whether we find anything or anyone, and then we go."

But Pete knew, now they'd begun, they'd keep searching until they were certain there was nothing to be found.

With rainwater filling the deep ruts left by the construction machines, and slippery mud coating everything else, they soon left the unpaved track and ventured into the trees, finding easier going between the towering pines. From the red and orange paint ringing the trunks, many had been marked for logging, but to them, at least, the apocalypse had brought a stay of execution. The paint gave an indication of the vast scale of Kempton's ambition for the observatory, though it was, and forevermore would be, no more than a circular kilometre of mostly cleared forest.

Ninety percent of the perimeter was marked by a low fence, sturdy enough to keep out a curious deer, though not a determined bear. However, close to the rolling gate, a hundred metres of fencing had been entirely removed.

Parked neatly near the gate was a row of saw-and-claw harvesters, while inside the fence were more cabins, of a similar style to those by the train tracks. The blue and gold painted huts were clustered together seemingly at random, but around one, a solitary cabin near the centre of the site, Pete saw the missing fencing.

"Are those people?" he asked. "Can you see where I mean, that cabin in the middle with the fencing around it?"

"They're zombies," Corrie said. "Dressed in blue and gold. It's the same kind of gear we found aboard Kempton's jet."

"That's what happened to them?" Olivia asked, leaning around the tree she was sheltering behind. "Kempton's people are zombies. But they built a smaller defensive perimeter around that cabin? That doesn't make sense. Not if those cartel people were living here. Why didn't they kill the zombies?"

"Because they're keeping someone prisoner," Pete said. "The zombies are the jailers. Ten bucks says Trowbridge is inside. And another ten says he's dead."

"But we'll have to check, won't we?" Olivia said. "Damn it. Why couldn't the general have taken that message from us in Wawa and told us to get lost? Those cabins look similar to the huts by the railroad. A bullet would go straight through. If I go get the TAPV and... and yes, drive it through the perimeter-gap where they removed the fence, then down that sort-of-avenue by the tree-harvesters, I can stop right next to the fence. That'll get the zombies away from the cabin. Corrie, you can shoot them. Pete, you can rescue our illustrious president, if he's still alive. And if he doesn't give you a seat on his cabinet for it, then we'll let him walk back to civilisation."

"I'll settle for a cold beer and a hot bath," Pete said.

"Times three," Corrie said.

With Rufus following Olivia, Pete and Corrie jogged in the other direction, through the trees, down the slope, and to the gap in the fence ringing the construction site. Up close, the facility was larger than he'd first assumed, though the fence was no higher. That was something, he thought. If Kempton had been prepping for the undead, she'd have built a taller fence.

Inside, blue ropes divided the mud that was intended to become road and the mud that was scheduled to be excavated for foundations, though with occasional yellow ropes ringing circles of ground-hugging yellow-petal flowers. He wished he knew their name. Above all, he wished they hadn't been there. Someone in the construction crew must have planted them. Perhaps rescuing them from the ground levelled for the train tracks. Their wages, after taking such meticulous care over the plants, had been to become one of the undead now guarding the fenced cabin.

More ropes branched left and right, marking temporary avenues. But though, on foot, the site seemed larger than it had on first sight, they soon reached the near-centre, and the cabin ringed by fencing. He and Corrie took shelter opposite the fence, behind the corner of a long cabin where four of the prefabs had been joined together, end to end.

"Seven," Corrie whispered. "Seven zombies. Definitely zombies."

Pete nodded. He could hear them beating against the solitary cabin. Whoever had dismantled the outer fence and rebuilt it here had realised that it wasn't tall enough to hold the undead. They'd built it to double-height, with the upper ring wired to the lower, the entire edifice held in place by an odd mix of poles and props, some metal, some timber, and all surely whatever had been close to hand. Though haphazard, it was sturdy enough to keep the undead inside.

Pete rolled back around the corner, leaning against the wall of the cabin. "There's definitely someone inside the cabin," he whispered.

"The way those zombies are trying to break in? Yep," Corrie said.

"Why would Kempton have brought Trowbridge here?"

"Winters, not Kempton," Corrie said. "And because of the helipad. That's how she was going to get out."

"The helipad?"

"You didn't see it? Down the avenue marked with flowers."

"Oh. Right. Sure." Pete peered around the corner again. "They're all dressed in blue and gold. The zombies. That's her people." He leaned back against the hut. "So that's what went wrong. Kempton's people were here." He frowned. "So were they infected? Or did they get infected afterwards?" He glanced at the ground, then left and right. "*How* did they get infected? How did zombies get here?"

"Good question," Corrie said. "A better one is how we're going to get through that fence."

Pete took one more look around the hut.

"I can't see a gate. It must be on the far side. I'll go look for it."

"No, wait," Corrie said. "There might be more zombies roaming the construction site. Better we stick together. We can figure out how to get inside after we've shot the zombies."

"Speaking of that, where's Olivia? Shouldn't she have got here by now?"

"Give her time," Corrie said.

Again, he listened for the TAPV. He should have heard it by now. What if there were more gangsters? What if they'd followed the sound of gunfire down to the train tracks?

There *were* more of the gangsters.

They *hadn't* gone down to the train tracks.

"Well, isn't this nice?" a woman said from above. "No, don't move."

Pete spun. Corrie did the same. Above, on the flat roof of the extended cabin, stood the CIA agent, Ms Winters, a gun trained on them both.

"We're not with the cartel," Corrie said quickly.

"Pity," Winters said. Her gun didn't move. "Drop your rifles. Thank you."

"But *you* are with the cartel, aren't you?" Corrie asked as Pete dropped his rifle, and she leaned hers against the cabin wall.

"Not *with*, no," Winters said. "Ah, Feldman. Watch them!"

A man in body armour over a blue and gold jumpsuit had appeared from the far end of the cabin. He carried a submachine gun to which was attached a suppressor.

Winters lithely jumped down from the roof, landing with a spray of mud on the loose-packed dirt. "I see you're members of the press," she said, pointing at the faded paint on their battered body armour. "Why are you here?"

"We're looking for fuel," Corrie said. "We're taking news of what happened along the Saint Lawrence to British Columbia."

"Except you're not, are you?" Winters asked, seemingly incurious as to what had happened on the Saint Lawrence. "I recognise you two. You were in Wawa. You had a dog, didn't you? And here you are, and you know about the cartel. So, who are you really?"

"Just curious journalists," Corrie said with an edge of desperation.

Winters shook her head. "No, that won't do." She extracted a small aluminium case from a hip pocket. "What are you two to each other? Friends? Comrades? Lovers? No... there's a similarity in appearance. You're related, aren't you?"

Pete said nothing. Nor did Corrie. Even so, Winters smiled.

"Ah, I thought so." She opened the case. Inside were five small vials and a pair of syringes. "This is *it*," she said. "Such a small thing. Such an innocuous thing. Yet it is the root of all our troubles, the seed of all our solutions." She held it up, smiled, and waited.

"That's the virus?" Corrie asked.

Winters gave a satisfied nod. "And I shall infect one of you. The other will live. So, I shall ask again, how did you come to be here, and who are you really?"

"Is that what happened to those people behind us?" Corrie asked. "You infected them deliberately? That's why you're happy standing here in the open? You know there are no more undead anywhere nearby."

"Indeed," Winters said. "But I'm very tired of people asking me questions without answering my own. One of you lives. The other dies. Decide."

Pete glanced at the soldier, but he was four metres away, with the barrel raised, his finger on the trigger. Winters was closer, but not close enough. He shook his head. Corrie simply shrugged.

"Ah, no, you misunderstand," Winters said. "I appreciate you would rather die than betray each other. But would you die to save the other? If you talk, I'll infect you, and let the other live."

Pete looked at Corrie and nodded his head. Corrie looked at Pete and shook hers.

322

"Yeah, fine," Pete said quickly. "I'll talk. If you let her go. Now. First."

"Oh, no," Winters said. "Not yet." She stabbed the needle into his arm, depressing the plunger even as he reflexively pulled his arm back. He swore. Loudly, and again, cursing in increasing volume because he was almost sure he'd heard something on the wind. Almost sure. Certain enough to take a gamble on being immune, but not so certain he'd risk Corrie's life, too.

"Oh, it doesn't hurt that bad," Winters said. "Not yet. The pain comes next, from what I've seen. Next and soon. So talk or I'll infect her, too."

The rumbling roar grew in volume.

"Fine," Pete said loudly, staring at Winters. "I'll talk. I work for Lisa Kempton. That's right. I sell carpets for her. Regional manager, for the Midwest, that's me."

Winters frowned, tilted her head, stepped back, and peered along the avenue, then up at the sky. "Feldman, go," she said, as she snapped the metal case closed and drew her sidearm, aiming the pistol at Pete and Corrie.

Feldman had managed two steps out onto the roped avenue when the TAPV, weaving erratically as it bounced over the rutted unpaved mud, sped towards them. Without slowing, the truck slammed into the corner of the wire fence ringing the cabin. Metal struts flew into the air. Wooden props snapped. The upper row of fencing collapsed as the TAPV kept going. The armoured vehicle carved through six metres of the barrier before riding up and onto a timber beam sturdier than the others. Wheels still spinning, it twisted, rolled, landing on the passenger side, the undercarriage facing the cabin and the now approaching undead jailers.

"Kill the hostiles," Winters said wearily.

Feldman raised his weapon and began shooting the undead. One shot, one kill, and each in the forehead.

Pete coughed. He clutched his stomach, doubling over.

"Ah, he turned quickly, this one," Winters said. "I wouldn't do that," she added as Corrie knelt down by her brother's side.

Pete groaned, hunching over, twisting so he was side on to Winters. Turning so the CIA agent couldn't see Corrie reach for his holster. Groaning loudly to cover the sound of the button being unsnapped. Behind them, from the direction of the cabin, came a loud bark, then an even louder burst of automatic fire.

As Winters looked up, Corrie drew Pete's sidearm, emptying three bullets into the CIA agent's head. As Winters died, Corrie spun to face Feldman, firing even as more bullets were fired from the shadows. By the time Pete had dragged himself up, Feldman was as dead as the zombies now dripping gore into the mud.

Rufus bounded forward, leaping up, paws forward, onto Pete's waist, nearly knocking him back over.

"Are you okay?" Olivia asked, stepping out of the shadows as Pete grabbed his rifle.

"I think so… maybe. More or less. Assuming I really am immune. Ask me again tomorrow. How did you survive the crash? You don't even look scratched."

"I wasn't in the truck," Olivia said. "There was another guy waiting by the TAPV when I got back." She shrugged. "I figured there might be more of them. So when I got back to the track, I stopped and came to take a look. I saw you two, and them, and did the rest with a rock on the gas and my belt on the steering wheel. That's Winters, isn't it?"

"It is," Pete said. "It was. And she was cartel." He bent down and took out the small case from the corpse's pocket. He extracted the vials and crushed them beneath his boot. "Let's go see if Trowbridge is still alive. Wow," he added, as they walked nearer to the TAPV. "That fence really did a number on the truck. I guess we're walking to Pine Dock."

It wasn't Trowbridge in the cabin.

The key was in the lock. Even as Corrie turned it, the door was pulled inward from the other side, revealing a dishevelled, unwashed, but smiling face.

"Lisa Kempton," Corrie said.

324

"Ms Guinn, did I not say we'd meet again? Mr Guinn, as always, it is a genuine pleasure to see you. And what did you say your dog's name was?"

"Rufus," Pete said.

"Rufus, wonderful. And have I had the pleasure?" she added, addressing Olivia.

"This is Olivia Preston," Pete said.

"His girlfriend," Olivia added. "And your former employee. Pete and I worked together in the carpet store in South Bend."

"Ah, you are the young woman to whom he was talking in the snow," Kempton said. "But how did you come to be here? No," she added, holding up a hand. "There isn't time. Not here. Not yet. How many are dead?"

"Of Winters's people? Five, plus Feldman and Winters herself," Corrie said. "Why are you here?"

"Where else would I be?" Kempton said, striding across the mud to where Feldman lay. She picked up the suppressed submachine gun from where it had fallen. "You said seven are dead? There could be two more," she said. "Hoyle left two days ago, with the majority of Winters's people. Two others disappeared last night. I think they decided a nuclear war voided all contracts and obligations, and that they would be better seeking employment in sunnier climes. It is possible I am wrong, so we must be cautious. And we must be quick. Did you come here to find me?"

"No, we're here more or less by accident," Pete said. "We're on our way to British Columbia, to see if help can be found for the army that was being formed along the Saint Lawrence."

"These are the soldiers who were in Wawa?" Kempton asked. "Led by General Yoon?"

"Them and others who've come to the colours since," Corrie said.

"A lot of others," Pete added. "Canadian and American. But they were close to at least one of the nuclear bombs. We're not sure how close, or how many are still alive, or what help can come, but we've got to try."

"Don't we indeed?" Kempton said.

"These zombies, they were your employees?" Olivia asked.

"The winter logging team," Kempton said. "Merely seasonal labourers employed to clear the land for this facility prior to the installation of phase-one, the more permanent base for staff. I assumed they had left. After news of the undead, after three weeks without pay, why would they stay?"

"They weren't soldiers?" Corrie asked.

"Soldiers are for armies," Kempton said. "And armies are for countries. When individuals like myself gather them, it is called a gang, and I despise those."

"Which isn't really an answer," Corrie said. "But at least it wasn't a question."

Kempton smiled. "Yes, I promised Tamika I would try to kick that habit. Speaking of her, we should get moving."

"Wait," Corrie said. "Why did you bring Winters here? You did, didn't you? Coming here was your idea?"

"Of course," Kempton said. "After I was captured, after she took me to Wawa, I needed an alternate plan. I led Winters to believe that this was an extraction site, a place where I kept supplies and a helicopter. In truth, assuming the site would be deserted, I thought it the best place to strand her. Here, somewhere the landscape would kill her. Unfortunately, the presence of the logging crew rather derailed my plans. No pun intended. This way," she added, picking her way across the mud, away from the cabin and its corpses. "From what you said, you are aware there has been a nuclear exchange?"

"Yes," Corrie said. "They dropped bombs on Montreal and Ottawa, and on Lake Superior. We're not sure where else, but there was at least one more mushroom cloud."

"Many, many more, I'm afraid," Kempton said. "Yes, I failed, Ms Guinn. I do not know the extent of my failure, nor whether I achieved more than the smallest measure of success. Regardless, responsibility lies with me. I did not try hard enough. I can blame the existence of the undead, but that will not cure the world of these new ills. No. But when I implied this might be a safe redoubt for Winters, I still hoped the nuclear

326

war might be averted. After Washington, after the British announced their evacuation, it was a slim hope. A forlorn one, as it turns out."

"Despair solves nothing," Olivia said.

"An apt saying for our times," Kempton said.

"It was something our old boss used to say. The woman you bought the carpet store from."

"Nora Mathers? A charming woman," Kempton said. "I wish I'd met her under different circumstances. Now, here we are." She'd stopped outside another cabin. This one had no fence, but there was a padlock on the door. "After we left Wawa, we came here."

"Wait," Olivia said. "You tried to stop this nuclear exchange?"

"Indeed."

"With Corrie's help?" Olivia asked.

"In part. And with the assistance of others, and through my own efforts. Yes. Obviously, I failed."

"Because the plans were already underway," Olivia said. "The orders had already been given before the outbreak, right? So if it hadn't been for the undead, the nuclear war might have been stopped?"

"And if it hadn't been for the nuclear bombs, the undead might have been stopped," Kempton said. "Though dwelling on what might have been is surely the shortest route to despair. It was about power. Politicians desperate to acquire it, and gangsters eager to avoid capture and death. That is how it began, years ago. The situation escalated. Their fears fed one another, became intertwined until their fates were linked. Their failure, and their deaths, was inevitable. Or would have been had it not been for the undead."

"How did you get to Wawa?" Pete asked. "How come you were a prisoner there?"

"Those are questions for another time," Kempton said. "And time is pressing. As I say, Hoyle left a few days ago with most of Winters's crew. She, and they, must be stopped. After we left Wawa, I still hoped that the nuclear war had been averted. I believed coming here, stranding Winters in the frozen north, would give a chance for the Marines to act. They died first. I still hoped the cartel thugs would have deserted, and perhaps, in time, they would. Ms Guinn, would you mind assisting me with the door?"

"You want me to open the cabin?" Corrie asked. "Who's in here?"

"Trowbridge," Kempton said. She slapped the side of the cabin. "Trowbridge? Are you alive?"

A pitiful groan came from inside that certainly didn't belong to a zombie.

"They brought the president here, too?" Olivia asked.

"Despite the ceremony you witnessed, he is not the president," Kempton said. "I don't believe Grant Maxwell is actually dead, and there are others more senior than Trowbridge still alive, or who *were* alive before I was so rudely detained. From what I have learned in the last few days, Trowbridge was the cartel's insurance policy in case the nuclear war was averted. Winters had her own plans, of course. She intended to be made Vice President, then she would have killed Trowbridge herself. The sisters, the women who run the cartel, wouldn't have stood for it. They don't want to be the people *in* power, but the people in the shadows, controlling those in high office. Without the nuclear exchange, the cartel and the politicians, and their agents like Winters, would have killed one another. The collateral damage would have been high, but that is the cost of such a venal pursuit of power. Of course, the nuclear war changes everything. Perhaps the sisters are dead. Perhaps the other pretender-presidents perished, too. We do not need presidents and prime ministers, but we do need leaders. We need to galvanise the survivors, to bring them together, to salvage what we can, to rebuild what we must, and replace what we need. The door, Ms Guinn."

With her bayonet, she broke the lock.

Kempton pulled the lock free, pushed the door inward, took a step back and sighed. She raised the submachine gun, and fired. Three shots, and then another three.

"Whoa, what!" Olivia exclaimed.

Oddly, Pete wasn't surprised.

"He didn't deserve to live," Kempton said.

"He was a prisoner, like you!" Olivia said.

"Not like me, no," Kempton said.

"Yes, no," Olivia said. "Because he ran a dozen charities while you were busy playing games with the lives of everyone on this planet."

"Ah, his charity work, yes," Kempton said. "He claimed to be rehabilitating and rehousing young offenders. Very young. You don't want to know what he really did."

"No, we don't," Corrie said firmly. "Okay, so Trowbridge is dead. But you say there are others calling themselves president?"

"There are, or there were," Kempton said. "Around themselves, they will gather military units and resources that would be better spent keeping the wider population alive. I will take care of them, one way or another. Unfortunately, that will not be an ending, but only the beginning. The nuclear war changed everything. Our purpose now, everyone's purpose, is to ensure our species survives."

"And you want us to come help you?" Corrie asked.

Kempton smiled. "No, I think not. There is someone on the U.S. East Coast whose assistance I shall enlist. Besides, I only have room in my helicopter for two."

"Your helicopter?" Pete asked. "I thought you said that was a ruse."

"Indeed it was," Kempton said, "but that doesn't mean I would be so foolish as not to make provision for my own escape. You said that you were on your way to British Columbia? You won't make it on foot. To the west is a river. Follow it north for ten kilometres. You will reach a small hut in which there are some dirt bikes. They won't get you to British Columbia quickly, but it will be faster than if you were on foot. In the hut is a small safe. Do not touch it. It's wired to blow."

"To blow?" Pete asked.

"Blow up," Kempton said. "That was my plan-C. Plan-A was to escape. Plan-B is the two-seater helicopter I shall be flying eastward. It is also wired to blow, but I can disable the device. The devices in the safe, I cannot. The codes were changed after the outbreak."

"That's why you really brought Winters and Trowbridge here?" Olivia asked. "So you could blow them up."

"I hoped I could persuade them to blow *themselves* up," Kempton said.

"Dirt bikes won't work," Olivia said. "Not for Rufus. We'll have to see if we can get the TAPV fixed."

"There isn't time," Kempton said. "But it is a two-seater helicopter. He can come with me. How do you feel about flying, Rufus?"

The dog twitched his head.

"You want me to give you Rufus?" Olivia asked.

"I am preventing you from having to make a very hard decision ten kilometres down the road," Kempton said.

Olivia shook her head. "You took my job, then you took my boyfriend, and now you're taking my dog."

"Mr Guinn has been returned to you, and so shall your dog be. British Columbia, you say?"

"British Columbia and Nova Scotia," Corrie said. "They're pulling back to the Great Lakes, to Thunder Bay, but then pulling out."

"West or east. Understood. Rufus, come. Ms Guinn, Mr Guinn, Ms Preston, until we meet again."

Epilogue - Rule Five
Ontario

"She took my dog," Olivia said as they trudged through the forest, looking for the river.

"He seemed to go willingly," Pete said.

"I know, that's what bugs me," Olivia said. "Rufus was never *my* dog. It was always more that I was *his* human. I'm going to miss him, that's all. What are you doing, Corrie?"

She'd taken out her phone. "Just deleting some footage," she said.

"You were recording?" Olivia asked.

"Yep. Not intentionally. I had it on while we were driving, and now I want to delete anything that might be incriminating."

"Maybe you should throw it away," Olivia said.

"No, we need footage to show that Winters and Trowbridge are dead," Corrie said. "For all that Kempton said, all that she assumed, people in Guam think Trowbridge is the president."

"Assuming Guam survived the nuclear attack," Pete said.

"Assuming that," Corrie said.

They walked on.

"So that was Lisa Kempton," Olivia said. "I actually met her."

"She's weird, isn't she?" Pete asked.

"She's not like normal people, no," Olivia said. "It was like... I don't know."

"Like she's already had half the conversation in her head, and expects you to still have heard it," Corrie said.

"I wonder how she ended up in Wawa," Pete said.

"I wonder where she's going next," Corrie said.

"I wonder if we'll really see her again," Olivia said. "By which I really mean Rufus."

"There, done," Corrie said. "But that'll do as proof Trowbridge is dead. I think that's the river."

The ground levelled, and the trees thinned, revealing a shallow bank and a wide river.

"We're going to have to cross it, aren't we?" Pete said. "Which means getting our feet wet."

"Let's leave that until we're closer to the hut," Corrie said. "Maybe there'll be a towel there. I left mine in the TAPV."

"I left the food," Olivia said.

"I've got the ration packs," Pete said. "Maybe we'll find some food with the dirt bikes."

"Assuming there is a hut," Olivia said.

Pete said nothing. He was sure there would be. If Kempton had simply wanted to get rid of them, she wouldn't have offered Rufus a ride. Probably. Almost certainly. It was difficult to know.

"Pine Dock next, yeah?" he said.

"I guess so," Corrie said.

"We should have asked her how she knew the bombs had fallen," Olivia said. "And we should have asked her where else they'd fallen. We should have asked her so much. But none of it really matters, does it? Not now. Not really. Trowbridge is dead. There won't be another president."

"There'll be someone in charge down in Guam," Pete said, clambering over a fallen log.

"Yes," Olivia said. "A leader of the survivors, but not a president of America. Not a prime minister of Canada, or Australia. Kempton's correct about that."

"It won't be us, though," Pete said. "But maybe, in Canada, it'll be Judge Benton. And maybe we'll get to be journalists after all."

"One day," Olivia said. "After the fallout's settled. Oh, and it can only have just begun to fall. The road ahead, it does seem long. That's something else Kempton got right, we're only at the very beginning."

Despite that, Pete found himself smiling. "I'm calling that rule five," he said.

"I thought you were up to rule fifty-something," Olivia said.

"I decided to start again at the beginning," Pete said.

"What are the first four?" Corrie asked.

"Rule one, check your boots," Pete said. "Rule two, remember rule one. Rule three, not everyone is special. Rule four, but some people are. Rule five, appreciate what you have. And I've got you two. I love you, Olivia. Love you, Corrie."

"I love you, too," Olivia said.

"You sure you're feeling okay, mate?" Corrie said. She smiled. "Love you, too."

Pete grinned, but then ruined the moment by tripping on a broken branch.

Despite everything, or perhaps because of it, he was happy. Trowbridge and Winters were dead. Kempton had gone to deal with the cartel. That part of his past was over. Done. Leaving him, walking through vast, empty woodlands with his once-lost sister and the woman he loved.

Life could be worse. A lot worse. And it had been. And it would be again, as the twin fangs of the outbreak and the nuclear war truly made themselves known across the world. But for him, now, walking away from a battle, in the company of those he loved, and who loved him, he truly appreciated how good life could be.

The End.

Printed in Great Britain
by Amazon